EXPOSED

R.A.D. exclusive edition

Dear readers,

I'm so pleased to be able to share Exposed with you.

I'm going to be honest here. Exposed was a selfish book to write. Why? Because I wrote it completely and utterly for myself, adding all the things that I love in a book.

Post-apocalyptic… tick. Most of the books that I read outside the MM romance genre are post-apocalyptic, and I also devour a lot of TV and films in this genre. If you've read the book, you'll see that there's a nod to Terminator in it, both in something that Tate says to X and Tate's reaction to being asked to pack hand grenades. I loved this film as a kid and had a huge crush on the character of Kyle Reese played by Micheal Biehn. It continued in Aliens by the way, but I'm getting slightly off-track.

Survival against the odds. Tick. I've often joked that I have a bit of a survival kink.

A dangerous character who comes across as cold but who really isn't. Or at least not for one person. Tick. That's my kryptonite in books. Describe a character as cold in a romance book and I'm there for it because I know he'll thaw by the end of the book. And so X was born.

Just because I wrote it for myself didn't mean that it was easy to write. Exposed had far more ups and downs than any other book I've written. I started writing it in August 2019 but then had to abandon it for a while to finish another project. Why is this important? Because I found myself continuing it in a pandemic where the first 20k I'd already written was something of a strange reflection of what civilization was actually becoming with people not allowed to go to certain places and curfews in effect. I'm not saying I'm psychic, but it was weird.

I'd gotten up to 40K on it when my laptop fell prey to a virus and I couldn't even get it to boot up on the same day the UK went into lockdown. You know those authors you hear about who forget to back up their work. Yep. That was me. I hadn't backed up a single word and suddenly found I couldn't access it. Would I have re-written it? I don't think I would have done. It would have been too hard. Luckily, I'm nothing but stubborn and after doing things to my laptop that meant I was very much in need of a new one, I got access to it. Phew!

Exposed was meant to be 80k when I first came up with the idea. The members of my FB group will testify to how frustrated I became as 'Stabby' (my pet name for the project) just kept growing and growing until it ended up at a whopping 132K. I have a habit of writing long, but not that long.

Anyway, it did get finished, pandemic or no pandemic, laptop or no laptop (thank you Amazon for keeping laptops on the essential equipment list that could still be delivered quickly in a pandemic) and to my surprise the book that I wrote for myself also found an audience with other people who loved it. I'm grateful for every message I've ever had professing love for Exposed and its characters. It was a lovely bonus on top of writing the book that I wanted to write.

P.S Don't tell X that I said he isn't really cold. Only Tate is meant to know that.

Other Books by H.L Day

13 Kingdoms series

The Reluctant Companion (#1)

The Stubborn Accomplice (#2)

The Wandering Prince (#3)

EagerBoyz series

Eager To Try (EagerBoyz 0.5)

Eager For You (EagerBoyz 1)

Eager For More (EagerBoyz 2)

Too Far series

A Dance too Far (Too Far #1)

A Step too Far (Too Far #2)

Temporary series

A Temporary Situation (Temporary; Tristan and Dom #1)

A Christmas Situation (Temporary; Tristan and Dom #1.5)

Temporary Insanity (Temporary; Paul and Indy #1)

Fight for Survival series

Refuge (Fight for Survival #1)

Rebellion (Fight for Survival #2)

Standalones

Time for a Change

Kept in the Dark

Taking Love's Lead

Edge of Living

Christmas Riches

Exposed

The Longest Night

The Beauty Within

Not So Silent Night

Five Night Stand

H.L Day's darker alter ego H.L Night

Twisted Web series

Shai

Elijah

EXPOSED
H.L. DAY

Copyright © 2020 H.L Day
All Rights Reserved
This special edition published in the United States by
Rainbow Crate llc and Rainbow Publishing ltd.
www.rainbowcratebookbox.com

ISBN 978-1-958974-38-4
Rainbow Crate Special Edition First Printing, 2024
Book originally published by H.L Day
hldayauthor.co.uk

No part of this book may be used or reproduced in any manner whatsoever without written permission from the author except in the case of brief quotations embodied in critical articles, reviews and social media features.

This book is a work of fiction. Names, character, places and incidents are either the product of the author's imagination or are used fictitiously and any resemblance to actual persons, living or dead, business establishments, events or locals, is entirely coincidental.

Cover art by Kendal Gates | @lonestarloser
linktr.ee/lonestarloser
Hardcase art and design by Soren Häxan | @t_hornapple
Endpaper art by Dibyoshree Sarkar
Cover design by Jamie Lynn Lano
jamielynnlano.com
Interior design/typesetting by Landice Anderson | @manicfemme
manicfemmecreative.com

Representation
mlm
Gay male main characters
Queernormative world

Content Warnings
Graphic violence
Knife play (consensual)
Breath play (consensual)
Mentions of **domestic abuse**
Police violence
Gun violence
Murder
Death
Stalking
Alcohol abuse
Sex work
Explicit sexual content
Death of a parent

Huge thanks to my beta readers Barbara, Sherry, Petra and Sarah

1
x

Somewhere on a large continent in the year 2076, after the end of the world as we know it.

My feet didn't make a sound as I followed him. I knew where to step, *how* to step so that I could move as silently as a wraith through the dark city streets. He remained unaware of my presence.

As always.

There were two men in my sights, the taller blond one wrapping his arm around the other's waist as he stumbled drunkenly and almost fell, his laughter bouncing off the walls of the surrounding houses. I gave him only a cursory glance before turning my attention back to my quarry, who was also struggling to stay upright. It was no wonder. He'd drunk seven vodkas tonight. His usual was only three or four. I didn't know why he'd felt the need to drink more tonight. Work stress, maybe? I might have assumed relationship problems, but the couple seemed happy enough, and trust me I'd looked closely, my scrutiny missing nothing.

The couple drew to a halt and I paused, stepping back into the shelter of a building, my black clothing making it all too easy to melt into the shadows as if I'd never been there in the first place. The tall guy—Joseph Turner, it hadn't taken me long to discover that piece of information, along with his address and the names of everyone he'd ever come into contact with since the day he'd been born—pushed his partner back against the nearest wall.

I watched closely for any sign of emotional strain from the shorter dark-haired man, anything that would make me believe that he didn't want it, my fingers moving to the handle of one of the knives I carried at my waist. But he simply laughed, winding his arms around the taller man's neck, their lips meeting in a passionate kiss. A kiss that went on for a long time.

Them kissing. Me watching. The pair oblivious to their audience. I tamped down on the emotions writhing underneath my skin, telling myself, as I always did, that I had no right to feel them.

Finally, the blond ended it, whispering something in his companion's ear. Whatever he'd said, it had the other man nodding eagerly.

Deciding whose home to return to, possibly? At the moment, they were equidistant between the two. As the pair moved away from the wall to continue their journey, I peeled myself from the shadows, allowing a distance of a few meters to build up before following. This late, with only an hour until the midnight curfew, there were few people on the streets. Those that were almost fell over themselves in their haste to get out of my way. Whether it was because they knew me by reputation, or could simply tell I wasn't someone to be messed with, I wasn't sure. I didn't care. They were right to steer clear. Less chance of them being introduced to one of my sharp friends that way. My blades weren't fussy. They didn't care whose flesh they sank into. They were equal opportunity knives—fat, thin, tall, skinny, black, white, male, female. They all bled the same way. And they all died with that same expression on their face, the one tinged with regret.

A rattle to my right had me spinning around, muscles

tensing, prepared for action in whatever form it might take. There was no threat though. Just a rat, its whiskered face poking out from between the pile of cans it had knocked over. It was tempting to take it down with a well-aimed knife, but I had more important matters to deal with first.

The pair came to a stop in front of a building. It was where the blond lived, his apartment on the fourth floor. The door had ceded entry easily enough to my trusty lockpicks while he'd been at work. I'd spent an hour in there, sifting through every drawer and every cupboard in search of anything that didn't match the squeaky-clean persona my background check had shown. There'd been nothing. If Joseph Turner was anything but the twenty-five-year old bank clerk he portrayed, then the evidence was cleverly hidden.

And that's why he was still breathing. So far, anyway.

There was very little coverage on this street if you didn't want to be seen. Even for me. I kept to the opposite side of it until I reached the building I was looking for. One fluid movement, a short climb up brickwork crumbling just enough to offer perfect foot and handholds, and I crouched on a fire escape offering an unobstructed view of the couple. There was more kissing against the wall of Joseph's building, hands groping freely over clothes, lips sharing a conversation I wasn't able to hear before resuming kissing. They finally parted, both of them laughing as Joseph took his partner's hand and led him into the building.

And still I waited.

I leaned my head back to look up, focusing on a window halfway up the side of the building. How long would it take them to get there? By my calculations, two minutes. But that depended on whether they could keep their hands off each other for the duration of the stair climb. From the evidence of the night so far, that seemed unlikely.

It was four minutes before a light illuminated the window. Two minutes of extra foreplay then. A silhouette appeared at the window but there was too little light to be able to tell which one of them it was. The figure reached up, tugging the curtains across and ending my view of anything that would follow. It didn't matter. Having seen it all before, I could picture it perfectly. Too perfectly.

I crouched there in the darkness, my hands forming into fists as I pictured the lovers tumbling onto the mattress. The mattress I'd lifted while searching Joseph's apartment just in case he was craftier than I'd given him credit for. He hadn't been. It was just as empty and uninspiring as the rest of his apartment had been. Joseph Turner was about as vanilla as they came.

Only when the siren for the curfew sounded, signaling that anyone caught outside would be shot on sight, did I drop soundlessly to the ground. Time to go back to where I belonged, to where the polished sterility of the streets, save for the odd rat, didn't make my skin itch. I belonged in the slums. Not here. I was just a frequent visitor on this side of the wall.

The street lights had all blinked out one by one as the curfew sounded. It was meant to act as a deterrent, leaving anyone rebellious enough to ignore martial law fumbling around in the dark. But in reality, it made it easier. It meant that people like me—if there was such a thing—could move around with less risk of being seen. Enough light spilled from windows that it wasn't quite pitch black.

I kept my ears open for any telltale signs of the Defenders of The Peace being close by as I walked. The DTP ran this city, and every other city on this continent. The title was a fucking joke. They were about as peaceful as a fucking riot. World War 3 had changed everything, knocking the majority of civilization back at least a few decades and making many parts of the world uninhabitable due to the radiation; populations regrouped to wherever they were told to go without any say in the matter. Global warming had played its part too, changing temperate climates into tropical ones, deserts forming where previously there had been none. It was a new world with place names changed to reflect that. Even the older generation could barely remember what they'd been before.

A new force had been brought into being. The history books said that it had been meant as a short-term solution until unrest settled down, but they'd never gone away. They were judge, jury, and executioner, running every town and city with an iron fist that knew no mercy. Gone were the days of democracy. Gone were the days of civil liberties. There were stories. Tales of places beyond their control. But for the most part, that's all they were—stories.

The city changed as I snuck across the boundary, the intact houses giving way to shacks, some built after the war from whatever material had been at hand, but most were houses that had suffered bomb damage and had been patched up. Not nuclear damage, or the city would have been yet another place in the world abandoned and left to go to rack and ruin. This part of the city—*my* part of the city—had a distinctive smell to it, a permanent scent of rotting rubbish and unwashed bodies. I smiled. It was the smell of home. Cofield could keep their posh brickwork and their clean streets, and they could keep their houses built from scratch for 'the business people,' made from materials shipped from afar.

This was where I belonged: in the filth of the slums where the only currency was violence and crime. There was much less of a DTP presence here, which suited me down to the ground. Sure, they showed their faces occasionally to gun down some bastard too stupid to keep his drug dealing on the downlow, but for the most part they left us alone, happy to have the vermin contained in one place.

I slipped between the buildings, pausing for a moment to consider my options. Home? Or elsewhere? Decision made, I headed toward the building at the end of the street, its neon sign extinguished as part of the curfew. During the day, it proclaimed

'*Dolly's*' in three-foot tall pink letters. Who the fuck Dolly was, I had no idea. A less fitting name for the dive I was about to step into would have been hard to imagine. I doubted that anyone called Dolly would have been into sticky floors and the permanent smell of lube and sex.

I'd barely stepped through the door when someone came barreling into me, their shoulder pushing me aside. Quick as a flash, I had them up against the wall, my knife to their throat. The man swallowed convulsively, the movement pushing his skin against the blade, a drop of blood slowly forming to drip down his neck. I watched its progress with morbid fascination. I'd always liked blood. There was something so pure about it, so transfixing.

"X, man. Don't kill him. He's one of my best customers."

I didn't need to turn to identify the voice. It belonged to Ren, the weaselly balding man who owned the joint. He hovered by my shoulder, knowing better than to get too close or to try and touch me. I focused my attention back on the man on the end of my blade, his eyes bulging and his forehead damp with sweat, which only seemed to have gotten worse with Ren's use of my name. Funny that. "Fucker needs to be more careful and look where he's going, or who knows what might happen to him."

Ren came forward to place himself in my line of sight. "He knows that. Right, Chris? Tell the man you're sorry for not looking where you were going."

I smirked, knowing full well that Chris wouldn't dare to say a thing for fear of the blade kissing his throat moving a millimeter closer to something delicate. "He doesn't sound sorry to me."

Ren tried a different tack. "Come and have a drink. I've got some expensive whiskey in just for you. It's on the house." I was beginning to suspect that the man was a friend of his. I'd certainly never seen Ren go to bat for anyone else before. Perversely, it made me want to kill him more, not less. Because I knew Ren wouldn't do a damn thing about it. He'd clean up the body, and then he'd offer me the whiskey anyway, along with anything else I wanted. That was the way it worked. I knew it. He knew it, and I expected even the sniveling wreck with the death wish knew it.

It would be so damn easy as well. All I had to do was press a bit harder and my freshly-sharpened blade would cut through his windpipe as quickly and easily as if it was made of marshmallow rather than bone and cartilage.

Ren coughed. "I've got a new boy in you might like. You've come here to let off a bit of steam, right? You'll like this one. Mid-twenties with dark hair and blue eyes. Fresh in last week, but he knows what he's doing. Can suck a cock like you wouldn't believe, and he loves taking it up the ass. Let's get a whiskey, and then I can introduce you to him."

I took a moment to fantasize about the fountain of blood that would flow from my victim's neck if I cut deeper, before removing the knife from his throat and pushing him away. He fell to the floor, wheezing and clutching at his neck in an over-dramatic fashion. The threat may have been there, but in reality, all he had was a tiny nick which would stop bleeding in a matter of minutes. I nudged him with my foot. "Piece of advice for you. You still being here really makes me want to change my mind." He took the hint, crawling the few meters to the door before struggling to his feet in order to open it and moments later spilling out onto the street outside.

Ren's exhale was loud as he walked over to the stack of wooden crates which represented a bar, plucking a bottle and glass from the top of one. His hands shook as he poured a generous measure into the glass before passing it across to me. I took it, taking a sip as I scanned the room. It was so silent that it could have been empty. But it wasn't. It was full, everyone in it so still that they might as well have been mannequins, their gazes fastened on anything that wasn't me. I recognized the game. It was an old one, as old as time: if we can't see you, you can't see us.

I held my knife in the air, turning it from side to side to examine its surface. "I need a cloth. Your friend got my knife dirty."

Ren fumbled for one, holding his hand out for the knife.

I regarded him steadily, tamping down on the flicker of annoyance. "No one touches my knives. No one. You know that."

Ren's smile in response to my words lacked conviction, trembling for a moment on his lips before disappearing completely. He held the fabric out, the tremor even more pronounced. Plucking it out of his hand, I wiped the blade clean before sliding it back into the sheath and flicking the cloth back at him. "So, where's this new boy you told me about? He better not be a fucking figment of your imagination!"

Ren's head lifted, his gaze searching the still silent room until he paused to focus on someone. "Bartholomew, why don't you come over here and introduce yourself to X?"

It was phrased as a question, but I knew it wasn't. I turned around, leaning my elbows back on the packing crates as a tall dark-haired man stood up from one of the tables and started to make his way toward us. Too tall. The hair would pass though, as would the blue of his eyes once he was close enough that I could see them. The lack of fear on his face was surprising. I would have put it down to him being new in town and therefore oblivious to my reputation, if it wasn't for the fact that he'd just witnessed it first-hand. One of those that got off on danger, perhaps? He was certainly looking at me as if I was all his wet dreams rolled into one, his heated gaze sliding down my body. His tongue moistened his lips as his scrutiny reached my crotch. Either he was a damn good actor, or I genuinely was his type. He propped one hand on his hip, tilting his head to the side in a provocative fashion. "Good to meet you, X. Why don't we go somewhere private? Work off a little bit of that… tension that you seem to have a lot of tonight."

I lifted the glass to my lips, draining the rest of the whiskey and enjoying the smooth burn as it slid down my esophagus. Reaching into my pocket, I threw a handful of coins in Ren's direction without bothering to count them. There was more than enough to cover the cost of an hour, and that was all I needed.

Bartholomew's mouth curved into a smile. He inclined his head toward the back of the building where the private rooms were. That's if you could call a space barely the size of a cupboard with nothing more than a bare mattress in it a room. "Shall we?"

I didn't bother to answer when the question was rhetorical anyway. My answer was implicit enough in the fact that I followed him as he began to wend his way between the tables, the people seated there seeming to shrink even more as I passed by.

The room he led me into was slightly bigger than the ones I'd been in on previous visits. I'd need to have a word with Ren. The bastard had obviously been holding out on me.

Bartholomew pointed toward a table next to the door. "Leave your knives there."

I pulled both knives out of the sheathes I wore at my hip with a flourish, laying them on the table with a slight lift of one eyebrow.

Bartholomew's eyes narrowed. "All of them."

Clever boy. That answered one question. He obviously did know who I was. Keeping my eyes trained on him, I reached down, sliding my fingers beneath the hem of the left leg of my trousers and unstrapping the smaller, but no less deadly knife that I kept there. I did the same with the one strapped to my back before extracting the throwing knives from the inside pocket of my jacket and adding them to the pile. "You think I'd need my knives to kill you?"

"Probably not. But let's just say that I don't need them accidentally sticking into me once we get down to business."

I advanced toward Bartholomew, causing him to back away until the wall prevented him from going any farther. His eyes widened as I wrapped a hand around his throat, his pulse hammering beneath my palm. "You talk too much. From now on, I don't want to hear you speak unless I ask you what your name is. Do you understand?"

He nodded jerkily, the muscles of his throat convulsing beneath my fingers. A look in his eyes said that he understood perfectly, his next words confirming it. "I understand. And if you ask my name, what name should I give?"

I hesitated. I hated this bit, even as I craved it. "Tate. Just say Tate." I let go of him, shoving him in the direction of the mattress. "Now strip. Face down. Ass in the air."

To give him his due, he didn't say another word, removing his clothes in a perfunctory fashion and arranging himself exactly as I'd described. Fastening my gaze on his naked ass, which was more than adequate, I unzipped my trousers and pulled my cock out, giving it a few clinical strokes until it was hard enough. A few steps brought me over to the mattress, my feet between his spread thighs. "What's your name?"

The figure shifted slightly, his naked ass tipping up provocatively in a clear invitation. "Tate. My name is Tate."

2
TATE

One week later

I held the glass containing the bright red liquid up to the light, wrinkling my nose at it. "What the fuck is this?"

Joseph snorted and nudged my arm. "I don't know. New drink. I thought we'd try it."

"Well, I've tried it, and I've decided that I'm not a vampire so I can't drink anything that looks like blood."

Joseph rolled his eyes while Trisha leaned across the table, her glass already empty. "Tastes alright though." She snatched the drink out of my hand, downing it in one gulp before I could even think of voicing a protest. "Now you can stop moaning."

I narrowed my eyes at her. "Now I'll moan about not having a drink."

Joseph stood, brushing his blond hair out of his eyes. "I'll get you something else." His smile grew seductive. "Maybe I'll get you drunk again. It was fun the other night. You were pretty wild."

I shot a glare at Trisha as she made a loud retching noise. I'd known her a lot longer than I'd known Joseph, having worked with her at the same pharmaceutical firm for the last couple of years. Whereas my relationship with Joseph was still relatively new. We were still in that phase of feeling our way around eac other and learning each other's likes and dislikes, both in and out of bed. He was handsome, kind, and thoughtful, so maybe this relationship would last for a change. I hoped so. "Vodka, please." He winked and was about to step away from the table when the siren went off. *Fuck*! Every single person, no matter what they'd been doing, froze in place with the same look of dread on their faces. I quickly pulled Joseph back into the chair he'd just vacated, figuring he'd be less conspicuous seated. My gaze met Trisha's at the same moment as all the overhead lights in the bar came on, both of us blinking as we tried to adjust to the sudden change in lighting. Joseph grabbed hold of my hand and squeezed, and I was glad for the comfort. I squeezed back as we all braced ourselves for the upcoming DTP raid. The sirens were an instruction. An instruction that the building was currently being surrounded and that everyone needed to stay exactly where they were. Failure to obey was viewed as guilt, the perpetrator shot where they stood. And it was no idle threat either. I'd seen it happen. I'd also seen someone drunkenly argue the DTP's interruption at their thirtieth birthday celebration. Thirty was as old as they'd ever gotten, their body leaving nothing but a stain in the middle of the nightclub floor. Obstruction of justice was what they'd called it.

I'd read the stories about countries with leaders: kings and queens, presidents and prime ministers. I'd seen the films as well. Well, those days were long gone. There was only the DTP now, with their own special brand of brutal justice. Crime rates were low in this part of the city. Of course, they were. How could they not be when the sentence, even for petty crime, was immediate death? There'd been uprisings, attempts to overthrow the iron fist of the DTP. They'd all failed, stamped out as quickly as they'd started.

Their presence apparently didn't have quite the same impact in the slums. But everyone with any sense stayed well away from that part of town, myself included. There were other elements besides the DTP you could fall foul of if you were stupid enough to cross from Cofield into the slums. The wall had been built for a reason. There might be access between the two places, but it was extremely limited and confined to certain hours when it was policed.

The double doors opened, and I braced myself. That first sight of the DTP never got any easier, my stomach churning on cue. Their units tended to vary from three to eight. Three or four usually indicated that they weren't expecting any resistance. A full unit of eight meant they were either searching for someone dangerous or for more than one person.

Today, there were five of them as they stepped through the door. They were dressed the same as always: head to toe in protective Kevlar, black military masks covering their face so that they all looked the same. The one at the front held up a small metal box, the usual recorded message whirring to life. I'd heard it so many times that I probably could have recited it for them if they'd asked. *"We are here to enforce the laws of the city. Laws that you all accept by choosing to live here. Do not try to interfere in our investigation in any way or there will be consequences. Do not attempt to harbor the criminal or cover up their whereabouts or there will be consequences. Stay still while we run facial recognition. Do not attempt to hide your face or there will be consequences."*

The only people who moved for the next few minutes were those stood directly in the path of the DTP, who melted to either side as one of the soldiers produced a scanner and began to run facial recognition checks. The DTP in all their righteous splendor were of course privy to technology that the rest of us couldn't even dream of possessing. If we were lucky, they'd come up empty and move on to the next building. If we weren't so lucky, then one of the people in our vicinity was about to get vaporized, and I'd have yet another nasty image to file with the rest.

I went rigid as a soldier carrying a scanner stepped up to

our table. No matter how much you knew that you hadn't done anything, your brain insisted on playing tricks on you, demanding evidence that you'd remembered to buy the groceries you'd obtained earlier, that you hadn't accidentally caused a gas leak which had killed someone. The soldier held the scanner up to my face, Joseph squeezing my hand tighter as the machine emitted a series of clicks. Was it taking longer than it usually did? What did that mean? It had to have been longer than a minute. A bead of sweat trickled down my face, but I didn't dare raise a hand to wipe it away in case it was viewed as trying to obstruct the facial recognition software from making an identification.

To distract myself, I stared at the faceless mask. *Who was under it? Was he young? Old? Did he have a family?* The DTP were a complete mystery. No one knew how they were recruited, where they came from, or even where they lived. The theory was that they had a number of compounds scattered across the continent, but no one ever seemed to have seen them, or if they had they hadn't lived to tell the tale. Wherever the DTP were based, it had to be a virtual fortress.

All of a sudden it was over, and I could breathe again. Joseph and Trisha got the same treatment with the exact same result before the soldier moved on. The checks continued on the rest of the crowd, but much to my relief no match was found. Less than ten minutes after their arrival, the DTP moved out, the siren stopping a few seconds later and the lighting dimming again. Conversations started up and glasses clinked as an air of normality started to filter back in.

Joseph let go of my hand, both of our palms equally sweaty. "I guess I'll get those drinks for us. Vodka, was it?"

I shook my head. "I just want to go home. Can we call it a night, please?"

I'd just reached the exit at work when my phone rang, the

security guard manning the desk giving me a nod of recognition as I scanned my ID as evidence that I'd left the building.
"Hello."
"Hey, it's me."
Joseph. "Hey." I'd barely seen him since the aborted night out a week ago. But we had plans to see each other tonight. His sigh echoed over the line. "I've got to work late. Something to do with a big cash transaction going astray. We've been told that we can't leave until it's been squared away. I don't know if I'll be able to make it to the club."
That's where I was on my way to now. Thinking of the club and its entrance fee had me patting the back pocket of my jeans. "Fuck!"
"Sorry. There's nothing I can do."
"No, not that. If you can't make it, you can't make it. I understand. You can hardly tell them to screw their job. I've just realized that I've left my wallet on my desk. I'm going to have to go back for it."
"Can't you send your guardian angel?"
I rolled my eyes, even though Joseph couldn't see me. The guardian angel thing was a running joke that no one ever seemed to get tired of repeating. So, I'd had a few runs of good luck from time to time, including Niles, an abusive ex-boyfriend of mine meeting a sudden end. I'd put that one down to karma, the universe recognizing that any piece of shit who hadn't thought twice about giving me a black eye wasn't worth keeping around. Suffice it to say, I hadn't shed any tears over his unfortunate demise. The world was brutal. Mysterious deaths happened. As far as I knew, they'd never caught the culprit, which I supposed proved that the DTP weren't infallible. The sudden windfall when I'd been in financial straits had been more difficult to explain. Facing the possibility of finding myself out on the streets, or at least having to foist myself on friends until I'd worked something out, I'd gotten home one day to discover a

brown envelope propped up in the middle of my dining table. There hadn't been a name on it. But who else could it have been meant for when I lived alone? The panic that someone had been in my house had quickly diminished once I'd opened it to discover it was stuffed with money—more than enough to solve all my problems and still have some left over. If I'd been conflicted about using it, it hadn't lasted long. The money was on my table. How could I not use it? Where it had come from, though, was a mystery. It wasn't from family, my mother, who'd been my last remaining relative, had died years before.

Even a couple of years down the line, I still didn't have an answer. Hence the guardian angel theory. Sometimes I wished that I'd never gotten drunk and shared the story. I'd never heard the end of it since, every tiny bit of luck I had put down to an act of intervention from my mythical guardian angel.

Therefore, when I answered Joseph, my voice was more clipped than it needed to be. "I don't think guardian angels fetch wallets. They're not dogs."

"Fuck!" Joseph's voice dropped to a whisper. "I've got to go, babe. My supervisor's doing the rounds. I'll see you later if we can manage to get this shit sorted."

He'd already hung up before I had a chance to respond. Sighing, I turned back to the building, squinting up at the exterior of the high-rise and noting the lack of lights on. Not a surprise, it was Friday after all, and late. Most people had already left before I had. I retraced my steps, the security guard raising an eyebrow at my reappearance. "Back already?"

I scanned my ID again while nodding. "I forgot something. I'll only be a couple of minutes."

The building was silent as I tackled the stairs that would take me back to my office. Once there, I didn't bother to switch the light on, my desk close enough to the door for light to spill in from the hallway. It was easy to make out the shape of my wallet on the corner of the desk. I must have put it to one side to make sure I didn't forget it and then done exactly that. *Idiot.* Mind, at least I'd only gotten as far as the street. It would have been far worse If I'd gotten all the way to the club before realizing.

I shoved it into my pocket and was about to leave when something caught my eye. There was a thin beam of light spilling from under my boss's office door. It was strange because he'd left an hour before I had. I'd witnessed him locking the door, the same way he did every night. That meant that no one should be in there. Had he come back? I doubted it. My boss wasn't exactly renowned for his work ethic. Once the weekend came, he was usually the first out of there, not wanting to work even a minute longer than he needed to. Besides, there shouldn't have been anything that couldn't wait until the following week.

Turning to leave, I hesitated, my feet moving in the opposite direction before my brain was fully on board with the idea. I'd probably discover that the door was locked and that Mr. Sinclair had simply forgotten to switch the light off before his departure. Except when I tried the door handle, it turned and opened.

There was a man sitting behind the desk. His head whipped up at my entrance, the expression on his face akin to shock. I did a number of quick computations. Mr. Sinclair's office was out of bounds. This wasn't Mr. Sinclair. It was Malcolm Jones, one of the lab grunts. Ergo, he shouldn't have been in the room, never mind typing something into the computer. A computer he shouldn't have had password access to. I was ninety-nine percent sure he hadn't been in here when I'd left, which meant he'd been hanging around the building and biding his time until everyone had gone home. Which I had done, apart from the small matter of forgetting my wallet. He shouldn't have had a key, so how had he even accessed the room?

I took a step into the room, my gaze automatically lifting to the security camera situated in one corner of the office. It should have been recording Malcolm's unauthorized activity, a blinking red light in the corner confirming its operational status.

But there was no red light. What did that mean? Was it broken? No, that was too much of a coincidence. Malcolm must have done something to it.

What the hell was going on? The whole thing stank to high heaven. I stared at Malcolm, trying to come up with the right thing to say. The two of us had never seen eye to eye in all the time we'd worked together. Malcolm was too much of an ass licker. Except, was he? Because that didn't equate with him sitting where he was now. I wanted to leave and forget I'd ever seen him, but it was too late for that. "What are you doing here?"

His earlier shock was quickly replaced by a sneer. He tapped at the keyboard, seeming more interested in it than me. "None of your business."

"Does Mr. Sinclair know you're in his office?"

This time the stare was cold when it landed on me, his fingers pausing on the keys. "You shouldn't have come in here, Tate."

The words sounded suspiciously like a threat. I took a step back. "I saw the light. I knew that Mr. Sinclair had gone home. I didn't know…"

"Go home, Tate."

I found myself nodding and edging closer to the door. Whatever was going on, I wanted no part of it. There was no logical reason for Malcolm to be in here. Therefore, he was up to no good, and the less I knew about it the better. I spun on my heel, walking quickly out of the office and back down the hallway, my palms a little bit too slick, and my heart beating faster than it should have been.

Whilst scanning my ID for the third time in the space of ten minutes, I scrutinized the security guard's expression, wishing that I could see into the room that housed the security feed from the numerous cameras stationed around the building. Did he know what was going on? Was he in on it? Whatever *it* was? Or had he just not noticed that he was missing one of the camera feeds? Should I say something? Tell him to investigate? Or better yet, should I tell him where Malcolm was?

The phone on the desk rang, the opportunity gone as he picked it up and turned away. It wasn't my problem. I gave the building one last look before heading to the bar. I needed a drink. And not one of those godawful red drinks either. A proper one. One that would start the weekend in style where I didn't have to think about work until Monday.

Trisha slung an arm around my shoulders, her red-painted lips hovering close to my ear as she shouted to be heard over the music. "I need a man."

I let out a snort at her bluntness, waving an arm to gesture at the mass of heaving bodies on dancefloor. "Take your pick."

She pouted. "No, like a *real* man. One who'll throw me over his shoulder and have his wicked way with me. Not these..." She threw a look of disdain in the direction of the gyrating bodies. "... suited pretty boys." She grabbed hold of my T-shirt, pulling me around to face her, her eyes alight with excitement. "I should climb over the wall and go to the slums. Apparently, there –"

I didn't let her finish. When she was this drunk, it was better not to pander to her. "Don't even think about it. You'd be dead within an hour."

Her face fell. "I might die happy, though."

"You might..." Whatever I'd been about to say was cut off by the simultaneous action of the lights coming on and the drone of the siren starting up. I let my head *thunk* back against the wall. "Oh, for fuck's sake! You've got to be kidding me. Twice in one week. How fucking unlucky are we?"

Trisha's eye roll said very unlucky. She squeezed my arm. "Ten minutes and it'll all be over. Then I vote that we pour a lot more alcohol down your system. Enough that you'll stop being such a stick in the mud and join in with my fantasy of stripping myself naked, arranging myself provocatively against the boundary wall, and luring a caveman from the slums for the evening."

The smile on my face in response to the picture she was painting crumbled away as the familiar figures filled the doorway, their black military masks sending the usual shockwave around the assembled crowd. The sight on the dancefloor was a strange one, people who only moments before had been gyrating to the heavy bass were now stock still, their bodies crushed together. Due to the number of people in the club tonight, this was going to take forever. Maybe Joseph hadn't been unlucky after all. At least being stuck at work was saving him from this.

I closed my eyes as the familiar recorded message started up. *"We are here to enforce the laws of the city. Laws that you all accept by choosing to live here…"* Someone needed to record a new message for them. They'd had the same one for years. There must be something else they could say instead that would shake it up a little bit.

"…do not try to interfere in our investigation in any way or there will be consequences. Do not attempt to harbor the criminal or cover up their whereabouts or there will be consequences." I thought about the old stories of a time where you were apparently innocent until proven guilty. Here, it was the other way around—guilty until proven innocent. It happened a lot: names being cleared after they'd already been executed. Not that the DTP gave a damn. They had no spokesperson. No governing body. There was never any apology or recognition that they'd killed an innocent man—or woman. No consequences for them—ironically. *"Stay still while we run facial recognition. Do not attempt to hide your face or there will be consequences."*

With at least twice as many people in the club as there had been in the bar, the scanning process took longer, just as I'd known it would. My phone chimed in my pocket, but I didn't dare reach in to silence it. It was probably Joseph, either ringing to say he was on his way, or that he'd gone straight home. At the noise, one of the soldier's turned in my direction. Sweat broke out on my forehead as the black eye sockets of his mask seemed to bore into me. The ringing seemed to go on forever, the soldier only turning away again once it had fallen silent. Trisha shot me an accusatory look as if it was my fault that my phone had been ringing.

About half of the people in the club had been scanned before they got around to us. Trisha was first, the machine making its usual chorus of hums and blips before giving the all-clear. I braced myself as the machine was pointed in my direction, reminding myself that I'd endured it only a few days ago. All I had to do was the same thing I'd done then. Stand there. Stay still without twitching. Let the machine do its job and then move on. Easy. Then why didn't it feel like that? Perhaps it was the oppressive presence of the man holding the scanner, his mask reflecting back my own face.

The scanner had barely been pointed in my direction for five seconds when a green light came on. That couldn't be right. That was what happened when the person they'd been searching for had been located. There must have been some mistake. Maybe there was someone behind me? But there couldn't be because I was leaning against a wall. A faulty scanner then?

Within seconds, a solid wall of DTP soldiers formed in front of me. One of them held up the recorder, the tinny voice springing to life with the second recorded message of the evening. *"You have been formally identified as Tate Gillespie. Tate Gillespie is charged with industrial espionage. You were identified on camera accessing an unauthorized part of your employment complex outside employment hours where sensitive information was exchanged for a fee with a rival company. In accordance with the laws of this city, you have been found guilty. Your sentence is execution to be carried out immediately. Tate Gillespie, do you have anything you wish to say before your sentence is carried out? Speak now or forever hold your peace."*

The words blurred together in my brain, and I struggled to make some sort of sense out of them. Industrial espionage… unauthorized… exchange of information… fee… guilty… execution. They finally coalesced into a stunning realization, all the blood seeming to pool at my feet. It had only been two hours since I'd left work. Two hours since I'd stumbled upon Malcolm in Mr. Sinclair's office where he shouldn't have been. Whatever he'd been doing, he'd somehow managed to make me the fall guy for it. How had he done it? Had he doctored the cameras? Made it look like I'd been the only person in the building? Had that been the plan all along? Or had forgetting my wallet meant I'd landed in his lap like some sort of sacrificial lamb? It must have been the latter. There was no way he could have known that I'd be stupid enough to investigate the light. Why hadn't I just left? Why hadn't I spoken to the security guard? Why the fuck hadn't I called Mr. Sinclair and told him what I'd seen? It would have been far better to suffer him chewing me out for disturbing his weekend than this.

The pharmaceutical company I worked for had top secret projects worth millions of pounds. I'd had to sign a waiver when I'd first started working there so it shouldn't have come as a surprise that someone might sell those secrets. Even the smallest tidbit of information was classed as potentially useful to rival companies.

What had Malcolm sold them? Blueprints for the latest drug synthesized by V-tech? Or something else? I guessed I'd never know because I was about to be… I fought against a wave of dizziness, my limbs twitching as if they wanted to run. But it wouldn't do me any good. It wasn't like I'd get far. Did I want to say something? My gaze strayed to Trisha, who stood immobile, her eyes wide and teary and her hand clasped over her mouth. "I didn't do it. It was Malcolm. Malcolm did it." The words weren't really aimed at her, but it was all I could think of to say.

She barely had time to shake her head before an DTP soldier

roughly manhandled her to the side and away from me. A sea of faces surrounded me, their expressions a mixture of relief—that it wasn't them—and horror at what they were about to witness. I turned my attention to the DTP soldier in front of me. "I didn't do it." The faceless automaton didn't react in any way. Speaking to him was pointless. How many times had I heard the same words spill from other men's lips? It always ended the same way with them being gunned down anyway.

Rough hands grabbed my elbows to frog-march me across the floor. The crowd parted, squeezing themselves into any available space until the DTP were satisfied that they had enough room. A shove pushed me to the floor. I stumbled and fell, my forehead hitting the floor hard before I could right myself. A cold inevitability settled over me as I struggled to my knees.

This was it. My life was down to seconds. For what? Being in the wrong place at the wrong time? For living in a world where this was how crime was dealt with?

The closest soldier lifted his gun and pointed it at me. There'd be a flash of blue, and then my body would simply disintegrate. There'd be no more Tate Gillespie, except in the memories of those that had known me. Trisha would be left sharing stories of her traumatic night out, telling everyone who cared to listen that she'd had no idea what I'd been up to despite working with me. Joseph would tell his next boyfriend during the past relationship discussion that I was dead. Yes, it was sad. No, he wasn't devastated because we hadn't been together that long.

Was I supposed to close my eyes? Keep them open? I supposed it didn't really matter either way. Breathing had become difficult, like all the oxygen had been sucked out of the room. Perhaps I'd suffocate before they ever got around to shooting me.

What was I supposed to think about? My father—God rest his soul? My mother—who'd lived for a few more years after my father's death? The fact that I was dying without ever having experienced love or been true to myself about what I really desired in a relationship?

There were too many things to think about and not enough time.

3
X

I patted my pockets even though I'd already done it once, checking that everything was where it was supposed to be. In the slums, it paid to be prepared for any eventuality. I might be relatively safe in my underground bunker, but up on the streets I was always going to be a target. My reputation kept the majority of people away, but I wasn't stupid, I knew there was a price on my head. There were people new to the town who wanted to make a name for themselves. People stupid enough to believe that they could be the one to take me down.

Over the years, there'd been several. Old and grizzled. Young and foolish. Individuals. Groups. Some came for me in broad daylight. Others relied on the cover of darkness. Some were even foolish enough to breach the bunker. They'd all fallen at the first hurdle, either to the sweet kiss of one of my blades or to one of the traps I

set up for such an eventuality. And they'd keep coming. Some for the money they'd been offered for delivering my head. Some simply for the kudos it would bring. There would always be men, and there would always be reasons.

On a day like today, it was just tiring. I grabbed hold of the feet of the man who'd lost his head—literally—when he'd sneaked into my bunker, the rigged-up shotgun dispatching him cleanly. A smear of blood marked the route as I pulled him across the floor. I had no idea who he was. Maybe if he still had a face, I might have had a chance of identifying him. But without one, he could have been anybody. Perhaps it was the man I'd nearly killed last week? The one Ren had worked so hard to save.

Crouching down to examine him more closely, I prized a pistol from his fingers, turning it over to look for any identification marks that might provide a clue as to where he'd gotten it. No firearms were registered these days, but if you knew who to ask—which I did—they could still provide information about whether its owner was part of a group or working alone. There were no distinguishing features on this one, though.

I nudged the body up against the wall with my foot, dropping the pistol on top of the headless corpse. He could wait. It wasn't as if he was going anywhere. Hand automatically straying to the knife at my waist, I headed for the ladder that led up to street level, pausing on the way to reset the tripwire and reload the shotgun. If the man was part of a group, I wouldn't put it past one of the stupid fuckers to try again.

The night outside was pitch-black. I stood for a minute, letting my eyes adjust to the gloom before making my way toward my intended target, a hut at the end of the street. I didn't have friends. Friends meant trusting people. Trusting people meant a risk of being betrayed farther down the line. As a child, I'd learnt that the hard way, and I'd never made the same mistake since. But the man I was going to see, while not technically a friend, was probably the closest thing I had to someone I could trust.

I found Cyrus at his usual spot, hunched over the computer he'd built from various pieces of junk. He raised his head as I pushed the door open, his rheumy blue eyes widening until he realized it was me. He acknowledged me with a curt nod. I threw a bottle of whiskey his way, his hand shooting up to catch it. For a man who was permanently three sheets to the wind, he had excellent hand-eye coordination. "X."

I returned his nod. "Brought you a gift, old man."
He let out a snort. "Like fuck you did. You don't do gifts. You do exchanges." He held the bottle of whiskey up, turning it around so that he could examine the label. Not that it mattered. I could have given him methanol and he would still have drunk it. "So what the fuck do you want?"
"Information."
"About?"
"I had a visitor this morning. One that's now missing his head. No ID. No distinguishing features. Wondered if you'd heard anything about anyone wanting to kill me."
He scratched at his long, gray beard, his lips curling up in amusement. "Everybody wants to kill you. Everyone apart from me." He twisted the cap off the top of the whiskey and raised the bottle to his lips, taking a long swig. "And I only don't want to kill you because you bring me this."
I perched myself against an old barrel. Most of the decor consisted of pieces of junk. It was what passed for the height of fashion in the slums. If your junk was intact rather than infested with woodworm, or slowly rotting to pieces, then you were doing well for yourself. "So, have you heard anything?"
Cyrus took another swig of whiskey before shaking his head, his tattooed arm flexing with the action. "Not so far. I'll look into it for you, though. Need help with the body?"
I shook my head. "No, I'll dump it tomorrow night. It can keep me company until then."
"Some company. But then you always were a perverse fucker."
Ignoring the jibe that only he could get away with, I gestured toward the computer. Purchased computers had inbuilt tracking, meaning that should the DTP choose to look, every key-stroke, every action could be traced. But if you built one from scratch, nothing was traceable. Add to that the fact that the sozzled old man was an expert hacker, and you had an unbeatable

combination safe from prying eyes. It enabled Cyrus to track anything that took his fancy, including keeping tabs on the DTP rather than them keeping tabs on us. "Any DTP traffic?"

He pulled a face, twisting the bottle of whiskey in his hands, one quarter of its contents already resting in his gullet. "No, it's been quiet." He tapped a few keys, grinning as he swiveled the monitor around so that I could see the naked centerfold filling the screen. "Found her, though. Look at the tits on her. It'd be like being on a bouncy castle."

I gave her only a cursory glance. Porn—like most things—was illegal these days. Cyrus had obviously been browsing the dark web again.

The old man's lips curved into a sneer. "Oh, sorry. You like a bit more cock than that, don't you?" He laughed as if he'd said something hilarious. It was time to go before I forgot how useful he could be and decided to put an end to the noise coming out of his mouth once and for all. "Let me know when you find out something." I got halfway to the door before he spoke.

"Hang on. We've got movement from the DTP. They've got a target."

I paused in the doorway, tempted to keep on walking. I didn't have the headspace tonight to give a fuck about what they were up to. Although, knowing their whereabouts could be useful. If they were chasing a target, then they weren't here, which was always a good thing. If they were busy, it might even be better to dump the body tonight rather than waiting. I turned back. "Location?"

Cyrus leaned forward, squinting at the screen, the latest dose of whiskey probably making it even harder to read. "Club in Cofield. The Frozen Duck. Fucking stupid name if you ask me. Guess there's going to be one less posh fucker by the end of the night."

"Name?" I didn't know why I asked, really. But occasionally it was one I recognized.

His fingers moved at lightning speed over the keyboard. "DTP fuckers have put a new firewall in. Give me a minute to get through it." His brow furrowed as he concentrated on what he was doing, the bottle of whiskey beside him momentarily forgotten. A smile slowly bloomed on his face. "One of these days, they'll actually manage to come up with something good enough to keep me out for more than thirty seconds. But not today, you bastards."

I had neither the time nor the patience to wait while he patted himself on the back and told himself how wonderful he was. "Do you have a name or not?"

He lifted his head from the screen. "Yeah, I have a name. Tate. Tate Gillespie."

I was already halfway down the street and running before the last syllable had left his lips.

4
TATE

If I'd ever asked myself whether I was a hero or a coward, I would definitely have gone with the latter. Yet there was something in me, something that made me open my eyes, lift my chin, and stare down the barrel of the gun that was about to extinguish my life. Maybe it was the desire to see one more thing apart from the darkness behind my eyelids. Or maybe it was just the damn stubbornness I'd always been accused of having. I didn't know. But I did it anyway, fixing my gaze on the masked man behind the gun. Would ending my life bother him after he'd pulled the trigger? Or was it just pest control in his eyes?

In those last few seconds of my life, all my senses seemed heightened, everything coming into sharp awareness. The floor was colder. The weight of a hundred stares all focused on me was that bit heavier. And the silence… God, the silence was deafening, accentuating the rapid thrum of the blood through my veins even more. The soldier hitched his gun a little higher, taking aim, his finger starting to curl around the trigger. I tried to swallow, but I couldn't remember how to do it, tried to breathe but that was difficult too.

Something whipped past my ear at rapid speed, landing in the crook between the soldier's mask and his shoulder, managing to find access space where I wouldn't have thought there was any. I stared at the handle of the knife sticking out, trying to make sense of it. I braced myself for the burst of laser fire but it never came. The soldier teetered for a few moments, his finger slipping off the trigger as the gun fell to the floor with a *crash*. It didn't remain alone for long, the soldier toppling over to join it within seconds. Was he dead? I guessed a knife in the neck would do that to a person. But who had thrown it? And why?

All hell broke loose then, the remaining three soldiers spinning around in an attempt to locate the unknown assailant who'd dared to take down one of their members. Another rush of air, the gleam of something shiny spinning through the air, and then another soldier fell, the knife hitting him in exactly the same spot as it had the first. Not quite as effective this time, though. He stumbled to his knees, putting him on the same level as I was. His hand lifted to his neck to pull the knife free, the armored suit darkening as blood began to gush out. He kept his other hand on his gun, the barrel strafing left and right, his gaze searching the crowd for the enemy.

As for the onlookers, they didn't seem to know what to do. I could see in their eyes that they wanted to run. But if they did, they were just as likely to be gunned down by the DTP as they were to be felled by whoever was being so free and easy with the knives.

One of the DTP soldiers, seemingly having worked out the direction the last knife had come from, pushed his way through the crowd on the dancefloor. That left the one bleeding profusely and one other behind me. Should I try to run? But where would I go? There was nowhere the DTP couldn't find me.

A figure detached itself from the shadows, a tall man dressed all in black that I'd never seen before. He closed the space between us in a couple of strides, his arm hooking beneath mine to drag me to my feet. I found myself crushed against his hard body, his body heat forcing warmth into limbs that I hadn't even realized were cold. The stranger yanked me to the side as the soldier bleeding from the neck lifted his gun and fired, the burst of laser fire hitting the spot where I'd been milliseconds before.

In my absence it hit someone on the dancefloor, vaporizing them in seconds, screams rending the air from the people who'd been standing next to that person. The muscled body I was holding onto jerked, his arm lifting to send another knife sailing through the air. It embedded itself in almost the exact same spot on the soldier as the first had. This time the soldier slumped to the floor, the hand previously clasped to his neck lying limp and still, his gun skittering away across the floor.

At the sound of the gun being discharged, the soldier closest to me whirled around. But I was already being hustled backward, the crowd swallowing us up and covering our retreat. I let myself be led, wondering whether I should have been struggling. But whatever else this man was, there was no disputing the fact that he'd just saved my life. Therefore, I went with it, my limbs so jelly-like that I struggled to keep up with him as he pushed people out of the way.

I had no idea where we were going. I just hoped to God that he did, and that he wasn't leading us into a dead end. But then, even if he was, I wouldn't be any worse off, given that I'd been seconds from death. His hand was a vise around my arm, holding me up as I stumbled.

The original message from the DTP started to play. I assumed it was for the benefit of my rescuer, the reminder that there would be consequences for harboring a criminal resonating in my ears as a door loomed in front of us. The stranger kicked it open, hustling me through the back of the club and into a long corridor, increasing his pace even more as he took us down it.

His T-shirt was bunched between my fingers, but as hard as I tried, I couldn't seem to convince my fingers to unfurl and let go. The feel of the fabric somehow grounded me, reminding me that I was still alive. One by one, my other senses started to spark back to life, the man's earthy—but not unpleasant—scent teasing my nostrils.

A door slammed behind us, one—or both—of the remaining DTP soldiers hot on our heels. I wasn't about to waste time turning around to count them. Neither was my companion, it seemed. He broke into a run, taking a sharp left and then a right, paying no attention to the open doors we passed as if he knew exactly where we were going. Another door appeared in front of us and we were suddenly out on the street, the crisp, cold air filling my lungs and feeling like heaven. And still he didn't slow down.

People stared as we passed, but none of them made any move to stop us. It showed that had he been my kidnapper instead of my savior, I would have gotten no help from anyone. Although, I suppose if that had been the case, I would have been shouting for help and digging my heels in, rather than keeping stride with him. Just as my lungs had started to burn and I wasn't sure how much longer I could carry on, he led me into an alleyway, pushing me into the space between two dumpsters, his bulk filling the gap and hemming me in. I sagged back against the wall, getting my first real opportunity to take a look at him while I tried to force some much-needed oxygen back into my lungs.

The stranger was hewn from granite, all sharp angles and shadows, his features slightly too acute to be deemed conventionally attractive. Eyes that could only be described as amber scoured the street, oblivious to my scrutiny. As I watched, he scrubbed a hand through his hair, or what there was of it anyway. It was buzzed to the point of being almost non-existent, the ends a mere shadow against his scalp.

He almost crackled with expectant tension, bulky yet still lean muscles filling out his T-shirt in all the right ways. My gaze dropped to the long, curved knives strapped to either side of his waist, his fingers resting on the handle of one of them. Whoever this man was, one thing was for sure, he was danger with a capital D. Had I just escaped one life-threatening situation, only to swap it for another? He seemed to be waiting for something, but I wasn't sure what? Was he checking to see if we'd been followed? If so, it seemed we hadn't or the DTP would already have been on top of us.

His gaze suddenly swung from the street to me. I couldn't help it. I backed away. It was only the brickwork behind me that stopped me from going any farther. Something flickered across his face, but it was so fleeting that it was gone before I could identify it.

I wrapped my arms around myself, rubbing my shoulders in some poor facsimile of comfort. "Who are you?"

He came a step closer, scrutinizing me as if he'd found an exotic new species. "You're scared of me."

His voice matched his appearance, all sharp-edged and lethal.

Swallowing with difficulty, I let my gaze drop to the knife his hand still rested on. "Shouldn't I be?"

"No."

There'd been no hesitation before he'd delivered the one-word answer, just that blunt rebuttal. Still, I needed more. "Are you going to hurt me?"

His expression didn't change. His face may as well have been a mask for all the emotion it showed. "Why would I save you, only to hurt you?"

It was a good question. "Why did you save me?"

He turned away, his face falling into shadow so that I couldn't make out anything on it. "Now's not the time. They'll be gathering more forces together. They'll coordinate a search through the city for us. We only have a small window of opportunity to get out of the city."

I nearly choked on my tongue. "Out of the city? I've never left the city."

His eyes narrowed, his face hardening. "You'd rather the

DTP gunned you down like a feral dog?"

"No, of course not."

"Then… it's our only option."

"I didn't do it." I had no idea why I felt the need to tell him that. He was a stranger, an unknown quantity. But it still felt imperative to defend myself, to let him know that he'd been right to save me, whatever his reasons were.

"I know."

The soft acknowledgement shocked me to the core. How could this complete stranger believe in my innocence? Even Trisha, in the few seconds before they'd dragged her away, hadn't looked that sure. I regarded him steadily, trying to see past the scary exterior. "What's your name?"

His fingers flexed, releasing the handle of his knife for a few seconds before tightening around it once again. Amber eyes locked onto mine. "X."

I frowned. "X? That's not a name. That's a letter." The words were out before I could ponder the wisdom of insulting the dangerous man with the knives. "Sorry. Mine's Tate."

"I know that as well."

"How do you—"

But he was already taking hold of my arm again and ushering me over to the opposite side of the alley before telling me that we needed to run again. I had a feeling that I was going to get more exercise today than I had in the previous six months put together.

But I was alive.

For now, anyway.

5
TATE

It wasn't until we were standing in front of the high wall covered by barbed wire that I appreciated where the mysterious X was taking me. He meant for us to cross over from Cofield into the slums.

He interlocked his fingers together, motioning that he would assist me in climbing the wall. I tilted my head back, assessing both its height and its danger. And that was without considering what lay on the other side of it.

If I was honest, most of my concern wasn't about breaching the wall, but about what lay beyond. I hadn't been joking when I'd told Trisha that she'd have to be an idiot to set foot in there. People like us steered clear of the slums because there were people like… well, like X there. People you didn't go anywhere near if you knew what was good for you. That's why the wall had been built in the first place. To protect the inhabitants of Cofield from the less savory elements on the other side.

X's body language radiated impatience, the barbed wire suddenly appearing less menacing in comparison to the possibility of facing his wrath. I braced my hands against the wall, the brickwork cool and gritty against my fingers and stepped onto the hands he'd left there for that purpose. Breath rushed from my lungs as I was hoisted unceremoniously upward without any warning, my fingers scrabbling for purchase at the top of the wall. "What about the barbed wire?"

"Try not to touch it." *Great fucking advice.* With the combination of X pushing from below and my own puny efforts at pulling myself up, I managed to heave my body onto the wall. There wasn't much space up there, so it was precarious to try and balance without touching the barbed wire. At least it was still pre-curfew, which meant there was enough light from the streetlights in Cofield to ensure we could see. God knows how we would have done it had it been a couple of hours later.

I'd often wondered what the slums looked like. The view in front of me couldn't have been more different from the streets I was used to. Behind me were polished glass buildings and perfectly paved streets. Whereas the slums looked like pictures I'd seen in history books of refugee camps with all the buildings patched together from whatever had been available, whether that was sheet metal or tarpaulin which looked like it had seen better days. And there were no pavements, just a dirt track which wended its way between what passed for buildings. What was supposed to happen now? I might have made it to the top of the wall thanks to X's assistance, but he was still stuck at the bottom of it.

I turned, intending to ask him, but the words died in my throat as he took a few steps back from the wall before coming at it in a run, executing a perfect flying leap to grasp the edge of the wall and expertly pull himself up with very little difficulty. I would have been impressed if... No, strike that. I was impressed. He had athleticism and strength all rolled into one. To distract myself from the possibility of saying something stupid about his muscles, I gestured at the barbed wire. "How do we—?"

I hadn't even finished my sentence before X was peeling off both his leather jacket and T-shirt, rendering me speechless as he uncovered a torso which could only be described as a work of art, each muscle perfectly defined. The man had to work out morning, noon, and night to have a body like that. If I'd been capable of speech, I would have blurted out something stupid like whether now was really the time to be stripping. Thankfully, the fact that I couldn't meant I stayed silent as he draped both items of clothing over the vicious-looking coils of wire, inclining his head in an unmistakable silent instruction. I lifted one leg gingerly, positioning myself so that I could straddle the wire.

For one horrifying moment, I teetered as I lost my balance. Firm fingers gripped hold of my arm, holding me still as I lifted the other leg and managed to clear the wire. X hopped over it as if he did it twenty times a day, which for all I knew he did.

The first obstacle navigated, I stared down at the sheer drop on the opposite side. The barbed wire wasn't the only deterrent. The wall had been built so that although it was on a level with Cofield, there was a gradient on the other side. If I broke a leg, I was a dead man who may as well wait around for the inevitable mercy killing from the DTP. X crouched, motioning me toward him. Like an obedient child, I shuffled across to him, making sure to avoid the barbed wire at my back.

X held his hands out in front of him, palms upward. "Take my hands. I'll lower you as far as I can."

It took some awkward maneuvering to get into the right position, X's hands clamping around my wrists, and then before I knew it my feet were dangling in mid-air, my heart beating an uneven rhythm against my ribs. I made the mistake of looking down, the ground looking too far away for comfort. Quickly averting my gaze, I concentrated on the bulging biceps straining beneath my weight, which were a much more pleasant sight to look at.

My feet wind-milled in the air, instinct causing me to search for something to stand on, but of course there was nothing apart from the vertical surface of the wall. The grip on my wrists loosened. "Wait." I just needed a few more seconds. Time to convince myself that this was necessary, and that if I didn't do it,

I was going to die anyway, so what did it matter if I fell wrong and bashed my brains out on the ground below.

"Time is a luxury we don't have."

The words were almost growled out, letting me know that his patience was starting to wear thin. Was he already regretting his intervention? Wondering why he was wasting his time with someone who couldn't even handle a fifteen-foot drop?

"Three..."

Fuck! He was counting. It was just a wall. Just fifteen feet or so. How far could a human fall safely? I tried to recall whether I'd ever read anything that had provided that information, but I drew a blank.

"Two..."

There was no other choice.

"One..."

And then X let go, and I was falling, my breath leaving my lungs in a rush as my back hit the ground. Hard. I lay stunned for a few seconds, carrying out a quick inventory of my limbs and finally concluding that apart from a few bruises, I was going to be fine. Nothing was twisted. Nothing was broken. There were no bones protruding from anywhere there shouldn't be. I looked up in time to see X lowering himself over the side of the wall. Without anyone to hoist him down, the drop was going to be even farther for him. I held my breath as he let go.

There was a couple of seconds of his body falling through the air, and then he landed on his feet, dropping straight into a crouch to absorb the impact. The man was part cat. Actually, a cat was the perfect comparison. He was all power and grace, and the knives were his claws. I was still contemplating the strange analogy as he came toward me and held out a hand. I took it, letting him help me up. "Now where?"

He hadn't let go of my hand, so when he took off at a jog without answering my question, I was forced to follow as we weaved our way through the dark, twisty streets, the only light on this side of the wall spilling from windows that we passed. I knew the slums were meant to be different, but the descriptions I'd heard really hadn't done it justice. For one, the smell was something else. The only thing I could equate it to was rubbish that had been left out in the sun for a week. I had no idea where the stench came from and to be honest, I wasn't sure I wanted to know.

Figures stood in doorways, turning their heads to track us as we passed them, curiosity evident on their faces. No one tried to stop us or questioned why we were running, or where we were going. Whether that was due to the aura X exuded or that they just didn't give a damn, I didn't know. My clothes had to give away where I'd come from. But for all I knew, maybe it was a common occurrence for a refugee from Cofield to try and seek sanctuary there from the DTP.

It couldn't be, though, could it? Or I'd have heard about people escaping from them before. Someone would have said something if an angel bearing knives had been rescuing criminals—or supposed criminals. Which meant this was the first time it had happened. Why? What made me so special? Why would someone risk their own life to save mine when I was a nobody? And what was X even doing in Cofield in the first place?

The questions raging through my head were silenced as X came to a sudden stop. Relieved, I bent over with my hands braced on my knees, looking around while I tried to catch my breath. We'd stopped in what looked to be a scrapyard. And not a very good scrapyard at that. It looked like it had long since been cleared of anything that might be useful leaving nothing but huge chunks of rusted metal, their initial purpose no longer obvious. I squinted at one, trying to work out if at one point in time it had been a car. But it could just as easily have been something else entirely. "Where are we?"

"My house."

"It's nice." The sarcastic words were out before I could

stop them. I didn't even try and hide my wince. *That's right, Tate. Smart-mouth the man with the blades, why don't you?* I half expected to feel the cold kiss of steel against my neck. But either he hadn't heard me, or he'd chosen to ignore me. He swept his foot across the ground, a metal hatch gradually appearing as he cleared the debris to one side. He bent down, twisting a circular handle in the middle of the hatch before lifting it. I stared down into the gloom, only the top rungs of a ladder visible. "Oh, I see. You live *here*. Not"—I gestured around the scrapyard—"here."

X stood over to the side, holding his arm out in a clear invitation. Apparently, I wasn't just scared of walls; dark, unknown spaces didn't really do it for me either. I stepped closer, hoping the bottom of the shaft would come into view from the new vantage point. It didn't. It might as well have been a drop into hell.

"Lights come on automatically near the bottom."

"Yeah?" That was quite possibly the best news I'd ever been given. X gave me a gentle but insistent shove. I curled my fingers around the cold metal of the ladder and took a few steps down.

"When you get to the bottom, stay close to the ladder."

"Why?"

But X was too busy pulling the hatch back into place over our heads and extinguishing what tiny bit of light the moon had provided. I could hear his feet moving downwards above my head, meaning I had no choice but to keep going, my hands and feet feeling blindly for each rung. How long was the ladder? How deep did this shaft go?

A dim light clicked on by my head. It was better than nothing but not by much. But it did enable me to see the bottom of the shaft and thankfully, it wasn't that much farther. I sped up now that I could see it, reaching the bottom within seconds and gazing with curiosity down the corridor that lay beyond it. I started down it, intrigued to see where it led. A hand gripped my bicep, yanking me back and pushing me against the ladder, the rungs digging into my back. X's face loomed close, the expression on his face none too pleased. "I told you to stay where you were. Do you have a fucking death wish?"

It was difficult to concentrate on his words with my body reacting so strongly to his proximity. Hard muscle pressed against me at every point, pinning me in place so that I couldn't have moved even if I wanted to. And I liked it. I liked it a lot, a certain part of my anatomy liking it even more than my brain did. I willed my cock to calm down. The last thing I wanted was for my unlikely savior to decide that I was some sort of pervert. Besides, I had a boyfriend. I tried to conjure up an image of Joseph, but next to the sheer presence of this man, it was like trying to compare a ghost to something flesh and blood. I needed X to move away so that my body could calm down and I'd be able to think again, but he seemed in no hurry to do so, the expression on his face expectant, as if he was waiting for something. What was it he'd said? Something about having a death wish, that was it. I stared at him. "Sorry. I forgot."

He shook his head. "You need to listen, Tate."

His casual use of my name reminded me of the fact that he'd said he'd known it already. But how could that be when I'd never seen him before in my life? At least pondering that mystery stopped me from focusing on how good he felt pressed against me. Finally, he stepped away.

He held up a hand to tell me to wait, my gaze automatically following his as it dropped to the floor. A thin piece of wire stretched across the corridor—a trip-wire. A trip-wire that my feet had to have been mere millimeters away from triggering. The question was what happened when it was triggered. As X crouched, his fingers deftly unhooking the trip-wire, I scanned the corridor, finally spotting the shotgun mounted on the ceiling, which would have sent a bullet straight through my brain if I'd so much as nudged the wire. "I guess you don't like visitors?"

No answer. X stood, waiting till I'd stepped past the wire

before hooking it up again. I only took two steps before coming to a halt. I'd learnt my lesson. "Any more booby traps I should be aware of?"

He shook his head. I was beginning to get the idea that X was a man of few words. The problem was, when other people didn't talk that much, I tended to try and fill the space with meaningless drivel. I made my way cautiously down the corridor to where it opened into a large room. Sparse didn't even begin to describe it. There was furniture—of a sort. But that was about it. There was nothing that could be classed as home comforts, not even a solitary cushion. But then X didn't exactly strike me as a man who was into soft furnishings.

I turned in a slow circle, my gaze raking across every nook and cranny in order to try and find out more about my mysterious... friend? Was he a friend? He'd saved my life. There was no disputing that fact. But what that made him, I wasn't too sure. Did he want something from me? If so, what? I didn't have anything to give him. I had some money in the bank, but nowhere near enough to make putting himself on the wrong side of the DTP worthwhile. I needed to start demanding answers from him.

Stepping back, my foot brushed something against the wall. I glanced down, expecting to see something innocuous like a rug, although my previous thoughts about soft furnishings should have told me that that wasn't possible. In the circumstances, the scream that escaped from my throat was unavoidable. I'd barely started before a rough hand clamped over my mouth and stopped in its tracks. It held fast as I automatically struggled against the pressure. A hand fastened across my chest, pulling me flush against his body so that we were pressed together. Again. The only difference this time was that my back was to his front. Lips hovered by my ear. "Shhhh... we might be underground but there are vents. If you scream, someone might hear. Nod if you understand."

Despite the surge of panic still turning my blood to fire, I managed a shaky nod, the hand fastened over my mouth shifting with the motion.

More words were spoken directly into my ear. "I'm going to let go now. Promise you won't scream."

I gave another nod, the fingers covering my mouth slowly loosening as X stepped away. My gaze immediately returned to the floor, nausea bubbling away inside me. "There's a dead body in your house."

X's gaze followed mine, raking the prone figure in an unconcerned fashion. "I'm aware of that fact."

"He doesn't have a head."

For a second, the corner of X's mouth twitched as if he might have been considering a smile. If so, it was a pretty strange thing to find amusing. "That happens when you trespass on someone's property."

It all clicked into place. The tripwire. The shotgun. The corpse with the missing head. It still didn't make it normal though. "And you just left him here?"

X tilted his head to the side. "He wasn't really up for going for a walk."

No matter how much I tried not to look at the body, my eyes kept straying back to it. Given the DTP's brand of justice, I was used to death. But death by laser gun left nothing but a pile of ash. I wasn't used to seeing bodies with nothing but a ragged stump of flesh where their head used to be. There was a sweet, cloying smell coming from it as well. Only faint, but it was still there.

X walked over to what passed as a sofa, sweeping a covering from it and laying it over the corpse. "Better?"

"Yes." It was better. At least I could stop looking at it now. I forced myself to walk away from it until I was in the middle of the room. But when my eyes strayed over to the bed in the corner, I almost wished I still had the corpse to stare at. It suddenly struck me that I was trapped. I didn't know how to deactivate the trip-wire myself, so I'd just walked willingly into a place where I couldn't leave. What if X's intentions were simple? Abduct someone who wouldn't be missed. He could keep me as some sort of sex slave. Chain me to the bed and do whatever he wanted to me, and why wasn't that thought as repugnant as it should have been?

But X didn't seem remotely interested in the bed. Or in me for that matter. He was over by a door in the wall that I hadn't spotted. He opened it, disappearing inside for a few moments. I raised my voice so that he could still hear me. "So, we'll be safe here? From the DTP, I mean."

He stepped back out, shoving a large backpack into my arms. "No. I expect it won't take them too long to work out who I am. We should be okay for about thirty minutes, and then they'll still have to cut through the hatch to get access. We need to be gone before they get here. The shotgun will only take out the first one."

I attempted to swallow, but saliva seemed to be in short supply. "How many do you think will come?"

The look he gave me was reminiscent of one you might give to a poor innocent child. "A lot."

"Right." I fidgeted with the bag. "What's this for?"

X gestured to a cupboard next to where we stood. "Fill it with grenades."

I blinked a few times. "Grenades!" Sure enough, when I pulled the door open, the shelves were stacked with weapons. X reached over my head, plucking a bunch of small knives from the middle shelf. They looked like the ones he'd used to take down the soldiers in the club so I guessed that they were replacements. It wasn't like we'd hung around to retrieve the ones embedded in the soldiers' necks. "Anything I should know about handling grenades?"

X opened a drawer, tugging out a black T-shirt and pulling

it over his head before donning a well-worn leather jacket in the same color. "Yeah. Don't pull the pin out. And if you do, don't hang on to it for longer than three seconds."

From anyone else I might have assumed it was a joke, but even after such a brief acquaintance I was pretty sure that he wasn't the type for levity. I reached out, gingerly wrapping my hand around one of the grenades and transferring it to the bag.

"Quickly."

Right. Because who didn't want to handle grenades quickly? I sped up, trusting that the pins were in tightly enough that they wouldn't be dislodged easily. "Bag's full."

Another backpack came winging its way across the room toward me. I caught it, almost dropping the full bag in the process. "Oh, good! Because I was worried that I wouldn't get my own bag of grenades. Now we can have one each."

I glanced over, but X was too busy filling another bag with God knows what to pay any attention to me. When both bags were full, I fastened them securely, almost having a heart attack as I straightened to find X standing directly behind me. The man didn't make a sound when he moved. Someone should put a bell round his neck. He stretched out an arm, a jacket similar to the one he wore dangling from one finger. "Put this on."

It was on the tip of my tongue to refuse, but seeing as I was dressed for clubbing and my arms were bare, it would have been cutting off my nose to spite my face. I reached out and took it, the leather surprisingly soft against my fingers as I shrugged my arms into it. It smelled like him, a tantalizing mixture of musk and spice.

He stepped closer, one hand fastening on the side of my head, the sure grip tilting my head to the side in a move that brooked no argument. I held still as he scrutinized the place where I'd banged my head in the club. His face was distractingly close, and I found myself staring at his stubble-covered chin. Had he not shaved today? Or was he one of those men who needed to shave more than once a day? I breathed him in, feeling like between him and the jacket I was surrounded by his scent. I'd never expected someone who lived in the slums to smell good, but he definitely did.

I found myself steered through a door and into a tiny bathroom, one of X's hands still holding my head at an angle while the other pulled a cabinet open and extracted items from inside it. My attempt to see what they were was met by a tightening of the grip holding me in place. I let out a curse as something that stung like hell came into contact with raw skin as he wiped away what I could only presume was dried blood. It felt like I had quite the bump as well, the skin tender as he probed it. I guessed when flesh met concrete, it was a common result.

X had to be the strangest nurse I'd ever had. Despite the initial burst of pain, his touch was surprisingly gentle, so gentle that with everything else going on, it brought a lump to my throat. I gave myself a mental shake, desperately searching for something to say to break the stillness before I did something stupid like burst into tears. "It's just a bump."

"Shhh."

Fingers continued to probe at my scalp, dipping briefly into my hair. Finally satisfied that he'd removed any traces of blood, he added a Band-Aid as a finishing touch, even going so far as to smooth the edges down. Then he let go as he stepped back.

My head felt strangely heavy now that I had to support its weight without help, and I was struggling with a strange sense of being bereft. I lifted my hand, feeling my way around the edges of the Band-Aid to try and gauge how big the lump was. A mirror, that's what I needed. I looked around, but there wasn't one. Who didn't have a mirror in their bathroom? The answer to that question was apparently X. "Thanks."

X shrugged, backing out of the bathroom and forcing me to follow in his wake. "What happens now?"

"I have a few errands I need to run, and then we get out of the city."

I was already shaking my head before he'd finished talking. He'd said a similar thing earlier, but I'd hoped it had been one of many options. It seemed it wasn't. "And go where?"

Something flickered across his face. Something that made me think that he wasn't quite as confident about everything as he was making out. But it was gone as quickly as it had appeared, his next words confirming that I'd been right. "We'll work it out."

"So… you don't even know where we're going? You did the whole 'come with me if you want to live thing' without having worked out how you were going to accomplish that?"

He frowned, the cultural reference obviously falling flat.

"Terminator?" Still nothing. I sighed. "It's a really old film. One of my favorites. Well, the original anyway. I stopped watching once they'd gotten to *Terminator X*. Films are kind of my thing. Anyway, in *Terminator* there was a man named Kyle Reese. He went back in time to save Sarah Connor from the Terminators so that her son could live. It all got very complicated, though, because he ended up fathering the child that hadn't been born yet, the one that had sent him back in the first place. And then he died. But when he first intercepted one of the Terminators, he told her to come with him if she wanted to live. And he was just a man and they were robots, so it wasn't really a fair fight."

I was babbling so I forced myself to stop. "It's a good film. You should watch it." I scanned the room, noting the lack of any electronic equipment whatsoever, never mind a TV. What did the man do for fun? Although, given his demeanor, I wasn't sure the word fun was in his vocabulary. "Maybe not. Anyway, it reminded me of us. You're Kyle Reese, and I'm… Sarah Connor."

X's eyebrow twitched. "You want me to call you Sarah?"

"I think I'll pass on that." I hoisted one of the backpacks onto my back, trying not to think about how many grenades

were currently jostling against me through only a few layers of fabric. "And the DTP are not Terminators, they're just men in combat armor, which is good I guess." Christ! I was still talking about it. I needed to change the subject. " I need to see Joseph before we leave the city, to say goodbye to him."
"No." The word was delivered without emotion, but still packed quite a punch.

I stared at him as he arranged the backpacks so that he could carry two—the advantage of having a broad, muscular back. Not that I'd noticed. "You don't understand, he's my boyfriend. I can't just leave. He's a good man. He's—" What was I doing? The man had a corpse in his living room, and I was trying to appeal to his better nature. I must have hit my head pretty hard to think that was going to work. For some reason, I kept forgetting that he was dangerous. I just didn't feel like he was a threat. Not to me anyway. Maybe it was because he'd just saved my life and given me medical treatment. God, I was naïve.

"We'll see."

The words came as a surprise, and it was all I could do to stutter out a "Thanks."

A muscle twitched in X's cheek. "I'm not promising anything. We'd have to work out a way of contacting him."

"That's not a problem." I rooted around in my pocket, pulling my phone out with a flourish. "I can just call him."

I couldn't honestly have said whether I made the connection before or after I saw the truth reflected in X's face. Only that I had. Therefore, it didn't come as a surprise when he snatched it out of my hand, dropped it on the floor, and ground it to smithereens beneath his boot. "Shit! They'll be tracking it, right?"

He nodded. "Our thirty minutes just became considerably less." As if to illustrate his point, heavy footsteps sounded directly above our heads, both of us automatically raising our eyes to the ceiling.

X grabbed my arm. "Time to go." He pulled me in the

opposite direction to where we'd entered, stopping in front of a solid wall. I watched in confusion as he smoothed his hand over it, his fingertips grazing over its surface carefully as if he was searching for something. Finally, he paused, pressing down, the wall sliding back to reveal a dark corridor not dissimilar to the one on the other side of the bunker. I didn't need any encouragement to step through the doorway. Not now that the sound of drilling had started up. X had said that it would take them five minutes to get through the hatch. Which begged the question how his dead friend had been able to gain access.

 X stepped through too, the wall sliding back into place when he pressed something. "That'll slow them down." He pulled a flashlight out of his pocket, lighting up the gloom in front of us. "Follow me."

 I followed. What else was I going to do? Unlike the other corridor, this one wasn't straight and went on for much longer. Ease of movement varied at different points, the passageway becoming so narrow at times that the only way to traverse it was to remove the backpacks and push them in front of us. At other points, the roof dipped so low that we almost had to crawl. Despite not being claustrophobic, I found myself struggling, having to force myself to breathe deeply in order to stay calm as I stared at X's back to remind myself that I wasn't alone. And then of course there was the fact that I didn't have a clue where we were going.

 We navigated one last twisting turn before the tunnel came to an abrupt halt, a metal hatch embedded in the wall in front of us. Expecting X to open it, I was mystified as he hammered on it with the palm of his hand. "Can't you just open it?"

 He shook his head. "It only opens from the other side. It's meant to be an entrance, not an exit."

 Fucking fantastic. "And who are you expecting to open it?" My question was drowned out as X hammered on the metal again. I glanced back down the tunnel, half expecting to see the DTP round the corner. If they'd discovered the tunnel, then they had to hear the noise. We might as well be announcing our whereabouts. Finally, the hatch was pulled open with a groan of metal as if it hadn't been opened for quite some time, the face of an old man with a long white beard appearing in the space. X pushed him out of the way. "About fucking time, Cyrus."

He crawled through the hatch, reaching back to help me clear the obstacle. Then he led me through a doorway. I looked around in curiosity. We were in the middle of a shack that looked like it had been patched together from any parts that they could find, the lighting system consisting of car headlights attached to a generator that sounded like it was on its last legs. It wasn't until I'd finished my scrutiny that I realized that the man X had called Cyrus was staring at me with his mouth wide open. I stared back, witnessing the moment when he managed to muster words. "Who the fuck is this?"

X regarded the man coolly. There seemed to be a strange energy between the two of them that had me pondering exactly what their relationship was. They bore no resemblance to each other whatsoever, so they couldn't be father and son, and it made it unlikely that they were even related. They weren't friendly enough to be friends, so I guessed they were business acquaintances—of a sort. X seemed in no rush to answer the old man's question, which left me feeling awkward and wondering whether I was supposed to introduce myself. Finally, X cocked his head to one side, delivering the answer with zero emotion. "He's Tate Gillespie."

Cyrus staggered backwards, his hand reaching out for the back of a chair for support as his features creased into an expression of shock. "No fucking way! What the hell did you do, X? Have you lost your fucking mind?" He pointed a tremulous finger in my direction. "He's meant to be dead." The finger swung back to X. "You're a fucking idiot! An idiot with a death wish, apparently. And you bring him here. *Here*, of all places."

Nice. I could see that Cyrus and I weren't about to be friends any time soon.

X's expression hadn't changed one iota throughout the old man's tirade. He waited until the man had paused for breath. "I need your help. Find out what you can about what they know. How many units have they sent? What do they know about me?"

The old man shook his head as he sat down at what I assumed passed for a computer on this side of the wall, his fingers already tapping on the keyboard. "You're going to get me killed."

X snorted. "Better be quick then before they get here."

Droplets of sweat had appeared on Cyrus's forehead. "What am I meant to say to them when they pop out of the tunnel? That's assuming they actually stop to ask questions and don't just gun me down."

X crouched, pulling two grenades out of the bag he carried. "They won't be coming out of the tunnel because I'm going to blow it."

"What about when you need it again? I ain't digging no fucking tunnel for you. Not for all the whiskey in the goddamn world."

"I'm not going to need it again." X's head lifted, his gaze alighting on me for a few seconds before his focus returned to Cyrus. "I won't be coming back."

Cyrus's fingers stilled for a beat. "I see."

X disappeared back through the door, Cyrus's hands continuing to move across the keyboard at lightning speed even as he shook his head again and muttered, "Crazy fucker," his gaze darting to me as if he expected me to argue with him. There was no chance of that though. Not when I didn't even know X. There was a muffled thump, followed by one more, the whole shack shaking but thankfully remaining standing.

X appeared shortly after. "Done."

Cyrus dug his fingers into his beard, scratching his chin. "My life's going to be much simpler without you around, you know that, right?"

Leaning forward over the makeshift computer, X gave the closest thing I'd seen to a smile. "A hell of a lot more sober as well. Let's hope the withdrawals don't kill you before the DTP does."

"Fuck off, you cocksucker!"

Maybe friends, then? Or what passed for friends in the slums, which I was beginning to think meant people who could be useful to you in some way. I guess that made sense. When you didn't have much, you hung on to anything you could.

X fidgeted impatiently. "What have you got? We need to get moving. I still need to get maps from Ren."

Leaning back in the chair, Cyrus linked his fingers behind his head. I tried my best not to stare at the dark sweat patches under his arms revealed by the change in position. He cleared his throat as if he was about to give a speech. "One small unit was initially dispatched"—his gaze lifted to mine—"as pretty boy here wasn't deemed a risk." He turned to look at X. "After the stroke you pulled… both soldiers died from their wounds, by the way, just in case you're interested… they upped that to two units." His eyebrows rose as he gave X a hard stare. "Once they'd identified you, they added another three so you currently have five units on your tail. One is in your bunker. One is stationed by the border gate so I wouldn't suggest going that way unless you're ready to surrender to the inevitable without a fight. One is currently patrolling so they could be anywhere. Last known position is in Cofield, but that was ten minutes ago, so…" He shrugged. "The other two have been dispatched, but haven't gotten here yet. ETA is thirty minutes." He lowered his arms and pressed another key before shaking his head. "You're both dead men walking. You'll be lucky to survive an hour."

Cold dread filled my body. It was one thing to know it, but another thing entirely for someone to lay it out like that without any sugarcoating whatsoever. Five units? Even at minimum unit size—which was unlikely—that was fifteen highly trained, deadly soldiers hunting us. And the worse-case scenario... forty of them. All because I'd walked into the wrong room at the wrong time and been too naïve to realize what was going on. I wondered what Malcolm was doing right now. Probably drinking champagne and congratulating himself on being a criminal genius.

X picked up the backpacks again. "We'll see. Let's see how they fancy a journey cross-country."

Cyrus shifted in his seat. "You're leaving?"

X quirked an eyebrow. "What did you think we were going to do? Play hide and seek around Cofield?"

"So, you really meant it when you said you were getting out of town?"

I pulled the jacket that smelt of X more firmly around me while I watched the interchange between the two men.

X nodded. "Bet you're gonna miss me, aren't you?"

The old man laughed, revealing a mouthful of rotten teeth. "Like fuck I am. Now get gone before they track you here and I find myself having to breathe the same air as a bunch of cock-sucking soldiers. I need to hide this computer and pretend that I'm a harmless old man before they start doing their house calls to search for your sorry ass. I always said you were nothing but fucking trouble. Look how right I was. You owe me a shitload of whiskey."

"I owe you fuck all."

Cyrus gave X the finger, but X had already turned away to head for the door. I followed him, all without having said a single word since we'd arrived at the shack. X was all that stood between myself and a bunch of DTP soldiers intent on obliterating me from existence.

6
X

Two hours ago, my biggest concern had been disposing of the latest fucker who'd stupidly taken the invitation of an unlocked hatch to become better acquainted with my shotgun. Now, I was on the run. There were thousands of names Cyrus could have let slip earlier that wouldn't have changed my life one iota, and he'd had to announce the *one* name that had.

I'd run like I'd never run before. There'd been no question of me coming to Tate's aid. The only question had been whether I would get there in time. I didn't believe in a divine being of any description, but I'd come closer than I ever had before to praying to whoever the fuck might be listening. Maybe they'd been listening anyway, or maybe it was just pure, dumb luck. I didn't care.

Tate was still alive. How long I could keep him that way, though, was another matter entirely. But one thing was for sure, I'd give it everything I had until my last, dying breath. Hustling him in the direction I needed him to go, I dismissed a fleeting thought about hiding him somewhere. Gaze darting left and right, I kept searching the shadows for any sign of DTP movement.

Only when I was sure we were alone did my gaze stray to Tate. He'd gone quiet, the events of the last hour finally seeming to catch up with him. He'd been scared of me at first. I'd seen the look in his eyes that I'd always known would be there should I ever step out of the darkness and try to interact with him, as if I could ever think anything other than that he was a precious jewel, and I was pond scum not fit to be on the sole of his shoe.

What was surprising was how quickly he'd seemed to get over it. Even when he'd been faced with the headless corpse in my bunker, it hadn't returned. I reminded myself that his opinion didn't matter. He didn't need to like me; he just needed to trust me enough to follow my instructions.

I grabbed his arm, ignoring the tingles that touching him evoked as I pulled him toward our destination. *Tingles?* What the fuck was I thinking? I was X—cold-blooded killer and a man not to be messed with. I didn't get tingles. Not even for Tate Gillespie. I needed to eradicate those sorts of thoughts from my head. Tate would no doubt be horrified if he caught so much as a sniff of the fact that I leaned that way. Tate was pure, and I was… well, I wasn't. I wore the stench of death like a cloak, and there was no way I was going to let it contaminate him.

This close to the curfew, the neon sign had already been switched off. They stayed open, but it was better to draw as little attention to themselves as they could. I hated bringing Tate to a place like this, but I hated the thought of letting him out of my sight more, even for a few seconds. Not when that's all it would take for there to be no Tate Gillespie left in the world. And then what purpose would I have?

"What is this place?" The quietly asked question was the first thing Tate had uttered since we'd left the tunnel.

"You don't want to know. Just stick close to me and you'll be fine."

He nodded as he followed me inside.

As usual, conversation stuttered to a halt at my entrance. People watched me while doing their best to pretend they were doing anything but, reflective surfaces and brimmed hats utilized to best effect. I ignored them. They held no interest to me tonight, not even for sport.

I made my way over to the wooden crates, searching out Ren. He had something I needed and if he wasn't prepared to give it to me, then I planned to take it anyway. A familiar figure stepped into my path, his gaze skirting briefly over me before resting on Tate for a little longer than I was happy with. It was Bartholomew, the guy I'd paid to fuck the other night. The guy I'd probably have continued to fuck had tonight's events not happened. With the two of them in the same room, the similarity between them was unmistakable. They could have been brothers. Bartholomew smiled, showing the same lack of fear and disregard for his own safety as he'd done during our previous meeting. "X, you've brought a friend."

"Get out of my way!" The threat in my tone was clear for all to hear.

Apart from shifting his weight slightly, Bartholomew didn't move. He had even bigger balls than I'd given him credit for. My fingers automatically closed around my knife. If he thought that me having fucked him gave him some sort of protection, he was about to discover the hard way that it did no such thing.

I hesitated though with the blade halfway out of its sheath, my fingers stilling. Did I really want Tate to witness me killing someone simply for the crime of standing in my way? That might be the sort of man I was. But if *he* saw that, would he still trust me? The likelihood was that he wouldn't want to be anywhere near me. He'd run, and probably straight into the path of the DTP. I wasn't used to exercising restraint. It was almost an alien concept. For that reason, it was difficult to force my fingers to relax enough for the knife to drop back into its sheath. "What do you want?"

Bartholomew's gaze had barely moved from Tate. "Who's your friend?"

"None of your fucking—"

"My name's Tate."

Trust Tate to feel the need to be polite. To give Bartholomew his due, if he was surprised by the name, he didn't show it, his face remaining expressionless apart from the slight quirk of one eyebrow. "Of course you are." He stepped aside in one fluid movement. "Good to see you again, X. Nice to meet you, Tate." His gaze slid slowly back to mine, a mixture of amusement and curiosity in his eyes. "Let me know if you need anything."

Before I could stop him, Tate stepped forward to grasp hold of the flimsy sleeve of Bartholomew's barely-there clothes advertising his wares. "I need to contact my boyfriend."

Just when I kept thinking he understood the situation, he did something to prove me wrong. Did he really think we had time to meet up with the insipid blond banker? "Tate!"

He ignored me, pressing on regardless, his fingers tightening on Bartholomew's arm to pull him closer. "I need someone to get a message to him, to tell him to meet me. Can you do that?"

Bartholomew's amusement grew. "Your boyfriend? Sure, I can do that for you. For a price."

Tate's face lit up. "Yeah! Really? He's on the other side of the wall. Joseph Turner." He rattled off his address while he patted his pockets, his expression turning distraught. "I haven't got any money. My wallet must have fallen out of my pocket while we were running."

Bartholomew smirked, inclining his head toward me. "You should ask your… friend for some."

Tate turned pleading eyes in my direction, and I was suddenly aware of just how many people were watching, including Ren who'd now appeared behind the packing crates. They were probably waiting for me to give Tate a lesson in what happened to people who thought they could make demands of me. Tate stepped into my space, his fingers wrapping around my biceps and gently squeezing. "Please, X. I know it's…" Tate paused as if suddenly becoming aware that we had an audience and he needed to watch his words. "... a risk, but I really need to see him before... well, you know. He can bring money, enough to pay you back and some extra. That'll be useful, right?"

I'd never had any problems saying no to anyone before. And it would be the height of stupidity to say yes. It could get us both killed, and for what? Just so he could share a touching farewell with a man he'd been seeing for less than five minutes? But then, I couldn't dispute that money would be useful, and we had to go back through Cofield anyway.

It wasn't until I noticed Bartholomew's fixation on my arm that I realized Tate was still touching me. That I was letting him touch me when someone else would probably have lost their fingers by now. Now that I was aware, each fingertip seemed to brand my skin. I had the ridiculous thought that when I removed my jacket, there'd be physical evidence that would never go away. "Fine." I rooted around in my pocket, pulling out a handful of bills and shoving them into Bartholomew's hand. "Tell him to meet us by the intersection of 4th and 5th at eleven thirty. Tell him that if he's followed, he needs to stay away, and that if he's so much as a minute late, we'll be gone. And tell him to bring as much money as he can."

Bartholomew winked and backed away, leaving me to contemplate that being around Tate was making me soft. I turned my attention to Ren, who was the whole reason for being there in the first place. We were supposed to have been in and out as quickly as we could, not hanging around chewing the fat with Bartholomew while the DTP got a lock on us. And now on top of everything else I'd agreed to a cozy meeting which didn't need to happen. Either the world had gone mad or I had, and I wasn't sure which one was preferable. I slammed my hand down on the packing crates, Ren's flinch somehow making me feel better. "I need maps. The latest ones."

Ren pasted a look of confusion on his face. "I don't know what you—"

I didn't let him get any further. Whether it was my uncharacteristic weakness when it came to Tate, or the fact that it had been witnessed by at least twenty interested onlookers, I wasn't sure. But I was done messing around and playing nice, anger bubbling inside me until it was almost overwhelming. I leapt over the crates and grabbed hold of the weasel's neck, backing him up against the wall and leaning in close so that my lips were against his ear, the scent of his sweat pervading my nostrils. "Here's what's going to happen because I have neither the time nor the patience to play games with you. You're going to stop pretending that you don't know anything about maps. You're going to hand them over free of charge. If you do that in the next five seconds, then I won't gut you like a fish and use your innards to add to the interior design of this shithole. Do we have an understanding?"

Ren gave a jerky nod, his eyes bulging. "I need to get them. They're in a safe in the back room."

I let go of him and he slowly edged away without taking his eyes off me while rubbing at his neck. It wasn't until he'd disappeared through the door that I remembered Tate and my earlier vow to keep my temper under control around him. Well, I guessed it was too late for that now. I turned my head slightly, just enough to ascertain that he was still there, but I couldn't bring myself to look at him properly, too scared of what emotion I might see on his face. What would it be? Shock? Fear? Disapproval? Anger? Whatever it was, I would rather remain in ignorance. He could hate me if he wanted as long as he kept on breathing. I'd get him somewhere safe, away from the clutches of the DTP, and then I'd leave him alone. He could grow to be an old man, and I'd… well, I had no idea what I'd do, but one step at a time.

Ren came bustling back through the door in less than a minute with rolled-up paper under his arm. He held them out, his fingers jerking spasmodically. "This is all I've got. They're

the most recent ones, I promise."
I took them from him, rifling quickly through them to check that he wasn't giving me blank paper. Everything seemed to be in order. "Thanks." The platitude was ridiculous considering that I'd threatened him to get the information, but he nodded anyway as if we were nothing more than acquaintances finalizing a business deal. I took one last look around the place. It wasn't that I was going to miss it exactly, but there was something to be said for familiarity, and where we were going, there wouldn't be any.

Making it back over the wall to Cofield had been easier this time due to the rope and grappling hook I'd brought with us. It had been as simple as one good throw and then showing Tate how to plant his feet against the wall while pulling himself up with his arms.

I checked my watch again. Loverboy needed to get a move on if he had any chance of making it home again before curfew kicked in and the lights went out. All had been quiet on the DTP front so far, but our luck wouldn't hold forever. If Cyrus was correct—and he'd never been wrong before—then the two extra units were due to arrive at any time. Which made it all the more ridiculous that we were hanging around, waiting for Joseph fucking Turner to make an appearance. If the man had any sense, he'd stay at home and lock the door. I dismissed the thought that I really wasn't the right person to judge what lengths people would go to for Tate Gillespie.

"Are you angry at me?"

I still hadn't looked Tate's way. Not at his face anyway. I'd deduced that things would be infinitely easier if I stayed away from the lure of those big blue eyes. That way I could remain impervious to whatever might be reflected in them and concentrate solely on keeping him alive. "Why would I be angry?"

Out of the corner of my eye, I saw Tate wave a hand in the air. "This. Insisting on meeting Joseph when I know you think it's a stupid thing to do." He paused for a moment before tagging something else on the end. "Talking to your friend without your permission."

"He's not my friend."

Tate shifted slightly. "I know what that place was."

I almost smiled at the defensive way he said it, like he was trying to prove that he wasn't a complete innocent. "Oh, and what is it?"

"It's a…" I did smile then as he searched for the right word. Luckily, I had enough presence of mind to turn my face away, the surrounding darkness doing the rest to hide my reaction, even if Tate was looking my way. "… a brothel. You'd… fucked him. I could tell from the way he was looking at you."

My fingernails dug into my palms, but I forced myself to shrug. "So? That's what people in…" I went with the same quaint old-fashioned word he'd used. "… brothels do."

"What was his name? Do you even know?"

I had no idea where this line of questioning was going and whether there was any point to it. Perhaps he just wanted to put a name to the person who'd offered to help him—albeit for a price. "Bartholomew."

"Do you think he took the message, or do you think he just took the money and ran?"

It was a good question, and at least it meant that Tate wasn't quite as naïve as he'd appeared so far. There were so many reasons we shouldn't be waiting around, so many variables that could go wrong. Yet, here we stood. "I don't know."

"Bartholomew looked a lot like me."

I forgot how to breathe, my chest refusing to cooperate in something as simple as taking in oxygen. There was no way Tate could know. He was just making an observation. I somehow managed to force words past the obstruction in my chest, impressed with how casually they came out. "Do you think?"

"Yeah. Dark hair and blue eyes. He was taller, though. I started wondering whether I had a long-lost brother. You didn't notice?"

"No." The lie slipped easily from my lips.

A rustle from the left had me pulling both knives from their sheaths and bracing for action until a blond head appeared cautiously from behind a bush. Tate rushed forward, throwing his arms around the man, and embracing him. "Joseph, you came."

Joseph stepped back to put some space between them so that he could cup Tate's face between his palms. Nausea bubbled in my stomach and I gave in to the fantasy of removing Joseph's fingers one by one so that he could never touch Tate again. He smiled, oblivious to the hatred pouring off me in waves. "Of course I came. Trisha called me and told me everything. At least she did once I'd managed to get her to stop sobbing so that I could understand her. She's devastated, the poor thing. There's obviously been some mistake. We'll get it sorted. Clear your name."

I couldn't help the snort of sardonic laughter that escaped from my mouth. Joseph's head whipped up at the sound, obviously noticing me for the first time. His eyes narrowed on me as if he was trying to take my measure. I moved slightly, ensuring that what little light there was caught the blade of my knife. I suppressed a smirk as his look of suspicion swiftly changed to something else, something far more wary. Good. He should be wary.

His gaze returned to Tate, although it kept straying back to me as if he wasn't entirely sure he could take his eyes off me for too long without me going on the attack. He grabbed Tate's arm, tugging him into the shelter of the bush, his whisper urgent. "Who's that?"

Tate lowered his voice too, but it was a wasted effort considering that they were no more than a couple of feet away, the leaves of a bush not providing much soundproofing. "His name's X. He's the one who saved my life. He reckons he can get me out of here. Out of the city. That's why I needed to see you, to say goodbye. I'm leaving, and I won't be coming back. Ever."

Joseph had already started shaking his head before Tate was halfway through his speech, his gaze darting in my direction every few seconds. "Are you insane? Have you seen him? He's clearly dangerous. He's probably pretending to help you so that as soon as he's gotten you away from here, he can do something awful to you."

I'd heard enough. It had been insane to let this little rendezvous happen in the first place, but to let it drag on while the DTP scoured the streets for us was ludicrous. I needed to toughen up when it came to Tate. And wasn't that a thing, X, demon of the streets, who'd never been soft in his life, needing to be less amenable. I stepped forward. "Tate, we need to go. Now."

Joseph, in all his brazen stupidity and misplaced loyalty, stepped in front of his boyfriend. "No. He's not going anywhere with you. He can come with me. I'll keep him safe. I love him so I wouldn't do anything to hurt him. You…" His voice cracked, but his protective stance didn't waver. "… are nothing but an opportunist. I don't know why you saved him, but I'm guessing it's for your own selfish purposes. But I'm not going to let you take him and rape him and do whatever else your sort of people do. Tate's too good for the likes of you."

I saw red, heat spreading quickly through my body as I struggled to hold myself in check. There was one reason, and one reason only, why Joseph wasn't already on the floor with a knife buried in his chest. Tate. He wouldn't thank me for killing the man he'd been so keen to say goodbye to, and if I did kill him, the chances of Tate still coming with me were slim to non-existent. Therefore, I breathed through the rage, his allegation that I could ever do anything to defile Tate lying heavy in my stomach, my fingers shaking with the effort of keeping them away from my knife.

Tate squirmed his way around his boyfriend's body, putting himself back between the two of us and effectively blocking my view of Joseph. Even though he was facing me, he spoke to the man at his back. "I have to go. I know you'd try and keep me safe, but you'd only succeed for so long. There's nowhere we could hide." His gaze lifted to find mine. "He might be dangerous." Tate hesitated, as if giving himself a moment to taste the words he'd just said. "But dangerous is what I need right now. Back in the club, he killed two soldiers. And I believe that he wants to keep me alive. Tell me you understand."

Joseph shifted slightly to the side, the new position bringing his face back into view, enough that I could see the expression of anguish on his face. As if sensing it, Tate turned back to face him. He tilted his head back as Joseph lifted his hand to stroke the backs of his fingers over Tate's cheekbone. "I don't want to let you go, but I do want you to live."

"Exactly." Tate leaned in, pressing his lips tightly against Joseph's, their lips parting as they deepened the kiss.

I'd watched them kiss before. Hell, I'd watched them fuck, but never this close, and never with them knowing I was there. It was like being the worst sort of voyeur, except I couldn't force myself to look away, even when the kiss grew more and more passionate. I wouldn't cut Joseph's fingers off; I'd remove his tongue instead. Finally, Tate stepped back, his cheeks flushed and his lips swollen. "Did you manage to bring any money?"

Joseph shook his head and I swore under my breath. *Useless fucker!* That rendered this meeting completely pointless. Tate didn't seem to think so though. "You need to go. The curfew will be sounding in a few minutes and if the DTP catch you out here, you'll be in the same boat as me."

Joseph nodded, taking a step back, and then another. He made no move to turn away, as if he couldn't bear to tear his eyes from Tate. I was surprised to find a twisted sense of solidarity settle in my gut. I could only imagine what it would feel like to realize that this view of Tate would be his last. Joseph stopped a few meters away, his gaze finding mine in the darkness. "Please be a better man than I think you are and keep him safe."

I gave a grudging nod. "I promise he'll be safe with me and that I'll defend him to my dying breath. That's the best I can do."

It was his turn to nod, and then with one last, lingering look at Tate, he turned and walked away, his steps quickening as he glanced at his watch.

My attention turned to Tate, who seemed to be struggling to keep it together. Another man would have tried to comfort him, but I wasn't that man and it wasn't the time or place. He turned away, and the best I could do was to give him a few moments to compose himself while I pretended not to notice that he was wiping his face. When he turned back to face me, his expression had hardened. Good. That was the Tate I needed. One who was determined to survive, despite the fact that the odds were clearly stacked against him.

Tate inhaled slowly before releasing it. "I'm ready to get out of here. How do we do it?"

A slow smile spread across my face. He wasn't going to like this. Not one little bit.

7
TATE

The farewell with Joseph had left me feeling like a hole had been carved in my chest. I might not have been in love with him… we'd never had the chance to get that far, but he represented all the things I was leaving behind: safety, familiarity, security. And the knowledge that I could never see him again, even if I wanted to, sat like a leaden weight in my chest.

Then there was his character assassination of X to think about. I'd be lying if I said it hadn't led me to question my own take on my unlikely savior. Because when it came down to it, I didn't know him. He may have saved my life, but he was clearly a violent man. The knives weren't just for show. I'd seen that when he'd grabbed the man in the brothel by the throat, and I'd also seen the way he'd almost lost control with Joseph before I'd interrupted. Yet… I still couldn't see him as a danger to me. It was the strangest thing. Perhaps it was because in all our brief interactions so far, he hadn't so much as raised his voice, never mind lifted a hand in my direction. He'd been nothing except protective.

I watched him as he crouched down, trying to work out what he was doing as he strained to lift something, the muscles of his arms bulging. I moved closer, only realizing as the metal disc came away in his hands that it was some sort of hatch. Another bunker? How much time was that going to buy us? And then the smell hit me, the truth smacking me right between the eyes—or should I say in the nose. I instinctively stepped back, shaking my head in denial. "You've got to be shitting me, not the sewers. Tell me that you've just stashed something down there? Anything but that that's our way out."

X straightened, his head tilting to the side as if he'd heard something. "This is our way out. It's our route past the Cofield boundary wall which will be heavily guarded by now."

I gestured at the hole in the ground he'd uncovered. "What makes you think they won't know about the sewers? There could be a whole squad of DTP soldiers down there already, just waiting for us."

He shrugged. "There could be. But we don't have another option."

They weren't the words of comfort I'd been hoping for. But I guess I only had myself to blame for that. I wrapped my arms around myself, still struggling to rationalize that stepping into the pitch-black unknown, which smelt like hell, was the better alternative. "I've heard it's like a maze down there. How will we even know where to go? I think I'd rather be vaporized by the DTP than die of thirst from wandering around the sewers aimlessly."

X's keen gaze swung my way. He stared at me for a few moments before tapping one of the backpacks he wore. "I have a map."

Right. One of the maps he'd picked up from the brothel. It didn't make me feel much better about it. I covered my mouth and nose with my hand before stepping closer to the edge to peer down into the hole. It was like the bunker all over again, except this time, I guessed there'd be no emergency lighting at the bottom. Just darkness and stench and whatever else might be down there. I'd seen a film once about an alligator that lived in the sewer. It had grown to giant proportions and then gone on a killing rampage. Apart from fictional monsters, my knowledge of the sewers extended to the waste that went into them. Waste I'd never expected to become reacquainted with. I swallowed nervously, fighting a rising tide of panic. "How are we going to be able to see? Can you see in the dark?"

Despite it being a stupid question, I wouldn't have been surprised if X had answered yes. The man had dispatched two DTP soldiers with nothing more than a flick of a wrist and a couple of knives, so superhuman capabilities weren't that much of a stretch.

He shook his head, feeling around in the backpack until he brought out two flashlights and handed one to me. I took it with my free hand, the other still glued to my nose as a very ineffectual barrier against the smell.

"You're going to need both hands to climb down the ladder."

I glared at him, forgetting for a moment that he was armed and dangerous. "Yeah, in a minute."

That's when we both heard it, the unmistakable rumble in the distance of an DTP tank. They'd sent a fucking tank out against me. *What the fuck!* Or maybe it wasn't for me. Maybe it was for X? Whoever it was for, I wasn't about to stick around to ask them. The DTP might already have a unit in the sewers, but one thing was for certain, they were definitely up here, not too far away, and getting closer with every passing second.

I took one last breath of relatively clean air before lowering myself over the side until my feet reached the ladder. The rancid air filled my lungs and I gagged, fighting the urge to throw up everything I'd eaten that day.

As soon as I'd cleared the top of the ladder, X came in after me, pulling the hatch over our heads and plunging us both into darkness. I clung to the ladder, my limbs seizing up as panic clawed its way up my throat. My fingers tightened spasmodically around the thing in my hand, my brain taking far too long to recall that it was exactly what I needed—the flashlight. I fumbled for the switch on the side, the beam of light appearing seconds before X's flashlight also lit up. It was thin enough that I could hold it and grasp the ladder at the same time. I aimed it between my legs, the beam bouncing off the water that lay at the bottom a good twenty meters below. At least now that there was some light, I could get my arms and legs to move again.

I made my way down the rest of the ladder, shining the flashlight left and right as I stepped off it into the foul-smelling water. Cold water covered me up to mid-thigh, the water deeper than I'd expected and making me gasp. Maybe I'd die of hypothermia before the DTP ever managed to get hold of me? That or septicemia from whatever I was going to be wading through. I made a mental note not to touch the wound on my forehead. Although, I was sure that there were probably plenty of airborne pathogens down here as well.

X landed with a quiet splash beside me. If the water bothered him, he didn't comment. He pulled one of the maps out of the backpack, focusing the flashlight on it. I peered over his shoulder, but it looked like nothing more than squiggles to me. Like whoever had drawn it had had very little in the way of actual map skills. But as long as X understood it, I guessed it didn't matter. I left him to his scrutiny, staring up into the darkness and trying to make out the shape of the hatch above our heads. Even when I shone the flashlight in that direction, it was impossible to see. It was like the sewer had swallowed us up. Eventually, X lifted his arm to point straight ahead. "This way."

We began to trudge through the water, the effort required immense when it was so high. For me, anyway. It didn't seem to bother X one little bit. Maybe he wasn't Kyle Reese. Maybe he was the Terminator. A maniacal giggle escaped from my lips before I could stop it, and X's flashlight immediately swung my way, making me blink as he shone it in my face. "Tate?"

"Sorry. I just… it's been a long night. My brain's playing tricks on me."

"You need to hold it together."

It wasn't as if I'd expected sympathy, but something a bit more encouraging would have been nice. It might have stopped me pondering what sort of man I was trapped underground with. Again. X took a sharp left, the tunnel gradually thinning out until we were forced into single file, X in the lead while I followed. At least the water level had dropped a bit. Now, it was only up to my knees, and I'd stopped noticing the smell as much, my nose apparently growing accustomed to it. I kept my flashlight trained on X's back as we made our way through the tunnels. I decided that tunnels and bunkers had become my number one hate. Actually, number two—I needed to keep the number one spot for the DTP. With little else to distract it, my mind wandered back to Joseph. "Thanks for not killing him." The words were out before I could stop them.

There was a momentary pause, the muscles in X's back seeming to tighten unless I was just imagining it. "Who?"

I skidded on something slimy at the bottom of the sewer—no prizes for guessing what it was—but managed to stay upright. "Joseph."

"Why would I have killed him?"

"Because... he insinuated you were a rapist, and I saw the look on your face. Anyway, thank you. I just wanted to say that. That I appreciated it. Even if I never see him again, which I guess I won't, then... I prefer to think of him as still being alive."

X stayed silent.

It would have been better to leave it at that, but I'd never coped well with silences. I'd always felt the need to fill them. "I don't think you are by the way... a rapist, that is. I mean, I know I have nothing to base that on. I don't really know you, but I just wanted to tell you that."

"Good to know."

"You don't say much."

X stopped abruptly at the end of the tunnel to scrutinize

the map again. There were three separate passages that led off in different directions: left, right and straight ahead. It quickly became obvious that he wasn't going to bother responding to my last comment. While we were stationary, I let the beam of the flashlight play over the walls of the tunnel, wishing I hadn't when all I found was dripping green slime.

The sewers were silent, save for the occasional splash of water, and I didn't even want to think about what might be causing the splash. But the silence was good, right? It meant that we were alone. The DTP might be many things, but able to move through water silently in full combat armor wasn't one of them. The question was, though, how long it would be before they exhausted all other avenues and switched their attention to the sewers? I just hoped we'd be long gone by then.

I was so lost in thought that it took me a few seconds to follow as X set off down the tunnel leading to the right. This one was a little wider, meaning that once I'd caught up, I could fall into step beside him. The water level had dropped again and was now only up to our ankles, making the going much easier. The gradient changed slightly, a gradual slope upwards, meaning that the farther we progressed, the more it dried out. It should have felt better, but all it did was focus my attention on the water squelching in my shoes. The shoes that had been my best pair at the beginning of the evening. But then I guessed I had far bigger things to worry about than my wardrobe.

Something brushed my leg. Something that moved. Heart pounding, I jumped, whirling around and blindly grabbing onto the closest thing, which happened to be X. If I could have climbed him like a tree, I probably would have done so. As it was, I had to make do with clutching onto him, my flashlight beam dropping to the floor just in time to witness the long tail disappearing into the shadows.

I was surprised when X's arms wrapped around me instead of pushing me away, his lips close to my ear. "It was just a rat.

The sewers are full of them. They're going to be wherever the water isn't deep because they're not keen on swimming."

I couldn't hold back my shudder. "I don't like rats." I didn't. There was something about their tails and their whiskers that set my teeth on edge, and no matter how many times I tried to convince myself that my reaction to them was irrational, I couldn't seem to convince my brain to get onboard with the idea.

I snuggled closer to X because at least he felt reassuringly solid. And warm. Even the handle of the knife I could feel sticking into my hip didn't make me want to let him go.

X cleared his throat. "You're not going to like this."

I turned my head, the steady beat of his heart thudding beneath my cheek. "Not going to like what?" I knew what he was going to say, even before he lifted an arm to shine the flashlight farther down the tunnel. "There's loads of them, isn't there?"

It was easy to interpret the way his body moved in response to my question as a nod. "You probably get loads of rats..." It didn't seem right to say the slums, so I corrected my wording. "... on your side of the wall."

"A fair few."

"We don't get many in Cofield." I was only delaying the inevitable. I knew that. The rats—however many there were of them, I hadn't dared to look yet—were in our path, meaning that there was no choice but to go through them. A squeak sounded from a few feet away and I clutched onto X even more tightly. "I'm not scared of them. Not really."

"Of course you're not."

Was that amusement in his voice? That was the second time I'd gotten the impression that something I'd said had amused him. I wouldn't have had him down as a man who was even capable of feeling that emotion.

And I was still holding onto him.

I forced myself to step away, glad that the dark hid the visual evidence of the heat that had crept into my cheeks. "Sorry about, you know, grabbing you."

"Hmm... How do you want to do this?"

I still hadn't turned around. I kept my gaze fixed on the indistinct outline of X, my flashlight dangling loosely from my hand to point at the ground. "I'm guessing we can't throw a grenade at them?"

"That wouldn't be a good idea unless you want to be buried alive."

"Not particularly. And you don't have enough knives?"

He shook his head. I was amazed at his patience. Shouldn't he be telling me to get a fucking grip and get my ass down the tunnel or he'd hand me over to the DTP personally? "They're just rats." I forced myself to slowly turn around, my hand shaking as I lifted the flashlight until the beam lit up the tunnel, easily picking out the mass of furry bodies. "Motherfucking Jesus! That's a lot of rats." There had to be at least a hundred of them, their bodies intertwined as they milled around with no seeming destination or purpose in mind.

"They'll move."

"Will they?"

"We're bigger than they are."

"Bigger. Right." I took a deep breath before moving forwards. I kept my flashlight beam trained on the floor, ready to kick one away if it even thought about coming anywhere near me. But X had been right. They parted as if by magic, so that although they were much closer than I would have liked, there was nothing more than a few fleeting brushes against my feet and ankles to contend with.

In the next tunnel, the gradient dropped again, leading us back into water. I'd never been more grateful to wade back into filth than I was right then. The rats could keep the dry tunnel. I'd happily stay submerged if it kept them away from me.

I wondered how long we'd been in the sewers. It felt like hours. But I doubted it had been anywhere near that long. I tensed as our trip through the maze of tunnels took us into another dry one. This one was blessedly rat free. Perhaps it was a dip between two waterlogged places so that the rats stayed on either side. I didn't care. I was just glad for a few minutes without rodents or water.

X paused at the end of the tunnel before starting along it. Unlike the other tunnels, it ended in a small room. It looked like it had once been some sort of handyman's room used to store equipment, the remnants of what looked to be an old water pump strewn across the floor. If it was, it must have been deserted for quite some time, though.

My gaze flitted to X, wondering what was so fascinating about it. It was a dead end. We needed to turn back and go another way. I started to turn away, intending on retracing our steps back to the last junction, but X grabbed my arm, his fingers digging in through the borrowed jacket. "I'm thinking we should stay here tonight."

For some reason I looked up, as if I might be able to gauge precisely which part of Cofield we were underneath. I couldn't, of course, there was just a layer of concrete above our heads, topped by however many feet of dirt before you reached the surface. "Shouldn't we be trying to get out of the city?" When X didn't respond, I shone the flashlight in his direction, feeling guilty as he cringed away from the bright light in his face. "Sorry." I moved it away, far enough to be able to see the expression on his face without rendering him blind.

A muscle twitched in X's cheek. "I'm trying to think like them. The first thing they'll do is rip the city apart and search every possible hiding place. They'll talk to your boyfriend. He'll tell them that you had plans to leave the city."

"He won't tell them anything."

X turned slowly to face me, his lips twisting into a sneer. "He won't even have lasted five minutes."

I opened my mouth to protest but then I pictured the scenario: armed DTP soldiers bursting into Joseph's apartment while he cowered on the floor. X was right. He would have said whatever he needed to say, and I didn't blame him. I would probably have done the same if our roles had been reversed. "I put him in danger."

X shrugged, leveling a flat look in my direction. "They would have visited him with or without your fond farewell. At least you gave him something to tell them."

It was a cold comfort. "So, your theory is that they'll think we got farther away? What if you're wrong and the first place they come is down here?"

He didn't need to answer the question; it was written all over his face. X wasn't pretending to have all the answers. He was taking a calculated gamble. It was possible that the moment we popped our heads aboveground, we'd be shot. It was also possible that the DTP were already on the way to the sewers to continue their search underground. There was no way of knowing for sure. My brain hurt just from thinking about it, so I could hardly expect X to have all the answers either.

I was suddenly completely and utterly exhausted. At least staying here would mean I could get some rest. I shone the flashlight around the room, examining every corner. It was dry. No rats, not that I could see anyway. It stank, but there was very little we could do about that. The floor was covered in debris, but it wasn't deep enough that it couldn't be cleared to one side to make a space.

I nodded, coming to a decision. Even though I knew it had never really been my decision to make. Chances were high that had I said no, X would simply have overruled me. And he had two particularly persuasive objects strapped to his waist that I wasn't about to argue with. Besides, it wasn't like I was going to leave him there and make my own way to the surface. "Okay. We'll stay here."

X was already laying his flashlight down, the fixed position providing enough light for him to start scraping the debris over to one side with the sole of his boot. "Take your trousers off."

For a moment of stunned silence, I was convinced I must have heard him wrong. It didn't help that when I turned to look at him, one of his hands was resting on the handle of his knife. I swallowed with difficulty, managing to croak out the word, "why?"

He frowned, the hard planes of his face seeming even more defined in the dim light as his gaze trailed slowly down the length of my body. "You're wet. You'll be more comfortable without them on. It's common sense."

Right! Didn't I feel like a complete idiot for jumping to ridiculous conclusions? X hadn't shown the slightest bit of interest in me, so why I would think he was looking to get it on with me in a sewer was beyond me. Shrugging my backpack off, I lowered it gently to the floor and propped it against the wall. I still had an issue with it being full of explosives, and I had absolutely no idea why we needed two bags full of them.

I copied what X had done with his flashlight, laying it down on the floor so that the beam crossed with his before toeing off one squelchy, sodden shoe, and then the other. Bracing an arm against the wall for balance, I removed my socks, the concrete floor icy beneath my bare feet. X had busied himself with wedging the door shut. The closed door giving a strange sense of safety while in reality providing none at all. One good kick and it would come flying open. Still, it was better than nothing. Better than there not being a door, or us having attempted to bed down in one of the many tunnels. My fingers paused on the button of my trousers. "Just my bottom half, right?"

X's keen glance flicked my way as he crouched down, opening up the second of the backpacks he'd packed, the one that had contained the rope we'd used to scale the wall. Although, he'd left that behind. "Anything else wet?"

"No."

His shrug said it all. I unfastened my trousers and stepped

out of them, unsure what I was supposed to do next as I stood there shivering. X pulled out a tightly rolled cylinder of fabric and held it out to me. It wasn't until I had my fingers wrapped around it that I realized it was a sleeping bag. I could have cried as I unzipped it, climbing in before easing myself into a seated position in the corner of the room. I closed my eyes, my frozen legs warming quickly. All I needed now was a coffee to drink and a doughnut, and I might have been somewhere approaching happy, in spite of my surroundings.

My eyes snapped open as something nudged my hand. X stood over me, holding out a bottle of water and an energy bar. It wasn't coffee and doughnuts, but it was the next best thing and I accepted them gratefully. What else had he put in that backpack? So far it seemed to be the next best thing to Mary Poppins's bag. I was tempted to share that observation with him, but he didn't exactly strike me as the *Mary Poppins* type. He'd never even heard of *Terminator*, so a quaint lady with a flying umbrella and dancing penguins was likely to be way out of his wheelhouse. Unscrewing the cap from the bottle of water, I took a long swig before leaning my head back against the wall. Unlike myself, X had made no move to shed his wet clothing.

I gestured at his lower half. "What about you? You're wet as well."

He settled himself on the floor opposite, his face disappearing into shadow. "I'll be fine."

"Do you have another sleeping bag?"

He shook his head. What was I supposed to do with that knowledge? Offer to share? That would be weird though, right? So I stayed silent. He'd given it to me. He could have just as easily kept it for himself. It wasn't like I'd have fought him for it. As if reading my thoughts, he shifted position, pulling one of his knives from its sheath and holding it in the beam of the flashlight as he turned it from one side to the other as if inspecting it for imperfections.

I swallowed nervously. "You like knives? I mean…" What did I mean? "Rather than guns? Guns just seem better."

Even in the dim light, I could sense X's stare. The silent scrutiny went on for so long that I began to feel as if I'd personally insulted him. In an effort to hide my discomfort, I concentrated on unwrapping the energy bar and taking a bite. It didn't taste of much, but at least it would prevent hunger pangs. When X still hadn't spoken after I'd chewed and swallowed my first mouthful, I felt forced into defending myself before he decided to show me just how effective knives could be by throwing one in my direction. "I just meant that given a choice between a gun and a knife, it seems like most people would pick a gun. I didn't mean to offend you."

"Guns jam. Guns need ammunition." He held the knife up to the light, the metal glinting. "This baby just needs sharpening."

Baby? Interesting turn of phrase for an inanimate object. Questioning him on it seemed like a bad idea, so I cast around for a different topic of conversation. "What's X short for?"

"It's not short for anything."

I took another bite of the energy bar, chewing methodically. "It must be."

"Why?"

"Because… nobody calls their child X."

"My parents couldn't read or write."

I was still trying to find a link between the strange statement and what he was trying to convey when he lifted the hand holding the knife and made a crisscross motion in mid-air. "Oh!" That was quite possibly the saddest thing I'd ever heard, the image of a child saddled with a name simply because his parents couldn't figure out how to fill in the compulsory documents any other way. "Are they…?"

"Dead. Both of them."

"I'm sorry."

"I'm not."

He didn't bother to elaborate, and I didn't ask. I finished the last of the energy bar, pondering what to do with the wrapper before coming to the conclusion that there was so much crap in the room, it really wasn't going to make the slightest bit of difference if I just added it to the pile. So I did, balancing it on top of something that looked as if it had once been a bag of cement. I pulled the sleeping bag up higher, the cold from the wall against my back starting to seep in. There was one question that kept rebounding in my skull and refused to go away. "Why did you save me? Why put yourself in danger when you don't even know me? I don't understand."

X shifted slightly, his head thudding back against the wall as he stared at me with hooded eyes. "You should get some sleep, Tate. I'll keep watch."

He couldn't have given me any clearer an indication that he didn't intend to tell me. But if he thought I was going to stop asking, he was mistaken. I needed to make sense of something. I'd started the night as a relatively carefree pharmaceutical employee, and I'd ended it as a wanted criminal who should have been dead. I might not be able to do anything about that, but surely I could unpick the mystery of the man sat opposite and work out why he'd come to my aid. My eyelids suddenly felt as if they weighed a ton and I slid down the wall until I was prone rather than seated. But maybe not tonight?

Tomorrow. Assuming I lived to see it.

8
X

I was surprised by how quickly Tate succumbed to sleep. One minute he was wide awake and asking questions I wasn't prepared to answer, and the next his eyes were closed and his breathing had slowed. But then, sudden bursts of adrenaline such as the ones Tate had been experiencing throughout the long evening could do that to a person. Or so I'd been told anyway. Not caring very much whether you lived or died seemed to negate such a thing from happening in my case.

In sleep, Tate almost looked content, as if far more pleasant thoughts than sleeping in a sewer had already begun. I'd watched him sleep before—many times. But never at such close proximity. Never at a distance where I could reach out and touch. And then what?

Why did you save me?

It had only ever been a matter of time before he'd ask. I was a stranger to him. A nobody. I'd hoped that with everything else going on, his mind might have stayed cloudier for longer. But this was Tate. He'd always been curious, always needed to know people's motivations, so of course he was going to want to put two and two together and work out why a man he'd never met would swoop in and show a vested interest in his survival. What was I supposed to say to him? The truth?

I ran the tip of my blade over the fleshy part of my thumb, drawing blood and welcoming the sting of pain. No, the truth wasn't an option. That would have him desperate to get away from me. That left me with a problem. Because Tate's curiosity and stubbornness were such that he'd keep asking. What should I do? Refuse to say anything? Or come up with a lie? A lie, though, had to be convincing enough for him to believe. What possible use could Tate have had to me without the prior knowledge of him I had? The answer was none. There was nothing remarkable about Tate, except for the fact that he was Tate.

I sucked my thumb into my mouth, the bitter taste of the blood reminding me that while Tate had eaten something, I hadn't. Reaching into the backpack, I pulled out another bottle of water and an energy bar. Finding supplies was just one of the problems that lay ahead. I hadn't stocked my bunker with food suitable for a long journey because I hadn't known I needed to. Besides, the backpack could only hold so much. If we rationed, it would keep us alive for a few days and then we'd need another source, which would mean hitting civilization of some kind. I unrolled the maps, finding the one I needed and spreading it out in front of me on the floor.

I'd been out of the city before, but not for many years, and since then the DTP had clamped down on what they termed migration. They wanted people to stay put, where they could keep their beady eye on them. The map I had in front of me was meant to be the most up-to-date version of the land. How accurate it was remained to be seen.

I pulled the flashlight closer to me, lighting up the map until I located the underground city of Maimos, my finger tracing the route that would get us there. It was the only place I could think of where Tate would be safe. Built underground, it was said to be a warren of winding passageways stretching for miles. Although the DTP knew about it, short of flushing its residents out like unwanted cockroaches, there wasn't a lot they could do about it. Rumor had it that they'd tried that once, only to meet a series of traps which had thinned their numbers, and to have wandered around for hours without discovering hide nor hair of its residents, who'd obviously devised a foolproof hiding position where they couldn't be discovered. False tunnels, maybe? They probably had secret exits as well. Because if not, what was to stop the DTP from just caving in the entrance? Therefore, the scumbags did what they always did when a problem couldn't be solved by a laser gun and brute force: they turned a blind eye, pretending that they had no interest in it and leaving it alone. Which meant it was a perfect place to take Tate. As long as he remained belowground, he'd be safe. It would be a very different life from the one he'd been used to, but at least it would be a life.

But Maimos was hundreds of miles away. My finger played over the route we would need to take, trying to visualize it in my mind. There was a train that would cut at least half of the distance, but that would put us right under the noses of the DTP, who would be stupid not to predict that that was where we would head once they worked out that we'd left Cofield. Which they would. It was a case of when, not if. The journey would have been difficult enough without the DTP breathing down our necks. With them, it would be damn near impossible. But what was the alternative? Stay down here until we died of thirst?

I blinked, my eyes burning as fatigue started to seep in. Sleep wasn't an option. I had too many variables to think through while Tate slept. I needed a plan A, B, C, and possibly a D as well if we had any hope of outwitting a number of highly-trained military units who had all the benefits at their disposal that we didn't: numbers, transport, and communication devices to name but a few.

Rummaging around in the backpack, I located what I needed at the bottom. I flicked a quick glance over at Tate to check if he was still sleeping before pulling out the pre-loaded syringe. Then it was just a case of removing the syringe cover from the needle, lining it up with the fleshy part of my thigh, and pressing the plunger. At first there was nothing, but then within a few minutes, the urge to sleep disappeared beneath the rush of chemicals trickling through my body.

I breathed deep, pushing past the unfamiliar feeling of a stimulant curling itself around my nerve-endings, my heart already beating more rapidly against my ribs. Drugs were rife in the slums, but I'd never fallen victim to their lure. Drugs might speed you up to start with, but there'd always be a period of slowness, of dullness that followed, and I relied on my reflexes, my ability to be faster than everyone around me too much to be prepared to suffer the after-effects. But desperate times called for desperate measures. It had just been pure luck that two nights earlier I'd relieved a two-bit drug dealer of his supply of Dextrostat.

The need to sleep averted, I got back to the important matter at hand, mapping out a dozen different routes we could take while considering the possible pitfalls of each one. A strange noise filled the room, a sort of strangled whisper, my head whipping up to identify the source of danger. My back was against the door so no one had gained access. There'd been no sign of the rats that Tate was so scared of, and I would have heard them before now if there'd been any holes in the walls where they could get in. And then the same sound came again. But his time, I saw it leave Tate's lips. He was still asleep, his closed eyes testifying to that. He must be dreaming.

As I watched him, he began to thrash, his limbs jerking in small movements beneath the fabric of the sleeping bag. Another sound left his lips, this one higher pitched and desperate. I revised my opinion: not a dream then, a nightmare.

Almost without conscious thought, I shifted myself closer to him, unsure what I was supposed to do. Situations that couldn't be solved with a sharp blade weren't my specialty. Tate thrashed again, words starting to spill from of his mouth. "No, no, please.

I haven't done anything. Please, don't." It didn't take a genius to work out that he was replaying the events of earlier tonight.

I had an instinctive urge to offer comfort of some sort, but the word itself was alien to me. And would it even be accepted? What if Tate opened his eyes to find me looming over him? He'd probably freak out. It was better to leave him to work through his nightmare on his own. After all, a nightmare couldn't hurt him, and we were deep underground, so it wasn't like anyone was going to hear him, unless they were already in the sewers, and if that was the case, then we were screwed anyway.

Indecision warred within me as I shuffled even closer. I reached out, my fingers hovering in mid-air a few inches short of touching him. His face screwed up in anguish, tears starting to roll down his cheeks even in sleep as his head tossed from side to side. "Please don't. Please don't. Please don't." The litany of repetition made my mind up for me, simply by the fact that I couldn't bear to listen to Tate sound that scared and distressed.

I lowered my hand slowly and hesitantly until it rested on his forehead, the skin clammy beneath my palm. And then the most amazing thing happened; Tate stilled and went quiet, as if my touch alone had been enough to calm him. I told myself that it was just a coincidence, that his nightmare had probably already run its course. But I kept my hand there until he rolled back onto his side, his breaths once again deep and even. I stayed there for the next ten minutes, just watching him, telling myself that it was only in case the nightmare returned. Nothing to do with the desire to be close to him. Finally, when I couldn't come up with any more excuses, I returned to my vigil by the door, poring over the map as I continued to consider different strategies.

Tate didn't so much awaken as sit up with a jolt and look around. I watched him as his gaze swept the room, taking in the piles of rubbish and the twin flashlights that were still the only source of light before finally alighting on me, his eyes pools of confusion.

I decided to help him out. "Can you remember where you are?"

"Sewer." His voice sounded hoarse. "With rats, and the DTP searching for me because they want to kill me." He lay back down, a laugh bubbling up that was far too close to hysteria for my liking. "Good times."

I checked my watch. "We move in an hour. I've calculated that's our best chance of being able to leave here without being seen."

Tate gave a weary sigh. "Great. I'll just watch some TV until then. Maybe have a shower and do ten minutes on the exercise bike." He reached for the trousers he'd discarded the previous night that looked no drier than they had when he'd taken them off, his nose wrinkling. "Work out how to get these back on."

A change of clothes wasn't something I'd considered. In the limited time we'd had, it hadn't been possible to think of everything so it was inevitable that things would have been forgotten. It was done now. We were both going to be stuck in what we currently wore until an opportunity presented itself to source replacements. Besides, it was odds on that there'd be more wading to do before we exited the sewer.

I rolled a bottle of water across the floor to Tate and he took it with a wan smile, draining almost half of the bottle in one go. "Thanks. Don't suppose you've got any more of those energy bars? I'm always grumpy in a morning before I've eaten."

Feeling around in my pack, I found one and tossed it in his direction so that Tate could catch it. He wasted no time in ripping it open and getting started on it. "Do you remember having a nightmare?"

He paused mid-bite before shaking his head. "Was it bad?"

I didn't know how to answer that question. I didn't have

any frame of reference with which to quantify a nightmare. I'd never had one. Not since I was a child, anyway, and even those I couldn't remember. I'm sure I'd featured in a few other people's nightmares though. Not knowing what to say, I simply shrugged.

Once Tate had eaten the energy bar, he struggled to his feet. I held my hand out for the sleeping bag and while he concentrated on peeling the wet fabric of his trousers back over his legs, I folded the sleeping bag back into the tightest cylinder I could manage. Not that space in the bag was a problem, not after leaving the rope and grappling hook behind on the wall. But I was hopeful of picking up supplies at some point. If we lived that long.

Tate's next question showed that his thoughts had traveled down a similar path. "What do you think our chances are?"

I studied him as he pretended a great interest in the debris on the floor. Did I lie or tell the truth? Was he looking for a false sense of security or trying to prepare himself for the worst? It was hard to tell. In the end, the silence had stretched on for too long for me to answer the question. Instead, I concentrated on readying for our departure, swapping the batteries out in both flashlights for new. The last thing you needed in the pitch-black was to find yourself suddenly without light and scrambling around to try and find batteries by touch alone.

"Is it light outside?"

At least that was a question I could answer. I shook my head, holding up my arm so Tate could see the illuminated face of my watch. "The sun will be close to rising in approximately twenty-five minutes, which should be about the same time that we reach the exit. It will be light enough to see, but dark enough that we'll still have a certain amount of cover."

Tate's eyebrows rose. "Sounds like you've thought about it a lot."

I had. All night. Every single permutation, the chemical concoction in my blood, which I could still feel swilling around my veins, ensuring I'd had plenty of hours to do just that. "We'll see if I'm right."

He nodded, and we exited the room a few minutes later, the corridors of the sewer seeming no more inviting than they had the previous day. It wasn't long before we were back in thigh-high water, Tate seeming relieved that at least it took rats out of the equation.

It was another twenty minutes before we reached the bottom of a metal ladder. I wrapped my hand around one of the rungs, testing that it felt secure. "This is it."

We both looked up, the metal hatch above our heads barely showing up as I shone the flashlight upwards.

Time to find out what was waiting for us at the top.

9
TATE

Numerous thoughts floated through my head as I followed X up the ladder, most of them negative. Would we be able to get the hatch open from the inside? What if it had rusted? X had said that this section of sewer had been abandoned for years, which was undoubtedly the reason the DTP had missed it. What if the only option was to go back the way we came? What if we did get the hatch off only to reveal the DTP all in a circle waiting for us at the top? My head was spinning by the time X reached the top and lifted his hand to give it an experimental shove.

I held my breath as nothing happened. No squeak of metal moving. Nothing. I couldn't help, all I could do was keep my flashlight trained on the metal hatch to provide X with some light to see by. X curled his fingers around the edge of the ladder, bracing himself so that he could put more effort into it. Again nothing. And then suddenly, as X's biceps strained, it moved an inch. I winced as a loud screeching sound filled the narrow shaft, even as relief that it was moving at all surged through me. At least we were getting out of here. To what, I had no idea. But it was baby steps. One thing at a time. That was the only way I could keep my feet both metaphorically and literally moving forward.

X glanced down, his eyes glinting in the glare of the flashlight. "Ready?"

I nodded, before it occurred to me that with the beam of my flashlight shining in the opposite direction, he might not be able to see the action. I made an effort to clear the choking fear from my throat and form words. "As I'll ever be." X had already gone through what would happen when we exited the sewers in detail. There were trees apparently, about a hundred meters away. A thick forest which would provide the best cover we were going to get. The only problem was that between us and the forest there was nothing. No hills. No bushes. Just a hundred meters of flat ground leaving us completely exposed to anything and everyone. Therefore, we needed to get to that cover as quickly as possible. It had sounded so simple when X had gone over it. But now faced with the impending reality, it seemed like a mammoth task. *One step at a time.*

X held up five fingers to give me a countdown. I clutched the ladder tighter, my palms sweating as I readied myself to ascend the rest of the ladder in the quickest time possible. The sound as X continued to push on the hatch was like nails down a chalkboard. And worse than that, anyone within a three-mile radius had to be able to hear it. Light flooded in. Not a lot of light. X's calculations had been spot-on, the sun only just beginning to rise.

X disappeared from sight as he levered himself out of the hole, my arms and legs moving like pistons to get to the top where he'd previously been standing. There was no sound from outside. No shouts. Nobody calling out to say that we'd been spotted. No gunfire. Just silence. That had to be reassuring, right?

A hand appeared to yank me from the hole as I reached the last rung of the ladder. Then we were running, my hand still clasped in X's as he dragged me in what I could only assume was the right direction. I couldn't see trees, but that was because I couldn't see anything, even the dim light playing havoc with my eyes after being below the ground for so long. And it was getting brighter, the sky lighting up with a reddish glow. All I could do was trust that X's eyes were faring better than mine, and that he was leading us toward relative safety.

And then I heard it, my blood freezing in my veins and my legs almost buckling
at the distinctive rumble of a vehicle followed by the electronic message to "Stay still. Do not move." X's fingers tightened on mine as if he thought I might be crazy enough to obey. I was stupid, but not that stupid. We both picked up speed. I blinked, still struggling to get my eyes to focus properly. "How far?"

"Farther than I thought."

The words weren't reassuring. Not in the slightest. The backpack bounced against my back as we ran at full pelt. Should you run with grenades? What if one of the pins came loose? I guessed if it did happen, it wouldn't really matter as by the time I became aware of it, I'd already be dead. My eyes finally adjusted to the light, enough to be able to see the outline of trees in the distance. Had we come out of the wrong hatch? Is that why it was farther? Or was it just a case of the distances on the map not being accurate? I hoped I'd get a chance to ask X later. If I was lucky, he might even deign to answer the question.

I wanted to look behind, to see how much space there was between us and the vehicle, but I didn't want to risk slowing down. They weren't shooting so that had to be a good sign. It probably meant that at the moment we were out of range. But they'd be gaining on us. I stumbled, X holding me up when I might have fallen, hissing at me to keep going.

Despite the acid burning in my lungs, I had no intention of stopping. I was twenty-six years old, and I wanted to survive to see thirty. And if survival meant pushing myself harder than I'd ever pushed myself before, then that's exactly what I'd do.

The trees were closer, but then so was the rumble of the vehicle. X tugged harder, and I somehow managed to find another gear.

And then suddenly we were in the trees, dodging left and right to avoid the tree trunks, the vegetation getting thicker the deeper we went. It was darker in here too. Most of the dawning light blocked by the thick canopy above our heads. We weren't safe. Far from it. But the DTP would only be able to follow us on foot, which at least leveled the playing field to a degree. We were louder now, dried leaves crunching beneath our feet and announcing our path through the trees. It wouldn't be hard for them to know exactly where we were. "X, they'll hear us."

"I know."

Of course he did. He was many things, but—even after only knowing him less than twenty-four hours—stupid wasn't one of them. He drew to a halt, pulling me back behind the thick trunk of a tree, our backs plastered against it. Or as much as they could be given the bulky backpacks we wore, which thankfully hadn't gone *boom* yet. I leaned back against the tree, sucking in as much oxygen as I could. Now what? Did X have some sort of plan? I hoped so. Turning my head, I watched him as he scanned our immediate surroundings. Nothing seemed to escape his scrutiny, from the branches of the trees above our heads to the small stream bisecting the land a few feet away.

X held out his hand. "Give me your backpack."

I shrugged it off my shoulders and passed it to him, biting back the questions that yearned to spill from my tongue. Now wasn't the time. He did the same with both of his, crouching to carve out a hollow with his hands in the soft dirt underneath a bush. When he deemed it was deep enough, he shoved the backpacks in, covering them with a thin layer of dirt and tugging the fronds of the bush back into place. It wasn't perfect but it was good enough that unless you were actively looking in that direction you wouldn't see a thing. And the DTP were looking for people, not bags.

X placed a finger on his lips before lifting his foot and placing it on the ground so slowly that it was painful to watch, his face a study of concentration. It wasn't silent, but it was a hell of a lot quieter than our progress had been so far. I could hear the familiar crunch of someone else making their way through the trees now, the sound distant but getting closer. I nodded to show I understood.

Pointing in the direction of the ditch that led to the stream, X began to make his painstaking way down the bank with me following as quietly as I could. As the ground became muddier, we were able to speed up, the leaves sodden enough not to make much noise. I had no idea where we were going. All I could do was step where X stepped and put my life in his hands. Again.

It was only as we neared the stream that I spotted what X must have seen from the top of the verge. There was a hollow at the side of the stream where some of the mud had been washed away. It wasn't big enough to be classed as a cave, but it was hidden from view to a certain extent by virtue of an overhanging tree and a bend in the stream. Hell, no! There was no way I was going to do what he thought I was going to do. There was barely room for one man in there, never mind two. We'd be packed together like sardines and even then, there was no guarantee of the DTP missing us.

X inclined his head toward the indentation, motioning silently for me to get in. I shook my head. His eyes hardened and a muscle ticked in his cheek, giving me the distinct impression that if I didn't do as he said, he'd stab me and stuff me in there anyway. I did what any sane person would do when faced with that situation—I got in. Dropping onto my back, I wedged myself as far into the tiny hollow as I could go. It didn't feel safe. I felt like a child attempting to hide from their seekers around a corner. I turned my head to the side, my gaze searching out the top of the grass verge where the DTP were likely to emerge. It was an obstructed view, but I could still see it, which meant they'd be able to see me too.

Then I had other things to think about as X squeezed himself into the hollow too, the only option when space was so limited was to wedge himself on top of me. I was suddenly surrounded by him, his chest and thighs pressing down on mine and his hot breath against my ear. I'd never been that close to any man that I wasn't in the middle of having sex with before. I shifted slightly, trying to find more room, but all it did was wedge us even more tightly together.

X's breath played over my ear lobe as he whispered into it. "Don't panic."

For a moment, I assumed he was referring to our proximity. But then he reached up, grabbing onto the overhanging part of the bank and pulling at the tufts of grass that grew there. It resisted at first but then the side caved to cover the gap and block out all of the light. Somehow, he'd managed to do it so that the earth above us stayed largely intact. Whether by luck or design, I wasn't sure. Some small stones and silt still rained down, though, only the fact that X was on top of me, saving me from the worst of it. I automatically closed my eyes, nothing but darkness greeting me when I finally opened them. We were trapped together.

"Breathe, Tate."

The harsh panting gasps I could hear were my own. I grabbed onto him, my fingers digging into his jacket in my desperate need to find something to anchor me. What if we couldn't get out? I didn't want to get shot by the DTP but I didn't particularly fancy being buried alive either. I forced myself to think rationally. It was doubtful X had brought enough of the soil down on top of us that we couldn't dig our way out. All we needed to do was wait until the DTP had given up on their search of the forest. How long would that be? Hours? A day? Longer? I needed to focus on the fact that X had successfully hidden us from view. Yet again, he'd found a solution to what had seemed like an insurmountable problem. It was back to one step at a time. I just needed to ride out one thing, and then I could worry about the next. Finally managing to get my breathing under control, I forced my fingers to relax their tight grip on X.

"Better?" X's voice was as quiet as he could make it and still be audible.

I followed suit, my answer barely more than a whisper. "Yes."

The only problem was that without the panic to distract me, I had nothing else to think about apart from X, multiple details all assailing me at once. Like his body heat and the fact that if I turned my head even slightly to the side our lips would touch. As it was, every time he exhaled, his breath skated across my cheek like a warm caress. Even worse, our crotches were pressed together. I could feel every defined muscle of his, and it was no exaggeration to say there were many. I did what I always did when I felt awkward, I whispered the first thing that came into my head. "Do you come here often?" No response. "Is that your knife digging into me or are you pleased to see me?"

X shifted slightly, the pressure that had indeed been the handle of his knife, moving from my thigh to my hip. "Sorry."

For some reason that one word got to me. I doubted X said sorry to many people. The X I'd seen back in the brothel had struck me as a man who apologized to no one. Yet, here he was, apologizing while saving my life. Acting completely on impulse, I lifted my hand, my fingertips finding his face and tracing the contours. He went rigid beneath my touch, the breaths that had heated my cheek stopping altogether. Despite the alarm bells ringing, I continued my exploration, the darkness giving me a sense of courage that I never would have possessed in the light. I let my fingers dance across one sharp cheekbone before trailing them over the stubble on his cheeks and down to his chin.

"Tate?"

The rasp in his voice broke the spell. What the hell was I doing? Less than twenty-four hours ago I'd had a boyfriend. A boyfriend I'd said a tearful farewell to. Now I was... I was what?

Capitalizing on our forced proximity by groping him when it clearly wasn't welcome given the fact that he may as well have turned to stone? I let my hand drop. "Sorry. I was just…" There was no explanation I could give that would make any sense. Not when I wasn't even sure why I'd felt compelled to do it.

"Shhhh." X pressed a finger to my lips as if he feared the instruction for quiet wouldn't be enough. I didn't need to ask why it was so important, I already knew. I could hear them, that familiar crunch of leaves that signaled someone was close by. There was conversation too. I'd never heard the DTP talk to each other before. They always used the recorded messages to talk to civilians.

"Combing area."

"Criminals' location currently unknown."

"Sweeping grid. Will report when targets located. They can't have gone far."

It was an effort to breathe, my body deciding it would be a good time to panic again. The sounds were so close now that if X or I made the slightest sound, then they would hear us. The knowledge that I needed to stay still made it almost impossible to do so. Luckily, I had the heavy weight of X bearing down on me. Far from feeling suffocating, it helped, reminding me that should I give our position away I wouldn't just be responsible for my own death, but X's as well. It surprised me that that would matter so much after so little time of knowing him, but it did. My teeth dug into my lip as I counted my own breaths. When that didn't work, I counted X's instead. His were deeper and slower, as if he were relaxing somewhere rather than veiled from a troop of trained killers by the thinnest veneer of dirt.

"River bank clear. Proceed to next grid point."

Did that mean they were going away? That they were satisfied we weren't in the area? God, I hoped so. And then came the sweetest sound, the crunch of leaves getting fainter and the voices becoming indistinct enough that I could no longer tell what they were saying. I waited as long as I possibly could, my voice the merest whisper. "X, have they gone?"

A hand pressed over my mouth. It was relatively gentle, but the meaning was clear. He needed me to stay quiet for longer. He probably had a point. One of them could still be standing there, waiting. If so, I risked giving our whereabouts away for the sake of holding my tongue for a few extra minutes. Even though it was dark, I closed my eyes. It felt safer somehow, like I could imagine I was in bed asleep and none of this had happened. Or at least it would if I could manage to ignore the feeling of X's fingers on my lips and the hard body pressing down on mine that felt nothing like Joseph's had. Joseph was lighter, less muscular, and he'd never have dared cover my mouth even if I'd have asked him nicely.

Finally, X took his hand away. I stayed silent. X hadn't steered me wrong so far, so I was more than happy to follow his cues. He shifted slightly, his lips returning to my ear. "They're gone."

"Are you sure?"

Instead of answering, his body strained against mine. It wasn't until a chink of daylight streamed in, enough that I could see his outstretched hand silhouetted against the light that I realized what he was doing. My eyes watered as they were assaulted by the light and I squeezed them shut. The constant switch between dark and light was disorientating. I made another attempt to open them, but this time there was even more light, X having been busy in the interim. Squeezing them closed again, I made a grab for him, my fingers tightening around hard, corded muscle. Just like when I'd touched his face, he went still. I ignored it, pretending I hadn't noticed his reaction. "Don't you think we should wait a bit longer?"

"No. If we wait longer, we risk them doing another sweep. At the moment we're in the safest place. The place where they've decided that we're not. As soon as they search the rest of the forest and come up with nothing, they'll realize they missed us, and chances are that they'll start over again."

It made sense. It was strange how the place that had felt like a tomb only minutes ago now felt like the safest place. My brain needed to sort itself out and make its mind up. Then the weight was gone from me as X managed to clear enough of the soil to be able to squeeze himself out. Without the protection of his body, earth and gravel started to rain down on me. I coughed silently, turning my head away in an effort to avoid the worst of it. I was still trying to clear my throat when the hand reached in and dragged me out of the small space until I found myself on my feet, blinking in the light. I couldn't help myself, I started laughing, managing even in my hysteria to keep it to a low rumble.

"What's so funny?"

The lack of humor in X's urgent whisper helped bring me back to earth with a bump, as did the fact that I could finally see. Although, that did mean I was witness to the tight expression on his face. I'd obviously done something to upset him. I just didn't know whether it was not being quiet enough or the groping in the dark, which outside of the strange intimacy of the enclosed hollow seemed even more invasive. What the hell had I been thinking? I shook my head. "Sorry. I guess it's just the fact that I'm still alive. Against all the odds." I held my arms out to the side as if I was about to carry out a slow twirl.

X didn't so much as crack a smile, his amber eyes seeming to look straight through me. "If you want to stay that way, we need to get out of here before they come back."

Stuck somewhere between apologizing and thanking him, I didn't manage to do either before he'd turned away. I followed him as he made his way back up the bank to where we'd hidden the backpacks, taking the opportunity to admire the tight muscles of his ass as they flexed during the climb. After all, I wasn't dead yet. I might as well wring any enjoyment I could out of this predicament. And it wasn't like I was brave enough to ogle it when he was looking my way. I doubted there was a man—or woman—alive that was that brave.

For the next few minutes, we edged our way silently through the trees. We fell into a pattern where X took a few steps, demonstrating where best to tread—he seemed to know instinctively which patch of ground would make a sound and which wouldn't—and then gesturing for me to follow when he was sure that the coast was clear. I did my best but seemed to fall far short of what was expected—in my mind anyway. X was all fluid lines and masculine grace, and I was more like a baby elephant crashing through the undergrowth. I wondered at what point he'd start regretting saving me. That was assuming it hadn't happened already, which again raised the question never very far from the surface, why had he?

He hadn't answered the previous night, but at some point in the future I needed to drag it out of him before it drove me crazy. X took a few paces forward, keeping himself obscured from view wherever possible. Sweat dribbled down my neck, mixing with the grit and dirt which had infiltrated my clothes during our time trying to blend in with the ground. X leaned around a tree trunk, scanning the view in front of us before raising his arm with the signal to follow. I grimaced as my very first step resulted in a loud crunch. I froze, half expecting DTP soldiers to rush from every direction. When there was nothing, save for silence, I continued, managing to do better with the rest until I'd fallen into step beside X.

I leaned out, wanting to get a better look at what came next. Fuck! We were nearly out of trees. A multitude of questions hovered on my lips. Had X expected this? Were we going the right way? Where were we supposed to hide if we left the trees? Was it good that we'd neither heard nor seen the DTP? Or bad because we didn't have a clue where they were? I bit them all back. X would tell me what I needed to know and no more. It was strange to place so much trust in someone I'd known for less than twenty-four hours, but he'd already earned it in spades. I certainly wouldn't have gotten this far on my own. In fact, my life would have ended on that dancefloor.

X glanced my way, his voice a low whisper. "We're going to keep to the edge of the trees as long as we can. Then when we hit open ground, we're going to run and get as far from here as we can. It's about a mile. How fit are you?"

"Fit enough to run a mile." X nodded. Luckily, he hadn't asked at what speed and whether I'd ever done it with a backpack, or he might not have been so satisfied with the answer. It was a mile. How difficult could it be?

The answer turned out to be pretty damn difficult when it meant running a mile with someone who was apparently half cheetah. I shouldn't have been surprised. Not really. Not given all the other examples of athletic prowess I'd already witnessed from him, including scaling a wall without even getting out of breath. Yeah, he was definitely not Kyle Reese. He was the damn Terminator. Which I supposed was good. Terminators were indestructible and just kept going no matter what. It was what I needed, even if it hurt like hell and made me feel as if my lungs were about to incinerate in my chest. What was undeniably good was the fact that there was no sign of a tank or a DTP foot patrol. No sign of anyone in fact.

X glanced back, his pace not faltering in the slightest. "Come on, Tate. Keep up. Not much farther to go."

I gritted my teeth, trying to close the gap between myself and the fitness coach from hell. He was barely sweating, whereas I was drenched in it. I hoped that wherever we were heading to would be a step up from the sewers. And by step up, I'd take anything with some sort of washing facilities. Hell, I'd have taken a freezing cold river right about then. In fact, I would have welcomed one. X had told me when I asked that we were heading for a bunker. He just hadn't said where that bunker was, or what it contained. Had he been there before?

He'd never said that he'd left the city, but from what had happened so far, I'd gotten the distinct impression he must have done exactly that. He was too comfortable with everything we'd encountered so far, not to have seen at least some of it. And how would he know there was a bunker if he hadn't seen it before? Or that we'd be able to access it? Except, perhaps he didn't, and he was just hoping for a stroke of luck. Fuck! I silenced the voice in my head that was getting far too annoying for its own good and concentrated on keeping my legs moving so that the gap between myself and Superman at least stayed constant rather than getting any wider.

10
TATE

I tried my best not to panic as X stood in the middle of a patch of grass that looked exactly the same as all the rest of the grass had since we'd left the trees. There were no rocks. No nothing. Just grass. Yet, he still seemed to be searching for something, his eyes fastened intently on the ground. At least it was affording me the opportunity for a rest, my lungs still feeling like they'd been scoured with sandpaper. I must have shaved at least two minutes off my personal best for running a mile. X had unfortunately skipped the part where he awarded me a gold medal for my sterling efforts.

Hefting the backpack more securely onto my back, I moved closer to X, intent on plucking up the courage to ask what he was doing. I paused halfway when something didn't feel right under my feet. It was like the grass was loose rather than rooted into the ground, like it was slipping on something as if it were a carpet. I slid my foot along the patch of grass, trying to work out whether it was just my imagination, concluding in the end that it wasn't. There was definitely something not quite right about it. "X?"

He glanced my way, his gaze barely making contact before returning to his scrutiny of the ground. I moved my foot again. Same result. "There's something wrong with the ground here.

I'm thinking you should probably come and take a look at it."

I moved out of the way as he walked over, watching with fascinated bemusement as he crouched down, his fingers delving into the earth and then starting to roll the grass back. It revealed a hatch similar to the one that had covered the entrance to the bunker where he lived. I corrected myself—the bunker where he used to live. Even if the DTP hadn't bombed it, which they probably had if only in retaliation, then it wasn't as if he'd ever be able to go back. "You forgot to say thank you."

His fingers paused momentarily in their work, the briefest glance thrown my way, his expression revealing nothing. "For what?"

"Finding the hatch for you. You'd been looking for it for ages. I mean... I probably could have found it sooner if you'd told me what it was you were looking for." I shrugged. "Just saying."

There was no discernible reaction from him, but I was slowly getting used to that. It was just the way he was. He'd finished clearing the hatch, the surface still somewhat soil-splattered but otherwise unobstructed. He sank back onto his haunches and stared at the metal surface of the hatch with a thoughtful expression on his face.

Unease stirred in my gut as I realized the ramifications of his scrutiny. He didn't know how to get in. I glanced around. There was no shelter for miles apart from the forest we'd come from which X had said they'd search again. We were completely and utterly exposed. All the DTP would have to do to spot us, even from miles away, was look in the right direction. We needed to get under cover as soon as possible. "We could try open sesame, or you know, turning the handle."

"It's locked."

I crouched down next to him, my shoulder nudging his. I was surprised when he didn't try and move away. "How can you tell?"

"I just can."

Great! Apparently, I could add psychic powers to the long list of skills that X possessed. It was oh so tempting to reach out and try the handle anyway, but I wasn't quite ready to lose a finger when X decided to skewer it to the hatch with one of his knives. Besides, he'd been right about everything else so far, so the least I could do was take him at face value. "So how are we going to get in?"

He turned his head slowly my way until our eyes met. There was some sort of emotion lurking in the depths of his eyes that I couldn't identify. "Have you ever heard the saying that there's more than one way to skin a cat?"

I stared at him, wondering if the stress had finally gotten to him. It was the only reason I could think of for him to suddenly start talking about cats. "Erm… yeah, I guess."

X stood suddenly, walking over to where he'd left his backpack and starting to unfasten it. "Well, it's not true. Not in this world anyway, and the sooner you realize that the better." I watched as he pulled out what looked like several blocks of plasticine and a spool of wire. He walked back over to the hatch, attaching one of the blocks of plasticine at each corner and then placing one in the middle. After a moment's silent contemplation, he added another one. "You get what I'm saying, right Tate?"

I didn't. I didn't have a clue, so I just shook my head. I was too tired for riddles. As he pulled a knife out and started cutting lengths of wire before pushing them into the plasticine, a connection finally pinged in my brain. It wasn't plasticine. It was explosives. He intended on blowing the hatch open. Saliva dried in my mouth, a whole host of problems with that scenario assailing me all at once. Would it even work? The hatch was solid metal. Was it going to be powerful enough? And what about the noise? We might as well call the DTP and tell them exactly where we were because surely to God, they were going to head straight to an unexpected explosion. And even if it did work, we were going to be sheltering in a bunker with an open entrance where anyone could stroll in without so much as a knock.

It hadn't exactly taken the DTP long to gain access back in the slums and that hatch had been closed and locked. Whichever way you looked at it, it seemed like utter insanity. Yet, I couldn't seem to find the words to protest, so I simply stood there and watched as X connected all the wires so that he had a single... fuse? Was that the right word?

X's fingers dipped into his pocket, something small and metal in his hand when he pulled them back out. It was only when he flicked the top back and I saw the flame that I realized it was a lighter. Fuck! He actually meant to do this. He held the flame steady, but didn't move it any closer to the fuse. He turned his head, his gaze finding mine. "Here's what's going to happen, Tate. You're going to pick up the backpacks and move them at least a hundred meters away because grenades and explosives don't mix, or we're really going to have a party. You're then going to move at least another fifty meters away so you're not close to the grenades." He scanned the horizon. "I'd say take cover, but there isn't any."

"What about you?"

His mouth quirked, one side turning up slightly. "Oh, don't worry, I'm not contemplating death by explosion. I'll be joining you once I've lit this."

There were so many questions buzzing through my head that I felt like I'd gone momentarily insane. But instead of voicing any of them I did as I'd been told, walking over to the backpacks. I heaved the one I'd been carrying all day onto my shoulder and then curled my fingers around the straps of the other two to drag them across the ground while I tried to calculate how far a hundred meters was. I wasn't keen on putting space between myself and X, but I was even less keen on hanging about near the plastic explosives.

I'd barely taken two steps when a strange creaking sound came from behind me. I whirled around just in time to witness the hatch door being flung open. It thudded back against the ground, a man's head appearing out of it a couple of seconds later. The color in his cheeks and the expression on his face said that he was none too pleased with what he could see. Sure enough, his eyes narrowed on X. "For fuck's sake, you couldn't knock like a normal person? You want to blow us all to kingdom come like some fucking mad scientist."

I might have been surprised by the man's appearance, but X barely blinked, almost like it was exactly the outcome he'd intended from the get-go. Had rigging up the explosive been purely for show? A threat rather than an intent? He took his time closing the lighter as if he had all the time in the world, placing it back in his pocket with the same slow, unhurried movement. The hand that had just been in X's pocket came to rest on the handle of one of his knives, the fingers flexing restlessly as if he'd like nothing more than to stab someone. When he finally responded, the tone of his voice was completely in line with his lack of reaction. "If I'd knocked, you wouldn't have answered."

The man's cheeks turned even redder. "For a fucking good reason, you're trouble with a capital T. Always have been, always will be. You think I don't know that the DTP are after you? You and him."

He punctuated his final words by throwing a venomous look in my direction. It was reminiscent of the reaction I'd gotten from Cyrus back in the slums. I was going to start getting a complex if many more people looked at me as if I was the devil incarnate. Deciding there was no longer going to be an explosion, I trudged back to where I'd started. X had wanted the hatch open and he'd gotten it open. I guessed this was what he'd been referring to when he'd said there was only one way to do things.

Getting closer meant I could take a better look at the man who apparently lived in this bunker. He was far enough up the ladder that I could see his torso. Not that there was a lot to see: he was quite possibly the skinniest man I'd ever set eyes on, his chest beneath the frayed shirt he wore almost concave, his arms like two twigs sticking out of the sides. His face was all angles as well, his chin and nose pointy enough that he'd have made a great stereotypical witch had his gender been different. Being close also meant I could smell him, the lack of hygiene becoming all too apparent when the wind changed direction. I turned away, attempting to disguise my cough at the stench drifting my way as something else. It wasn't quite as bad as the sewers, but it came a close second.

Thankfully, X's response to the man's accusation provided enough of a distraction for me to be able to school my face. "That's why we're staying here tonight, Jim."

Jim went so red in the face that I thought for a moment he was going to blow instead of the plastic explosives. His head shook back and forth, bits of spittle flying from his mouth as he struggled to form words. Finally, they came out in a splutter. "Over my dead body."

A coldness crept over X's face. It was the same expression he'd worn in the brothel when the man had claimed not to know anything about any maps. It was an expression that said that he wasn't someone to be messed with, his next words quiet but carrying a great deal of menace. "That can be arranged. I wasn't asking you. I was telling you. You can agree and you might still be breathing tomorrow morning, or you can disagree and we'll use your corpse for a table." He whipped something out of his pocket, stepping closer to the open hatch before holding it out over the shaft, his fingers hovering over the pin to the grenade, the message clear.

My gaze darted back and forth between Jim and X. Was this another threat? Another staged bid to get what he wanted, or would he really do it? Jim seemed to be going through the exact same thought process, a muscle ticking in his gaunt face as he stared unblinkingly at X. I could hardly breathe as the silence stretched on in this weird stand-off between the two men. Should I try and interject? It was doubtful X would thank me for it. There was obviously some sort of history between them, enough for them to know each other's names anyway. It was better not to get involved in something that I didn't really understand.

I tried to weigh up what might happen. Jim could make a grab for the hatch and close it, but I'd bet anything that X was faster and that Jim would find himself in his bunker with a grenade about to blow. And even if he did get the hatch closed, we'd be back to square one with X ready, willing, and able to use the plastic explosives.

X's finger twitched closer to the pin on the grenade, Jim throwing his hands up in the air with a look of alarm on his face. "Wait! Wait! One night. That's all. You need to be gone by first light. Because you know if they find you here, I'm a dead man."

X's cold stare never wavered from his adversary. "It seems, Jim, that whichever way you look at it, you're a dead man. Maybe you could do something useful before you die."

"Fucking dick!" Jim spat the words out with as much venom as he could muster. However, they became trapped in his throat as X's hand shot out, grabbing him by the neck and squeezing, Jim's face slowly turning purple. I automatically stepped forward, although to do what I had no idea. X leaned in, bringing his face close to the other man's. "It's not nice to call your guests names. Now why don't you invite us in?"

Jim's eyes bulged and he made a strangled noise that sounded a little like "let me go" but could just as easily have been something else entirely. X shoved him backwards as he released him, Jim starting to cough as he hooked an arm around the rung of the ladder to stop himself from losing his balance. The coughing went on for a while, X looking bored of the whole thing. Finally, Jim hacked up a mouthful of phlegm onto the grass, his face almost back to its original color. He glared at X, his eyes saying what he seemed to have decided was inadvisable to say with his tongue. "Not this entrance. I'll open the other one. Put the grass back unless you want company tonight."

There was another entrance? I looked around, trying to work out where it could be. I guessed it made sense. X's bunker had had two entrances as well, only one of them had gone into the strange little shack where Cyrus had lived. No shacks around here though. X's voice cut into my thoughts. "Don't try and pull anything."

Jim gave a strange little head bob of acknowledgement before disappearing down the ladder and out of sight. I let go of the trapped air in my lungs, sensing that the worst of whatever that had been was over.

I found myself studying X as I dragged the backpacks over to where he stood. I should be scared of him. He threatened men as easily as I might take a drink of water. Yet, I wasn't. Far from it. In fact, there was a slight tingling in my groin that I didn't even want to think about. Once I was close enough, I nudged him with my shoulder. "It's always nice to drop in on old friends, isn't it? Nothing beats that warm glow when you've got your hands wrapped around their neck." The words slipped out without me having run them through my brain first. Fuck! What was I doing? I might not be scared of him, but that didn't mean it was a good idea to antagonize him. Keyed up from his run-in with Jim, it was probably nothing short of suicide. I was probably about to feel those hands around my own neck and then my whole theory about not fearing him would be disproved in a matter of seconds.

X's only response was a shrug. For some reason, I seemed to be immune from his wrath. One more thing that didn't make sense. Was it because I wasn't a threat? But then, neither was Jim unless body odor counted as a deadly weapon. It was just another piece in the puzzle that made up X—a puzzle that was starting to itch beneath my skin, begging to be solved. I didn't get a chance to ponder further as the ground a few meters away started to open up, grass and all, the two sides slowly folding back to reveal another entrance.

X gave it a brief glance before crouching down and starting to dismantle the plastic explosives he'd rigged. Each piece was wrapped again before being placed back in the bag. He finished by rolling the grass back into place and smoothing over the edges until there was no sign of anything having been there. Jim's head popped out of the other entrance to inspect X's handiwork. Seemingly satisfied, he disappeared again. I waited for X, having no intention of venturing inside without him there. He held his hand out for the other bag and I passed it over.

I followed him over to the second entrance to find another ladder leading down into yet another dark shaft. I was getting mightily sick of both. Reminding myself that it was better than waiting around for the DTP to locate us, I gingerly placed a foot on the ladder, peering down into the darkness below. If people had to live in bunkers couldn't they at least rig up some sort of lighting? Was it really too much to ask? I climbed down a few steps before hesitating. Was it only Jim who lived here? It would have been nice to know what I was getting myself into. But it was too late now.

It took a few minutes to reach the bottom, the same stench that had been coming from Jim much stronger, and not just because he stood at the bottom with a lantern, scowling, like the world's least welcoming host. X landed with cat-like grace next to me, not waiting for an invitation to venture farther into the bunker. Where X's bunker had been minimalist to the extreme, Jim's was the opposite. There was barely an inch of space in the place that wasn't covered with something, everything from old magazines yellowed with age, to an assorted jumble of electronic equipment. I wondered how he survived out here. Where did he get his food from? Although, going by how skinny he was, perhaps he didn't.

X cleared a path through the junk, Jim clearly itching to tell him to watch himself but wisely managing to hold his tongue. Instead, he busied himself with picking up anything that X had knocked over, or touched, smoothing the cover of a magazine as if it was something of great value. X flicked a glance Jim's way. "We'll take your room."

Jim's face screwed up. "Now hang on. I might be offering you my hospitality, but you can't just waltz in here and take whatever you want, including my room. It doesn't work like that."

X spun around. "It works however I say it works. Tate's tired, and we both need a shower."

I perked up at the last word. There was a shower. Maybe this place wasn't so bad after all.

At the mention of my name, Jim's gaze slid my way, making no effort to hide his curiosity. But it quickly faded, giving way to something that resembled pity. "Whatever it is that he wants from you that's worth keeping you alive, I hope you realize that once he's got it, he'll slit your throat. X cares about nothing and no one. You're no different. What have you got that he wants anyway? Information? A map to buried treasure? Keys to the lost city of Atlantis?" He began to cackle at his own joke, trailing off with a strangled wheeze as X's hand strayed back to his knife. Jim held his hands up. "Jeez man! Just a joke. I'm not stupid. I have a failsafe built in where the doors work on a code that only I know, so you need to keep me alive or you're not getting out. I suppose you could blow them open, but..." Hands still in the air, he waggled his fingers in a gesture clearly meant to represent the roof falling down.

X stared at him coolly. "Or I could carve little pieces off your body until you're begging for the opportunity to tell me the code."

Jim took a few steps back, his throat working overtime. "Not necessary. I'm going to be over here. You make yourself at home. One night though, remember. No thinking you can set up home here. Jim lives alone."

X didn't grant him a response, heading instead toward a door at the back of the room. It led into a smaller room that contained little more than a single bed. But at least it was free of junk. Another door led into an even smaller room with a sink, toilet, and shower. It wasn't the height of luxury, but it was better than nothing. And even the thought of running water caused my heart to beat faster. I suddenly became aware of X's eyes on me. The weak smile I gave him wasn't returned. He inclined his head toward the door that led to the main part of the bunker. "Jim's full of crap. Don't listen to him."

It took a moment to work out what he was so concerned about. Right! Jim informing me that once X was done with me, he'd slit my throat. For some reason, I hadn't believed it for a second. I wasn't sure whether that made me stupid or naïve. Probably both. I'd always been told I was far too trusting. This just went to prove it. It raised that same damn question again though. "What *do* you want from me?"

X's head was down as he rifled through one of the bags before pulling something small and flat out. He handed it over to me. Excitement bubbled in my veins. Was I finally going to get an answer? I took the object from him, holding it up so that I could see what it was. A mirror. What the fuck! What did that have to do with anything?

Despite my confusion, I stared at my reflection. I'd spent the night in a sewer and hidden in an indentation belowground to evade the DTP. I could also see what X looked like, so I don't know why it came as such a surprise that I looked like a swamp monster. Actually, X had come out of it looking far better than I had. Even dirt didn't dare stick to him. A smile crept onto my lips at the thought, X's eyes narrowing on me. "What?"

I shook my head. I doubted he'd find my observation quite so amusing. "Nothing. Just… sometimes strange things amuse

me. You should know that about me… maybe. Or maybe not."
I walked over to the bed, staring down at the crumpled sheets that I suspected had once been white. Now they were most definitely gray. I found myself missing the sewer accommodation from the previous night. At least that hadn't pretended to be anything other than it was. There was no way I was going to sleep in that bed. Jim could keep it. I'd rather make myself a bed out of magazines and sleep there.

A rustling sound brought my scrutiny of the bed to a close. I was just in time to witness X pulling his T-shirt over his head, his jacket already gone. He was facing away so there was nothing to stop my gaze from roving over his muscular back, marveling again at the fact that there wasn't an inch of fat on him. My strange companion exuded power and physical strength. My mouth dropped open as X didn't stop there, bending to remove his boots before his hands dropped to the fastening on his trousers. Was he…? It would seem he was. I watched in stunned fascination as he stepped out of his trousers and underwear, leaving them in a pile on the floor, to reveal a bare muscular ass.

I swallowed, trying to summon saliva from a mouth that had forgotten how to produce it. I needed to say something, but then if I did X would turn around and I'd be subjected to the front view. Subjected? Right, like that was the correct word to use. What was his cock like? *Stop thinking about his cock.* I couldn't. In fact, it was all I could think about. I tried to bring an image of Joseph to mind, but it was like trying to forget an intricate wood carving by staring at a tree. The two just couldn't be compared.

There was no denying it any longer. It was stupidly impractical given that we were on the run and he'd given every impression of being a homicidal maniac. But I wanted him. Or maybe it was because of those reasons. I didn't know. My brain had ceded control to my cock, and I couldn't find it within me to care.

11
X

There hadn't been any other option but to come to the bunker. If there had been, I would have taken it. But there was nowhere else for miles. Therefore, despite being fully aware that I couldn't trust Jim as far as I could throw him, it had been the only play available. Our paths had crossed years ago, shortly after population control measures had been brought in, when Jim had ratted out a family for hiding a secret baby. The result of his whispered words into the right ears—one dead baby, a publicly executed father and a mother who'd been left in such a fucking state that nobody seemed to know what had become of the other child. Unable to cope with her grief, the mother had eventually thrown herself off the tallest building she could find, not tall enough unfortunately to prevent her clinging to life for an extra week before she eventually succumbed to her injuries. And what had Jim been paid for that information? Either money or food. Or maybe that's where the bunker had come from.

Yeah, Jim was one of those people who only looked out for himself no matter what the collateral damage might be. I imagined that if I carved his chest open, I'd find a black heart, or none at all. My fingers itched to find out. Some people might have drawn comparisons between the two of us. But there was one major difference: unless people got in my way, they were of very little concern to me. I certainly didn't sell my soul for a few extra rations. And I'd rather skewer my own eyes out than align myself with the so-called Defenders of The Peace.

Therefore, I needed to keep Tate away from him. Just in case Jim had any ideas about serving up Tate's dead body to the DTP for a reward. They wouldn't care who did it as long as the sentence was passed and he was dead. It would have been far easier to kill Jim, but I knew Tate wouldn't understand, and stupid as it was, I couldn't bear for him to look at me like the murderer I was. I liked him looking at me as if I was some sort of hero. I wanted to hang on to it for a few more hours, maybe even days if I was lucky.

I ran through the plan for the next few hours in my head. We both needed to shower while the opportunity was there. Who knew when we'd next get the chance? I began to undress, already intent on putting the first part of the plan into action. There was nothing we could do about our clothes, but I figured Tate would still feel better to wash some of the mud off. He'd need to sleep for at least a few hours as well. And then as soon as it was light, we'd be on our way again. Food was a priority too. Hopefully, something more substantial than an energy bar. Despite Jim's emaciated appearance, I didn't doubt that he had a secret stash somewhere. The man was just too miserly to actually eat it.

Tomorrow we'd head to the train that would take us cross country. Despite the fact that I knew the DTP might have foreseen that as being our destination, it would halve our journey time so it just wasn't feasible not to try. If we were lucky, maybe they'd discount it as being too obvious.

A strange noise cut into my thoughts. Alarmed, I spun around, scrutinizing Tate's flushed cheeks and glazed expression. I crossed the floor in a matter of strides, tipping his chin up so that I could get a better look at him. "What's wrong? Are you ill?" I lay my hand on his forehead, but he didn't feel particularly warm. Was it possible that he'd picked up some sort of bacterial infection from the sewers? I pushed his hair back to probe the wound at his temple, the Band-Aid long since having been lost. I could feel a scab, but it was impossible to tell whether it was sore or enflamed when it was caked in dirt. I'd be able to tell more once Tate had showered. I cursed the decisions I'd made for the last twenty-four hours. Who took someone with an open head wound into the dirtiest places they could find? Perhaps Jim's hoarding habits extended to antibiotics? If so, he could hand them over if he wanted to keep his genitalia attached instead of in a jar.

"You're naked."

I pulled back, searching Tate's face and noting his steadfast determination not to let his gaze dip anywhere below my chin. Was my naked body that offensive to him? "We need to shower."

He nodded a little too eagerly, the movement almost spasmodic. "Yeah! Shower. Water. Right. Sounds good."

I grabbed his wrist, pausing to collect my knives from where I'd left them before pulling him into the small bathroom and closing the door. He stared at me wide-eyed. "Why do I have to be here?"

"We stay together." I didn't want to explain more. Having Tate scared of Jim wouldn't serve any purpose apart from panicking him unnecessarily. He thought he was safe, and I wanted to keep it that way. His gaze flicked downward for the briefest moment before returning to my face, a heated flush turning his cheeks crimson. He forced a smile, but it was less than convincing. "Great! Just me, you, and your knives. I should have known you showered with them as well."

I lay them gently on top of the toilet cistern. "Jim likes to collect things that he deems useful. I don't want him getting his hands on them." Painting Jim as a thief wouldn't do any harm. Far better that Tate thought that than to believe that Jim would be only too happy to use one of my knives to gut him and serve him up to the DTP as the dish of the day. "Do you want to go first?"

Tate coughed, his gaze dipping briefly again as he crossed his arms over his chest. "You're the naked one."

He had a point. I reached for the lever, a painful prolonged clanking sound finally resulting in a pathetic stream of water. At least it wasn't freezing cold. It couldn't be classed as hot either. Tepid would probably be the best description for it. There was no shower curtain, meaning that Tate was forced to plaster himself against the wall as water came his way in the tiny enclosed space. "I don't know how much water there will be. It's probably reliant on a supply of rainwater. You may as well get in."

Tate's eyes opened so wide that for a moment they were nearly all white. "Together? Naked?" He seemed to have some strange fascination with the word naked. Unbeknownst to him, I'd watched him with numerous boyfriends, and he'd never been shy. Therefore, it was strangely uncharacteristic of him. But then, I wasn't his boyfriend, and I needed to remember that. I was a stranger.

I turned around, trying to angle the thin stream of water so that it trickled over my back, the water running down the drain a distinctive muddy-brown color. Lack of noise and movement from behind me made it obvious that Tate hadn't even started to remove his clothes. What was he doing? "Come on, Tate. I need to clean your head wound."

He muttered something but it was too quiet to make out over the sound of the water. "What?"

"Nothing." A lengthy sigh echoed through the room before the telltale rustle of clothes being removed. I tipped my head to one side, running my fingers over my scalp in an attempt to comb out all the soil and grit that had gathered there. I ignored the voice in my head that kept asking what the fuck I was thinking by inviting Tate to shower with me. It was practical, that was all. Nothing more. Beyond a slight morbid curiosity, he'd never look twice at someone like me. I knew that, and I was fine with it. He might have checked my cock out a couple of times, but that didn't mean I needed to start weaving crazy fantasies that could never come true.

"How do we do this?"

I turned around to be confronted by a naked Tate. A naked Tate who was doing his best to pretend that his nakedness didn't bother him when it clearly did, his fingers flexing as if he was finding it difficult to resist the urge to cover his groin.

This was a bad idea. A very bad idea.

Even knowing that, I stepped aside to make room for him. He squeezed in, both of us quickly realizing that there was no way we could share the space without body parts touching. The only question was which body parts they'd be. I turned him so that his back was to my front, the curve of his ass pressing against my cock. His skin was smoother than I'd imagined, and softer. And I'd be lying if I said I hadn't imagined it a million times, both asleep and awake. It was so tempting to let my fingertips explore. Just for a second. Just so I could experience it once. I pulled my hands away from his chest as if they'd been burned, swallowing with difficulty.

Focus! I tipped his head back so that the water sluiced over his head, starting to wash away the ingrained dirt while Tate made a valiant attempt to scrub at his torso. The friction of him moving against me producing a predictable result.

Tate froze. "Oh!"

"Ignore it." The words came out sharper than I'd intended, making it sound like I was mad at him rather than myself. "I'm like any man. All it takes some days is a strong breeze. Don't take it personally." *Liar!* There wasn't another person on the planet who could have made me that hard that fast. But he didn't need to know that. I didn't need to be the recipient of his pity for believing that there could ever be anything between the two of us.

"You're not like any other man."

The words were spoken quietly, leaving me unsure whether they were meant as an insult or a compliment, so I did what was becoming standard procedure with Tate; I pretended I hadn't heard them. I still wasn't sure whether his lack of filter was a blessing or a curse. Possibly both. I needed to concentrate on what was important, which at the moment was Tate's head wound. I scrubbed my fingers through his hair, a satisfying amount of dirt spiraling down the drain.

"Are you washing my hair? Because I don't mind admitting that I find that a little strange. You're not exactly the hair washing type. Not that that's a bad thing. Most people aren't. I mean... I wouldn't say that I am either. Although, it's never really come up, so maybe I am. I guess it's one of those don't knock it till you've tried it things."

Tate was nervous. The only time his mouth truly ran away with him was when anxiety made his brain run so fast that he lost awareness of which parts were transmitted to his mouth. "I need to see your head wound to check if it's infected. I can't see it with all the dirt." He was clean enough now that I could see the enflamed skin. Only, I was at an awkward angle. I turned him to face me, probing the wound gently for any sign of infection. I'd been right in my earlier assumption that it had scabbed over. The skin around it was red and sore, but it looked no worse than you'd expect for an injury that was less than a day and a half old. I just needed to keep an eye on it. "Any dizziness?" Tate shook his head. "Do you have a headache?"

"Not particularly."

"What does that mean?" I tilted his head back so that he had no choice but to look at me. "You either do or you don't?"

He swallowed. "It means... it's been a long day and a lot has happened and I'd be surprised if I didn't have one. But I don't think it's got anything to do with the knock that I took to it."

It made sense. Now that I'd stopped focusing on the wound, I suddenly became aware of the answering stiffness pressing against mine. I glanced down to where our lower bodies were pressed together, Tate's cheeks flaming anew as I lifted my gaze back to his face. He began to babble. "That thing you said… you know… me too… strong breeze… sorry. Only, it's not the strong breeze thing for me. I guess it's when someone else gets hard around me. It gets strange ideas."

I disentangled myself from him before I got any crazy ideas of my own like offering to solve the problem with my hand. Stepping out of the shower, I picked up one of my blades, examining its surface for blemishes to keep my gaze away from the siren call of Tate's erection.

"Is this where you threaten to cut it off?"

I forced myself to look at him. The flushed cheeks were still very much present, but there was an added sheen of something else in his eyes. I frowned. "Cut what off?"

He gulped, his gaze dropping briefly to the stiff appendage between his legs, his fingers hovering over it as if he couldn't quite decide whether to cover it or stroke it. It took me a few seconds to work out what he was alluding to. When I did, I almost laughed. "You think I'm the sort of man who would castrate you simply for getting aroused?" Of course he did. What had I ever shown him that would make him think otherwise? I'd done nothing but threaten and kill since he'd met me. It was the way I lived my life and the way I ensured my survival. But that didn't mean I was completely oblivious to how it looked from someone else's point of view, particularly someone who'd led a sheltered life by comparison.

I collected my things before Tate could answer the question and I was faced with having to hear something I didn't want to. "I'll leave you to finish up. The water will probably run out soon so you need to be quick." I left the bathroom without a second glance, although the sight of Tate's pretty pink cock would no doubt be burned on my retinas forevermore. Dressing quickly in the room outside the bathroom, I grimaced at the feel of the dirt-encrusted clothes as they slid over relatively clean skin. The rest of the bunker was silent, which made me wonder what Jim was up to. I'd wait for Tate to appear, and then I'd go and find out.

When he finally did join me, he was already dressed. He seemed about as happy as I was to be back in the same clothes. I wished I had something else to give him, but raiding Jim's wardrobe wasn't an option. Not unless we were both happy to swap dirty and smelly for dirty, smelly, and torn, which reminded me. I strolled over to the bed, staring down at the cesspit where Jim apparently lay his head every night. If he'd ever changed the sheets in all the time he'd lived here, there was no evidence of it. It was impressive given that I'd been born and raised in the slums that Jim had managed to elevate himself to the scummiest person I'd ever met. I cast a quick glance in Tate's direction. "You want to sleep here?"

He came to stand next to me, his shoulder touching mine. The contact was a habit of Tate's, one I was beginning to like rather too much. His face screwed up as he eyed the sheets. "Is it rude if I say I'd rather sleep on barbed wire?"

"You could take the sheets off."

Tate shook his head so vehemently that the vibration rattled through his entire body. "It would take a nuclear warhead to fix a bed like that." He jostled me. "Hey! perhaps you should get the C4 out again. That might work."

"Hmm..." I took a step back, reluctantly breaking the contact between us. "Let's go and break the good news to Jim that he gets his bed back. I need to know what he's up to anyway."

We found him crouched in a corner. He looked up at our approach, holding up two cans that looked as if they'd seen better days. Neither of them had a label. He held them out to me. "Here. You wanted food. Here's food. Don't say I never give you anything."

Tate leaned over my shoulder to peer at the cans. "There's

no label. What are they?"

Jim eased himself to a standing position, his knees cracking loudly. He lifted his shoulders in a shrug. "Fuck knows. If you're lucky you've got stew or beans. If you're not so lucky you've got a can of peas... or dog food." He cackled at his own hilarious joke. "Take it or leave it. I don't fucking care. You barged your way in here. It's not a fucking dinner party." He gestured over to the far corner of the bunker. "Stove's over there. Knock yourself out."

For a moment, I allowed myself the extremely pleasurable thought of removing Jim's tongue so that those words would be his last. I could remove his eyes as well, the same eyes that had just strayed over to Tate, which I didn't like... I didn't like it one little bit because I knew he was calculating something. I'd relied on Jim being too slow to put a plan into action earlier. But now that he'd had more time to think about it, I needed him away from Tate, and away from any equipment which might enable him to contact someone. There had to be a reward for information leading to Tate's capture, and Jim had already let it drop that he knew we were on the run. The sooner we were out of here, the better. Unfortunately, that wasn't possible until morning.

I gave brief consideration to whether we would have been better circling back to the trees and camping there, but I dismissed it just as quickly. It would have been too cold, too exposed. Tate deserved better, even if the only better I could give him at the moment was a stinking bunker with a sniveling weasel of an old man.

Leveling my gaze on him, I waited until he'd dragged his eyes away from Tate. "Bedtime, Jim."

He blinked a few times before lifting a grimy arm to stare at his watch. "Too early."

I took a step forward, Jim predictably taking a step back. "Have an early night. I insist."

He finally seemed to pick up on what I was getting at, his face twisting into a look of displeasure. I wanted him to argue so that I could stop playing nice. I wanted an excuse to gouge out his eyeballs. If he couldn't see, he wouldn't be contacting anyone. His mouth opened and then closed again without him having said a single word. Finally, he gave a jerky nod. "Reckon you're right." His eyes narrowed suspiciously. "Thought you told me you were taking the bedroom?"

I shrugged. "Change of plan." I took another step forward. "You should go now."

He backed away so fast that it was a miracle he didn't fall over anything. The door closed behind him and I looked around for something to block it, my eyes falling on the pile of dusty magazines. They might not be enough to stop him from opening it, but they'd make enough noise to serve as a warning so that he couldn't creep up on me.

"Is that necessary?" Tate's forehead creased as he eyed my makeshift fortifications. "I know you're worried he might steal something, but barricading a man in his own bedroom after we've already pushed our way in here seems a bit like overkill."

I added another pile on top of the first, stacking them as high as I could without them toppling over. It was difficult to know what response to give to Tate when I was still determined to protect him from the truth. The safer he felt, the better he'd sleep, and then the more prepared he'd be for the next day. "I don't want him to interrupt us."

"Ooh! Why? What are we going to be doing?" I saw the moment when Tate's own words registered. Yet another case of him speaking before thinking. He mumbled something inaudible, dipping his head as he picked up the two cans and turned tail, almost running over to where Jim had said the stove was. I followed him at a more sedate pace, giving him time to recover his composure as I cursed myself for getting aroused in the shower. Before that, everything had been fine. Now Tate was like a cat on a hot tin roof with God knows what thoughts going through his head. My cock had a lot to answer for.

Tate was in the process of trying to open one of the cans with a rusty can opener. I took it from him, accomplishing what he hadn't been able to in half the time. Peeling the lid back, I brought the can to my nose and took a sniff. Tate's eyebrows lifted in question. "Well, what have we got? Please tell me it's not dog food." He frowned. "Although, I'm probably hungry enough to eat it. Is it dog food?"

I shook my head. "Beef stew, I think."

A huge smile bloomed on Tate's face. "Jackpot." He eyed the only available pan before deciding to place the can directly onto the gas ring he'd already lit. He handed the other can to me. "Start praying for two out of two."

That one took a little longer to open, long enough for Tate to have located two spoons and two plates, and for him to have done his best to clean them. I passed the second can over. "Ravioli."

He nodded and placed it on the second gas ring. There wasn't a lot of power in the gas stove. It was closer to being a camp stove, so it took a few minutes for the contents to start to bubble as Tate occasionally stirred them. When Tate was satisfied, he shared the contents out onto the two plates before offering one to me. With no sofa, or chairs, I settled against the wall, Tate coming to sit beside me and doing the shoulder thing again—a warm, comforting presence.

"What would you normally be doing now?"

I turned my head slightly, enough to be able to see him in my peripheral vision. "What do you mean?"

Tate chewed a mouthful of food and swallowed. "If you weren't here, I mean, and life was normal, what would you be doing instead? I'm curious."

"That depends."

"On what?"

I scooped up a piece of ravioli, giving it far more attention than it deserved while I contemplated my answer. The truth was that it depended on what Tate would have been doing. I calculated what day it was—Saturday. That meant he wouldn't have been at work. Chances were that unless I'd had some sort of money-making opportunity lined up—weapons and information courtesy of Cyrus were my usual trade—that wherever he was, whether that was out, or at Joseph's, I would probably have been less than twenty feet away, watching. But I could hardly tell him that. "On whatever was going on at the time."

Tate frowned at my lack of a clear answer. "What did you do in the…" He checked himself. I assumed he'd been going to say slums. "… on that side of the city for fun?"

Emptying my plate, I placed it down on the floor. "You can say slums. Most people do."

Tate grimaced. "I don't want to offend you. You'll probably stab me." Despite him phrasing it as a joke, there was a ring of truth in the way he said it.

"I wouldn't stab you."

"Ever?" Tate laughed. "Don't answer that. Besides, you have my permission to stab me if the DTP are about to vaporize me."

I turned my head to stare at him. "That doesn't make any sense. Vaporization would be far less painful." I clicked my fingers, provoking a wince from Tate. "It happens like that."

Tate blinked a few times, the spoon in his hand going lax. "I know. I've seen it. I was seconds away from it happening to me." His stare grew distant. "Imagine they're behind me, though, and I don't even know it. One minute I exist, and the next…" A muscle in his cheek twitched. "… so yeah, I'd rather know that I'm about to die. I'd rather feel it. At least then I get a chance to think about things for a few seconds."

"What would you think about?"

It was a stupid question, not to mention intrusive. I wasn't entitled to his private thoughts. I was about to tell him that when he started talking.

"People, I guess. My parents. Friends. Regrets. Things I should have tried harder to find that would have made me happier."

"Like what?" I was genuinely curious. From the outside, Tate's life had been close to perfect: a good home, a nice if slightly insipid boyfriend, money, a job, and a host of other things. I knew numerous people that would have given their right kidney to have a tenth of what he'd had.

He shrugged, his expression shuttering. "Nothing I want to talk about." His face suddenly brightened. "Anyway, you haven't answered my question. What did you get up to in the… slums? Apart from fucking, that is."

Tate said fucking like an accusation. Like I was supposed to be celibate. Perhaps he was still sore about what had happened in the shower? "You wouldn't want to know."

His eyebrows shot up. "That interesting, hey?"

Interesting wasn't the word I would have used. Violent and necessary, maybe? But I doubted he wanted to hear about that. Not a man like Tate whose life hadn't been built around day-to-day survival. He finally gave up on waiting for an answer, changing the subject. "So… tell me what the plan is from here."

I was surprised he'd taken this long to ask, but then we'd been busy. "Tomorrow, we travel cross country. I've worked out a route. We get the train, which will take us most of the way to Urstone. I've got the name of a contact there who can sort us out with supplies. From there, we make our way to Maimos, which will be your new home. It's underground, and the DTP never venture down there so you'll be safe."

Tate's brow furrowed. "I knew there were still trains running but I thought they were just freight trains."

"Most are."

I was saved from having to elaborate more when Tate was unable to suppress a loud yawn. Getting to my feet, I cleared a space on the far side of the room before laying magazines on the floor to form a makeshift mattress. It wasn't exactly the height of luxury, but it would be marginally better than the floor. Once it was done, I indicated to Tate that he should lie down. He did, turning his face into the magazines, the expression on it saying that if he so much as caught a whiff of anything bad, he was going to be on his feet in a flash. When his nose wrinkled, but he didn't comment, I assumed there was nothing worse than a slight mustiness, which was understandable given how yellow and aged the paper was. I fashioned a similar type of bed on the opposite side of the room, despite having no intention of sleeping. I lay on my back, arms tucked behind my head as I stared up at the ceiling.

"X?"

"Yeah?"

"Can you come over here?" The note of pleading in Tate's voice immediately rang alarm bells.

"Why?"

"To sleep. I don't see why you have to be all the way over there. I'm scared that I'm going to wake up, not know where I am, and freak out."

"And you think waking up next to me would offer some comfort." I didn't phrase it as a question. Not when the notion was so ludicrous.

"Yes." There was no hesitation before Tate answered. "At least, I'd remember that I wasn't on my own. That you were there looking after me, protecting me."

Something stirred in my chest, something warm and delicate and completely alien. I remembered the nightmare Tate had had the previous night. He hadn't remembered it when I'd questioned him about it. Was he worried about having another? Was that what had triggered the request?

The reasoning didn't really matter. The bigger question was what was I going to do about it? Was I going to ignore him, or was I going to do as he'd asked? After all, it wouldn't exactly be a hardship to lie next to him. Emotionally though, it would probably be better to stay put.

"Please."

I got up, collecting together the magazines that had made up my bed and crossed over to his side of the room where I laid them down again next to his to turn it into one big bed. He leaned up on one elbow, watching me until I'd finished and only relaxing back again once I was lying next to him. I assumed the same position, only this time my examination of the ceiling was more a cover for the fact that I was painstakingly aware of the man lying next to me, of every breath, every movement. I didn't know what to do, what to say. I should have stayed on the other side of the room. I was no one's source of comfort. Not even Tate's.

"Can I cuddle you?"

"What?" My voice came out as a rasping croak.

Tate laughed. "Cuddle. It's—"

"I know what it is. I'm not exactly…"

"Cuddly." Another laugh. "I'm aware of that, but I can make the best of it. All you need to do is lie there. I'll do the rest. I just need your permission."

"I…"

Tate moved closer. "If you don't say no, I'm going to take that as permission, because I suspect that you're a man who finds it hard to say yes."

At the moment, it was hard to say anything, so I stayed silent even as arms snaked around my waist and a head settled on my chest. Tate let out a noise which sounded suspiciously like satisfaction. "We were closer than this earlier today anyway."

My brain had ceased functioning. All I could think about was the head burrowing into my chest as Tate tried to find a comfy spot, that and the hand resting dangerously close to my groin. "What?"

Breath fluttered across my neck as Tate turned his head.

"When we did our little hiding in the ground thing. We were squashed together. We were closer then so this shouldn't be a problem."

I remembered. I remembered his body pressed to mine and I couldn't rid myself of the memory of his fingertips exploring my face. "Who said it was a problem?"

Tate chuckled, creating an interesting vibration across my chest. "You're as still as a corpse. Your body language isn't exactly screaming enjoyment. You could... you know, wrap your arm around me. Make me feel like it's consensual. I feel like I'm cuddle-raping you."

I lifted my arm, draping it across his back, my fingers curling around his shoulder. "Is that better?"

He snuggled closer, his palm resting on my chest. "It's a lot better. Warmer. Thank you." He sounded drowsy, his words starting to slur as sleep threatened to pull him under. "I have questions I need to ask you."

My thumb started stroking his shoulder of its own accord. "What questions?"

"About why you're helping me. You keep dodging it."

I lowered my head to his hair, breathing him in. "Do you have to know why? Can't you just accept it?"

His fingers tightened around the fabric of my T-shirt. "So, you admit there is a reason?"

Stupid! I was letting the intimacy lull me into a false sense of security. I knew better than that. I needed to be on my guard with Tate—emotionally anyway, and wasn't that a kick, me admitting I even had emotions when there were hundreds of people who'd be only too happy to attest to the fact that I was the most emotionless bastard they'd ever had the misfortune to meet. "Isn't there always a reason for everything?"

Tate didn't reply and it took a few moments to register that his breathing had evened out. He was asleep. I pulled him closer, giving myself a few minutes to enjoy his warmth before I moved away. I had no plans to sleep. I hadn't the previous night and tonight would be the same, another of the syringes would make sure of that. Sleep was for the safe, and we were a long way from it.

12
TATE

I watched X as he gathered our few things together. He'd woken me at the crack of dawn, or what I assumed to be the crack of dawn. It wasn't like there were any windows in the bunker to be able to check. X was all business, his movements quick and efficient. In the light of day, it was hard to believe that I'd managed to talk him into sharing a bed with me, let alone the fact that I'd been brave enough to snuggle up to him like he was the world's most unlikely teddy bear. "Do you think Jim will give us anything for breakfast?"

X paused for a moment, flicking a glance back over his shoulder. "Doubtful."

I nodded. He'd just confirmed my own suspicions. He'd been reluctant enough to hand the two cans over the night before. He was probably going to be devastated to find out that they hadn't been dog food after all. As if I'd conjured him up, a string of muffled curses emanated from the other side of the room as Jim attempted to open the door, only to find it blocked by the stack of magazines X had left. There was a savage kick to the wood and then a *thud* as the magazines toppled over. A very disgruntled face appeared in the space, the door still not fully able to open, Jim proceeding to force his skinny body through the gap. "For fuck's sake! What do you think you're playing at? A man can't even go to bed in his own home without being barricaded in." Finally through the door, he bent over to pick up one of the magazines, examining its cover carefully. "You better not have ruined any of these. They took me years to collect."

Casting a guilty glance in the direction of the makeshift bed that we hadn't bothered to disassemble, I was glad that Jim hadn't noticed it yet. He was still focused on examining the magazines that had blocked the door. As for X, he hadn't shown any signs of hearing Jim's complaints, despite the fact that they were still ongoing. Therefore, it was left to me to try and keep the peace. "Sorry."

X thrust the backpack at me. "Don't apologize to him. *You* didn't do anything, and no one needs to apologize on my behalf." X seemed crankier than usual this morning. I stopped short at the thought. How the fuck would I know what X was like in the morning? I'd spent a grand total of two mornings with him, with this being the second. It was strange. It seemed like much longer, but then we'd spent every single second together for the last God knows how many hours. I'd probably dated Joseph for a month before we'd spent the same amount of time together. And then there was the fact that X and I had already shared so much. We'd been crammed together, faced rats, scaled a wall, shared a shower, and then of course there was the previous night's cuddling, even if the majority of that had been me. A frisson of something danced down my spine at the realization that X had let me. The man who was supposed to be a cold-blooded killer had let me snuggle up to him without a single word of complaint. And I'd slept much more soundly than the night before. Or at least it felt like I had. I certainly couldn't remember waking up until X had roused me this morning.

Thinking about Joseph gave me a bit of a jolt. He already seemed like a distant memory. Did I miss him? Not really. Did I wish that Joseph was here instead of X? Definitely not. For one, I'd already be dead. Joseph had never been great in a crisis. Whereas X…

Jim was still grumbling in the background, his hands smoothing over the surface of the magazines as he tried to erase invisible creases. I shifted the backpack over to one side, ready to put it on whenever X gave the signal, smiling as I realized who Jim reminded me of—Gollum from the film *Lord of the Rings*. All he needed to do was start calling his magazines precious things and he'd be a dead ringer, gaunt face and all. I lifted my head to find that X had paused from whatever it was that he'd been doing and was staring at me with a quizzical expression on his face. I shrugged. "Something amused me. I'd explain it later, but it's another film thing so you probably wouldn't get it."

"It's good that you can find something to smile about." X delivered the words with an intensity in his dark eyes that I found almost impossible to look away from. Something unfurled in my stomach, and I wondered how I'd ever found his features to be too sharp when we'd first met. Now I just thought of him as... I swallowed as the reality hit me square in the solar plexus. Handsome. I thought he was handsome. He stepped forward and I had to tilt my head back to maintain eye contact. His head lowered, and my heart started to beat double time. What kind of kisser would he be? The probability was rough and demanding. I wanted that. I wanted it so much.

His head tilted at the last moment, his lips hovering somewhere near my left ear rather than where I wanted them. In my state of arousal, it took far longer than it should have to work out that that had been his intention all along. His breath was a warm caress against my earlobe as he began to speak in an urgent whisper. "The likelihood is that Jim will report our location to the DTP the moment we've left. You should go and wait by the entrance. I won't be long."

Still reeling from the disappointment that the imagined kiss had never been going to happen, it took a moment to connect the dots. When it came to me in a rush of clarity, I didn't bother to hide my look of horror as I searched his face. I shook my head while I tried to force my mouth to form words. "You can't."

X's jaw firmed, his gaze focusing somewhere above my left shoulder. "I have to. Trust me."

His fingers curled around the handle of the knife on his left-hand side. Without thinking it through, I placed my hand over the top of his, holding it in place so that he couldn't withdraw it from its sheath. It wasn't until I'd already completed the action that I wondered what the hell I was thinking. But it was too late now. I'd already done it. I braced myself to be pushed away, or worse, but all X did was freeze in place. And he still wasn't looking at me. I needed him to look at me. "X?"

His gaze slowly swiveled in my direction. I put all the pleading I could muster into my face and voice, dimly aware of Jim still muttering in the background, completely unaware that I was in the process of begging for his life. "Don't... please. There must be another way."

X shook his head, a hard look in his eye. "He's not a good person, Tate. I know you want to think that he is. You look for the best in people, but he really isn't."

I squeezed X's hand. "I'm not saying he is. But whatever he's done or is likely to do, he's still a person, and I know I'm different from you..." Frustration built inside me as I struggled to find the right words. It was crazy to think I could have any influence over a man like X, but I had to try. "... I don't want that on my conscience."

"It won't be on your conscience. It will be on mine."

The implication was clear without X having to say it. He didn't have a conscience so he didn't give a damn. I forced myself to breathe evenly, my mind racing to come up with an alternative. Jim was nothing. A nobody. A vile, smelly old man. But that didn't mean I could live with contributing to his death. X could have killed him last night, but he hadn't. That had to mean something. That I had a chance to change his mind. "We just need to delay him, right? We could..." I wasn't used to having to solve problems like this. It was about as far removed from my normal life as you could get. Inspiration suddenly struck. "... we could tie him up. Make it so that he can't get loose for hours. By that time, we'll be well away, and it won't matter if he gives them our location. The DTP know roughly where we are anyway." I held his gaze, trying to read the various micro-expressions that flickered across his face. Because I was studying him so closely, I could tell the exact moment he resigned himself to doing as I'd asked.

He stepped back, my hand falling away from his. I missed the warmth and the feel of his skin immediately. His gaze swept the room, falling on a box full of old electronic equipment, including a mass of wiring. "That should do the trick. Can you grab those?"

I hurried over to it, my hand pausing in mid-air as Jim finally pulled himself away from the magazines. He announced his presence with a loud belch and his distinctive body odor, his narrowed gaze sweeping over both of us. "Are you two fuckers still here? I thought you'd be long gone by now. Actually, I didn't hear any fucking last night. You must be losing your touch, X." He chuckled to himself.

Tensing, I watched X to see what he'd do. It wouldn't take much to change his mind. If only Jim knew that provoking X was the very last thing he should be doing at that moment. X ignored Jim, his gaze moving past him to find mine. "Have you got it?" I shook my head, dipping my hand into the box and tugging out a large handful of wires. Never having tied anyone up before, I had no idea how many it would take.

"Hey! Don't touch any more of my fucking stuff, or I'll—"

Whatever Jim intended to do, he never got a chance to voice as X came up behind him, locking his forearm across his neck and wrenching his head back so that the words died in his throat. "Let's take a walk to the bedroom." Jim made a futile attempt to resist, but he was no match for the strength and power of X as he was half dragged into the bedroom while I trailed after them with the wires. Once they were in the room, X dumped Jim on the floor, the old man dropping like a stone. Unfortunately, the fall wasn't heavy enough to prevent him from spinning around and spitting in X's face before he could move out of the way.

Fuck! I intervened quickly, putting myself between the old man and X as X wiped at his cheek with a look of disgust on his face. Lifting my foot, I kicked the old man in the shin, and I didn't bother with gentle either. "That was a really fucking bad idea. I've just talked him out of killing you, but you seem to want that so maybe I should just step out of the way and let him do what he wants." I wasn't sure whether I was bluffing or whether X's approach to life was starting to rub off on me. But I was certainly getting less bothered about what happened to the malodorous old man. He shook his head so hard that more spittle flew out of the corner of his mouth, narrowly missing my trousers. "No, please. I thought he *was* going to kill me. I'll be good. Just don't kill me. What are you going to do me?"

X stepped forward before I got a chance to answer, still wiping at his cheek. His voice was soft but still managed to carry a clear thread of menace. "I've had a better idea. If we blind him or cut off his hands instead, that'll do the trick."

It was no exaggeration to say that Jim turned an ashen-white color. Only a ghost could have managed to be paler. I let the silence hang for a few seconds longer than I needed to. "Let's stick to the original plan." I handed the wires over to X. "Unless of course"—I let my gaze drift down to the man on the floor—"he struggles, and then we might not have a choice."

X smiled. He actually smiled. At me. For a moment, I was so dumbstruck that I couldn't stop staring at him. I hadn't even known the man was capable of such a feat. Never mind that it would transform his face into something that transcended handsome. I forgot about Jim. I forgot about the fact that we were on the run from a military unit determined to vaporize us both out of existence. Nothing mattered except for the fact that X had smiled at me. Like we were some sort of team, rather than me being nothing more than a useless lump.

"Tate?"

He was looking at me like I was crazy. I probably was. I gave myself a mental shake as I gestured toward Jim. "What do you need me to do?"

Oblivious to the thoughts going through my head, X had already started combining the wires together to make a thicker one. "Find a blunt knife. The blunter, the better."

I was grateful for the excuse to leave the room. I needed to give myself a good talking to while I was away from X. A talking to that consisted of dropping any romantic notions about the two of us. We weren't Bonnie and Clyde. And despite the dramatic way he'd rescued me, we weren't even Sarah Connor and Kyle Reese from *Terminator*. We were just X and Tate. And X was... well, I was still learning what X was.

The obvious place to search for a knife was the corner of the bunker masquerading as a kitchen. Finding some drawers, I pulled one open to find it jam-packed with junk, everything from takeaway menus for places that hadn't existed since the war to pieces of metal that looked as if they were of no use whatsoever. It seemed that Jim wasn't prone to getting rid of anything. I pocketed a few items that looked as if they could be useful, thinking that after tying the man up, stealing some of his things paled in comparison. Besides, it would be a miracle if he even noticed. Unless he had an inventory of everything in the bunker, he probably didn't even know what was there.

I drew a blank with a knife, having to rifle through three more drawers before I found a butter knife with only half a handle. That should do. I hurried back to the bedroom to find that X had been busy in my absence. Jim's legs were bound from ankle to thigh, the wires digging in tightly over his clothes. One of his arms was bound to the leg of his bed, but the other was free. I held the knife up for X to see and he nodded. A strange rush of pleasure went through me at the knowledge that I'd gotten something right. He took it from me, placing it in Jim's unbound hand.

Jim held it up in front of him and stared at it, his voice taking on a wheedling tone. "You've got to be fucking kidding me. It'll take me days to cut through the wires with this. You gotta give me something sharper, man. I wasn't going to grass you up. I wouldn't do that. Jim likes to keep himself to himself. Jim doesn't need any trouble. He doesn't need the pigs crawling all over the place. Jim doesn't—"

I drowned him out as he continued to talk about himself in the third person, focusing all of my attention on X and speaking to him as if the old man wasn't even in the room. "He'll be able to cut through it though, right?"

X nodded, nudging the old man's bound thigh with his foot. "Sure. The only problem will be if he's a lazy fucker, and he just sits there and does nothing."

Jim's face twisted. "What about going to the bathroom? What about food?"

X crouched down in front of him. "I guess you'll piss yourself and I guess you're going to be hungry by the time you get free. Now, how about that code?"

A mutinous expression settled on Jim's face, but it didn't last long before resignation replaced it. He was hardly in a position to be withholding information. All X had to do was take the knife away and Jim would be left in the position of slowly starving to death, a far worse fate than he would have received on the end of one of X's blades. His tone flat and every inch of fight gone from his expression, he recited a six-digit number.

X stared at him for a moment before straightening up. "That better be the right number, or I'll carve every wrong digit into your skin."

If Jim gave any response, I didn't hear it as I followed X

out of the room. He headed straight over to the control panel, his fingers hovering over the keys as he paused for a moment and looked my way, something indefinable lurking in his eyes. I met his stare head on for a few seconds before having to look away, mumbling, "What?"

"When did you start kicking people?"

I couldn't hold back a smile. "Just now. It was kind of satisfying, to be honest. Maybe it will become a habit."

X turned his attention back to the keyboard, starting to input the digits he'd been given. "I doubt that somehow."

I watched with bated breath as he worked his way through the sequence. I'd already decided that if Jim was stupid enough to play silly games and give him a false number then I wasn't going to stand in X's way anymore. Jim had it coming. I had a few seconds to consider whether that was too harsh and what it meant I was turning into before a creak of metal signaled the panel opening.

Grabbing the backpack, I headed down the corridor to the exit, waiting at the ladder for X to catch up. I tipped my head back and stared at the small square of blue sky above, sudden doubts assailing me. I voiced them as soon as X was standing next to me. "Maybe we'd be better off staying here? For a while anyway."

X shook his head. "Do you know how often the train runs for passengers?"

I hadn't even known there was a train that took passengers until he'd mentioned it the day before. Movement between towns usually required several permits or connections to someone with less than savory contacts. I'd expected to spend the whole of my life in Cofield and I'd been fine with that. Therefore, I answered his question honestly. "No."

His gaze met mine. "Once a week. If we're not on it tonight, then we have to wait another seven days."

I nodded slowly as the information sank in. Seven days

would give the DTP plenty of time to search every nook and cranny of the area we were in. They were sure to find us. X was right. We needed to keep moving. I pointed to the ladder. "Shall I go first, or…?"

X's response was to step forward, his fingers curling around the metal. I waited until he'd climbed a few meters above my head before trailing in his wake. The hatch would automatically close within a couple of minutes. The silence left me feeling uneasy as we climbed. "How far away is this train?"

"About fifteen miles."

My heart sank. That was a full day of walking. "What time does it leave?"

X's hesitation was brief, but long enough for me to catch it so that I already knew I wasn't going to like what came next even before he said it. "I don't know. They don't run on a set timetable apart from the day."

The backpack weighed heavily as I concentrated on the coordination needed to scale the ladder. "So we could walk fifteen miles to discover that we've missed it?"

X clambered out onto the grass, lowering his hand to help me do the same. The bright light stung my eyes, but despite the fact that they were watering, I kept them open, needing to see his face when he answered my question. He stared off into the distance for a few seconds, thinking about God knows what before meeting my gaze once again. "Possibly."

"And then what? What do we do if that happens?"

He hefted the two backpacks more firmly onto his shoulders. "We'll cross that bridge when we come to it. The faster we can do the fifteen miles, though, the less likely it is to happen."

I took a deep breath, trying to steady my rapid pulse rate. "So, what you're saying is, shut up, Tate, and let's get going?"

A glimmer of humor sparked in his dark eyes. "Basically, yes."

He needed to stop it with the smiling, humorous thing. It

made him seem far too human... not to mention attractive.
"Which way?"

He lifted an arm, gesturing in the direction of a flat piece of wasteland, which looked exactly like all the other flat wasteland that surrounded us. God knows why there was a bunker here in the first place.

I squared my shoulders. "Let's go then."

The day was long and hard. I gave up trying to make conversation after the first few miles for a couple of reasons: X wasn't exactly the best conversationalist unless grunts counted, and the effort required to keep up the punishing pace he set meant it was better to conserve my energy for that. At least he seemed to know where we were going. To my eyes, there was nothing but a whole load of nothingness, interspersed with the occasional period of tree cover which we usually veered toward, X flitting from tree to tree like some sort of lethal panther while I did my baby elephant impression again. Eventually, we'd be forced out into the open again. The main thing was that we saw neither hide nor hair of the DTP. "Perhaps we've lost them."

A less than flattering glance was thrown in my direction. "The moment you start believing that is the moment they'll catch up to you."

Well, that was me told. "I'm just trying to be optimistic."

"Being realistic would be better."

"Realistic. Right. Got it."

I thought about it for a moment, unable to let it go quite that easily. "But... if I'd been realistic, I'd never have expected someone to swoop in and rescue me."

"How are your feet?"

The change of subject took me completely by surprise. "What?"

"Your feet..." X gestured at the ground as if he thought my

lack of response was down to me not knowing where they were. "You're not dressed for hiking."

I stared down at my black shoes, which after being submerged in sewer water looked nothing like they had before that. "They're fine. These are my dancing shoes." The phrase sounded absurd given our current circumstances, but it was the truth.

X nodded. "Once we get to Urstone, we should be able to source new clothes and sort you out with better shoes. You don't have any money, right?"

"Money?" I shook my head, trying to break free from the strange stupor making me sound like a complete idiot. "No, I lost my wallet in our escape from the club, remember? Not that there was much in it. I thought I was going out for the night, not about to embark on a life on the run. And Joseph didn't bring any." It seemed strange to mention his name, like he was already in the dim, distant past. "Do we need money for the train?"

He shook his head but didn't bother to elaborate. "Doesn't matter, we brought capital."

"Capital?"

"Munitions."

We'd walked for another minute before I worked out what he was referring to. "Oh, you mean the grenades and stuff? You intend to sell them?"

X's shrug was noncommittal. He was busy scouring the scenery, his eyes seizing on anything of interest like a hawk. A hawk… a panther… I really needed to stop comparing him to members of the animal kingdom. I stopped talking, concentrating on putting one foot in front of another in rapid succession. I didn't want to ask how many miles he thought we'd done in case I didn't like the answer. It was better to just keep going until he told me to stop. My stomach rumbled, reminding me that all I'd eaten all day was another energy bar provided by X from his magic bag just after we'd left the bunker. I couldn't really complain, not when he hadn't eaten anything. He must be hungrier than I was.

I couldn't have said how much longer we walked, but it was definitely hours. I lifted my head and blinked, wondering if the building I could see in the distance was the countryside version of a mirage. Only when we were virtually on top of it did I concede it was real and not a malfunction of my exhausted brain. I grabbed X's arm, the muscles bunching under my fingertips. "Is that it? Are we here?"

He nodded, coming to a sudden halt a couple of hundred meters away from it. I stopped too, taking the time to examine the building. In its heyday, it had probably been fancy. There were still signs of it now, the molding that lined the roof bearing a number of decorative touches. But at some point over the last fifty years, it had gone to rack and ruin, the stonework crumbling and the once red paint peeling off in multiple places to show patches of blue and brown beneath it. There were people as well, most of them looking as if they'd walked just as far as we had. I watched a couple approach the doors, a little girl I assumed was their daughter sandwiched between them. All three of them were dirty and bedraggled. It didn't surprise me. I already knew that people didn't leave their designated town unless there was a good reason. Few people would choose to come here except as a last resort, a means to try and get somewhere else without dropping dead from exhaustion. These were probably the lucky people that had managed to get permits.

I glanced X's way. "What now?"

"We wait."

"Wait for what?"

"To see if people are leaving. If they don't, that means the train is still expected."

That made sense. I sank down on the ground, figuring that if we were going to be stationary for the next few minutes, I might as well make the most of it. It was the first opportunity I'd had all day to rest. I hadn't wanted to complain, hadn't wanted to seem ungrateful or come across as pathetic, but my legs were aching.

Hell, everything ached. It would have been easier to categorize what didn't hurt. Whereas X still looked as if he could tackle another ten miles without breaking a sweat.

He watched the station, and I watched him. I wondered what I might have made of him if we'd met under different circumstances. But then, when would our paths ever have crossed? It wasn't like I'd ever have set foot in the slums. Besides, I could still remember that initial jolt of fear in the alleyway when I'd gotten my first proper look at him after he'd saved my life. I knew what would have happened. I would have walked away, or more likely run. The thought made me sad when he'd done more for me in the last forty-eight hours than most people had in my entire lifetime. And I still didn't know why. He had to be hiding something, but the question was what.

X reached down, grabbing my hand and pulling me to my feet, a look of urgency on his face. "No one's coming out. That means the train hasn't left yet." I interlocked my fingers with his, reluctant to let go as he tugged me in the opposite direction to the entrance. "Aren't we going in?"

He picked up speed, heading around the side of the building toward the back. "You want to just stroll in the front? Let everyone get a good look at us? Never mind the fact that we don't have a permit so we wouldn't be allowed onto the platform."

Well, wasn't I being a stupid idiot? Again. I would have been dead at least five times over by now if it weren't for him. "So… what is the plan?"

He didn't answer me until we stood in front of a ten-foot fence, the train track visible a few meters away on the other side of it. I tilted my head back until I could see the top of the fence, covered of course, as all good fences were, in barbed wire. I added it to my list of things, along with bunkers, that I was developing quite the aversion to. "I hope you're not about to tell me that we're going over this?"

X dropped to his haunches, fumbling through the contents

of the backpack until he pulled something out. "Not over. Through. Keep watch. Let me know if you see anyone."

At least that was a job I was capable of doing. The thing in his hands turned out to be wire cutters as he set to work on the fence, snipping through each small section with the aim of making a big enough hole for us to be able to squeeze through. Given how long it took him to snip through one small section, it was going to take him a while. He had far more patience than I ever could. I took my job seriously, constantly turning around every thirty seconds or so to check a different angle. I couldn't help but draw a strange parallel between what X was currently doing and what we'd left Jim to do. I wondered how far he'd gotten with freeing himself.

"Tate?"

I pulled my attention back to X. "Yeah?"

He didn't pause from working on the fence as he spoke. "The plan is that we wait for the train to arrive." He lifted his head to squint at the tracks. "We should be in line with the back of the train."

I wasn't keen on the use of the word "should" but I knew better than to say that out loud. "Right."

X continued. "When I give the signal, we run for the train. They don't let people onto the platform until the train arrives. There'll be a crowd of people. We'll need to blend in and be as inconspicuous as we can. Whatever you do, stay with me. Don't get separated."

Even though he couldn't possibly be aware of it with all his focus on the fence, I stared at him in horror. The fact that he'd thought it worth mentioning meant it was a possibility. "I won't. And we'll be on a train, right? So, if it did happen, we could find each other because there's only so many places that the other could be." I was babbling, but I couldn't seem to stop myself. X was my lifeline. Without him, I may as well just give myself up and bow to the inevitable.

X finally seemed to pick up on my panic, the high pitch of my voice probably giving me away. He lifted his gaze to meet mine, his stare as cool and steady as always, and just what I needed. "I'll find you. If we do get separated, which we won't, stay in the same place and wait for me. It'll be fine."

I nodded, swallowing with difficulty as I tried to school my face into a facsimile of someone who looked like they believed him.

Ten minutes passed with no sign of anyone stumbling across our location as X made steady progress on the fence. It was easy to see what he was trying to achieve as he worked his way upwards from the bottom. Once he got high enough, he'd be able to peel that section of fence back to make a space big enough for us to step through. Easy. Hopefully. Despite the fact the sun was starting to set, sweat gleamed on X's forehead. It turned out he was human after all. I had to fight the urge to wipe it off for him. "Is there anything I can do to help?"

He shook his head without looking up. "No, I only brought one pair of wire cutters. I didn't think to bring two."

"I can't believe you thought to bring one. You can't have already had this planned?"

"I didn't. I—" He paused, tipping his head to the side for a few seconds. "Fuck!"

"What?"

The answer was in the frenzied way he continued to cut the wire, the calm methodical process of earlier completely abandoned. And then I heard it too. The low rumbling that signaled an advancing train. The only one that would stop here for a week if X was to be believed, and I had no reason to doubt him. Another link gave way beneath X's fingers as he quickly moved onto the next. There were still too many though, the train now in sight. I tried to tell myself that it didn't matter, that X would have an alternative plan up his sleeve. That we could go back to Jim's bunker and hide there for a week. But if either of those things were a viable option X wouldn't be so determined to achieve the impossible. Sweat was dripping from his brow now as he continued to clip and move on. I felt helpless, knowing that there was absolutely nothing I could do to help.

The train drew to a stop, a great big hulking beast of a thing that didn't look in any better condition than the station. It belched great clouds of smoke like the steam trains of yesteryear I'd seen in black and white films. A crowd of people erupted from the station building, pushing and jostling each other in their haste to bag the best spot on the train—whatever that was. There were ten carriages to the train and there appeared to be far more people than could comfortably fit on it. I bit down on the urge to announce that the train was here, knowing X was fully aware of it.

He let loose a string of expletives, standing before planting the sole of his foot against the fence and pushing. The cut links separated away from the rest of the fence, but the hole wasn't big enough. It barely reached his knees. X grabbed hold of the cut section, using brute strength to peel it back like the top of a tin can as far as it would go. "Can you get through?"

The train was still filling up, a crowd of people six deep queueing to get on, some displaying more patience than others. "I can try." I took the backpack off, shoving it through the hole first before squeezing my body into a gap that looked far too small. Jagged pieces of wire tore at my clothes and my skin as I contorted myself into the smallest shape possible. There was a moment where I was sure that I was going to get stuck and then suddenly I was free. I reached back through the fence, grabbing both of X's backpacks and transferring them over to my side. That only left one problem: X himself. He was bigger than I was, therefore logic would dictate that if I'd struggled to fit through the fence when he was holding it back, there was absolutely no chance of him being able to do it.

The expression on his face said the exact same thing. I

glanced back at the train. The crowd had thinned, only a couple of rows of people left to board. X's fingers closed around mine through the fence. "You should go!"

I couldn't help it; I laughed. "Yeah, right?" My voice dripped with sarcasm. "We both know I wouldn't last two minutes on my own." I pasted a bright smile on my face, even while my pulse thundered in my ears. "So, you better get your ass on this side…" I glanced back over my shoulder. Only one row to go. We were rapidly running out of time. "… quickly would be good as well. We both go, or we both stay, so if you want me on that train, you better get a move on."

My gaze locked on X's, something passing between us for a few seconds that I couldn't even begin to quantify. Then he was a blur of motion as he attempted to force his body into a space where it clearly didn't fit, no matter how lean and athletic he might be. I grabbed his arm, pulling as he pushed and deciding that logic could take a running jump. We hadn't come this far to be stopped by a fucking fence of all things.

There was a moment where our efforts seemed completely hopeless and then X shifted slightly, his body slipping forward a few precious inches. I tugged harder, putting all the strength I had into it. It was strange but it felt as if I was fighting for far more than just the possibility of getting on the train. The opportunity for answers, maybe? Or the means to explore the strange attraction which kept on growing? For me, anyway. For all I knew, X felt nothing. But at the very least I wanted the opportunity to find that out. I just needed to come up with a way of broaching the subject without ending up with a knife in the heart—both metaphorically and literally.

And then X was through.

There were no people waiting to get on the train.

I grabbed his hand as he scooped up the backpacks and we both made a run for it. We were only ten meters away, a horn sounding to announce its departure. There were no doors on the train, or at least if they were, they didn't close. We'd gotten to within five meters when it started to move. X was faster than me, his hand holding mine tightly and dragging me along with him as he took the flying leap needed to board the train. There was a strange moment where I was anchored to X, but with the train moving faster than I was. My fingers started to slip from his, images of him sailing off into the distance without me already flashing through my mind. But then he readjusted his grip, giving me no choice but to make the same flying leap he had if I didn't want to end up getting my arm ripped off. I landed against his chest, his firm body absorbing the impact. I started laughing because against all the odds we were on the train.

We were on the fucking train.

The laughter died in my throat as I scanned the carriage to find all eyes on us. Men. Women. Children. Everyone. So much for blending in. We couldn't have been less inconspicuous if we'd tried. I'd been so wrapped up in my celebrations that I hadn't stopped to consider the ramifications of our last-ditch effort. The carriage was packed as well, just about every inch of space taken. X's fingers tightened around mine as he surged forward, making space with his pure physical presence where there was none. I couldn't see his face, but I could imagine the expression on it which ensured that no matter how cramped they were, people were still trying to move aside.

He brought us to a stop in the middle of the carriage, our backpacks, along with the lack of space meaning that we were crushed together. It seemed to be how we kept ending up. I lifted my arm, surprised to see blood on my fingers. It hadn't come from me, which meant… I lifted X's hand, wincing at the sight of the angry red furrows covering his palm. An inspection of his other hand revealed it was in the same state. It must have happened when he'd held the fence back for me, all those jagged ends of wires that he'd snipped cutting into his skin. Yet, he'd never once complained, never even mentioned it. Although they'd stopped bleeding, the cuts looked vicious and they had to hurt like hell. "Fuck, X! Your hands."

He snatched them back out of my grasp, his fingers curling into fists which hid the wounds from sight. "It's fine. They'll heal."

I wiped my hands on my trousers, figuring that since they were already encrusted with mud and dirt, a bit of blood wasn't going to do any harm. I hoped X was right about us being able to get clothes from somewhere. I didn't even care what they were, anything clean sounded liked luxury. The train had gathered speed, the scenery passing in a blur of green and brown below the darkening sky. Despite the circumstances and despite the fact that we were hemmed in like cattle, I couldn't help feeling a tiny bit of excitement that I was on a train. I tipped my head back to look into X's face, needing to share the experience with someone. "I didn't think they'd go this fast." When his expression remained blank, I elaborated. "Trains. I've only ever seen them on the TV before. They looked slower."

A man of few words at the best of times, he simply nodded.

I needed to talk though. I needed to rid myself of the mixture of adrenaline and nausea still coursing through my veins from our near miss. "How long are we going to be on it?"

"Eight hours."

For a moment, I thought I'd heard him wrong. Either that or he was joking. Then I remembered it was X and he didn't joke. I tried to change my position slightly, but I was hemmed in from all sides, a woman turning to glare at me as I accidentally knocked her elbow. Eight hours of this. Great. The euphoria that had been bubbling up inside me withered away to nothing.

X studied my face as if he was trying to read me. He probably could. It wasn't as if I'd ever been a master at hiding my emotions. He could definitely teach me a thing or two when it came to that. "You should try and sleep. We'll be traveling most of the night."

A chuckle escaped from my mouth at the absurdity of the suggestion. "Yeah, right. I'll just push some people off the train and then stretch out on the floor. I'm sure they won't mind."
"I didn't mean like that."
I frowned. "Like what, then?"
X lifted his right hand, bringing it across his chest to pat his left shoulder. "On me."
I stared at him incredulously, but his gaze never wavered from mine. Was he seriously suggesting that I use him as some sort of standing pillow? Last night, I'd had to use emotional blackmail to even get him on the same side of the room as me. What had changed? But I guessed I was probably reading far too much into it. X was just trying to be practical. I shook my head, fixing my stare on the moving scenery rapidly disappearing into the approaching night, and borrowing his words from earlier. "It's fine."
It wasn't long before I had to revise that opinion. I wasn't fine. I was exhausted, the lack of sleep, the fifteen mile hike, and the soothing motion of the train all combining to leave me dead on my feet, my eyelids starting to droop. Each time it happened, I had to keep jolting myself awake. On the fifth or sixth occasion—I'd lost count—X made a disapproving noise in the back of his throat. "Don't be a dick, Tate. Sleep. We've still got a long journey ahead."
A laugh bubbled out of me. How had we spent so many hours together and he'd only just called me a dick? It usually happened much quicker than that. I moved forward, closing the little bit of space that existed between us. Still, I hesitated. "Are you sure?"
"Tate!" That one word contained so many different layers: annoyance, frustration, and something else that in different circumstances I might have interpreted as fondness. I liked him saying my name. I wanted to hear him say it in another context entirely—the heat of passion. What would X be like in bed?

Would he be the same calm controlled man he was the majority of the time, or would those occasional flashes of temper I'd seen from him come to the fore? Something unfurled deep inside me at the thought, a craving that I'd spent years doing my best to ignore. A darker part of me that I didn't let anyone see. Something that would probably shock anyone that knew me. I doubted it would shock X though. I doubted anything could.

I lay my head on his chest, his body heat leaching through the thin T-shirt he wore. His heart thudded beneath my cheek, a slow steady rhythm which coordinated with the train's. My eyelids drifted shut, but I didn't try to sleep. Not yet. I wanted to enjoy the moment for a little longer, wanted to enjoy just how solid, how dependable X was. I knew that I could go to sleep and he wouldn't let me fall, wouldn't let any harm come to me whatsoever. It was a strange feeling to recognize how much trust I had in him. "I like you, X."

I didn't realize I'd said it aloud until the muscles beneath my cheek turned to granite and he almost seemed to stop breathing, the heart beneath my cheek beating faster. It didn't matter. I wasn't going to take it back. Not when it was true. From what I'd seen of X, I couldn't imagine that anyone had ever said it to him before. But I didn't need his permission. He could take my liking and do with it whatever he wished, but it wouldn't make it go away. I smiled, adding an extra bit to make him feel even more uncomfortable. "I like you a lot."

X swallowed, the vibration travelling through his chest. "Go to sleep, Tate."

"Go to sleep, Tate," I mimicked. I slid my arms around his waist, my wrist brushing the handle of one of his knives. Knives that no longer seemed even remotely scary. In fact, they provided a twisted sense of reassurance. "You tell me what to do an awful lot. You know that, right?"

"It's necessary."

I turned my head slightly to the side, burying my nose in

his neck and breathing him in. He smelt of musk and sweat, and… X. "And what about if there comes a day where it's not necessary anymore? Will you still tell me what to do?" I sighed when no response was forthcoming. The man was an enigma and the urge to solve the mystery of what made him tick was quite possibly the strongest desire I'd ever had. I just needed to work out a strategy.

That was my last conscious thought before I succumbed to sleep.

13
X

Tate didn't sleep like he was standing in the middle of a train full of people with a military unit hot on our heels. He slept like the proverbial baby, his hand fisted in my T-shirt and his mouth open. The temptation just to watch him was so strong that I had to keep reminding myself that I needed to stay alert. I fought a constant battle between scanning the carriage for suspicious behavior and watching over him. Anyone on the train could be an informer—man, woman, or child. I was envious of Tate's naïveté in that regard, the fact that he was innocent enough to take people at face value. I hadn't been in a position do that for years—maybe not ever. Sometimes, it felt as if I'd been born with a blade in my hand.

"*I like you, X... a lot.*" Tate's softly spoken words played in a constant loop in my brain. They were ridiculous words, spoken by a man who'd already been half asleep. He was probably confusing gratitude with genuine emotion, but there was a tiny part of me that clung onto them with the ferocity of a wild animal who'd discovered a tasty morsel of meat.

The train was only due to stop three times during its route. Tate had already been asleep before we'd reached the first. I'd been hypervigilant for the few minutes that the train was sta-

off but no one of any note getting on. According to the sources of information I had, the second stop would come five hours into the journey, about another three hours from now. Therefore, when the train slowed after less than four hours had passed, my hackles were most definitely raised. I cursed the fact that we weren't close enough to the door to be able to see outside, but I'd wanted to shelter us from prying eyes.

I forced myself to work through all the possibilities before I jumped to a wrong conclusion. The information I'd been given could have been out of date. The train could have scheduled an extra stop, but unlike the first stop, which had been minutes long, the second had only lasted about forty-five seconds before it had started up again. It had been far too short to allow anyone to get off, but possibly just long enough to allow a military unit to board. Besides, my gut was telling me that something wasn't right and listening to it had kept me alive on more than one occasion. I lowered my lips to Tate's ear in an urgent whisper. "Tate! Time to wake up."

He stirred but didn't wake. I tried again, nudging his shoulder at the same time while trying to ensure that we didn't look too conspicuous. "Tate! We have to go."

This time, he awoke with a start, his eyes blinking open in confusion. To give him his due, it only took him a few seconds to work out where we were. "Are we here? Did I sleep through the entire journey?"

Keeping my lips close to his ear, I shook my head. "I think we've got visitors."

I inclined my head toward the connecting door between the carriages on the far right-hand side. "They'll have boarded on the left, so we go that way. "Are you ready?"

Despite the fact that I could tell Tate was still trying to shake off the last vestiges of sleep, he gave a shaky nod.

Pushing our way through people wasn't easy. They were clearly exhausted and not in the mood to make way for two men who'd suddenly decided to switch carriages for no apparent reason. My hands itched to draw a knife; they'd certainly move then. But that would create a scene, bringing the DTP down on us that much quicker. Tate's hand slipped into mine again as we inched our way through, and I was surprised by how natural it felt.

By the time we'd reached the next carriage, there were already signs of a disturbance farther down the train and it didn't take a genius to work out what had caused it. The only factor in our favor was that they were going to have exactly the same problem navigating the crowds as we had. At least until they grew bored and started throwing people off the train to make their passage easier. The time advantage would give us a few precious minutes to be somewhere other than the train by the time they reached the carriage we were in.

I pulled Tate across to the doorway, nothing but blackness and rushing wind beyond it as far as the eye could see. I could tell the moment he worked out what my intention was, his eyes going wide and his head shaking from side to side in an abnormally rapid motion. "No! No way! Not a chance in hell! I'm not fucking suicidal."

I grabbed his shoulders, turning him to face me and leaning in close. "Listen to me. Here's what's going to happen. You're going to take the backpack off and hold it in front of you with yours arms wrapped around it so it's held close to your body. I'm going to count down from five. On one you're going to jump. Keep your body tight and bring your knees in so that when you land, you roll. And then stay put. Don't go wandering around in the dark. I'm jumping straight after you. I'll find you."

Tate's next words came out almost in a hiss. "Even if I was going to jump, which I'm not, I'm not going to jump with a bagful of grenades. What kind of crazy fucking lunatic do you think I am?"

I ignored his protestations. "Take your backpack off."

He slid the strap off one shoulder. "I'm not jumping." I waited until he'd done the same with the other strap and was holding the backpack in front of him just as I'd directed him to do. "Five."

"Don't start counting. I'm not going to do it."

I shrugged my arms out of both of the backpacks I wore, moving them in front of me the same way I'd asked Tate to do. "Four." There was no sign of the DTP arriving in our carriage yet, but I sped up anyway. "Three." I shoved Tate forward so that his toes hung over the edge of the train, people around us starting to take an interest in what we were doing. The DTP would know that we'd jumped, but they'd have to get the train stopped, and it would take time for them to return to the same location to even begin their search. As long as we stayed one step ahead of them, we'd be alright. Tate said something, but I couldn't make out what it was over the noise of the wind. He was probably telling me that he wasn't going to jump again. Except, I knew he would. His mind might be rebelling against it, but his body was ready. Besides, he hadn't come this far only to surrender to the DTP and there was only one way off this train. "Two."

"Fuck!"

I caught that word, screamed as it was into the night. "One."

There was a momentary hesitation and then he was gone. I followed him as quickly as I could. The closer I was to him, the easier he'd be to find. The flight through the air lasted only a few seconds before I met the ground with a crunch, my shoulder impacting first. For the next few seconds, I was a tangle of uncontrollable limbs, flailing head over heels until I finally came to a stop. Winded, I lay on my back staring up at the starlit sky and concentrating on dragging some much-needed oxygen into my lungs. I waited until the sound of the train receded into the distance before dragging myself into a seated position and carrying out a quick inventory. Both backpacks—check. All knives accounted for—check. All limbs still attached – bruised, but check. I just hoped that Tate had fared equally well, which brought me to the next thing on my list. I needed to find him. I listened for movement, but the night was completely silent save for the wind.

"Tate!" No response. I cupped my hands over my mouth, affording the shout a lot more volume than I had the first time. There was a risk of someone else hearing me, but finding Tate took precedence over that. Even after repeating the call in every direction, there was nothing, the silent night continuing to mock me.

He couldn't be too far away considering there had only been seconds between his departure and mine. Even given the train's speed, he should have been close enough to hear me, which meant there was some other reason he couldn't—or wouldn't—answer me. The most obvious answer was that he was unconscious. Tate already had a head wound. What if he'd hit the same spot? Adrenaline spiked as I fumbled for one of the backpacks by touch alone, opening it and searching for the familiar shape of the flashlight. The first backpack revealed nothing, forcing me to repeat the process with the other. Finally locating it, I flicked the switch on with my thumb. The darkness gave way to a small sphere of light as I swung the beam around the surrounding area in an attempt to get my bearings. Rocks. Grass. And in the distance, the direction I calculated Tate had to be—trees.

I'd barely taken a few steps before my name echoed through the night air. The few milliseconds of relief that Tate wasn't lying dead in a ditch somewhere quickly faded as I registered the note of panic in his voice. I broke into a run, heading in the direction the noise had come from. "Keep talking."

"I'm not sure that's a good idea."

"Why?"

There was no answer. The undergrowth was dense, hampering

my progress as I weaved my way through the trees. I had no idea how Tate had ended up here. The trajectory from the train didn't make any sense meaning he must have ignored my directive to stay put and headed in this direction under his own steam. Catching sight of a glimmer of light in the distance that could only have come from Tate's flashlight, I sped up. It was then that I heard the growl. I burst through into the clearing, taking in the tableau in front of me at a glance. Tate, and one very pissed off looking cougar. In order to evade its snapping jaws, Tate had wedged himself into a rocky outcrop, the cougar not liking that at all. It prowled back and forth, lashing out every now and again with a powerful paw topped with razor-sharp claws. Luckily Tate was too far back for it to be able to reach its prey, producing a stalemate between man and beast.

Intent on its prey, it hadn't yet noticed me. I needed to take it down before it noticed my scent and realized there was more than one option for dinner available. Acting purely on instinct, I went for a throwing knife first, taking aim for only a few seconds before unleashing the power of my wrist. It was rare for me to miss and I wasn't about to start now. The blade embedded itself in the cougar's neck, the big cat unleashing an almighty howl before whipping around to face me. If I'd thought it was pissed before, that was nothing in comparison to now. It crouched, preparing to leap. If it did, it would wrap its powerful jaws around my throat and it would be goodnight, X.

I didn't give it time, unsheathing one of the long blades at my waist and launching myself onto it, its muscular body full of coiled power, bucking and writhing in an attempt to shake me off. The stab wound in its neck oozed warm blood over my hands as I gripped its fur tightly, keeping its sharp teeth away from me. There was almost a sexual thrill to it, perhaps because Tate was watching. Or perhaps because it had been so long since I'd taken on a truly worthy adversary. If it wasn't for Tate being in danger, I might have felt bad as I slid the knife into its brain. I understood creatures like the cougar; we were one and the same. It gave a couple of spasmodic jerks, and then lay still. Adrenaline was still coursing through my system, my blood rushing around my body at a million miles an hour.

Feet appeared in my eyeline and I looked up to find Tate glaring at me. He must have extricated himself from the gap he'd wedged himself in while I was getting my breath back. His eyes glinted in the light of my discarded flashlight. "Jump off the train, Tate! Well, I jumped off the train, and guess what the first thing I saw was when I managed to get my flashlight working. That fucking thing growling at me! Maybe next time you could mention that there might be wild animals about."

It was good that he was angry. Anger pushed down the fear and kept it at bay. He could be as angry at me as he wanted, and I'd quite happily take it. I grasped the handle of the blade and pulled it out of the creature's brain, wiping it on the cougar's fur before sheathing it again. I'd clean it properly later. Retrieving my fallen flashlight, I scanned Tate from head to toe. "Where's your backpack?"

A maniacal laugh burst from his lips. "Oh, don't worry. I'm fine. Thanks for asking. Funnily enough, while fleeing from the overgrown cat I decided that it wasn't in my best interests to lug it along with me so I left it… somewhere." He squinted into the darkness as if he'd be able to see it if he looked hard enough. Although…" His brow furrowed. "… maybe abandoning the hand grenades wasn't the best idea. Fuck! I could have thrown a hand grenade at it. I didn't even think about it."

I lowered the beam of the flashlight. "I'm glad you didn't."

Reaction finally seemed to set in as Tate sank to his knees, the position bringing him level with me. "Why?"

"Two reasons. An explosion highlighting where we are wouldn't have been a good idea, and"—I lifted the cougar's head turning it from one side to the other as I evaluated the amount of flesh on its body, concluding that it hadn't been short of a meal or two—"our dinner is better off in one piece."

Tate's eyes grew round as saucers. "We're going to eat it?"

There was that refreshing naïveté again. "What have you eaten today, Tate?"

"An energy bar."

"How many calories do you think it had?"

"Not many."

"How many calories do you think you've burned today?"

He forced himself back to a standing position despite the fact that his legs were shaking. "Yeah, yeah. I get it. I can't help feeling bad though."

I stood too, grabbing the cougar by the scruff of its neck to lift it. Such was its size that even lifting my arm high, its back legs still trailed on the ground. "It would have eaten you."

Tate laughed, but it sounded weak and reedy. "Good point... so what's the plan? You always have a plan."

"Locate the backpacks. Put some distance between us and where we came off the train. Find shelter. Make fire. Eat the cougar."

Tate turned in a slow circle, the light picking out nothing but trees on all sides. "Good luck with all that."

Tate quickly got over his aversion to eating the cougar once he'd tasted it, devouring every last little bit of meat I sent his way until he couldn't eat any more. After locating the backpacks, we'd covered as much ground as we'd dared in the darkness before stumbling over a ramshackle cabin in the middle of the forest. It had seen better days, but it was a roof over our heads, and at least it gave us some semblance of security. Besides, it was definitely a step-up from the sewers and arguably better than Jim's bunker as well. Tate had stayed quiet while I'd sorted out a fire and set to work on carving up the cougar to roast over the flames.

There was enough meat left for breakfast in the morning and

perhaps even enough to take with us the following day, providing we could find something to wrap it in to keep it relatively fresh. Neither of us needed food poisoning. Tate might not be glad that he'd stumbled into the beast, but I was. I'd barely eaten anything for close to three days, so I'd needed the protein. As for the looming presence of the DTP, I was relying on them not having enough information to find us that quickly. Even if they'd gotten as far as roughly pinpointing the area where we'd jumped off the train, there was still a lot of ground to cover. Being in the forest would make things more difficult as well. I just had to hope that those things combined would be enough to keep us out of reach until morning. But it was disconcerting to know how close they'd gotten to us. Their intervention left us with a lot more ground to cover on foot than I'd ever planned for as well.

I could feel Tate's eyes on me as I poked the fire with a stick. He'd watched me for the duration of our makeshift meal, and I didn't know why. Perhaps he was planning his revenge for me making him jump off a train, working out the best way to grab one of my knives and slit my throat. I didn't look up as he clambered to his feet, moving around the fire so that we were on the same side. I continued to stare at the flames as he sank to the ground right next to me. I'd always loved fire. Not as much as the cold metallic glint of metal, but it came a close second. There was something beautiful about its destructive nature.

Over the next few minutes, Tate gradually inched closer until his knee nudged mine. He still hadn't spoken, and I still hadn't looked his way. He was too close now though for me to pretend I hadn't noticed him. "Are you cold?"

A long hesitation, long enough for me to think he wasn't going to respond and then a single word delivered in a whisper, "No."

Tate suddenly lunged forward, his hand on my thigh while his lips fastened over mine. I froze, going impossibly still, the cabin and the world outside it ceasing to exist. There was only the pressure of his lips against mine, the feel of his fingers digging into my thigh, and the hot rush of blood around my body as I confronted the truth that Tate was kissing me. I wanted to grab him and throw him down on the ground. I wanted to grind my lips down on his, to make him open up so that I could taste him properly. I wanted to slide my hand inside his underwear and feel the throbbing heat of his cock against my palm. I wanted heat and nakedness, touch and sensation. The desire was almost overwhelming in its intensity.

But as quickly as it had started, it ended, Tate jumping back with such a look of horror that I would have killed anyone else responsible for putting that expression on his face. The kiss had barely lasted for a second. In fact, calling it a kiss would probably have been grossly overstating it. It had been a mere press of lips. Only in my head, had it been so much more.

Tate scrambled backwards across the floor, putting space between us as if I'd been the one to kiss him rather than the other way around. He shook his head from side to side, a cold deadness settling in my gut at the regret he wasn't even attempting to mask. "I'm so sorry! I don't know why I did that. I just… you were there, and I'm here, and…"

"Don't worry about it." My voice was flat and unemotional, completely at odds with the maelstrom inside me. "You're tired and stressed. You weren't thinking properly."

Tate dropped his head into his hands. "But I was. I've been thinking about doing that all day. What kind of terrible person does that make me?"

I shifted around so that I was facing him, struggling to follow his logic. "Terrible person?"

"Joseph… two days ago he was my boyfriend. I'm supposed to be upset about leaving him. I'm supposed to be missing him. I'm not supposed to be trying to kiss someone else."

I let out a snort. "Don't beat yourself up over Joseph. He was hardly the love of your life when you'd only been seeing him for three months."

Tate's head whipped up, his eyes narrowing on me. It was only then that I realized what I'd said. One touch of his lips and I'd let my guard down. He tipped his head to one side, his eyes never leaving my face. "How do you know that?"

I had two options: come up with a convincing lie or tell the truth. The truth… well, the truth would lead me down a very rocky path. A path that there was no coming back from, one I wasn't ready to travel down. Therefore, I went for the lie. Lies usually spilled off my tongue as easily as breathing, but there was something about staring into Tate's expressive blue eyes that caused my throat to close up. "You must have mentioned it. You talk a lot. You say a lot of stuff."

I could almost see the thoughts flickering across Tate's face. Just as I thought he was going to buy it, he shook his head, his mouth twisting. "You're lying to me. The only time I've ever said anything about Joseph was in the sewers, and I never mentioned how long we've been together. I've never said anything about our relationship." His voice dropped an octave. "So, how do you know, X? Tell me."

14
TATE

I hadn't been able to stop myself from kissing X. Something about the way his features were illuminated by firelight had made him damn irresistible. And maybe I'd wanted him to pay attention to me as well. Ever since we'd gotten to the cabin, I'd felt invisible, X more interested in butchering the damn cougar and staring into the flames than me. He was closed off at the best of times, but at that moment it had bothered me. I wanted to know what sorts of things went on in his head, what sort of thoughts preoccupied a man like him so much that he didn't even seem to be aware of my presence.

The kiss hadn't been planned. But once I'd been that close, I'd followed a base impulse. I'd realized my mistake as soon as my lips had touched his. It was in the stillness of his body and the firm line of his mouth. He hadn't acted like a person who wanted to be kissed. Far from it. I'd been mortified at forcing myself on someone who didn't welcome the attention. And only then had I remembered Joseph, my boyfriend of only two days ago, the man I was supposed to have been falling for. The man who had barely crossed my mind, if I was being truthful.

Everything was X. Everything that mattered anyway.

And then X had dropped his bombshell, casually mentioning that he knew how long Joseph and I had been together. That was bad enough, but then he'd lied, trying to make me believe that I was the one who'd told him that. He'd almost convinced me as well. Maybe he would have if we'd had numerous lengthy conversations. But this was X. Prizing words out of him was a feat of endurance. No, the only conversation we'd ever had about Joseph was the one where I'd thanked X for not killing him after Joseph's jibe about him being a rapist.

Was I supposed to let him get away with lying, let him fob me off like I was an idiot? We were stuck in this goddamn cabin together for the entire night. There was no way I could just let it go. I'd combust with frustration and resentment long before the sun ever rose, so despite my pounding heart, and my subconscious screaming at me that it was a bad idea, I forced myself to face him. "You're lying to me. The only time I've ever said anything about Joseph was in the sewers and I never mentioned how long we'd been together. I've never said anything about our relationship."

The only telltale sign that X had even heard me was in the sudden rigidity of his shoulders. "So how do you know, X? Tell me."

He'd returned to staring at the flames, his face in profile. Was he going to ignore me altogether? Finally, he deigned to glance in my direction. "You'd be better off not asking questions you won't like the answer to."

What the fuck was that supposed to mean? Seconds ticked by as I waited for him to elaborate but he'd returned to his wall of silence like a crab scuttling back into its shell. Anger burned inside me brighter than the flames of the fire that he was so obsessed with. "You could at least look at me."

X stood, turning slowly to face me. The expression on his face was as cold as I'd ever seen it. His hand moved to the handle of his knife but the action didn't scare me. I'd already seen it for what it was. For him, it was a source of comfort. He did it the same way someone else might hug themselves or bite their lip.

I didn't believe for one second that he'd actually use it on me, which was probably strange in itself to trust him so much after so little time together. "What do you want me to say, Tate?" I let out a mirthless chuckle at the stupid question. I fought to keep my voice even as I responded. Letting my anger out wasn't going to solve anything. "I want you to tell me the truth. That's all I ask. You keep avoiding my questions and then you expect me to just let something like that go. Well, I can't. You know something about me that you shouldn't have any way of knowing. All I want to know is why?" I studied his face, but he was the master of the impenetrable mask. His gaze flicked toward the door, his thought process clear to see. Fuck! What could be so bad he assumed I might rush out into the night and risk the cougars and the DTP? I might be angry, but I wasn't stupid. "I won't leave, no matter what you say." X looked less than convinced so I added a bit more. "I promise."

X's gaze drifted to a point behind me on the far wall. "Why do you think I just happened to be in that club?"

I shook my head, releasing a sigh. "I don't know. I've been asking you that same question over and over again. It's one of the many that you've refused to answer. I'd love to know the answer to that."

Amber eyes fastened on mine, a ticking muscle in his cheek revealing his discomfort at the turn the conversation had taken. "I'd been following you."

The four words hit me like a lightning bolt, reverberating around my skull as I struggled to make sense of them. "What?"

X shrugged as if he'd said nothing more momentous than a casual remark about the weather. "I told you, you wouldn't want to hear the truth."

His body language and tone of voice kept fluctuating between signs of extreme discomfort and a casual insouciance, and I couldn't work out which was real and which was fake. Sweat trickled down the back of my neck, making my skin itch.

"Why? Why were you following me?"

A cool gaze swept down my body, pausing at my crotch for longer than it needed to before returning to my face. "Why do you think?"

My skin was one throbbing mass of nerve endings, and I was finding it difficult to remember how to breathe. But I needed him to say it. I needed to hear him confirm it. "You were stalking me?"

Another shrug. "If you want to call it that."

I licked my lips, trying to force some saliva into my mouth. "What would *you* call it?"

He turned away, busying himself with unfastening one of the backpacks. He pulled the rolled up sleeping bag out of it and threw it in my direction. "You should sleep. We need to move at—"

"Dawn." I finished the sentence for him. It was the same speech he always gave. "I slept on the train." Something twanged in my chest, the mention of the train conjuring up the memory of falling asleep on him. I'd cuddled up to a man who was apparently my stalker—on the train and the previous night in the bunker as well. Was I that bad a judge of character? Or was X just good at hiding his true intentions? And what were his true intentions? Confusion swirled through my veins as thick as mud.

"Not for long. You need more. We'll have another long hike tomorrow."

I picked up the sleeping bag and retreated over to the far side of the cabin, as far away as I could get from X. I didn't look his way but I could feel his gaze on me. My brain was fuzzy. It felt like there should have been more questions, more things we both needed to say. But I couldn't seem to formulate the language I'd need to ask them. I got into the sleeping bag without removing any clothes, rolling over so that I could place my back to X. I stared sightlessly at the large logs which made up the wall of the cabin. There was one question that refused to go away, one thing I thought I knew from what he'd said, but I wanted him to admit it. "Did you watch us? Me and Joseph that is. Together?"

The crackling of the logs on the fire sounded abnormally loud as I waited for the answer. It was long enough that I had time to pray for a denial, for him to tell me that that was a ludicrous accusation to make. I wasn't facing him so this time I would have no idea if it was a lie.

"Yes."

I closed my eyes, refusing to think about his answer. Eventually, I succumbed to sleep but I was plagued by strange dreams of being back in Cofield, a shadowy figure following me wherever I went.

"How are your feet holding up?"

My answer was terse. "They're fine."

We'd set off at dawn, X silently handing over pieces of cold meat from the cougar that we hadn't devoured the night before. We hadn't spoken much while walking the day before, but at least when we had, it hadn't been smothered in tension and frozen politeness. I didn't know what to say to him and it seemed as if he was suffering from the same affliction. Hell, it wasn't even just talking to him. I couldn't bring myself to look at him either.

There'd been a moment that morning where I'd seriously considered setting off on my own, or making the cabin my permanent home. There had to be more wild animals out there, and forests had things you could forage, right? Berries and such. I'd figured I could talk X into leaving me one of his knives, which would have given me a weapon. The cabin was in the middle of nowhere, so who was going to find me? The presence of animals meant that there had to be a water source close by. But deep down I'd known it was just a pipe dream. Even with a knife, the probability of me being able to take down a cougar was slim to none. Whatever my personal feelings, my chance of survival lay with X. And wasn't that a peculiar twist of fate—stuck with my stalker.

Somewhere in the drudgery of putting one foot in front of the other, a strange clarity had started to arrive, though. A clarity which made a mockery of everything X had told me and forced me to ask myself why I'd been so ready to believe him. He'd made out that he'd stalked me for nefarious purposes. Yet... I'd shared a shower with him, with both of us naked, and nothing had happened. He hadn't even laid one finger on me despite his obvious state of arousal. I'd cuddled up to him in the bunker, and the result had been the same. He'd had plenty of opportunity to take what he'd implied he was after, but he hadn't.

And then there was the kiss. I'd kissed him and he hadn't responded. Perhaps he just wasn't a kisser. But the rest was harder to dismiss. Nothing in the last few days fit the picture that he'd been so determined to paint of himself. I believed that he'd been following me. Because... how else could he have been able to put such an accurate timescale on mine and Joseph's relationship? But I was beginning to think that that wasn't the full story. Far from it. He'd used my confusion and anger as a means of veering me away from a bigger truth, which meant he was still hiding something. But what? What could be so bad that he'd rather defame his own character than admit to it? I couldn't get to the bottom of it while we were hiking cross country, but once we stopped for the night, I had every intention of asking the right questions this time, and I wouldn't take no for an answer. We weren't done with this conversation. Not by a long shot.

The only problem was that my epiphany left me right back at square one and fighting my growing attraction to him. I went from refusing to even look in his direction to being barely able to tear my eyes away, admiring the muscular lines of his body and the way he moved so effortlessly. That poor cougar hadn't stood a chance. It had come across a much bigger predator than it was.

X's glances in my direction were brief and perfunctory, as if he was merely checking I was still there. I found myself smiling though. He didn't seem to realize how often he did it, the action completely involuntary. It gave me a strange sense of security. We didn't see any more wild animals, which was probably good in one sense, but I'd be lying if I said I wanted to go back to eating energy bars, and that was assuming X had any left. I hadn't asked.

The terrain had begun to change the farther north we traveled throughout the day—flat grass and occasional woodland giving way to more hilly and rocky outcrops. And it just kept getting hillier. I paused to take a breath, halfway up the steep hill we were currently traversing. Even focusing on X's muscular ass as I'd been doing for the last half a mile couldn't get me up this one without stopping for a rest.

It took a few steps for X to realize that I was no longer behind him. He stopped but didn't turn around. "Just this one and then we'll try and find shelter somewhere for the night."

Something caught my attention and I tilted my head to the side, listening. "Can you hear that? It sounds like a waterfall."

X mirrored my movement. Finally, he nodded. "I think you're right."

The thought of cool, clear water got my feet moving again and at a much quicker pace than I'd managed for the entire day. I was a sweaty mess and bathing sounded like a slice of heaven. I heaved myself up the side of the hill, using my hands to propel me when my thighs started screaming in protest, even managing to beat X to the top.

My lips curled into a smile at the sight that met me. There was indeed a waterfall, less than a mile away. Even better was the lake that the water ran into. I could almost feel what it would be like on my skin. Energized, I broke into a run, ignoring the warning note in X's voice as he called my name.

He must have realized eventually that there was no stopping me, catching me up midway and then matching my pace easily. Forgetting that I was supposed to be annoyed at him, I grinned.

Skidding to a halt at the side of the lake, I let my backpack slide off my back and drop to the ground. I'd given up worrying about it containing hand grenades. If they hadn't gone off during my less than elegant departure from the train, then it was unlikely that anything short of pulling the pin was going to make them go off at any other time.

I set to work on my clothes immediately, tearing at zippers and buttons. It wasn't until I was naked with my clothes in a pile on the ground next to me that it dawned on me that I'd been the only one undressing. X was still stood in the same spot, those amber eyes fixed on me without any indication of what he was thinking. I held my hands out to the side, letting him see everything. I might not have the same honed physique that he had but I had nothing to be ashamed of. "What?" When he didn't say anything, I continued. "You've seen me in the shower… and…" I let the silence hang for a few seconds, drawing the moment out for dramatic effect. "You've been stalking me, so you'd seen it all before anyway."

He winced, and an evil part of me I hadn't even known existed rejoiced at being able to wring some sort of reaction out of him. It was noticeable that he made no effort to deny it.

Turning my back on him, I gingerly stepped into the water. It was colder than I'd anticipated, but I pushed onwards until the water was up to mid-thigh. In the new mindset that I'd reached today, the thought of X watching Joseph and I fuck no longer seemed like something disgusting. In fact… my gaze dropped to my rapidly swelling cock. I took a few more steps toward the waterfall before turning back around, the water still not deep enough to hide my arousal. I smothered a smile as X's gaze quickly darted away telling me in no uncertain terms that he'd been staring at my ass. There was no way he could have missed the state of my cock. I parroted X's own words back to him, raising my voice so it carried across the distance between us. "Oh, don't worry. It's nothing personal. It only takes a strong breeze."

Amber eyes found mine again, narrowing at my words. "What game are you playing, Tate?"

I let my head fall back, my fingers tracing lazy circles in the water. Now that I'd been in there a while it didn't feel quite so cold. "Who says I'm playing a game?"

"Wash. I'll keep watch, and then I'll take my turn." X's voice was gruff, warning me that I shouldn't attempt to push it too far. I sighed, wading out farther until I stood below the water cascading down from the rocks. It was a far cry from the trickle of water in Jim's bunker.

Thinking about the old man gave me pause. Was he free yet? Or was he still trying to work his way through the wires? Did I care? I was surprised to find that the answer to that question was probably not. I'd changed a lot in the past three days, hardening in ways I'd never envisaged. I smirked, glancing down at my cock which was still at half-mast. I'd definitely changed. Who'd have thought I'd be trying to seduce a man who'd admitted to stalking me?

Assuming X was still watching, I made a big show out of cleaning myself beneath the spray of the water, letting my hands stroke over my body and delve into places where I wanted X's to go. The only thing missing was soap. Then I could have really put on a show. By the time I'd finished I was half wrinkled prune and half red tomato, but I felt clean for the first time since leaving Cofield.

I made my way slowly back to the shore, X's lidded gaze remaining on me. I was surprised to find my clothes laid out on the rocks. X flicked a lazy hand toward them. "I washed them." So much for him not having taken his eyes off me. I was caught somewhere between abject gratefulness at such a thoughtful gesture and disappointment at my clothes proving more interesting than my naked body. It did leave me with one dilemma: absolutely nothing to wear. X inclined his head to where he'd already unwrapped the sleeping bag. It seemed he'd already thought of that. I picked it up, wrapping it around me before lowering myself to sit on the ground. "Your turn."

X didn't move.

I frowned at him. "Seriously, it feels great." Yet, he still seemed reluctant. He'd stripped off without a second thought back in Jim's bunker, so it couldn't be that. I cast around for some other possible explanation. "If you're worried about your knives, don't be. I'll look after them. They'll still be here when you get back and… I promise to resist the temptation of throwing any of them at you while your back is turned. Even if you are a stalker." I couldn't seem to stop myself from using the word. Maybe I was trying to pave my way to the conversation I'd psyched myself up to have on the journey here.

X shook his head but didn't make any comment. I was getting tired of him not bothering to defend himself. He was clearly determined to paint himself as a villain. I watched as he divested himself of a number of knives, some I'd known about and others I'd had no idea he was carrying. They seemed to appear from every part of his clothing. He apparently came prepared for any eventuality. He lay them down in front of me until I felt like a knife salesman peddling his wares, only with no one to sell to. I opened my mouth to share my amusing observation, but the words dried up in my throat as he started to strip.

Two nights ago, X's nakedness had come as a shock, and I hadn't known where to look. Well, what a difference forty-eight hours and an admission of stalking could make. I had absolutely no qualms about looking now, letting my gaze wander hungrily over every inch of bare skin that was revealed. He was fucking gorgeous—muscular, tanned, and perfectly proportioned in every way. I leaned back on my elbows as he waded into the water, almost drooling at the sight of his bare ass. He didn't turn around until he was beneath the waterfall, tipping his head back the same way I had and letting the water sluice down over him. What I wouldn't have given for a camera. I let my imagination go wild, picturing my hands where his were as he scrubbed himself. I wanted to touch and taste. I wanted it so much that I was dizzy with desire, my cock throbbing urgently.

Pulling my gaze away from him with difficulty, I tried to focus on something else, my gaze snagging on where he'd left his clothes. I supposed that the least I could do was repay the favor. Therefore, while I couldn't exactly say that my full attention was on dipping the clothes into the water and scrubbing them, they were laid out beside mine by the time he made his way back to the shore. He gave them a cursory glance. "Thanks."

I lifted the edge of the sleeping bag in an invitation, unashamedly flashing my naked body at him with a smile. "Want to share?"

He shook his head, more interested in scanning the surrounding area. Lifting an arm, he pointed across to the other side of the lake. "Did you notice the cave behind the waterfall?"

I hadn't. But then, I'd been too busy putting on a show to think of anything important like shelter. "No."

X tilted his head back to stare up at the sky, the sun already starting to sink lower. "We'll get our clothes as dry as we can out here and then move to the cave. It looks as if it goes quite far back so we should be safe."

"What if it's got a bear in it?"

X smiled, a cold and deadly smile, his shoulders rolling back as if he was gearing himself up for something. "Then I guess bear will be on the menu tonight. We'll be able to compare the taste of it to cougar."

15
X

It had been a long day and I didn't know what was going on with Tate. His reaction the previous night had been everything I'd always expected it to be should secrets start to unravel. I'd deserved him looking at me as if I was the scum of the earth, and trying to get as far away from me as possible. The important thing was that he hadn't tried to leave. What would I have done if he had? Tied him up, maybe? It would have killed me to do it, but I'd rather deal with an angry Tate than a dead one.

Predictably, his attitude had bled into the morning, and he'd barely been able to look in my direction, never mind speak to me. I'd told myself that I didn't care, that as long as he wasn't going to bolt, it didn't matter. But that was a lie. I'd missed the chatty Tate, the one that had looked at me as if I was worth something. It might have been nothing more than a fantasy, but I wished that fantasy had lasted just a little longer. I had no one to blame but myself. I was the one who'd let slip the information about his and Joseph's relationship.

And then out of the blue, something had changed, Tate's shoulders relaxing and his whole demeanor changing. Where before he'd barely glanced in my direction, it was like he couldn't take his eyes off me. Things had only gotten worse once we'd reached the lake, his behavior giving me whiplash. One minute he was dropping the word stalker into every other sentence as provocation, and the next he was flirting and parading himself naked in front of me. I couldn't keep up. I had absolutely no idea what was going on in that pretty little head of his.

Much to my disappointment, the cave had turned out to be empty. I could have done with something to fight, something to take my aggression out on. A bear, another cougar, a DTP soldier? I didn't really care. I'd been right about it going far back, which meant we'd be well out sight. Even better was the fact that it was high enough for us both to be able to stand. There was only one exit point, though, which was the way we'd come in, but there was nothing I could do about that. Once Tate was asleep, I intended to station myself at the mouth of the cave anyway. I'd already worked out the best vantage point, which would allow me early warning of anyone approaching. I ignored the nagging voice in my head that was beginning to tell me that I needed sleep, refusing to give in to it. Even with the constant chemical concoction running through my veins, I was starting to feel the effects of exhaustion in the slight tremor in my hands, in the added few seconds that it took me to string a thought together. I had to wonder whether that was the true reason for letting my guard down the previous night. I'd hate to think that a fully alert X would have made such a rookie mistake. I'd have to sleep soon, for more than the occasional hour that I'd been allowing myself, but not tonight. Not when there could be anything out there.

I'd started a fire, managing to collect enough tufts of grass and branches together to get a decent blaze going. It wouldn't last the whole night, but it would serve the purpose of heating up the cave and removing the last vestiges of dampness from our clothes. I'd settled for putting my trousers back on while they were still slightly damp, and, thankfully, Tate had followed suit. Having to view his semi-erect cock for over an hour had been the worst sort of torture. In the cave, we were back to playing the game where he stared at me and I pretended not to notice. It was the same game that we'd been playing for most of the day. Therefore, I was aware from the very first second when Tate started to edge closer. It was just a waiting game to see what he was up to. But even I couldn't have predicted his next move, as he moved faster than I'd thought he was capable of, plucking one of the knives at my waist from its sheath and pressing the blade to my own neck. It was a move I'd done myself a thousand times. Yet I'd never been on the receiving end of it.

Until now.

Tate was just full of surprises. He applied pressure, forcing me backwards until I was laid on my back and he was straddling me. His face was wild, something almost feral in his expression, his eyes gleaming with the smug satisfaction of thinking he'd truly caught me off-guard. I kept my hands flat on the ground, giving him a few seconds to enjoy his victory before speaking. "You realize that I could take that knife off you in a matter of seconds if I really wanted to?"

Tate leaned forwards, his chest rising and falling with exertion. "So why haven't you?"

"I'm interested to see what you think you're going to gain from this."

"Maybe I just want to kill you."

"Then you missed your chance. Never waste time delivering pointless monologues, or before you know it, the opportunity has gone. If you really intend to kill someone, strike, and strike quickly. Slit their throat before they even know you're there."

"You don't. You toy with them first. You enjoy it."

"You've never seen me threaten anyone I actually wanted to kill."

A furrow formed on Tate's brow as he considered my words. I could see him recalling all the people whose throats he'd seen me hold a knife to. "You didn't want to kill Jim?"

"Not particularly. I just needed him to know that I would if I had to. Now, the cougar I wanted to kill. Did I hang around talking to him?"

Tate's lips twitched with barely suppressed amusement. It was like being held at knifepoint by a mouse. "You might have if you thought he'd understand you."

I stared at Tate's fingers wrapped around the handle of my knife. I never let anyone touch them so the sight should have infuriated me. It didn't. It seemed strangely intimate. In fact, the whole thing seemed strangely intimate, not helped by the fact that Tate's ass rested over my crotch, my cock beginning to make it known that it wasn't averse to the pressure of Tate against it. I searched for a distraction. "By the way, your technique is all wrong."

Tate quirked an eyebrow. "Oh, really. What am I doing wrong?"

"Your hand is too loose. Any sudden movement and you'd drop the knife. Tighten your fingers. Your elbow's out too far, meaning that you lack stability. And you're not exerting enough pressure to be taken seriously." I raised my head an inch, pushing my throat more tightly against the blade. "It needs to be at least that close." I pushed up a few more millimeters knowing exactly what would happen. What I couldn't have predicted was the alarm that blossomed on Tate's face. The knife slipped from his fingers, falling to the floor as he recoiled in horror, his fingers darting to my neck. "Fuck! You're bleeding. Why did you have to go and do that? I would never have…"

I grabbed his wrist to still his movements, waiting until he met my gaze, the blue eyes still clouded with concern. "I know. Which made your whole charade about as convincing as a nun with a shotgun. The last lesson I have for you, Tate, is that it's in the eyes. You can tell whether someone is capable of doing what they're threatening to do from their eyes. If you can't go through with it, you have no business picking up a knife in the first place."

He swallowed, his gaze returning to the trickle of blood from my neck.

I lifted my hand, wiping the blood away with my fingers. "It's just a scratch. Nothing to worry about."

His blue eyes found mine again. "You're a crazy fucker. You know that, right?"

I couldn't help it; I smiled. And for one frozen moment there was just the two of us, Tate's lips curling into an answering smile as we stared at each other. It was a struggle to bring myself back to earth and remember what I was supposed to be thinking about, and it didn't include blue eyes and pretty lips. "What did you want, Tate? What was all of this meant to prove?"

He sighed, a long heartfelt sigh as if he carried all the weariness in the world. "I thought I could get you to give me some answers."

"At knifepoint?"

He nodded.

I wiped the rest of the blood from my neck; it had already stopped bleeding. I knew those knives like they were an extension of my own arm so I'd known precisely how deep it would cut. There'd never been the slightest risk of serious injury. "I thought we did that last night. Even though I warned you that you didn't want to hear it. And I was right, wasn't I?"

Tate had already started shaking his head before I was halfway through my little speech, the look on his face nothing short of belligerent. "No, you fed me some bullshit that might contain an element of truth, but it's a long way from the true story. That's what I want. I want the unvarnished truth. The facts that'll make everything make sense. I don't know whether you're trying to protect me or yourself, but I can't handle it, X. I can't handle you lying to me on top of everything else. And you keep lying. Your lips say one thing, but your actions say another. You might be a stalker, but there's more to it than that. You're not some sort of pervert who skulks in the shadows. I know you're not, so it's no good pretending you are." He shifted slightly, his ass grinding down on my crotch. "You're hard now, but you haven't done anything about it." His gaze shifted across to the knife he'd dropped. "You could pick that up, roll me over and do whatever you want to me. It's not like anyone would hear me scream."

Tate was breathing hard by the time he'd finished speaking, his cheeks flushed.

I was faced with the realization that he wouldn't stop asking, wouldn't stop pushing. I'd seen his dogged determination from afar, so it was naïve to think that he would take anything at face value when he never had before. I'd just never been on the receiving end of it before. I became fixated on his last words, the ones that had created an ugly picture of me forcing myself on him. "I wouldn't do that to you."

Tate let out a long, shaky breath. "Exactly. Do you know what sort of person would do that?" He didn't wait for a response before answering his own question. "A stalker would. Especially a stalker who's killed God knows how many people." His brow scrunched up. "How many people *have* you killed?"

When his stare went on and on, it became obvious that he actually expected an answer. I shrugged, wondering whether I should make a number up, but I'd already paused for too long, his eyes growing wide. "Oh my God! You don't even know. You've lost count. That's"—his gaze slid away to the side— "I don't even know what that is. Did they all deserve it? Wait!" He held up a hand. "Don't answer that. I don't need to know."

"I've never pretended to be a good person." The words were like a rusty nail in my heart even though I'd been the one to speak them. That's what it all boiled down to, didn't it? Tate was a good person, and me? Well, I wasn't. I'd killed and I'd maimed without discrimination. I'd walked away when I could have helped people. My crimes against humanity were numerous.

Tate climbed off me, and I felt his absence like a physical blow. He didn't go far, sitting cross-legged in front of me as I eased myself back to seated. He propped his chin on his hands and simply stared at me. "I'll be the judge of that."

"What's that supposed to mean?"

He smiled. "Once I've heard the truth, the whole truth, and nothing but the truth, then I'll give you my judgement."

I frowned, the saying familiar yet alien at the same time. "Where does that saying come from?"

"They used to say it in the courts, back in the good old days where you were innocent until proven guilty, and even if you were guilty, they used to lock you up instead of vaporizing you." He gave a wry smile. "Just think if this was fifty years ago, I could be lounging on a bed behind bars now."

I gestured around the cave. "And miss out on all of this fun?"

"Yeah, there is that." He shuffled closer, his knees pressing against mine. "I'm going to ask you some questions. And all I want is the truth. Can you do that, X? For me."

Could I? If he asked the right questions, it would strip me bare. There'd be nothing and no one left to hide behind. And where would that leave us? I swallowed with difficulty, my throat suddenly dry. "I can try."

Tate nodded slowly, his expression turning pensive. "Okay then. Here we go. You should probably know that I can tell when you're lying."

"Can you?"

"Yeah." He tilted his head to one side, regarding me as if I was the most interesting thing on the planet. He gestured at his own face, his fingers waggling near his brow. "You get this eyebrow twitch thing."

"Eyebrow twitch?"

He nodded emphatically. "Trust me, you do."

"If you say so."

He sat up straighter. "How long have you been watching me for?"

Boom! He wasn't messing about. That was probably the

worst question he could have asked. I picked the knife up from the floor, the one Tate had dropped, and smoothed my hand over the handle as the silence lengthened between us. I lifted my head and looked him straight in the eye, needing to see his face as I answered. "Fourteen years."

From the way, Tate rocked backwards you would have thought I'd physically struck him. His eyes widened as he stared at me, his mouth twisting into a number of shapes before finally managing to force it into a shape where he could form words. "Fourteen years! But that would mean I was only twelve when you started. You would only have been…" He paused, his brow furrowing. "How old are you?"

That was an easier question to answer. "Twenty-nine."

Tate did a quick calculation in his head. "So, you would have been fifteen at the time." He let out a long, slow breath. "You've been watching me since you were fifteen. X, that's…" He shook his head, seemingly unable to find the words he wanted.

I did it for him, giving him a list to choose from. "Sick, perverted, scary?"

Tate leaned in, his expression intense. "Is it though? I still can't believe that. You've never once treated me with anything other than respect. In fact, you've let me get away with stuff… with doing stuff… saying stuff… that I don't think anyone else would get away with. And you've never even raised your voice to me, never mind…" He made a wild gesture at the knife in my hand. "… threatened me." He shook his head. "Why, X? Why did you start following me?"

I sucked in a breath, the urge to just get up and walk away almost overwhelming. I didn't, forcing myself to stay put. The truth was going to come out whether I wanted it to or not. "How much do you remember about your father?"

Tate frowned. "My father? He died when I was…" I saw the moment when the correlation in ages hit. "… twelve." He lifted his hand to massage his neck. "What's my father got to do with anything?"

"What did you know about him before that?"

Tate's face screwed up. "What's there to know? He was a doctor, and he was my dad. He went to work. Came home again. We had a good relationship, and then he died of a heart attack way before his time."

Despite the matter of fact way that he'd stated it, I could tell that the memory pained him even this many years later. "So, he never told you what else he did?"

A muscle ticked in Tate's cheek. "If you're about to tell me bad things about him then I don't want to know. He was a good man. I—"

"He was a good man."

"You make it sound like you met him?"

I'd come this far. There was no going back from it, despite the fact it meant discussing things I'd never shared with anyone before. I fixed my gaze on the cave wall, watching the shadows from the flames of the fire leap across it and hoping that the words would come easier if I didn't have to look at Tate when I said them. "Your father was a great man. He used to visit the slums to give out free medical treatment. He was generous with medical supplies as well. One day when he was in the slums, he stumbled across a child. That child was eight and had already been living on the streets for over a year. The child had pneumonia and was at death's door. He would have been lucky to last another week. Most people would have kept walking and decided that there was nothing they could do. He didn't. He paid for drugs for the child from his own pocket and he didn't stop there, he found the child a place to stay as well. Even when the child was better, he insisted on visiting them. And the child didn't do grateful or thankful, didn't even do nice. Yet, he never gave up on them. He made sure they had food and clothes and spent time with them even when he got nothing back."

"The child was you."

Tate's words were so softly spoken that I almost didn't hear them. I nodded without looking at him. "He knew he was ill." I risked a glance in Tate's direction wondering if this would come as news to him, but when he didn't flinch, I carried on. "He came to see me a week before he died. He told me things he'd never mentioned before, that he had a wife and a son, that he was worried about how they'd cope if anything happened to him. He'd never asked anything of me before. For years he'd been helping me, and not once had he even asked for so much as a friendly greeting. So how could I say no?"

"What did he ask of you?"

"To look out for you. Both of you. He already knew I'd been straying into Cofield on a regular basis out of curiosity, so he wasn't asking me to go anywhere where I wasn't already going. So, I did. I watched out for both of you, at least until your mother... Well, you know what happened." Tate's mother had died when he was sixteen. "And then... I just watched you."

Tate took a moment to contemplate the information I'd just given him. "I don't think my dad expected you to watch me forever. You could have stopped when I was eighteen." Tate's stare was intense, his brow wrinkled as if there were still things he couldn't quite work out. "So... you just followed me around?" I didn't get a chance to answer as a dawning realization blossomed on his face. "The money... the money that appeared out of nowhere when I was in debt. That was you? You did that?"

I hadn't expected him to put two and two together quite so quickly. "You needed it."

Tate laughed, a bright, bubbly sound which echoed in the cave. "All these years people have been winding me up about having a secret guardian angel and I actually had one."

"I'm hardly an angel."

Tate raised an eyebrow. "No, you're right about that. A guardian devil then." He sighed, but then his face suddenly paled. "What else did you do? Please don't tell me that you had something to do with Niles's accident."

I lifted my chin. "He hit you, Tate. More than once."

His breath escaped in a whoosh. "Fuck! You can't kill people because they don't treat me right. I'd kicked him out. He'd gotten the message. He wasn't going to come anywhere near me."

"So you were happy for him to do it to someone else?"

He looked affronted at the idea. "No, but… you didn't have to kill him." He drew his legs up, wrapping his arms around them and resting his chin on his knees, his eyes troubled. "You know everything about me. You've watched me day after day and I was completely oblivious. I just don't understand why you carried on. Your debt to my father… if there ever was one… was paid. He wouldn't have expected you to devote your whole life to ensuring my safety. No one could expect that. It's too high a price to pay."

I turned away from him, watching the flames slowly devour a branch. I'd spilled more of my history than I'd ever dreamed, especially to Tate of all people. But that was as far as I was going to go—ever. The rest I'd never admit. Not while there was still breath in my lungs. Tate's stare burned into the side of my face and I could almost hear the cogs going around in his brain. I'd wait him out and he'd get bored eventually.

"Holy fuck!"

I didn't lift my head. "What?"

"You love me."

If a lightning bolt had arced down from the roof of the cave and struck me, it couldn't have packed a bigger punch. For a moment even breathing was difficult, stars dancing in front of my eyes. I fought against the reaction, quickly gaining control of my motor functions again in the space of only a few seconds. I let out a deliberate laugh. "Love is a social construct designed to provide a multitude of excuses so that people can do whatever the fuck they want. In reality, it doesn't exist. And even if it did, what kind of fool could love someone they've never met?" The lie tasted bitter in my mouth, but it was necessary.

For the next few seconds, the only sound was the crackle of smoldering branches. I held my breath, waiting for Tate to get up and move away now that I'd shattered his romantic flight of fantasy. He didn't move. I braced myself for his next words, expecting them to be laden with scorn and hurt, the imagined rejection forcing him to lash out.

But when he did speak, his voice was soft, conviction ringing from every word. "No. I'm not buying that. It's the only thing that makes any sense. It's the reason why you continued to follow me long after you could have stopped. It's the reason why you came into the club and saved me." His voice rose in pitch and I could hear the smile in it. "You've been gentle, almost sweet. Other people aren't even allowed to touch you. But I can. You let *me*. You even let me snuggle up to you the other night. You let me sleep on your shoulder on the train. You let me touch your knife—"

"I didn't let you. You took it."

"Oh, come on." Tate's voice was full of the scorn I'd expected earlier. "You let me. You saw me coming a mile off. You just wanted to see what I'd do, how far I'd take it. And then there's the fact that you won't even look at me now because you know that everything I'm saying is true."

"I *can* look at you. I'm just choosing not to." Even to my own ears, I sounded like a petulant child.

"So... look me in the eye and tell me that you don't love me. It should be easy for you to do if you think love doesn't even exist."

There was no mistaking the challenge in Tate's voice. I was stuck between a rock and a hard place. If I didn't do as he'd asked, he'd take that as confirmation anyway, and if I did... Even my knives couldn't get me out of this one. Not unless I was prepared to stab Tate, and I'd rather peel the skin off my own cock than do that.

I swiveled around to face him again, Tate resting his chin

on his knee and smiling sweetly at me, the light from the fire casting interesting shadows across his face. He raised an eyebrow, his expression turning smug. "Go on then."

I couldn't do it. There were so many lies I could tell... had already told, but I couldn't form the words to even attempt to tell this one. I did love him. At some point in time when he'd matured from a gangly youth to the man he was today, I'd stopped seeing him as a duty and I'd seen him as something else. It had started as a tiny ember, a realization that I found him attractive. But from there it had grown to so much more. He was everything I wasn't: kind, caring, popular, always smiling. Tate had consumed my thoughts and my dreams for years. He'd been my reason for waking up in the morning and my reason for staying alive. I stared into his blue eyes, and I just couldn't do it.

His smile grew wider and he nodded, his eyes gleaming. "See! I knew I was right."

I felt like a fish on the end of a line and Tate had just reeled me in. There was no point in denying it. I'd given him the means to work out the full story when I'd revealed the rest of it. I needed to remember, though, that it didn't change anything. "It doesn't matter."

Tate's smile died on his lips. "What do you mean it doesn't matter?"

"It doesn't change anything. Me and you... we're from different worlds."

Tate lifted his head to stare around the cave. "Looks like the same world to me."

I shook my head. "You know what I mean."

"So..." His expression turned ponderous. "You've got me here and you're not going to do anything about it?" His voice dropped to a low, seductive note. "Did you like watching me fuck, X? Did you ever pretend that it was you in that bedroom with me? I bet you did." His gaze dropped to my crotch. "I bet you went home and you stroked yourself while you thought about me, didn't you? How many times, X? Hundreds? Thousands?"

There was only one way to handle that level of provocation. I stood up and walked away and I didn't stop walking until I reached the mouth of the cave. I leaned against the rocky outcrop, letting the cool breeze wash over me and dampen my ardor. My whole body was trembling with the temptation to let myself go and follow my base desires. But Tate didn't know what he was asking for. If he did, he wouldn't be stupid enough to be asking for it. I took a deep breath, dragging as much clean air into my lungs as I could.

16
TATE

I stared at the empty space where X had been only seconds before with the sinking realization that I'd gone too far. High on discovering that, far from him being immune to my charms, it was quite the opposite, I'd felt empowered enough to goad him. I'd wanted him to jump me. I'd wanted to feel that hard body pressed against mine and revel in the feel of his stiffening cock, the same way I had when I'd sat astride him. To me it was simple, if he loved me, then he wanted to have sex with me. And why the hell, shouldn't we? We could die tomorrow so what was stopping us from grabbing every bit of pleasure we could. I couldn't figure out what had gone wrong. He'd run off as if he had the hounds of hell after him. Did X think I was using him? Was that it? But it didn't ring true. My gut told me there was more to it than that.

The sensible thing to do would be to give him time to work through whatever was bothering him, to stay where I was and give him the solitude he apparently needed. I'd never been that sensible, though, or maybe it was more about being selfish. I wasn't sure, but I gave him less than a minute before making my way to the cave entrance. I found him leaning against it, staring out into the pitch-black night, one hand predictably resting on the handle of his knife. I wanted to step up behind him and wrap my arms around him. I could soak up his body heat and rest my chin on his shoulder. And he'd probably let me. But it wouldn't solve anything. Not until I worked out what was going on inside that wonderfully complex yet illogical brain of his.

"Come back inside."

He jerked slightly, giving away the fact that he'd been so lost in thought that he hadn't sensed my arrival. "Not yet."

"You can't stand out here all night just to avoid me."

The only answer he gave was a slight shrug.

I sighed, frustration starting to burn through me. The urge to hit him was starting to take precedence over the desire to touch him. I swallowed it down. The last thing X needed was someone getting angry at him. That's probably what he was used to from people. I wanted to be different. I wanted to be the person to treat him better. Like my dad apparently had.

"I'm sorry."

He didn't turn around. "For what?"

It was a valid question. What was I sorry for? Some of the frustration leaked into my voice. "I don't know. For goading you. For pushing you. I'm sorry for whatever it is that's driven you to come out here and stare moodily into the night." My fingernails dug into my palm as I carried on. "I thought that you loving me meant you wanted me. I... fuck it! I'm just going to say it in case it's not obvious. I want you, X. I shouldn't because it's way too soon after Joseph, but—"

"Don't bring him into it."

The words were delivered harshly, leaving me frowning. What was that? Jealousy? Or something else? I felt honor bound to stick up for Joseph. "He was a good man. He was kind to me. He was—"

"He was a stopgap until you found something better. You were never going to be with him forever."

Ouch! I couldn't deny the truth in it, though. Joseph had been fun, but I'd never once pictured spending the rest of my life with him. I guessed that explained why he'd been so easy to put out of my mind. Well, that and spending twenty-four hours a day with a man who oozed testosterone. "Why don't you want me?"

X's sigh was long and heartfelt. "Wanting and having are two very different things."

Great, now we were playing cryptic clues. My blood started to heat again, and I took a few deliberate breaths. X might be sexy as hell, but he was quite possibly the most insufferable person I'd ever met. "What the fuck does that mean?"

X's next words were measured and careful as if he was testing every word out before releasing them. "It's possible to want something but to not let yourself have it."

I laughed. "You don't need to *let* yourself. I've done everything short of spread-eagling myself in front of you and begging you to fuck me. And if I thought for one minute that would work, I'd do that as well."

"Be careful what you're asking for, Tate." The warning in his tone was implicit.

Despite the rapid thrum of my heartbeat, I made myself take a few moments to think back through all the conversations we'd had tonight. In some ways it felt as if we'd taken a massive step forward, yet gone nowhere at all. X's arguments were always about me. Everything was about me. Therefore, it stood to reason that his reluctance to give in also had to be about me rather than him. I just needed to work out where it stemmed from. He wanted me. That much was clear. But something was stopping him, and I wasn't fooling myself that it was all about gallantry.

Gallantry and X didn't exactly go hand in hand. But then, I'd never lain in bed and dreamed of a white knight. That wasn't where my fantasies lay. Not even close. "What are you scared of?" Fixated as my gaze was on his back, it was easy to see the muscles stiffen. It told me that I was right. That whatever was holding him back was about fear rather than lack of desire.

I carefully stepped around him so that I stood in front of him, giving him very little choice but to look at me. We were close. Close enough that I could have kissed him again. I wouldn't though, not when it had yielded such spectacularly poor results the last time.

Just when I thought he wasn't going to answer, he spoke, his voice sounding as if he'd been gargling with glass. "I don't want to hurt you."

I nodded, everything suddenly falling into place, from his comment about us being from two different worlds to his reluctance to kiss me back. It all came down to that one simple truth. He thought I was delicate and fragile. He might have watched me, but he'd never been able to see what lay beneath my skin. Nobody had, because I'd kept those dark desires to myself, never giving them the air to breathe, scared that if I ever unleashed them there was no going back. I took a deep breath, preparing to speak my own truth for the first time. "How many boyfriends have I had, X?"

Lines appeared on his forehead. It obviously wasn't what he'd expected me to say. "Do you want an actual number?"

I snorted. Given a few minutes to work it out, he could probably have given me one as well. As well as a physical description and breakdown of each one. "No, just a rough approximation."

"A few."

A few was an understatement. I'd had my first boyfriend at sixteen, a few months after my mother's death and I'd never stayed single for long since then. "And how long did my relationships last?" It was weird to be asking someone I'd only known for a few days for personal information about myself, but I knew he'd know the answers.

"Not long."

"Yeah, and do you know why that was?"

"No."

I forced my esophagus to carry out the necessary processes

required for swallowing. "Because none of them could give me what I wanted."

X's gaze remained fixed on me. "What did you want?"

I stepped closer so that our bare chests touched, my nerve endings tingling in response to the contact. Was I actually going to say this aloud? Was I going to reveal the fantasies that had plagued me almost before I'd even known I was gay? I'd never dared to tell anyone before. But X was different. He wasn't an urbane banker or a fellow pharmaceutical worker who'd recoil in shock. He was a man who didn't play by the rules, a man who threatened and by his own admission killed indiscriminately. He wouldn't judge me for what I was about to say, and if my gut feeling was correct, we'd fit together like two pieces of a jigsaw puzzle. I just needed to man up and admit what I wanted. I lifted my chin, looking him straight in the eye and refusing to be ashamed. "What I want… what I've always wanted…" The words got stuck in my throat and I had to cough to clear them. "…is someone who doesn't treat me like I'm made of fine bone china. I want someone to bruise me. I want…" Now that I'd started, there was no stopping the words from flowing as I laid everything that I'd always considered a secret perversion at his door. "… I don't want gentle. I want rough and ready. I need to feel like they mean it, though. Not that they're just playing some part. I tried that once and it didn't work. They weren't convincing enough. I need…" I let my lips curl into a slow smile, desire unfurling like a flower starting to bloom. "I need a man like you. A man who's violent but knows how to control it. A man who—"

"You don't know that I can control it."

They were the first words X had spoken since I'd started my heartfelt speech. It was a relief to hear that they were free of censure. "I do know. I've seen it, and I also know that you'd never hurt me… not really, not any more than I wanted to be hurt." I could see from the look in his eyes that I was winning, that he was wavering. I'd taken the one thing he was scared of and turned it back on him. I held my hand out, palm upwards. "Let's go back inside, X."

During the momentary hesitation that followed, I could barely breathe, but then his hand slid into mine, the callused fingers fitting perfectly in mine. I led him into the cave, only stopping once we were back where we'd started, the fire still burning. I let go of his hand and leaned back against the rocky wall, my chest rising and falling rapidly with a mixture of excitement and anticipation. My cock throbbed urgently in my trousers, begging to be touched. I lifted my chin and issued a challenge. "Show me what you've got."

The gleam in X's eyes as he advanced on me took my breath away. There was a split second of time where I was so damn scared that he was going to change his mind, but then he lifted his hand, his fingers closing around my neck. At first the touch was gentle, but when I didn't offer any sort of objection, they gradually tightened. I wondered if he could feel the rapid hammering of my pulse beneath his fingers. "Is this what you want, Tate?"

I nodded, the ability to form words completely beyond me. X leaned in, bracing his free hand against the wall, his breath ghosting across my cheek for a few seconds before his lips moved close to my ear. "All you need to do is say the word stop and I'll stop. Can you do that for me, Tate?"

The man who'd questioned whether he had control was apparently gone, and in his place was the predator I'd been craving. I managed another shaky nod, his fingers now pressing even harder into my windpipe. It hurt. And I loved it.

"I need to hear you say it."

Say what? There was no blood left in my brain. It was all in my cock. Stop! That was it. X needed confirmation that I understood. I made a superhuman effort to form my lips into a shape capable of forming words. "Stop."

X's hand dropped like a stone from my neck. I let out a moan of protest, the skin where his fingers had been feeling cold and bare. His gaze, though, burned into me. "Say it and it will happen, just like that."

I made a grab for his wrist, capturing it and putting it back where it belonged, the world feeling right again once it encircled my neck. We were both breathing hard now, X clearly just as affected as I was. And we hadn't even done anything yet. We were going to burn hotter than the fire a few feet away. I smiled at the thought, X's gaze homing in on the movement of my lips. He lowered his head and I would have met him halfway like a flower seeking the sun if the grip on my neck hadn't made it impossible. As it was, all I could do was wait and pray for it to happen, every painstakingly long second lasting an eternity. I braced myself for a hard kiss, expecting to be plundered, expecting X to show me exactly what I'd let myself in for. And I would have welcomed it too.

But when the kiss came, it was achingly gentle, his lips applying only the slightest pressure as his tongue teased the seam of my lips in the sweetest request to open up that I'd ever received. The twin sensation of brute strength and pure gentleness was my undoing. I whimpered, sliding my hands along the length of his muscular back to pull him into me as my lips obediently parted.

Had it been a kiss with anyone else, I would have tilted my head and searched for that perfect angle to deepen the kiss. But X controlled everything. I could only move my head if he allowed me to. His fingers slid higher, his thumb digging into my jawbone as his tongue gained access to my mouth. His thigh pushed my legs apart, sliding into the space between and holding me immobile against the wall. I was pinned by him in every way.

This. This was what I'd been searching for, for years. Someone prepared to completely overwhelm me and bend me to their will.

Little had I known they'd only been a few feet away from me, watching and waiting. I let out a moan as X deepened the kiss, but it was still gentle, still teasing. The kiss completely at odds with the bruising strength of the hand around my neck. I lost myself in it, happy to let him lead, happy to have him dictate everything about it. His hips ground against mine, hard cock pressed against hard cock.

Finally, X drew back a little, the grip of his fingers loosening slightly as he rested his forehead against mine. I drew slow circles on his back as I tried to work out what was going through his head. But then I realized that I'd probably die of old age if I waited for him to speak first. "I thought when I tried to kiss you before and you didn't respond that maybe you didn't like kissing. But I'm guessing you do. What I'm trying to say in my own individual rambling way is that you're a great kisser."

I felt his exhalation of breath in response. Had he laughed? Surely not. If X turned out to have a sense of humor as well as everything else, I may as well hand my heart over to him now. "We're going to fuck, right?" *Sorry, Joseph. I truly hope you find someone perfect for you and that in a couple of years you barely remember me.*

"I don't have protection."

Protection, right? I searched deep inside myself for the man who'd always been so careful during any hook-up, the one who'd have run a mile if anyone had even hinted at not using a condom, but I seemed to have left him in Cofield. He was probably still kneeling on the nightclub floor waiting for the burst of laser fire to strike him down. "I don't care. We could both die tomorrow."

"You should care. I've not been as careful as you."

That was probably an understatement. My only sex had been with boyfriends. I hadn't even done one-night stands, whereas X was the type to hang out in brothels. Thinking about the brothel triggered a memory. I planted my hand in the center of X's chest and pushed him back so that I could see his face. "That guy. The one I met. Did you fuck him because he looked like me? Did you pretend he was me?"

Amber eyes held mine and I could see the answer in them even before the husky "yes" left his lips.

I let my head thud back against the wall as I struggled to process just how deep X's obsession with me had gone. It should have made me feel uncomfortable. It should have made me want to call the whole thing off and go back to whatever we'd been before tonight. Friends? Maybe not. More like traveling companions. But it didn't. It just firmed my resolve even more. I smiled. "It's probably time you had the real thing then."

17

X

The last few minutes had seemed like a dream. A dream where paradise was possible, with paradise being Tate's plush lips and his body. Kissing him was everything I'd always thought it would be, and more. Despite what he'd said, I'd expected him to balk when I'd shown him with my hand around his neck what he was asking for, but he hadn't. The way his breath had hitched and his cock had grown even harder against my thigh couldn't be faked. I'd had to stop to gather myself. And wasn't that a fucking revelation. The man who was scared of nothing, completely undone by a single kiss.

"It's probably time you had the real thing then."

Whether it was the words themselves or the fact they were delivered by kiss-swollen lips, I wasn't sure. But they lit a fire inside me. Tate was right. The DTP could catch up with us tomorrow and there was no way I was going to my grave without having him. Heat slowly unfurled within me, the possibility of all the things I wanted to do to him running on a constant loop.

I stepped back, ignoring the confusion that settled on Tate's face at my retreat. I didn't give him a chance to protest, my gaze drifting down his body to the bulge at his crotch. "Strip!"

He inhaled sharply, twin flags of color blossoming on his cheeks as his hands immediately dropped to the fastening of his trousers. What a contrast it was to earlier when I'd done my best to avoid his nakedness as he'd paraded provocatively in front of me. Now I savored every inch as he bent over to roll his trousers down his thighs before stepping out of them. He hadn't bothered with underwear so there was only the glorious sight of his hard cock to stare at. "Stroke it."

His gaze never wavered from mine as he spat in his palm before dropping his hand to his cock and wrapping it around his length.

"Slowly."

His lips quirked, but he followed the directive to the letter, sliding his hand with agonizing slowness to the head of his cock before dragging it back down to the base. Tate's teeth bit into his lower lip as he repeated the movement another half a dozen times. Without taking my eyes off him for even a second, I shed my own trousers, Tate's gaze fastening hungrily on my cock, the hand on his speeding up almost of its own accord. "Tate." I threw the word out sharply and he immediately stilled, his chest rising and falling with the effort of holding back.

"Bastard."

I stepped forward, plucking his hand from his own cock and wrapping it around mine instead. "And don't you forget it."

Tate didn't bother to respond. He was more interested in fondling the cock he now had hold of, his fingers learning its shape and heft as if it was some sort of amazing discovery. He gave it a couple of exploratory strokes, his lips curling into a smile at the way my abdominal muscles fluttered at the touch of his hand. I was so primed for this that it just wasn't funny.

Placing my hand on the top of his head, I pressed down. Tate immediately understood what I wanted, dropping to his knees on the hard, stone floor, his hands clutching onto my thighs as his mouth enveloped my cock. Most of the men I'd had over the years had been whores and therefore experts at knowing how to please a man. Yet, none of them had ever come close to making me feel the way Tate did. He looked beautiful in the firelight, his eyes closed and his cheeks hollowing as he sucked. I ran my fingers across his forehead, his temples, his cheeks, my thumb tracing his bottom lip as it stretched around my cock. Tate's hands weren't idle either as he sucked me, exploring everything he could touch from my abs to my thighs before fastening on my ass to greedily pull me deeper into his throat.

Only when I was so close to coming that every muscle of my body strained with holding back, did he stop, sitting back on his haunches to observe me from lidded eyes. "I have a present for you."

I stared at him, dumbfounded, wondering why he thought now was a good time. He smiled as he scrambled over to where he'd left his trousers, briefly dipping his hand into the pocket. Within seconds, he was back, lifting a closed hand to me in offering. I peeled back his fingers to reveal what lay in his palm. I laughed when I saw what it was—a sachet of lube. Tate winked. "I had it at the club. I found it the other day and hung onto it just in case. Luckily, it survived you washing my trousers."

I plucked it off his palm, bringing it to my mouth and ripping off the corner of the foil packet with my teeth. Tate held his hand out, and I dutifully squeezed the contents onto his palm, the faint aroma of strawberry filling the cave. He wasted no time in slicking my cock from root to tip before smoothing the excess on his own rigid length. He clambered to his feet, returning to the wall of the cave and bracing his arms against the rock, his ass tipping up in invitation as he glanced back over his shoulder. "Is this okay?"

Blood thrummed in my ears so loudly that for a moment it was all I could hear. I fought for control as I closed the space between us. And then I remembered that he didn't want control. He wanted the ugliness, craved it even. Tate wanted to be possessed, and I wanted, no needed, to possess him in a synergy which was frighteningly pure. I left no space between our bodies, my cock sliding between his tight ass cheeks. Tate didn't have the same defined muscles that I had, but to me he was perfect. I plastered my chest against his back, my forearm snaking across his neck and pulling his head back. There was no pressure. Not yet. Just the promise of what was to come. I bit his earlobe, soothing the bite with my tongue as he hissed. "What do you need to say if it gets to be too much, Tate?"

"Stop." He sounded drunk, the single word dragged out for far longer than it should have been. "I won't say it."

I tightened my arm exerting enough pressure to start to impede the oxygen to his brain. He didn't stiffen. If anything, he relaxed into it. He trusted me. The realization was heady. I slid my hand down, collecting some of the lube from my cock on my fingers before pressing on his hole. His back bowed as I inserted first one finger and then another once he'd loosened up enough. The noises he made as I stroked his prostate were divine, so divine that I needed to taste them as well as hear them, my lips seeking his to drink them from his mouth.

Tate squirmed against me, trying to force my fingers into a deeper and faster rhythm. I didn't oblige, keeping him teetering on the edge of needing more for as long as I could. He was a mewling mess by the time I replaced my fingers with my cock, giving no resistance as I slid deep inside him with one thrust, the lube doing its job.

I paused for a moment, giving myself time to commit the moment to memory, taking in the way he pushed back against me, his sweat-slicked, heated skin, and the sheer desperation for an orgasm seeping from every pore. On the edge myself, I didn't intend to make him wait long.

"X." Just that one exhalation of my name on his lips carried so much longing. If anyone had told me a few weeks back that Tate Gillespie would ever say my name with so much pent-up desire, I probably would have slit their throat for taunting me with the impossible. Yet, here we were. I lowered my head, dragging my tongue along the length of his neck, the taste of his sweat like ambrosia. "What do you need, Tate?"

If he'd said the moon on a stick, I would have tried to find some way of giving it to him. Luckily, his demands were much simpler. He lifted his hand, his fingers curling around the forearm I had across his neck. "Tighter… and hard. Don't hold back. Give me everything."

My smile was wicked as I did as he'd asked. I increased the pressure as I started to thrust, Tate's tight ass sucking me deeper with each movement. I changed the angle until I found the one that forced the loudest moans from his lips. From there it was just a waiting game, Tate finally unable to resist wrapping his hand around his cock. I counted two strokes and then he was coming, his body sagging against the wall. I pushed him against it, letting go of his neck to dig my fingers into his hips. A few strokes more and I was shuddering against him, wrapping my arms tightly around him while I groaned my satisfaction into his ear. I didn't withdraw from his body, wanting to draw out the moment for as long as I could, wanting to pretend that nothing in the world existed except for Tate. We remained like that for an age, fingers still stroking lazily over skin, bodies fitting together like they were made for each other. Every now and again, Tate would give a little hum of pure satisfaction, seeming in no more rush than I was to separate. Whatever the future might bring, I knew that I would treasure this moment forever.

Tate slept more peacefully than I'd ever seen him sleep before. We'd gone at it a second time before retiring to the sleeping bag, Tate claiming that it would be a crime to waste the lube when it was all we had. He'd said he wouldn't be able to come again, but I'd taken great delight in proving him wrong on that score, his body shuddering to an even more intense orgasm with my hand wrapped around his cock. I'd come again as well, his ass clutching me just as tightly as it had the first time.

Once I'd laid the sleeping bag out, Tate had wound himself around me like a monkey clinging to a tree, falling asleep almost instantaneously with his head on my chest. I'd lain there for as long as I dared, replaying the events of the night, struggling to believe—despite the evidence in front of me—that it had really happened. When the sound of Tate's steady breathing had threatened to pull me into sleep, I'd reluctantly disengaged my limbs from his, wrapping the sleeping bag around him as he curled up on his side.

It was so tempting to sleep. But I couldn't. Not when there could be anything or anyone out there, ready to discover our hiding place. I put my trousers back on before making my way over to my backpack. I pulled one of the syringes out, doing a quick inventory of how many were left. Three, not including the one I was about to inject into myself. That should be enough, even with the extra days added on by our early departure from the train.

Uncapping the syringe, I squeezed my arm until I'd located a vein, sliding the needle in. About to press the plunger, I froze as a voice rang out. "What the fuck do you think you're doing?"

I lifted my head to find a naked and clearly irate Tate making his way toward me, his expression hiding none of his displeasure.

My fingers tightened around the syringe. "It's not what it looks like."

Tate dropped to a crouch in front of me. "And what do you think it looks like?"

That was easy to answer. "You think I'm a junkie shooting up. I thought you were asleep."

"I was. And then I woke up." Tate's sharp eyes spied the other syringes. He picked one up, turning it round to look at the label, his expression clouding.

"It's—"

He lifted his head, his glare cold enough to freeze lava. "I know what it is. I worked for a pharmaceutical company. You know, the one that thinks I committed industrial espionage against them and had me earmarked for execution without even a thanks for all the years you worked for us for shitty pay." He waved the capped syringe in my direction. "This is a stimulant, a strong one." He rifled through the rest of the syringes before eyeing the one still sitting in my vein. "How long have you been taking this crap? Have you any idea what this shit can do to you if you take it for too long?" His voice altered to a more even tone. "Please tell me you haven't been taking this shit ever since we left Cofield? When was the last time you slept, X?"

I couldn't answer either of those questions. The first because I couldn't give the answer he wanted to hear and the second because it would only confirm the answer to the first. "Someone needs to stay vigilant."

Tate shook his head, something fierce burning in his eyes. "Not the whole night. Or if we do, we take turns. I'm not a useless damsel in distress even if I might come across as one sometimes. I'm capable of pulling my own weight. All you ever had to do was ask."

My thumb hovered over the plunger, Tate's hand shooting out to cover mine. "Don't you dare! You're not going to stick any more of that crap in your veins while I'm around. You're going to sleep, X. I highly doubt that anyone is going to find us here, but if it makes you feel better I'll keep watch, and if anything more momentous than a leaf moving happens, I won't hesitate to wake you up and describe it in excruciating detail until you wish I hadn't."

Nobody had ever told me what to do. And if they had, well, I'd either ignored them or their ability to breathe had ended that day. But Tate wasn't just anyone. Tate was the man I'd poured every last ounce of my devotion into over the last fourteen years, whether he knew it or not. And if what I was doing made him unhappy, I didn't want to do it anymore.

He lifted his hand from mine, his eyebrow quirked in question. I pulled the needle out of my vein and capped the syringe again, Tate looking much happier once I'd done it. Without the promise of a chemical pick me up, exhaustion hit me like a punch to the gut. The two bouts of energetic sex leading to a brain full of dwindling endorphins probably didn't help either.

I was powerless to resist as Tate led me over to the corner, tucking his folded shirt under my head as a pillow and pulling the sleeping bag higher so that it rested beneath my chin. "Sleep well, X. You've earned it."

He might have said more, but they were the last words I remembered before sleep pulled me under. I dreamt of walking hand in hand with Tate through a forest. It wasn't a normal forest though. It was a forest where wherever you looked cartoon animals and birds hopped to and fro, twittering and fluttering their obscenely long eyelashes. Tate was of course delighted, and as for me, well, I couldn't take them down with a carefully aimed knife because it would upset Tate. Therefore, I put up with being surrounded by the strange creatures and agreeing that yes, they were the most beautiful things I'd ever seen. Second only to him.

18
TATE

It was one thing to promise X that I'd take a watch, but it was another thing entirely to be able to stay awake long enough to do it. Even the colder air outside the cave only helped to a certain degree. In an attempt to keep my mind active, I'd settled for recalling every second of X and I having sex—both times. X in the throes of passion was everything I would have dreamed about if I'd ever known what I truly wanted before meeting him. He'd provided a tantalizing mixture of violence and gentleness at the same time.

I lifted my hand to my neck, running my fingertips over the place where it felt like I could still feel the imprint of his arm. I'd come like I'd never come before with him restricting my oxygen. He'd known just the right pressure to exert without taking it too far, never once making me feel like I was in any sort of danger. Not even for a second. In fact, I'd felt safer with him around me and inside me than I had in a long time. As if he were a suit of armor I could wear that would protect me from all the evils in the world. I chuckled at the ridiculous thought. That was definitely not one not to share with X during my moments of rambling nonsense. Besides, X might be many things, but he was still just a man. Despite his physical prowess, he bled just like anyone else did.

After jerking myself awake for the second time, I gave in to the inevitable, heading back into the cave and waking X. The warm space in the sleeping bag felt all the better for bearing his warmth and scent, and I fell asleep almost instantaneously, waking a couple of hours later to take over again. That meant I was the one who got to witness the first strains of dawn as they started to make themselves known.

X was curled up on his side as I approached him, a couple of gaps in the cave roof that I hadn't noticed the night before letting in enough sunlight to illuminate his face. He looked younger when he was asleep, more innocent. I lowered myself to the ground next to him and sat cross-legged, resting my chin on my hands. I figured a few extra minutes couldn't make that much difference, and who knew when I'd next get a chance to study him. At least not without the keen gaze that missed nothing on me. With him asleep, I could study him and maybe touch as well.

My fingers crept across the space of their own accord, fastening on the edge of the sleeping bag to pull it down slowly. I uncovered one muscular shoulder first, remembering his strength as he'd pinned me to the wall. Not satisfied, I pulled the cover lower, baring the rest of his chest to my hungry gaze. I let it settle at his waist, knowing that if I went any farther, I'd start having crazy ideas about whiling the morning away with sex rather than covering the miles we needed to in order to stay alive.

Planning on waking him with a kiss, I leaned over. I paused before my lips made contact, scanning the floor for X's knives. I would have laid bets on him sleeping with one in his hand, or at least tucked under his pillow. But there they all were lined up neatly, apart from the one I'd stolen and held to his throat. That one lay close to the smoldering embers of the fire. Anyway, it meant I was safe. Well, safe… ish. This was X we were talking about. I doubted that he really needed a weapon to provide a threat. Before I could think better of it, I pressed my lips to

X's, letting them linger. I'd expected him to hit out, to wrap his fingers around my throat and really mean it this time. But he did none of those things. He did the one thing I would never have predicted in a million years: he smiled, his lips curving beneath mine for a few seconds before his eyelids slowly lifted.

I jumped back, staring at him as if he was someone I'd never seen before, which in a way he was. *Jesus! Had I fucked a smile onto his lips?* If so, I was putting myself forward as the eighth wonder of the world, not that more than three of them still existed. His brow wrinkled at the expression on my face. "What?"

I waved a hand in front of his face. "That thing on your face..." The frown grew more pronounced. "... the thing that your lips were just doing. You know, the smile. I didn't know you were capable of doing that."

He slid a hand around the back of my neck, pulling me back down, his expression earnest. "I wasn't sure whether you'd have had second thoughts in the light of day."

I shook my head. "I didn't even get as far as first thoughts really. Although... I did think about when we might find somewhere with a bed. A proper bed, not a stinking cesspit like the one Jim had... because my knees are bruised." The hand wrapped around my nape dipped to touch the side of my neck, and I followed his train of thought immediately as his fingertips stroked over the skin, answering the question he hadn't actually asked. "My neck's fine. Sore enough that I have it as a reminder, but I like that."

X moved so fast that I didn't see it coming until I was already flat on my back with him kneeling over me. There was no time to feign any sort of protest before his lips were on mine. I used to complain about morning breath when Joseph, or other men whose names I couldn't even recall, had tried to kiss me in a morning. But with X, I didn't care. Nothing mattered except the feel of his mouth on my own. I wished that I could just sink into it, that this was a world where we could spend the day exploring our feelings for each other. A day where we could experiment and I could find out just how far I wanted him to push me. But that was a fantasy, a pipedream, and I could tell the exact moment he came to the same conclusion. His lips lingered for a few more precious seconds before he reluctantly pulled away, the keen amber gaze moving to the shafts of sunlight growing stronger by the second. I said it before he could, hoping it would make me seem less desperate to do the opposite. "We have to go."

He nodded, but made no move to let me up, his burgeoning erection still pressing into mine. I scrutinized his face, looking for some sort of clue to what he might be thinking, but apparently sex wasn't a magical spell for unlocking the inner thoughts and feelings of X, and he was just as inscrutable as ever. Therefore, I had no option but to use speech instead. "What?"

His hesitation lasted for a few extra seconds. "All that stuff I told you last night, none of it bothers you? I've been watching you for years and following you around."

There was a coiled intensity to his body as he asked the question, as if he expected me to suddenly go, oh yeah, and push him away. I shrugged, or at least I tried to shrug. It was difficult when you were lying on a hard rock floor with however many pounds of solid muscle on top of you. I settled for raising an eyebrow instead. "And how lucky are you? Now, you've got me following you around instead. I guess it's only fair, though. It is my turn."

The smile didn't appear this time, but I could feel it lurking beneath the surface. It just needed the right words to tease it out. Maybe one day when we'd reached this supposed safe place, I'd be able to make that my target—make X smile. It sounded good to me. But unfortunately, today wasn't that day.

X's weight was already easing off me as he got to his feet. I watched him for a moment, mourning the loss of the beautiful view as he pulled his T-shirt over his head. At least our clothes were dry. I'd checked them before waking X. They wouldn't win any style awards and couldn't really be classed as clean, but they were slightly more respectable than they'd been prior to washing them in the lake.

The atmosphere between us as we left the cave couldn't have been more different to the previous day's departure where we'd barely been speaking and had avoided even looking at the other. Now, you could argue that there was a ridiculous number of glances being thrown around considering the situation we were in. At this rate the DTP would stumble across us, only to find us staring lovingly into each other's eyes.

Lovingly? The thought brought me up short. Was I going there already? I'd only known X for four days and I barely knew anything about him apart from the fact that he'd fended for himself from a young age, he would kill someone rather than look at them and that he'd—with a bit of prodding from my poor deceased father— appointed himself as my guardian angel. A role he took very seriously indeed.

We were walking much closer than we had the previous day. Close enough that I could bump my arm against his in a bid to get his attention. There was an easy way to rectify the fact that I knew very little about him. After all, how else were we going to fill our time while we walked however many zillion miles were on the schedule today. I'd stopped asking. Knowing the number made it more difficult, not easier. Apparently, we were heading for a town where X planned for us to stay the night. "X?"

He made a noise which didn't resemble any sort of word in the slightest. I pressed on regardless. "Can I ask you some questions?" Another noise, this one sounding even less agreeable. "I know you've had sex with…" Christ! What was the politically correct term for it? Bartholomew had helped me to say goodbye to Joseph. Even though he'd never be aware of it, I didn't want to paint him with a derogatory term. "… erm… men who work at that place that you took me to. But... there must have been someone apart from that? Someone you cared about, maybe? A boyfriend?"

Tension slowly crept into X's shoulders, and I cursed my curiosity. Perhaps I should have started with a less personal question. I could have asked about the bunker he'd lived in, or about his semi-friendly relationship with the drunken old man I'd briefly met. But no, I'd had to go right to the good stuff. I wanted an answer, though, so I waited him out.

"Why must there have been?" X's gaze was firmly fixed on the path in front of him.

"Because..." I thought carefully about my words. "... its human nature, isn't it? To seek out relationships, to try and find other people that you have something in common with." I remembered his words about love being nothing but a social construct. Even if they'd been meant as a way of distracting me from uncovering the truth, they had to have come from somewhere. "If not, it's... lonely. So... was there? Someone you cared about I mean?"

"There was no one."

Four simple words that seemed to echo through the canyon we walked through.

"Oh! I'm sorry." It left me with a strange feeling in my gut. I might not have been in love with any of the men I'd dated, but I'd had good times with them. Most of them, anyway. X had missed out on so much: dates, shared memories, make up sex to name but a few.

"Don't be. I never needed it."

I didn't know how true that was, but if X wanted to believe it then who was I to smash that idea to smithereens. It made the desire to survive even stronger. Just so I'd get a chance to show X some of the things he'd never gotten to experience. The thought made me smile. Poor guy didn't know what he was getting himself into by admitting his love. I had the two of us married off. And of course, me being me, I couldn't keep that thought to myself. I had to share it with him. "I'm going to take you out once we've gotten to somewhere safe. Just me and you. No knives—"

"The knives come."

I rolled my eyes. "Like I was saying, just me and you… and the knives. Just your everyday threesome. We can have dinner or something. You can try foods you've never tried before and try not to stab the waiter for taking too long."

"Sounds riveting."

I laughed at the dryness in his tone. "You'll love it."

"Will I?"

"Sure!" I let a bit of cockiness bleed into my tone. "Because I'll be there." My smile grew wider when he didn't bother to dispute the fact. In fact, he didn't make any further comment at all, and I vowed to do whatever it took to live long enough to take X out on that date. It would be worth it, just to see him scowling at everything. "Hey! If the date goes well and we make a go of things, we could get matching his and his knives?"

"You'd probably stab yourself."

I whirled around to face him, only to find his expression as deadpan as usual. I narrowed my eyes at him. "Did you just make a joke? I'm not going to know what to do with you if you start smiling *and* joking."

My stomach interrupted by choosing that moment to rumble. Loudly. God, I was hungry. It had been over twenty-four hours since I'd last eaten, X handing over the last energy bar. Knowing what I now knew about him existing on very little sleep, I suspected that the majority of the food had come my way as well, so he was probably even hungrier than I was.

"We should be able to eat something tonight."

I nodded, searching for a different topic of conversation to distract me from the feeling of hollowness in my gut. Complaining about it wouldn't make me less hungry so there was no point. "How do you know all this stuff about where we're going if you grew up in the slums?" He didn't seem to care what I called it, so I'd given up on censoring myself. I'd always assumed until the revelations of the previous evening that X had come from somewhere else, that we were retracing steps he'd made years ago.

"Research."

When he didn't bother to elaborate, I nudged him with my elbow, the technique working as words started to spill from his lips again. "I'd planned on leaving a few years back. I didn't end up doing it, but as you can see the information is proving useful."

I was still hung up on the first part of his sentence. "You were going to leave me?" My question was heavily weighted with accusation.

X snorted. "You didn't even know I existed."

"That's not the point."

He turned to look my way. "I planned on it. It didn't happen."

"Why?" That telltale hesitation that meant X was calculating how much to say followed my question.

Finally, he answered. "It was around the same time that you started having problems with that guy."

"The one you killed."

"The one that hit you. More than once."

X was right. It had happened more than once. But I hated being reminded of that fact because I'd been the one to give him that opportunity by forgiving him the first time and accepting his assurances that it wouldn't happen again. It was standard abuser technique, and I'd fallen for it hook, line, and sinker. I'd never understood how people could do that until I'd found myself in the same situation. But it was so easy to concentrate on the charming and attentive man he'd been before he'd lashed out because I'd said or done something he didn't like. I couldn't even recall which it had been. I could remember covering the black eye with make-up and lying about how I'd gotten it. It hadn't been my proudest moment. Reliving it did raise one question though. "I'm surprised he survived the first time?"

"There was no opportunity."

Such a simple answer. An answer that told me all I needed to know. I guessed that killing people, especially in Cofield, took planning. If X had just walked up and offed him in broad daylight in front of everyone, he wouldn't still have been alive to rescue me from the DTP. He would have been executed himself and I would never have known him. "How did you…?" I stopped myself from asking the question. No good would come of knowing the answer.

X answered the question anyway but thankfully without going into detail. "Quickly and painlessly, which was more than he deserved."

There was something else which had always bothered me about my short-lived relationship with Niles. Something I'd never been able to voice to anyone else because they didn't know my secret. But X did know, so if I couldn't ask him, I couldn't ask anyone. "I always wondered…"

"Wondered what?" X's voice was sharp.

"If he sensed this thing inside me, and he thought he was trying to give me what I wanted. Maybe I brought the violence on myself."

X stopped dead, whirling around to face me. I could see from his expression that he thought my theory was absolute bullshit. "Do you want me to hit you?"

I frowned at him. "No. I get off on the threat of violence, not on violence itself."

"Exactly. So he couldn't sense something that wasn't there."

He set off again, and I hurried to catch up. X might not have the best delivery, but he had succeeded in putting my mind at rest. We walked in silence for a few minutes until I got bored.

"So… this place where you think we'll be safe… Is that where you were going to head to?" X shook his head, and I pondered his non-answer for a few moments. "Where then?"

"Farther. There's a story about a place beyond the desert. A place that's similar to the way the world used to be, where there's less regulation and people are treated as equals. There's no DTP and the people govern themselves."

"Is it real?"

The answer was probably already there in the amount of time X took to consider the question. "I don't know. People have set out to find it, but if they did, they never came back, so no one really knows. It's probably a myth and anyone who tried to reach it died. Their bones are probably in the desert baked by the sun."

I stared at X. "Great story. Thanks. Very uplifting."

He didn't reply.

We reached the city earlier than X had anticipated. This was the place where the train would have brought us had we managed to stay on it for the duration of the journey. In a strange way, it felt like we'd caught up. To me, anyway. I had no idea what was going through X's head. He'd returned to being his usual taciturn self, any hint of the smiling man from that morning just a memory. I supposed it was to be expected, though, considering that for the first time in days we were about to enter a space teeming with people. The city itself didn't look like much. It was no Cofield, that was for sure. Cofield had been far more modern. Whereas this place, Urstone, X had called it, was far more rustic. It wasn't quite the patched together houses of the slums that I'd seen on my brief visit, but it wasn't that far off, given the plethora of materials that had been used to build it. I had the absurd urge to grab onto X's hand and hold on tight as we passed through the gate, but I doubted he'd thank me for it, and it was probably better not to bring any more attention to ourselves than X's presence already did. He leaned down to whisper in my ear. "Remember everything I said, Tate."

I nodded to show I'd heard him. He'd given me strict instructions including following his lead on any story he chose to construct to explain our arrival in the city. It had been unnecessary advice. I'd been following X's lead ever since he'd shown up on the nightclub floor and plucked me from the DTP's grip. I swallowed nervously as a few people lifted their heads to look our way. X gave them a nod but didn't bother to offer any sort of greeting so I didn't either. I was tempted to poke X and point out how well I was following his lead, but I managed to restrain myself.

Most of the people looked away again, but a few pairs of eyes strayed down to where X wore his knives, lingering with interest. I received a lot less scrutiny, glances my way barely lasting more than a few seconds. I didn't mind. I was happy to be inconsequential in their eyes. Inconsequential meant that they weren't recognizing me as a wanted man which could only be good news.

X veered off down a side street. I remained at his side, my heart hammering against my ribs and my palms turning sweaty. We were in search of a contact, apparently, one who could help us with supplies, as well as setting us up with somewhere safe to spend the night. My question to X about whether the place would include a bed had gone unanswered, leaving me to daydream about all the things I could do to X if it did.

I'd returned to those thoughts as X came to a sudden halt outside a door. He pulled a piece of paper out of his pocket, checking it against the numerals which looked like they'd been drawn by someone who'd had a bad case of the shakes at the time. I tried to relax as X lifted his hand and knocked. Although, I didn't know whether I was more nervous to go inside or to stay out in the street. It was probably a close call either way.

The seconds seemed to tick by in slow motion as I stared

at the closed door. But no matter how much I willed it to, it didn't open and there was no sign of life from behind its wooden exterior. I glanced around nervously, sure that by now people were starting to view our actions as suspicious. I jumped as X's next knock shook the wood, far more violent than the first had been. "What if nobody answers?"

X's cool gaze turned my way but before he could either offer an assurance or slam me with the pure unvarnished truth—the jury was still out on which one of those would have been more likely—a sound came from behind the door. I stepped forward, pressing my ear against it and as a result almost falling inside when the door suddenly swung open. Whoever I'd been expecting to see, it wouldn't have been a tiny stooped old lady eyeing us as if the devil himself had come to call. It seemed harsh until I remembered my first impression of X and admitted that she might have a point. "What do you want?" Her voice sounded surprisingly firm, forcing me to revise my initial impression of her. Stooped she might be, and she definitely looked to be on the wrong side of eighty, but weak she wasn't, sporting wiry muscles beneath the wrinkled skin.

X took a step forward. "I'm looking for a man by the name of Talon." I nodded, figuring it was better to act like I at least had an inkling who Talon was, and why we needed to see him beyond the obvious.

She tipped her head to one side, her gaze raking slowly down over X. "Who's asking?"

"I heard he was a man who might be interested in a trade. I have some good deals for him."

"You heard wrong, on both counts." The door started to close, giving us only a small window of opportunity to change her mind before we were back where we started which included no food.

Something about the way she'd sneered every time X had said the word "man" caused the synapses in my brain to make a startling connection. I stepped forward, not enough to block the door, but hopefully enough for her to notice the movement. "It's you, isn't it? You're Talon? He's not a man. X has been… misinformed."

She paused with the door halfway to closed. It eased open a few inches again, her chin lifting. "So what if I am?" Acting purely on instinct, I shrugged the backpack off, quickly unwrapping the ties and flipping the top back so that she could see its contents. After all, X had said that the grenades were to trade, and this was apparently the person we were meant to be trading with. She leaned forward in order to get a better look, her eyebrows rising. I couldn't help but wonder what a little old lady planned to do with grenades, but I wasn't stupid enough to ask. She still didn't seem wholly convinced though.

X must have thought the same as he interjected. "There's more where that came from. Plus, some C4 as well if that's of any use to you?"

She returned to scrutinizing X, but this time there was a flicker of interest in her eyes that had nothing to do with his muscles and sharp cheekbones. Finally, she gave a curt nod as she stepped back from the door. "You better come in so that we can talk properly."

Most of the women I'd known over the years were won over by flowers and chocolates, not by hand grenades and C4. It was yet another reminder that this was a different world than the one I'd known for so long. X gestured that I should step inside first. Despite his intention undoubtedly being born more of practicality than chivalry, it still made my heart skip a beat. That's what happened once you brought sex into the equation; your brain started playing tricks on you. I followed Talon as she walked into an adjoining room, the comforting presence of X at my back.

I stopped dead at the sight that met me. There was barely room for three people in there, crammed as it was from floor to ceiling with every conceivable item you could think of. I'd thought that Jim's bunker was cramped, but he was clearly an amateur in comparison to this. The only difference was that some of this 'junk' actually looked as if it might be useful. I reached out, running my finger over a gold statue of a cherub. Yeah, the word was definitely some.

"Don't touch!"

At Talon's outburst, I snatched my hand back as if I'd been burnt. I wondered if Jim had ever considered getting married. The two of them could have been perfect together as long as Talon wasn't put off by a bit of body odor. They could spend long evenings together stroking their collective riches. "Sorry."

She gave me a glare, the apology obviously falling flat. I did what I always did when I felt flustered: tried to make things better while actually making them worse. "Unusual name, Talon. It's pretty though. You know, makes me think of an eagle or some other sort of majestic bird. Were you named after an eagle?"

"Tate!" X didn't actually say shut up, but he may as well have, the message clear enough from the tone of his voice. I shut up. And I didn't touch anything, crossing my arms over my chest in case I was tempted to go in for another stroke of the cherub or touch something else like the peacock feather taunting me from its position hanging from the ceiling.

Talon lifted her chin, her attention back on X. She'd obviously decided to concentrate on the organ grinder rather than the monkey. "Show me what you've got."

X held out his hand and I passed the backpack over, holding onto a bottle of water which was about the only thing I owned apart from the clothes I was wearing. X plucked one of the grenades out and handed it to Talon. She pulled a pair of glasses from her pocket and put them on before subjecting the grenade to an extended scrutiny, turning it over and over in her hand while she examined every inch. I had no idea what she was looking for. Were there good grenades and bad grenades?

I'd always assumed that grenades were just grenades. Finally, she nodded. "How many?"

"Fifty." X's response came quickly considering I'd been the one to pack both bags at his request, and I certainly hadn't stopped to count them. Is that what he'd been doing at night when he should have been sleeping? I needed to teach him how to count sheep instead of grenades.

"And the plastic?"

X crouched down, pulling package after package from one of his bags. Talon's nose wrinkled. "Why is some of it unwrapped? I don't want used crap."

X's lips quirked at the memory. "It was unwrapped for less than a minute. I needed to convince someone to do something. It's still fully operational."

It felt like weeks since we'd stood outside Jim's bunker, when it was only what… two days? Three? I was losing track of time. Talon stretched out a hand, her fingers barely managing to graze the fabric before X pulled it back out of reach. "You only get these if you can provide everything we need."

Talon placed one scrawny hand on her hip, regarding X as if he were a bug who'd just crawled in from outside. "What do you need?"

"Clothes—"

"Just for you"—she flicked a glance in my direction— "or for the boy toy as well?"

Boy toy! I'd been called many things in my life, but that was a new one. I opened my mouth, ready to let rip, but X's hand on my arm stopped me, the fingers gently squeezing. I got the silent message he was delivering. If he could play nice, then so could I, even if it included taking derogatory comments from little old ladies on the chin. Besides, thinking about it, there were far worse things in life than being placed in the role of X's sexual plaything. Last night had proved that beyond a doubt.

"For both of us." X's gaze dropped to my feet, my once

snazzy clubbing shoes looking sad and forlorn as I flexed my toes. "He'll need boots as well. We'll also need food to last us a week and a safe place to spend the night."

Talon's eyes narrowed with a speculative gleam. My heart began to pound as I saw her putting two and two together and coming up with the right number. "What do you class as safe?"

X didn't miss a beat. "Somewhere where no one asks questions and can be trusted to keep their mouth shut should someone come sniffing around." I winced. He may as well have announced that we were on the run, but then, I was probably being naïve. She'd no doubt already worked it out. We didn't even know if she was trustworthy, never mind her contacts.

The whole thing suddenly seemed pointless. How deluded were we to think that we could stay one step ahead of the DTP? Maybe we could in the middle of nowhere. But in the midst of civilization, where people would do anything for a reward? They didn't care about trying to put one over on the people who doled out rough justice. They only cared about filling their stomachs and keeping a roof over their heads.

Talon's glance was long and considering. Just as I was sure she was planning how many more gold cherubs she could add to her collection once she'd collected the reward, she spoke. "They took my son."

I glanced at X, but it didn't take me long to realize that anything in the empathy department was definitely going to be down to me. "Who did?"

Her mouth curled into a sneer, but not before I'd already spotted the barely perceptible lip wobble. "The DTP bastards, that's who."

"I'm sorry." I didn't know what else to say.

"Do you know what he did?"

I shook my head.

"He got drunk and knocked into someone, a girl. She fell on some glass, claimed he'd done it deliberately." Her eyes filled with tears. "It was an accident. All she needed was a few stitches, while he…"

I didn't need her to finish. I'd been there. I could still feel the hard ground under my knees as I'd stared down the barrel of the gun. I doubted that memory would ever evaporate entirely. It would be engrained in my brain until the day I died, whether that was today, tomorrow, or a few decades from now. Short of telling her I was sorry again, there wasn't a lot I could say that would make her feel better. "So you'll help us?"

She took a deep breath in, squaring her shoulders as she lifted her chin, the tears disappearing as if they'd never been there. "While I sympathize with your plight, the payment"—she gestured to the bags—"is enough for the food and clothes, but if you want somewhere truly safe to stay, that's going to cost you a bit more." She turned her attention to X, her gaze straying over him until it settled on his waist. "One of those knives ought to do it."

It was a toss-up which one of us became stiller at her request, myself or X. She might as well have demanded that he chop one of his balls off and hand it over. I shifted uncomfortably, half expecting X's thin thread of control to snap. Even wiry as she was, this old woman would be no match for X, given that he was about a foot taller than her and armed. The silence seemed charged as I waited for him to tell her what she could do with her suggested method of payment. Instead, his hand dropped to his waist, but not in a 'I'm about to stab the bitch' way, more in a 'I'm not happy about it but I'll do it anyway' way. I grabbed his hand, holding it in place before he got as far as unsheathing the knife. "Wasn't that the one I used last night?"

His eyebrow arched. "I think so."

"Then not that one. I like that one. It holds good memories." He tugged his hand free, going for the one on the other side. "Not that one either. I have plans for that one." I ignored the loud tutting emanating from Talon as she watched us. I cast about for an alternative, the solution finally hitting me. Delving deep into my pocket, I pulled out the ring that was too big to wear on my finger but that I always carried around as a good luck charm. I'd even taken it clubbing with me.

I held it up so that Talon could see it. "Would you accept this instead? It's gold."

She held her hand out and I dropped the ring into the center of her palm. She began an inspection similar to the one she'd carried out on the hand grenade.

X's gaze bored into the side of my head, my skin tingling beneath it. "That was your father's ring. I can't let you do that."

"How do you…?" I bit down on the stupid question. Of course he knew where it had come from. He knew everything about me. Besides he probably remembered it decorating my father's finger. "It's just a ring. It's not going to serve any purpose apart from making us some money."

X's gaze bored into mine, the all-knowing amber eyes meaning I needed to lay it on a bit thicker. I inclined my head toward his weapons. "Whereas those… we might need those, and the thought of you just having one is weird. You'll be all unbalanced." Our gazes locked, heat building between us.

It wasn't until Talon cleared her throat that I remembered the reason we were even discussing it. I dragged my gaze reluctantly away from the chiseled features of X and back to the much less alluring sight of Talon.

She looked slightly amused as she rolled the ring around on her palm. "As it's gold, it will do. So… which is it going to be? The knife or the ring?"

"Knife."

"Ring."

We both spoke at the same time. I ignored X, reaching forward to close Talon's fingers around the ring, her skin dry and leathery beneath my fingertips. "The ring. It's the way my dad would have wanted it." I may have spoken the words to Talon, but they were for X's benefit.

Talon nodded, slipping the ring into her pocket. Despite it having been at my insistence, I still suffered a pang of regret. It was the last piece of my father I had, the last piece I'd ever have, given that all the photos, all the memorabilia I had linked to my parents was back in my apartment in Cofield. I squared my shoulders and tried to pretend that it didn't hurt to think about the home I'd never see again, the home that the DTP had no doubt ransacked and destroyed anyway.

"Stay here!"

She shuffled into the next room, X tensing beside me at the sound of muffled voices. Who was she talking to? I turned to him, speaking in a whisper. "Do you think we can trust her?"

He took far longer to think about it than I would have liked, which was answer enough. "We don't have any other option."

And there was the truth spelled out in no uncertain terms. Without Talon, we were just two men being hunted down in an unknown city, with a bagful of grenades and no idea what to do with them. X might be the toughest man I was ever likely to know, but he wasn't a magician. There was nothing to do but hope for the best. The voices continued for a few minutes, but there was no urgency to the conversation, nothing that had alarm bells jangling too loudly.

When Talon finally reappeared, her arms were full of clothes, as were the young man's who trailed in her wake. He looked to be no older than twenty, his red hair shaved so close to the skull that in places it was difficult to tell it was red. They dropped the clothes on the floor, Talon straightening as much as she was able to. She inclined her head in the direction of the youth. "This is Psyche. He's my grandson."

Psyche! Another lovely name. I wondered what moniker her deceased son had gone by, but I managed to muster enough self-restraint not to ask, simply offering a nod of greeting in his direction. Talon waved a hand over the pile of clothing. "Take what you need, and then Psyche will take you to your accommodation for the evening. He'll bring the food to you there, enough for three or four days."

X was already hunkered down, his fingers combing through the garments as if he knew exactly what he was looking for. Every now and again, he flicked something in my direction and I dutifully picked it up, bundling everything together in my arms. Psyche disappeared only to return with a pair of boots which he dropped at my feet. "Boots."

I bit down on two urges, one to reply, "Yes, they are, well done," and the other to question how he knew my size. Did he have some sort of superpower which enabled him to tell shoe size at a glance? Is that where his name came from? I almost snorted at the thought.

X seemed to be done with sorting through the clothes, which was good, seeing as the ones he'd chosen were now piled so high that I had to tuck them under my chin to avoid them spilling on the floor. At least, wherever the clothes had come from, they smelled fresh and clean. It gave me some hope that wherever our accommodation for the night was going to be, it might be similar. I still had my fingers crossed for that bed. X retrieved the boots from the floor but noticeably didn't offer to carry anything else. But then I supposed that should an attack come from somewhere that, out of the two of us, he was the best one to have his hands free. Because what was I going to do? Throw a shirt over their heads and make a run for it in the few seconds that they couldn't see? Psyche led us to the door that we'd come in through, Talon already having disappeared without so much as a goodbye.

Psyche, it turned out, was a talker. "… don't get all that many strangers around these parts. Most of them get off the train at Tordi rather than coming here. I assume you're heading to Maimos. No, don't tell me. Gran told me that you needed to keep things on the downlow." He paused to tap his nose. "Don't worry. I'm the soul of discretion. If I wasn't, Gran would have removed my tongue with a pair of rusty pliers years ago. I've thought about it… you know, getting out of here, seeing some other things, experiencing a bit more of the world… even threatened it a couple of times, but when it comes down to it, I can't leave Gran. Maybe I'll do it do it once she's not around anymore. Although, everyone round here is pretty sure that she's immortal. She's so stubborn that there's no way she's gonna die until she wants to."

If I was struggling with the constant barrage of words and information, then God knows how X was faring. He was probably nearing the point of slitting Psyche's throat just to shut him up. Luckily at that point, Psyche came to a stop in front of a door before my theory could be proved either way. He took a surreptitious look around before using his knuckles to rap out a succession of rhythmic taps which had to be some sort of code. Whatever it was, it made me feel better. It was unlikely they'd bring us to a genuine safe house if they intended to alert the DTP to our presence. The door swung open within seconds, a bald man's face appearing in the crack.

Psyche smiled broadly at him as if this was nothing more than a social call. "Got two guests for you."

I was beginning to wonder whether Psyche was all there, particularly when he continued to smile even as the door was opened farther and the bald man's expression demonstrated his lack of joy at the events unfolding in front of him. A welcoming party he certainly wasn't, and that was before his scrutiny reached X. At that point, he looked as if he'd just sucked a lemon, a very bitter lemon. "How long for?"

It was X that answered. "Just one night."

The man muttered something under his breath which sounded like "that fucking bitch, Talon" but could have been something else. I doubted I'd heard wrong, though, not when his face gave off exactly the same sentiment. For a moment, I thought he was going to shut the door in our faces, but then he stepped back with a long, weary sigh to reveal a kitchen behind him. X's hand on my lower back encouraged me through the door with him bringing up the rear. Psyche didn't step inside, giving us a cheery wave and assuring us that he'd be back within the hour with food. And then he was gone.

Silence descended on us, our new bald friend seeming a lot less inclined to chat, or to say anything really as he stared at us as if trying to take our measure. I offered him a friendly smile, hoping it would be enough to nullify whatever expression was on X's face. This wasn't like the situation with Jim where he'd known the man before, however briefly. Everyone in this city was an unknown quantity, and I got the feeling that that was the only thing keeping X in check. "I'm Tate, and this is…"

"I don't need to know your names. In fact, it's probably better that I don't."

It was a valid point and I cursed myself for giving out my real name so readily. Was I supposed to have come up with a pseudonym? I tried again, determined to bring an end to this strange standoff in the man's kitchen that seemed to be going nowhere. "So… you have somewhere for us to stay?"

He nodded, but still didn't move.

I was beginning to wonder if the kitchen was it. Maybe I was supposed to bed down in the fridge while X squeezed himself into a cupboard. "Can we see it?"

He nodded again and much to my relief, turned on his heel and started to walk away. Assuming we were meant to follow, I took the lead as he led us down a hallway past several closed doors. Finally, he stopped in a room that seemed to be used mainly for storing junk. Using his foot, he peeled back a large rug on the floor to reveal a hidden trapdoor. "Basement. There's a shower of sorts down there. Lights. Camping stove as well for whatever Psyche brings you. I'm not going to be feeding you."

"Of course not. We wouldn't expect…" My words trailed off, spoken as they were to the bald man's rapidly disappearing back. It was an understatement to say that he didn't exactly seem to be overjoyed at helping us. I wondered what the deal was there, whether Talon had something on him. I couldn't think of another reason that would explain the apathy bordering on antagonism toward us. He hadn't even told us his name. I turned my attention back to X to find him examining the trapdoor, his hands running over its surface with a slight frown on his face. "What's up?"

He lifted his gaze to mine. "No lock, which is good."

"Is it?" I didn't bother to try and hide my confusion.

His lips quirked. "You want him to lock us in?"

I considered it. "Not particularly." My gaze trailed over all the junk in the room, some of it heavy-looking furniture. "But… all you'd have to do is put something on top of it, right?"

X gave a long, slow nod. "Correct." He actually looked pleased that I'd worked it out all on my own. I tamped down on the warm glow threatening to spread through my body in response to X's approval. The hatch creaked as he pulled it open, and we both stared into the dark abyss. This was starting to be a reoccurring theme, but instead of a ladder leading down, there were stone stairs this time, only the top couple of stairs visible before they disappeared into black nothingness.

I sighed, trying my best not to let the thought that there could be rats sneak into my brain and take up residence. "We don't have any choice, though, do we?" I wasn't sure whether the comment was for X's benefit or whether I was trying to convince myself.

"No." He pulled the flashlight out of the bag, switching it on and shining it down the stairs. It wasn't powerful enough to reach the bottom. "Stay here while I go and check it out."

I nodded a little too eagerly, not taking my eyes off him until he'd disappeared out of sight, the darkness swallowing him up so completely that I couldn't even see the beam of the flashlight. Seconds dragged by, turning into even more seconds. "X?" No response. I leaned forward, peering into the darkness in the hope of being able to spot a faint light. What if it was a trap? What if someone had been lying in wait down there? Talon could be a double agent, someone who pretended to help refugees while secretly working for the DTP. That whole story about her son could have been utter bullshit designed to get people to trust her. There'd been no sound of a struggle but all it would have taken was for someone to step out of the shadows and chloroform X and he'd have dropped like a stone, sharp blades rendered useless.

I was still working through every horrific scenario my brain could conjure up when a light came on in the basement. Not a very bright light, but enough for me to be able to see the bottom of the stairs. X appeared at the bottom, annoyingly unflustered considering the mental gymnastics I'd just been doing. "Close the trapdoor and come down."

I walked down a few steps until I was low enough to be able to pull the trapdoor over my head, the maneuver taking some effort when my arms were still full of clothes. I continued the rest of the way until I found myself in the basement. It was huge, apparently stretching beneath the entire house. In one corner stood a large rustic-looking shower with a drainage ditch which diverted the water from it to God knows where. There was a toilet and a sink as well, and one cupboard which X was currently pulling open to see what was inside. The camping stove that our mysterious 'friend' had mentioned took pride of place in the middle of the floor. There wasn't much else apart from a bare double mattress over by the wall with a pile of bedding wrapped in transparent plastic next to it. I smiled as I walked over to it, unable to resist waggling my eyebrows at X in a provocative fashion. "We have a bed."

He came to stand next to me, his shoulder nudging mine. The mattress looked clean, or at least in the dim light from the one lightbulb swinging over our heads it did. I wasn't about to examine it too closely. I'd just call to mind the memory of Jim's bed and it would be pure luxury in comparison.

I couldn't tell whether X's huff at my announcement was a pleased huff, or a sardonic huff at me being so excited over a mattress. But if it was the latter, I wasn't about to let him ruin my enjoyment of the moment. If anyone had told the Tate Gillespie of a week ago that in times to come, he'd get excited by a plain mattress, I would have told them to fuck off and get real. Yet, here I was, already planning all the things I could do to X on a surface which wouldn't bruise my knees. Not yet though. Unfortunate as it was, fucking needed to wait.

Dropping the clothes in the middle of the mattress, I sorted through them to see what delights X had picked out. I smiled at the sight of underwear. Maybe there was something more exciting than the bed—clean underwear. I'd spent the last week wearing the same pair with only the occasional wash in a sink or a lake. If it was a choice between X and wearing underwear that hadn't dried to the consistency of cardboard, then there was no contest. The thought made me throw a fond smile in X's direction. He stilled from pulling items out of the backpack.

"Now, what's got you so happy?"

"Underwear."

"You're so weird." There was no venom in X's comment, just the opposite.

It gave me enough encouragement to continue the teasing. "If I'm weird, what does that say about you? You've followed someone weird around for years? That makes you... weirder."

"I always liked it."

My fingers curled around the shirt I'd been about to inspect. "Liked what?"

X's gaze met mine, the look in his eyes suddenly making it difficult to breathe when it was intensity, passion, and fondness all rolled into one. I'd never have suspected the man I'd first met of being capable of looking at anything that wasn't long, metal, and capable of stabbing someone, like that. Yet, it was all directed at me. It made me feel warm, safe, and… loved. Yeah, he was so getting it tonight. I tried to concentrate on what he was saying. "… the fact that you were different and didn't care what anyone thought."

I laughed. "Pot and kettle there, my friend. Because I hate to break it to you, but no one's more different than you. And I don't remember seeing you give a damn about what anyone else thinks."

"That's different. None of them were friends."

The words saddened me, and I suspected he could see it written all over my face, so I made an effort to lighten the mood. "They could have been friends if you hadn't introduced yourself by holding a knife to their neck."

"It wasn't always the neck!"

At my frown, X mimed holding a knife slightly below waist height.

I winced. "Right! Because nothing says pleased to meet you like someone threatening to cut your cock off. I think I can see why they gave you a wide berth."

There was the sudden sound of footsteps on the stairs behind. I spun around with my heart in my mouth, X clearly feeling the same, defensive posture at the ready and both blades already in his hands.

"Whoa!" Psyche held both hands in the air as he stared at X with wide eyes, the plastic bag dangling from one of his hands swaying in the air above him. "Not necessary, man." He inclined his head toward the bag while still keeping both hands in the air. "I brought you food and shit." He kept one eye on X as he walked across to the cupboard, only lowering his hands and starting to take items out of the bag once X's knives were sheathed again. "I guess I should have knocked, but most people that stay here aren't scary dudes."

Psyche flicked a glance at me. "Him, not you." His gaze darted back to X. "No offense. But I think that's why G has got his knickers in a twist. Thinks you're going to stab him in the middle of the night." His brow furrowed. "You're not, are you?" He waited for X to shake his head before continuing. "G might come across as a little gruff, but he's a good man, really. He's just had some shitty things happen to him in the past, so he has a few trust issues."

I could only assume that G was the name of the bald man, but given that Psyche had already moved on there was no opportunity to ask. At least his constant running commentary proved useful as he pulled items out of the bag. "… mostly canned stuff because you know it keeps. Brought you a can opener as well, though, don't you worry. Included baked beans because everyone likes beans, right? I should have probably asked you if you had any allergies or if you were a veggie, but I forgot so I just brought a mixture… some meat… some veggie." He lifted a tin, holding it up so that we could see the label. "Chicken soup. Everyone likes chicken soup. Got you a couple of cans of that." Some packets joined the cans on the counter. "Crackers. Pasta. Probably more than you need for a few days but if you don't tell Gran then neither will I. I figured you both looked hungry so at least you can have a slap-up meal tonight without having to worry about running out over the next few days. Got you some shower gel, because food isn't everything, and quite honestly neither of you smell that fresh so I figured you needed it. Deodorant for the same reason because even though I know personal hygiene isn't the number one thing on your list, you should think of other people. And…" He pulled two items out of the bag with a flourish. "…the piece de la resistance…" He mangled the words badly, but I got the gist. "I got you chocolate and some bananas. I had to promise to suck the guy's cock for these, but just between you and me, it's no hardship and he usually feels the need to suck mine in return, so you don't have to feel guilty or anything, and he's hot. Really hot. I'm trying to get him to fuck me, but he still swears he's straight so we're not there yet." He winked. "Soon though." His face brightened. "Oh, and that reminds me. I got you this as well. Just in case you need it." He delved deep into one of his pockets, repeating the same flourish from earlier but this time with a small bottle of lube which he added to the pile with the rest of the things.

The silence was jarring once he'd stopped talking. "Thanks, Psyche. We appreciate this." I didn't have to fake sincerity. He'd clearly gone above and beyond, and it made me feel better about the whole thing. No one lured someone into a trap and then took the trouble to think about their likes and dislikes as he clearly had, never mind provide them with lube. Unless, of course, he wasn't in on it. I dismissed the thought immediately. He'd know if good old granny Talon was a secret double agent.

Psyche raised his hand in a salute before walking back over to the stairs. "I'll leave you two alone now. Guess I won't see you again, but it's been good to meet you. I hope you make it to wherever you want to get to."

"Thanks." I felt like I needed to offer something in return. "I hope you get that guy into bed."

He gave another wink. "Oh, I will. Psyche doesn't give up. And there's always Rohypnol." He laughed at the expression on my face which I hadn't been able to hide. "Just joking."

The only problem was I wasn't too sure he had been. It had rolled off his tongue a little too easily. But he was gone before I could question it.

19
TATE

I felt like I'd been reborn as a new man. After more than twenty-four hours without food, we'd dined on sausages, beans, and pasta before sharing the chocolate between us. We'd showered separately, but that was fine. There was no shower curtain, so I'd gotten to watch X soap himself down, and I had to say he'd been nothing but thorough. It proved that even X could tease with the best of them if he put his mind to it. I, of course, repaid him in full, taking an inordinate amount of time to soap every inch of my ass with my back to him. And unlike when I'd pulled the same trick under the waterfall, this time he did watch, his heated gaze branding my skin.

And then there were the clothes. Despite the fact that they weren't the best fit, it was just a joy to dress in items that weren't splattered with mud, caked in dust, or that smelled of stale sweat. X had already picked out anything black before I'd gotten to them. Love apparently didn't extend to entertaining the thought of wearing bright colors. "Why did we get dressed when we're not going anywhere?"

X lifted his head from where he was busy filling the bags that had contained hand grenades with the food Psyche had brought. I guess that meant breakfast wasn't in the cards for the next day. "So we know what's good enough to take and what we can leave behind."

That was X to a T—always practical. I didn't want practical though, not now that we were both clean and no longer hungry. I wanted to christen the mattress. I watched him for a few minutes as he split the remainder of the clothes between the bags as well before finally conceding that he'd run out of things that needed to be done.

I prowled around the space restlessly until he lay back on the bed I'd already made. Seizing my opportunity, I pounced, jumping on top of him and straddling him, the sides of my knees pressing into his chest. I didn't waste any time in divesting him of the clothes that he'd been wearing for all of thirty minutes, X offering not a single word of protest. "So much black. What would happen if you wore white? Would you melt?"

X lifted his arms to assist in peeling the shirt over his head. "White shows up at night."

"Ah, right." I let my fingers play over his chest, tracing the clearly defined muscles. "You wouldn't be able to stalk people."

"I don't stalk people. I stalk you."

He'd said "I stalk you" the same way another person might have said I love you. It made me wonder if I'd ever hear him say the actual words. He might have admitted it indirectly, but he'd never actually said it. And I found myself wanting to hear those words from his lips. I wanted to hear Mr. Love-is-a-social-construct-and-nothing-else admit that I'd wormed my way beneath his barriers like no one else ever could. Yes, I was apparently that egotistical. But us both knowing it and him saying it were two different things, and I didn't know how much time we had. It could be hours, days, or years. "If all of this hadn't happened, would you ever have approached me?"

X propped his hands behind his head, lifting his chin as he stared at me. "Imagine I had. Imagine that one day as you were leaving work, I'd walked up to you and I'd introduced myself. Maybe I'd have said that I used to know your dad. What would you have done?"

My fingers stilled on his chest, the truth taking my breath away. I could imagine it, and there was no doubt in my mind that I'd have assumed he was full of shit. I'd have gotten as far away from him as I could, probably relaying to Trisha and Joseph the next day how I'd had a lucky escape from some sort of dangerous weirdo. We'd have laughed about it over a drink and they would probably have ribbed me for the next few days and then we would all have forgotten about it.

X crooked an eyebrow, responding to the look on my face without me having said anything. "Exactly, and I always knew that. So no, I wouldn't have approached you. You would have continued to live your life oblivious to my presence, and I would have…"

I finger-walked my way over his pecs until my fingertips rested against the curve where neck met shoulder. "Continued skulking in the shadows. Continued fucking men who look like me but aren't me. Continued pretending that you need nothing and no one in order to get by."

X grabbed my hand, his fingers wrapping around mine tightly, the look in his eyes one I'd never seen before. "Do you know what I need, Tate?"

I leaned forward, resting my elbows on his chest as I stared deeply into his eyes. "No, you're pretty much a closed book, so unless the words actually spill from your pretty lips, I usually don't have the slightest idea what you're thinking." It wasn't quite true, or how would I have guessed his feelings in the first place? But if it got him talking more, then the small white lie would be worth it.

He swallowed and I could tell he was fighting years of ingrained habits. I held my nerve, refusing to look away and willing him to be truly honest for once without me having to prize it out of him. "I…" He lapsed back into silence before trying again. "Just you. That's all I need."

There was no holding back the huge grin that spread across

my face. I ducked my head unable to resist brushing a kiss across his lips. "Lucky you got there in time then, isn't it? To rescue me, I mean... my own..." I hesitated, changing what I'd been going to say to something that fitted better. "... black knight with his collection of shiny knives." I sat up slightly, the quick movement of my wrists meant to depict X's quick dispatch of the soldiers in the club that night.

His brow furrowed, his chest rising and falling beneath me. "What was that?"

I repeated the movement. "Knife throwing."

X shook his head. "That is *not* how you throw a knife."

I turned my hands around, staring at my wrists as if they were to blame. "No?"

He gave another slow shake of his head. "When we get to..." He paused, grimacing before correcting himself. "...*if* we get to..."

I stopped him. "*When.*"

He conceded the point. "When we get to where we're going, I'll teach you how to throw a knife properly."

A warm glow spread through my chest. I really had changed in a very short space of time if knife throwing now counted as something romantic. "Deal. I promise to be a very attentive student."

"I doubt that."

I grinned wickedly. Yeah, he was probably right. He'd probably be modeling correct form and posture and I'd be ogling the flex of his biceps or admiring how good his ass looked in the correct stance. All of which served to remind me how distracted I'd become from what we were supposed to be doing. The future could wait until... well, the future. I was more interested in the here and now. I dropped my fingers to the fastenings of X's trousers, spending the next few minutes carrying out a close scrutiny of every patch of bare skin I uncovered until X was gloriously naked, his sizeable cock half erect against his abdomen.

I repeated the same process with my own clothes, making a show out of it and loving the way his eyes followed my every move as I wriggled out of them, all without losing my position astride him. It took a lot of willpower to focus on myself when all I wanted to do was touch. Within seconds of discarding the last piece of clothing my hands were back on him, tracing the curve of his collarbone as his lowered gaze followed my every movement.

Last night had been hard and fast, the little niggle at the back of my brain that had been too worried he might change his mind making it hard to be anything else.

But tonight felt different, as if we had all the time in the world. Something suddenly occurred to me, something I found strange as I explored his unblemished chest. "I thought you'd have scars. You know, dangerous life and all that. But you're as smooth as a baby."

X gave a slow blink. "Scars would mean I'd been too slow. Attack is the best form of defense."

The words were said with confidence rather than arrogance. And confidence was always a turn on. Especially when it reminded me that I had a dangerous creature between my thighs, even if he was lying there as politely as any corporate businessman. Actually, too politely. I shifted back a bit, X sucking in a breath as my ass brushed his cock, imbuing me with a heady sense of power. "Don't you want to touch?"

He nodded, but made no actual move to do so. Finally, just as I'd decided he was waiting for written permission, he lifted his hands tentatively, fingers coming to rest on my shoulders. And then they just sat there. I glared at him. "Pretend I'm one of your knives."

He smiled, and my heart skipped a beat. *Bingo!* One smile achieved—ten points to me. It did the trick though, his hands beginning a slow glide over my skin, alternately stroking and pinching, the calluses on his palms eliciting goosebumps wherever they touched. I arched my back as one hand slid from my abdomen along the length of my torso to grip my throat in a parody of what we'd done the previous night.

My hips started thrusting of their own accord, my ass crack riding his rapidly swelling dick as my cock thrust against the perfect muscles of his abdomen, leaving a trail of pre-cum behind. I closed my eyes and tipped my head back to give him better access to my throat. A moan escaped my mouth as I considered the fact that I could come from nothing more than the friction of his abdominal muscles against my sensitive glans and the head of his cock brushing my hole. Did I want to though? Or did I want more?

Something cold and alien touched my chest and I froze, all my movement ceasing immediately as my eyes snapped open. X's gaze met mine, the heat in their depths a startling contrast to the cold blade of the knife that he was moving in slow circles around my nipple. God! If he pressed that little bit harder, I'd bleed. Bleed for him. The thought should have horrified me, so why then was my cock harder than ever? And why were my breaths now short little pants? I tried to tell myself it was fear, but even I recognized that it was a complete lie. Fear didn't cause your nerve-endings to sing in glorious anticipation. Not just fear, anyway.

My gaze met X's as I continued to hold myself rigid, the point of the knife still moving, still creating a sensation like no other I'd ever experienced. I gasped as the point traced over the incredibly sensitive skin of my nipple. There was a question in X's eyes, one that he eventually put into words. "Tell me to stop, and I will. No questions asked."

Did I want him to stop? Wasn't this what I'd insinuated I wanted when I'd said I had plans for the other knife in front of Talon? When I'd told him that I got off on the threat of violence? X was just following my instructions, right? He'd understood and this was just him putting it into practice, testing my boundaries in a way no one else had ever been able to do. What did I feel? Dizzy—definitely. But not the bad dizziness. It was the sort that promised you an orgasm the likes of which you'd never had before, one that would wring me out with its intensity. I was hot and cold at the same time, my mouth too dry to form words, and my tongue felt like it was double the size it should have been.

The pressure of the blade started to lift, and I shook my head, swallowing furiously in an attempt to make my vocal cords do the job that they were designed for. "Don't."

X paused. "Don't what? Don't stop, or don't carry on? I need you to be clear here, Tate."

I held his gaze, my cock throbbing urgently. "Don't stop."

He nodded, acknowledging my response. "Then all you need to do is trust me. Can you do that?"

Could I? But I was already nodding, my body out of sync with my mind.

X's voice when it came was a slow, seductive purr. "Move again, Tate. Like you did before."

Something sizzled down my spine, an awareness of what he was asking me to do. "Kiss me first." I needed to feel a deeper connection before I let myself go so completely. X arched up as I bent forwards, our mouths meeting halfway, his tongue wasting no time at all in introducing itself to mine. The kiss was both soft and bruising, hard and gentle. It was a paradox, just like the man himself. And all the while, the blade pressed against my chest, a whisper at the back of my mind asking how he could possibly control it when his mouth was busy plundering mine.

The kiss went on for a while, achingly sweet and satisfying. I was the first to pull back, glancing down at my chest as our bodies separated and expecting to see blood. But it was just as unblemished as it had always been. If there had been blood, would I have stopped? I doubted it. I probably would have just brushed it off as a scratch.

"Move, Tate."

The instruction was urgent, the voice delivering it husky with arousal. I picked up my movements from earlier, the caress of hands replaced by the kiss of the blade as it moved to my abdomen, giving that area of my body the same attention as it had my nipple. My breath hitched at the thought of X lowering it farther. I trusted him. I did. But the thought of a knife near my cock was a step too far. I held my breath as it painted a trail around my belly button, only releasing my breath when it headed upwards rather than down.

A cold and dangerous line was drawn around each nipple, my hips still thrusting as the blade explored my collarbone on the way to my throat. My head was forced higher as the point was pushed against the soft skin underneath my chin. And then almost without any warning, I was coming, my back bowed as my cock emptied itself across X's abdominal muscles.

The orgasm carried on for longer than I was used to, all of my muscles tight as my body jerked. Just when I'd think I was done, my cock would pulse again, managing to find more cum from its seemingly never-ending reservoir.

When I finally came down from the plateau of sensation, I jerked upright, my fingers desperately exploring my skin to work out where the knife had traveled to while I'd been so lost in my orgasm. But wherever I touched, my hands came away free from blood, not even a scratch on my skin.

"Tate. Look at me." I obeyed the instruction immediately, lifting my head to meet X's gaze. "You're fine. I made sure of that. I'd never hurt you. Not unless you asked me to."

I nodded, my breathing still a succession of rapid pants. I hung my head as I tried to wrap my mind around the fact that I'd come so hard with just the knife touching me. The knife that now lay seemingly forgotten next to the mattress where X must have placed it. Sweat cooled on my skin as I concentrated on breathing, X's fingers tracing lazy, comforting circles on my back as the stiff erection pressing against my ass reminded me that only one of us had come. Surprised by the fact that I was still hard, I sat up, wrapping my hand around my cock to give it a couple of experimental strokes. It skated the very edge of being too sensitive, X's keen eyes following my movement. "I think I can come again."

"Yeah?" There was a gleam in X's eyes that said that was good news. "We should test it out."

I leaned over the edge of the mattress, plucking the bottle of lube Psyche had brought from where I'd left it. I took back every negative thought I'd ever had about him as I uncapped it to pour a generous amount onto my palm. Keeping my gaze fixed on X's face, I smoothed the majority of it onto his cock, eating up every little flare of nostrils and hitch of breath that gave away his pleasure. It was so enjoyable that I gave him a couple of extra deliberate strokes, dragging my hand from root to tip and admiring the way his cum-painted abdominal muscles flexed.

Deciding to multi-task, I loosened myself with lubed fingers while continuing to slide my fist over his cock. I wondered whether I could make him come like this. All the evidence pointed to the answer being yes. I might have tested it out if I didn't need his cock in my ass more. There would be time for other things later. Reality stole my breath away for a moment. Time. That was the one thing we didn't have. Not really. I made a huge effort to shove the thought from my brain, refusing to dwell on it.

"Tate?"

He didn't need to say more. I could read him just from the way he said my name. I stopped teasing him, lining his cock up with my hole and pushing back to take him inside me until he was fully sheathed.

"Kiss me."

Just like all his other instructions, I obeyed immediately, the two of us managing to twist ourselves into a shape where we could kiss deeply without my body separating from his. His mouth provided the perfect distraction as I struggled to adjust to the sizeable cock in my ass. X began to rock, our mouths still entwined. I broke free, needing to concentrate, needing to force my post-orgasmic muscles to relax and take him.

My fingers dug into his skin as I found a rhythm which enabled us to move together. There was a distinct moment where it switched from slight discomfort to pure pleasure, X reading my face as he began to thrust deeper. He wanted something more though; I could see it on his face. I didn't hesitate. "Whatever you want. Take it!"

The last word had barely left my lips before X withdrew, expertly flipping me over and pushing my thighs apart. His entry back into my ass without prior warning took my breath away, and I cried out into the pillow. He didn't hold back, pounding me mercilessly with long, deep strokes, his fingers bruising my skin. I soaked up every thrust, every touch of his skin against mine, and I loved it. All of it. Managing to wriggle a hand beneath me, I stroked my cock lazily as he continued to fuck me without restraint. I was barely aware of the fact that I'd taken to saying his name over and over again, falling into the rhythm of his thrusts as I repeated it like some sort of silent prayer. His groans in my ear were like sweet music as I pushed back against him, encouraging him to take whatever he needed. Not that he seemed to need the encouragement. He was like a one-man fucking machine, muscles straining, fingers digging into my skin as he arranged me how he wanted me, lifting my hips and spreading my thighs wider when he wasn't quite satisfied by the position.

Just when I thought he was going to last forever, his body stiffened and he moaned, long and loud, his body jerking on top of mine. A couple more strokes and I came for the second time that night, his orgasm triggering mine.

We both collapsed onto the mattress, X's weight pushing my

face into the pillow. Hard as I tried, I couldn't seem to summon the energy to mind. There were far worse ways to go than to be suffocated by a wall of muscle after two orgasms. I finally managed to turn my head to the side to draw in some much-needed oxygen. "Holy fucking Christ!" X shifted on top of me, rocking his hips as if he wanted to remind me that he hadn't withdrawn yet. I moaned at the feeling. "You're going to kill me."

Husky words were whispered into my ear. "You! Never."

I laughed. "Sweet talker." I closed my eyes for a moment, my pulse still racing. I needed to move. I needed to shower again and do something about the wet spot I'd created. My body, though, just wanted to sleep. I was dimly aware of X's weight lifting from me. That was fine. I didn't need to be squashed. He could take a shower first and then I'd have one in a bit when I could move again. It was only when I heard the telltale rustle of fabric that my eyes snapped open to find X donning his old clothes, which didn't make any sense. "What are you doing?"

He paused to pick up the knife from the floor, the memory of it moving across my skin making my dick twitch, even though there was no way in hell I was getting hard again any time soon. "I have to go and do something. I won't be long."

I struggled up to one elbow. "What do you mean, you have to go and do something? I mean… I didn't expect prolonged pillow talk from you, but I thought you might actually stay in the same room."

X's lips quirked as he dropped to his knees next to the mattress, brushing a strangely gentle kiss across my forehead. "Once I'm back, I will be. Trust me, it's important, or I wouldn't be leaving you."

Still reeling from the unbelievably sweet gesture, which didn't fit X at all, I didn't manage any more words until he was already at the bottom of the stairs. "And then you'll sleep, right? You won't inject any more of that crap." I should have pushed him to get rid of it. I would have felt better knowing it was at the bottom of the lake, rather than lurking at the bottom of the bag.

He gave a curt nod, but it wasn't enough to satisfy me. Not when after years of working for a pharmaceutical company I knew exactly how much damage drugs like that one could cause. "Promise me."

"I promise." And then X was gone, the creak of the hatch signaling his exit. I was left staring at the empty stairs and wondering what was so important that he was going to roam around an unfamiliar city in the dark. I resolved to stay awake until he came back so that I could ask him, but I don't think I even lasted five minutes before sleep wrapped me in its embrace.

I couldn't have said how much time had passed before I was woken by cold skin against mine as arms wrapped around me. It could have been five minutes or five hours. There was the tiniest stirring of panic before X's familiar scent made its way to my nostrils. I turned in his arms, draping my body around his and going back to sleep with the comfort of his rhythmic breaths against my neck.

20
X

It was strange. For years I'd faced the reality of knowing that my watch over Tate would never be anything more than that. That he'd never say my name, that our eyes would never meet, that we'd never exchange words. And in some twisted way I'd been fine with that. Had actually preferred it over the possibility of him treating me like a leper, of him looking at me with deep-seated fear in his eyes. And that look had definitely been there in the beginning when he'd finally had a moment to take stock and wonder who the hell I was.

The surprise had been how quickly it had worn off, and how little time had passed before he'd been ready to put his life in my hands. A cynic would argue that he'd had little choice, but they certainly couldn't have envisaged the way things had turned out after that, to the point where not only were we having sex but Tate had begun looking at me as if I was the answer to all his prayers. He was doing it now, a slight smile on his lips as he pretended not to be watching me. That feeling was more potent than any drug could ever be. It left me adrift, trying to fathom emotions I wasn't used to feeling. He'd always been the one thing that made me feel human. But now… I felt like something more. Something that mattered to someone. And not just someone. But Tate.

Fingers snapped in front of my face. "Earth to X. You still with me, sexy?"

Sexy! I raised my head to find Tate grinning at me as if he was well aware of the word he'd used and was waiting to see my reaction to it. "Do you know what happens to people who test me?"

Tate's eyebrows rose and he crossed his arms over his chest. "Ooh, no! But I can't wait to find out. Hang on! Let me have a few guesses first before you tell me. Do they get a…" He waggled his eyebrows. "… a spanking?"

My gaze automatically dropped, vivid images of delivering what he'd just suggested causing my cock to swell. "Not usually… but…" I forced my eyes back to his face, completely having forgotten how this conversation had started. "Is that something you might be interested in?"

"Possibly. I'd certainly think about it for the right person."

I stepped closer to him, arousal spiking. "And am I the right person?"

There was a gleam in his eyes as he plucked my hand out of mid-air, wrapping his fingers around my wrist to bring it up to eye level. He turned it over, pretending a careful scrutiny of the palm of the hand. "Maybe. I'd definitely consider a trial. You know, one practice smack to see how you do." His fingers traced the lines on my palm and the scratches that still remained from the jagged edges of the metal fence before brushing over calluses honed from years of handling a knife.

"That's a lot of pressure."

"Well, if you're not up to the job I can always find someone else." Tate nullified his words by dropping a quick kiss on the palm of my hand. It made me want to close my fingers, as if the kiss was something tangible I could hold on to. Only, there was a burning jealousy as well at the mere thought of someone taking away what I'd gained over the last few days. "You could, but then I'd have to remove that person's intestines and make them wear them as a scarf."

Tate's head tilted to one side. "Huh! I guess I better stick with you then. That's never going to be in fashion." He stepped forward, lacing his arms around my neck and staring up at me. Back when I'd followed him around, there'd been days where I'd forgotten how beautiful he was only to be reminded anew. It felt like that now, and all I could do was stare at him. Tate bumped his chest against mine. "That was meant to be a subtle hint to kiss me."

I didn't need telling twice, lowering my lips to his and letting myself get lost in the feel of him, the taste of him, everything that made up the only man I'd every truly wanted, the one I thought I'd never have. Yet here we were, with his fingers clinging to me like I wasn't close enough and his mouth moving greedily over mine. I pulled him in tighter, crushing our bodies together as we kissed with an increasing urgency.

There was a loud crash, followed by the sound of pounding footsteps down the stairs. Instinct kicked in immediately as I stepped in front of Tate, knives at the ready to face whoever it was. The balding man whose house it was burst into the basement seconds later, his face red and sweat rolling down his brow. He didn't mince his words. "You have to go. The DTP have been sighted close by. I assume they're looking for you. They can't find you here."

Realizing the threat wasn't from the man in front of us, Tate stepped around me, the color gone from his face. "Can we stay here?" He pointed up to where the hatch was. "You could lock it and put something over the top so that they don't know it's there. We can stay quiet. Wait till they've gone away." Tate was always so idealistic that sometimes it hurt. In his experience, hiding was always the best policy. Left to him, he'd probably have taken up permanent residence in the sewers beneath Cofield and never come out again, rats or no rats.

I shook my head, interjecting before Baldie had a stroke at the thought of hiding fugitives under the nose of the DTP.

"No, it wouldn't work. They'll search the entire city, rip the place apart until they find us." I picked up Tate's backpack, shoving it into his arms before shrugging my shoulders into mine. Tate's face was drawn and tight as he fastened it on his back. I wished there was some way of making him feel better, but there were no platitudes I could offer without lying to him, not when they were so close. "Ready?" He nodded, his expression about as far from ready as anyone's I'd ever seen.

I focused on Tate, trying to work out whether there was anything I could do to dial his panic down a few notches. Panic meant not thinking clearly. Not thinking clearly meant making mistakes that didn't need to be made. But unfortunately, the developments in our relationship hadn't made me any better at offering comfort. I turned to Baldie. "Give us a couple of minutes." He opened his mouth to object but a hard stare had him retreating up the stairs without another word. Wise choice. I forced Tate to meet my gaze. He wasn't in a good way, his forehead beaded with sweat and his stare glassy. For some reason, this was hitting him harder than any of our previous close shaves. I spoke slowly and calmly, hoping to imbue him with some confidence. "When we get outside, we're going to head north. There's another exit I discovered last night. We'll keep to the shadows where we can. Step where I step. If I hold my hand up"—I modeled the gesture for him—"that means stop." I curled my fingers. "That means go. Have you got it?" He nodded even more jerkily than he had before, his breathing rapid. I laid my palm against his cheek. "Look at me, Tate." He did, and this time there was more of the Tate I was used to seeing behind his eyes, as if my touch had calmed him, the same as it had the time when he'd had a nightmare. "We're going to get out of this! Trust me. Say yes, X."

There was the faint glimmer of a smile, Tate's hand lifting to cover mine. "Yes, X." The words sounded like they'd been forced out between two rusty sheets of metal, but it was better than nothing. I let my hand linger on his cheek for a few more selfish seconds, savoring the feel of his skin before reluctantly pulling away. But then I gave in to a crazy impulse, stepping closer to drop a gentle kiss on his lips. After all, what if it was the last time.

"Can you say it?"

I didn't need to ask what he was referring to; I knew exactly what he meant. The only problem was I wasn't sure of the answer. It might only be three words, but I'd never said them to anyone, not even my parents. But I couldn't ignore the longing in his eyes. He needed this, and it wasn't as if it wasn't true. I'd uprooted my whole life for him without a moment's thought, and I'd do it again in a heartbeat without regret. If I died today, I still wouldn't regret it, not when the alternative would have been leaving Tate to die alone on the nightclub floor.

If that wasn't love, then I didn't know what was. But saying it, forcing those words from my lips, that was a big ask. Tate's gaze hadn't wavered from mine, and although it had been only seconds since he'd asked the question, it felt like much longer. "I..." I swallowed, trying to force some saliva into a mouth rendered completely dry. Resignation started to seep into Tate's eyes, making me feel like a huge fucking coward. He wasn't asking for the world, just a verbal declaration of what he already knew to be true. Words that millions of people threw out without a moment's hesitation every single day. Words that some of them didn't even mean. Well, I'd say them, and I'd mean it, and the rest of the fucking world could go to hell. "I love you, Tate."

The world didn't come crashing down. I didn't disappear in a puff of smoke. In fact, a strange sense of satisfaction settled in my chest. It only grew as Tate smiled, his hand reaching for mine and intertwining our fingers. "I love you too."

What? I almost staggered backward, my mind unable to decipher the words that had just spilled from his lips. I searched his face, looking for any telltale signs that he was winding me up, or wielding his usual sarcasm. But his expression held nothing but sincerity.

Tate looked sheepish for a second. "I know it sounds crazy after such a short time and"—he rolled his eyes—"you're probably just going to put it down to me being grateful or something, or it being some sort of irrational reaction to danger because that's the way your mind works. But"—his chin tipped up stubbornly—"that doesn't mean it's not true, so I'm not going to take it back. You're going to have to accept it whether you want to or not."

Earlier it had been Tate who'd struggled for words. Now I couldn't even remember what they were, never mind manage to string some together to make a sentence. If Tate loved me… no, I couldn't even go there. It was preposterous. It was far beyond anything I'd ever dreamed of, even including the times where I'd allowed my imagination to run riot and Tate had submitted to having sex with me. And submitted was the right word. My fantasies had never come anywhere close to the consensual sex which had occurred between us over the last few days. I needed to say something. Something that didn't shit all over the gift he'd just given me whether it was true or not. But nothing came to mind, and we needed to move. The delay had been worth it, though. Tate looked far more with it than he had before. Who knew that a declaration of love could be the magic cure for settling nerves?

I led him up the stairs, Baldie looking mighty relieved at our appearance. He slammed the hatch closed as soon as we were out of it as if he feared we might change our minds at the last minute and run back to the safety of his basement. My fingers itched with the urge to demonstrate that had that been the case, there wouldn't have been a damn thing he could have done about it.

Baldie continued to hover around us like an annoying wasp as we headed to the door we'd come in through the previous evening. If he thought we were about to head out there blindly, he was in for a shock. Flattening myself against the wall near the window, I positioned myself so that I had a view of the street, Tate having enough presence of mind to stay well back.

There was nothing. No people. No commotion. Just an empty street. Too empty. My guess would be that word had gotten around that the DTP were on their way. People were no doubt cowering behind their doors and waiting for the storm to pass. That would leave us as the only people on the streets—good for people not getting caught in the crossfire, but not so good for leaving us standing out like a sore thumb. *People not getting caught in the crossfire?* Where the fuck had that thought come from. Since when had I given a damn about collateral damage? Tate's influence was starting to change the way I thought about things.

"Open the door!" I barked the instruction at Baldie, who immediately jumped to do as he'd been told, either because he realized that the tone of my voice brooked no argument, or more likely because he'd worked out that the sooner the door was open, the sooner he could put us on the other side of it. I grabbed Tate's arm, pulling him toward the open door as I whispered urgently in his ear. "You need to do exactly what I say. Even if you think it doesn't make sense. Can you do that for me, Tate?"

He nodded. We'd barely set foot on the street before the door slammed in our wake. "Yeah, goodbye to you as well, you motherfucker." The words didn't elicit any reaction from Tate, who'd plastered himself to my side as if he hoped that close proximity to me would offer some sort of magical protection. Tate grabbed my arm, panic twisting his features as his fingers dug into my skin. "Tank!"

I could hear it too, the familiar low rumble. "Follow me."

Tate was my shadow as I stuck close to the buildings, wending my way through the streets in the direction we needed to go. Every now and again, faces would peer at us from behind gaps in closed curtains. We may as well have been carrying a sign that said "fugitives on the run." I didn't pay them any attention, too busy trying to see the bigger picture. How many units had they sent? My money was on just the one.

There was no way they could have known for sure that we'd stop in Urstone. Therefore, they would have split the units to cover any eventuality. One unit still meant eight armed and dangerous men… and a tank. The odds of eight against one weren't in my favor. I wasn't including Tate in that equation because he had no training. His only use would be as a… the thought brought me up short, but the more I thought about it, the more a plan started to crystallize in my head. It was the only chance we had.

I swung Tate around to face me, the glassy expression back on his face. "Listen to me carefully. You remember that street, yesterday. The one where Talon's house was, the narrow one?" Tate's brow furrowed in confusion for a second, but then he nodded. "I need you to head for there. It was a dead end, remember?" Another nod. "The DTP need to see you and follow you." His eyes widened in alarm as he started to grasp what I was asking of him. "The street is too narrow for the tank, which takes it out of the equation."

"But—"

"I don't have time to explain. Do you trust me, Tate?"

There was a momentary hesitation before the nod this time, but I didn't blame him. I was setting him up to be bait, and although I had a plan, there was no guarantee it would work. There were so many things that could go wrong. If there had been any other way, I would have taken it. But past Urstone, there was only open ground for the next fifty miles or so. Even if we could manage to evade them for long enough to get out of the city, we'd be sitting ducks, and it would only be a matter of time before they took us out. Our only chance lay in the element of surprise and using the geographical advantages that the city provided.

I lay my hand on Tate's arm, the muscles trembling spasmodically beneath my fingers. "You can do this, Tate." I didn't wait for a response, pushing him gently in the direction I needed him to go. He gave one last glance over his shoulder, his blue eyes clouded with a mixture of confusion, hurt, and sorrow before turning away and jogging in the direction I'd instructed him to go.

I watched him for longer than I should have done before tipping my head back to scope out the surrounding buildings. I needed to go up, and unlike the buildings in Cofield, there were no handy fire escapes to aid my progress. Shrugging my shoulders out of the backpack, I stashed it in an alcove before starting my climb using only jagged brickwork and the occasional window ledge. It was difficult, but not impossible given my upper body strength. Curtains twitched as I heaved my body up to the top floor, dangling by one hand for a moment before managing to find a handhold that enabled me to pull myself up to the ledge. I took a short breather before the final push to the roof. The proximity of the buildings to each other in Urstone had been one of those things that I'd filed away in the part of my brain labelled "things that might be useful."

Well, it was about to be useful—hopefully. I flexed my shoulders before embarking on the final climb to the roof. That part proved easier: the brickwork more prone to crumbling so that even if there were no handholds to be had I could quickly gouge my own.

A few minutes later and I was standing on the roof with the whole city spread out before me. It didn't take long to locate what I was searching for—the tank stood out like a beacon as the procession of DTP soldiers made their way through the city. Just as I'd calculated there were eight soldiers, nine if you counted whoever was driving the tank. Two of them stuck close to the tank while it trundled through the streets while the other six fanned out, carrying out a search of every building they passed. I jolted at the tell-tale flash of laser fire. Someone obviously hadn't been cooperative enough for their liking and was now nothing more than a pile of ash.

I watched them for a few minutes, trying to work out the pattern of their movements, concluding that the path they were taking would bring them into contact with Tate's route in less than five minutes. He would need to stay ahead of them for three minutes in order to have sufficient time to get to the point where he needed to be. That only gave me seven minutes. Seven minutes to get there before Tate and to find a position where I could implement the plan that I'd cobbled together.

The time crunch was narrower than I'd have liked, but it had to work. Otherwise I was never going to get the opportunity to look into those blue eyes again, to see how much darker they became when Tate was aroused. I'd never get a chance to unpick why he'd said those three words, which still had me reeling, or possibly even hear him say them again, if there was any truth behind them.

Leaping from roof to roof didn't prove as straightforward as I'd hoped for a number of reasons. Distances between the houses tended to vary so while they didn't exactly require death-defying leaps, they were a challenge even for someone as surefooted as me. Loose roof tiles regularly slipped from under my feet to crash to the ground below. I counted the seconds in my head, taking more risks than I should have done in order to reach the destination before Tate. It didn't matter if my muscles were burning, or if my lungs were starting to feel as if someone had sandpapered them from the inside. All that mattered was getting there first so that I could get into a position where there was a sliver of a chance of pulling this off.

I breathed a sigh of relief as I reached the street where Talon's house lay. Scanning the roofs of the surrounding buildings, I finally spotted a perfect vantage point where part of the roof was flat. Keeping one eye on the street, I made my way toward it.

The street remained empty. No Tate. I ignored the nagging voice in my head which insisted on letting me know that the task I'd set him had been too hard, that the DTP had already caught up with him and that I'd left him alone in his hour of need. There hadn't been another flash of laser fire, not since the first. They weren't going to take him prisoner; they were only interested in executing him. Unless… they were going to use him as bait to get to me? Would they do that? Would they bother to set up a trap to lure me in their direction?

The probable answer was yes. I couldn't have made it any clearer that Tate was important to me. They had to know that I'd come for him. And they were right, I would if it came down to it. I stepped onto the flat roof, lowering myself into a cross-legged position, half hidden out of sight behind a chimney. Plucking the throwing knives from my jacket pocket, I arranged them in a neat line in front of me, all apart from two which I kept in my hands.

I rolled my shoulders back, breathing deeply and trying to relax my body, trying to get into that zone where movement came automatically without conscious thought. I needed to trust my years of training. I needed to remember that I could count the number of occasions I'd missed a target on one hand. *You have missed, though.*

Still no Tate. He should have been here by now. I went back to contemplating the DTP having him. If they set a trap, I'd walk right into it. Walking away wasn't an option. Either we both lived, or we both died. There was no additional option.

Just as I was beginning to despair, Tate came skidding around the corner. He was as desperate as I'd ever seen him, sweat pouring off him in droves and his hair sticking up in several directions. Yet, he was still the most beautiful sight I'd ever seen. Alive. Not imprisoned by the DTP. Beautiful *and* clever.

He didn't slow, passing the door where we'd sourced supplies only yesterday on his way to the end of the street just as

I'd directed him to do. Only then did he stop, bending over as he struggled to catch his breath. He looked so lost and alone. Did he think I'd left him? I ached to call out, to tell him where I was, but one glance in my direction at the wrong moment and my plan would crumble into dust. Pain in the short term was unfortunately necessary in order for there to be a hope of a long term.

Where were the DTP? There shouldn't have been that much space between them. My vantage point didn't allow me to see past the curve in the road. And then there they were, the familiar masked and uniformed figures—eight of them making their way onto the street. I gripped onto the knives so tightly that my knuckles turned white as I performed complicated calculations in my head, trying to work through all the possible permutations.

I could tell the moment that Tate saw them, his body going rigid and his knees buckling before he managed to straighten them. *Just hold on, Tate. Let them get closer and whatever you do, don't look up.*

The procession made their way slowly down the street, seeming in no rush to get to Tate. Behind the masks, they were probably laughing at his stupidity for running into a dead end. Tate meanwhile still seemed frozen, which wasn't a surprise considering he had eight guns pointed at him, all capable of vaporizing him in less than a second. The DTP had regulations though, a supposed code of conduct which required them to relay the sentencing before carrying out the execution. I just needed to work out who'd been tasked with carrying it out. Was it the soldier slightly ahead of the others? Or the one directly in the middle? Timing was everything. That soldier needed to go first, or the whole plan would tumble like a house of cards. If I miscalculated and Tate paid the price, then my life wouldn't matter. The only thing that would matter would be taking as many down as I could before they turned their guns on me.

The soldiers came to a halt about three meters away from

Tate. There was no recorded message this time, the tinny voice emanating from a speaking apparatus built into the mask. "Tate Gillespie, you were charged with espionage in Cofield and sentenced to execution. You failed to cooperate with the law, an action that led to the death of four military soldiers."

A pointless piece of information if ever I'd heard one. What were they going to do—kill him twice?

"...you have evaded capture on several occasions in a direct rebellion against the laws of this country. You will kneel and receive your sentence."

Tate seemed almost relieved to sink to his knees. My eyes weren't on him, though, my eyes were on the soldiers' body language, greedily soaking up any clue I could about who'd been tasked to pull the trigger. Not him—the gun wasn't held high enough. Not him—his body was angled ever too slightly in the wrong direction. I had it down to two. I was nearing the point of having to take a 50/50 chance when one gave it away, his finger moving just ever so slightly toward the trigger as he went to press it.

I took one last breath, lifting my hand on the exhale and with one flick of my wrist letting go of the knife in my hand. My aim had never been intended for the soldier, but for the gun instead. It discharged, a bright arc of blue light streaming from the barrel ready to disintegrate anything in its path. Only instead of the flesh and blood target it had been intended for, the impact of the knife knocked it off-center, a tree exploding in Tate's stead. I didn't waste any time, unleashing the second knife within a second of the first and already picking up the third. Just as it had in the club, the knife found its optimal target, sinking into that vulnerable sliver of neck between helmet and armor. I took down another almost instantaneously.

There was no time to celebrate, not with the element of surprise now lost and the rest of the soldiers turning and starting to look up in a bid to find out where the attack was coming from. Knives three and four found fleshy targets. Four down. Four to go. The next soldier took two knives to incapacitate, the first bouncing harmlessly off his chest plate to lie uselessly on the floor. I rectified the mistake with the second, ducking behind the chimney as a stream of blue laser fire came my way. Half of the chimney gave way, showering me with chunks of brick.

No longer hidden from sight, I launched myself to the edge of the roof, leaping from it in one smooth movement to land on the soldier who'd fired. As he crumpled under my considerable weight, I jerked his gun up and around, the laser beam vaporizing the other soldier instantaneously. Another throwing knife took down the remaining soldier on my right, and from there it was easy, just a case of holding the head of the soldier I'd landed on with my foot and sliding a blade into his neck, his body jerking a few times and then going still. I did the same to any of the other soldiers still showing signs of life, retrieving my throwing knives at the same time. I turned to survey the damage: bodies scattered all over the street. None of them moving. None of them a danger any longer. Eight for eight.

Tate.

He was still knelt, his head hanging down and his hair covering his face. I walked quickly toward him, his head lifting at my approaching footsteps. Stopping in front of him, I held out my hand. He took it and let me pull him to his feet. Whatever I'd expected to happen next, it wasn't for him to whack me in the middle of the chest. I took a step back, more out of surprise than because the attack carried much force, but still…

Tate's eyes blazed fire as he stepped toward me, delivering another whack identical to the first. "Could you have cut that any fucking finer?" He gestured wildly toward the smoking stump of the tree, the tree that had been no more than a meter away from him. "I nearly fucking died. Again." His voice was shrill and kept rising in volume. "Lead them here, Tate. Stick yourself on the end of a fishing line so they'll take a nibble and come after you, Tate. No fucking mention that you were going to let them deliver their fucking speech first." I received another thwack in the chest to punctuate that statement. I wasn't worried by his anger. It was the same way he'd dealt with the threat of the cougar. And just like then I was prepared to be his whipping boy if it meant him finding a way to deal with it. "Well?" He arched an eyebrow. "Nothing to say?"

"I needed to know who was going to pull the trigger."

"Oh really! You couldn't have..." He made a half-hearted attempt at imitating knife throwing, which was even less convincing than his effort the night before had been. "... done it at the end of the street before they got to me?"

"They weren't close enough, and the angle was all wrong. They would have been able to see me and take me out before I could kill them."

His blue eyes were unblinking as he stared at me. "Good choice then. Because although you're a bastard and I think I hate you right now, I still want you around."

I wanted nothing more at that moment than to pull him in and hold him close, to test how much of a bastard he really thought I was. Only, there were more important things to worry about. "There's still a tank. As soon as he realizes that radio communication has stopped, he'll call for reinforcements."

Tate flinched. "Right." He lifted his hand to my face, his fingers coming away stained red. "Are you alright?" I dashed a hand across my forehead, finding a bump from where the brickwork on the chimney had exploded. I hadn't even realized it had done any damage, too wrapped up in what needed to be done. I didn't know what was worse, Tate shouting at me or the look of concern now pasted on his face, his fingers still hovering close to my cheek.

"I'm fine."

He nodded but didn't look convinced as he lowered his hand back to his side, focusing on the prone body of the soldier who'd been going to carry out his execution. "Maybe we should take their guns? I know you don't like guns, but…" He made a fake gun out of two fingers raising them as he made a noise. His impression of shooting was on a par with the one of knife throwing—that was to say not very good at all.

"No point. They're biometric, fingerprint activated so they can't be disarmed and used against them." It was a toss-up whether Tate looked more relieved or disappointed by the news. Shock was starting to set in, though. As I started to lead him down the street, I needed to shake him out of it in some way. "You took your time getting here?"

He whirled around, his jaw dropping open and his eyes narrowing. "What? Are you fucking kidding me? I had to take the hard route, not take a little jaunt across the rooftops. And I had to hook those bastards to get them here, all while you were sitting on your ass."

That was better. "Hardly a jaunt."

Just as we passed a familiar door, it opened, Talon and Psyche stepping out. Talon's sharp gaze scanned the street for a few moments, taking in the scene before landing on us, her face expressionless. "Quite a mess you've made here."

While she was calmness personified, Psyche was a different matter entirely, almost bouncing up and down with excitement, his gaze entirely focused on me as if Tate wasn't even there. "Fuck me! The way you took those soldiers down was poetry in motion. The bastards didn't even know what had hit them. And it only took like a fucking minute as well. One minute they were there and the next"—he pointed at the ground—"they were fucking there."

I wasn't used to being on the receiving end of adoration from people, particularly not for doing what I did best—killing people. It seemed I'd been killing the wrong people all these years. Shame, I hadn't realized that. I would have been quite happy to make a sport out of hunting the DTP. Having no idea how I was supposed to respond to Psyche's childish enthusiasm, I simply ignored it. "We have to go."

Grabbing onto Tate, I pulled him along with me, already planning our route out of the city. I doubted there was more than two soldiers in the tank so they should be easy enough to avoid. As long as we were out of the city before the reinforcements arrived, we'd be alright. I'd barely taken two steps before Talon barred my path. I halted, regarding her coolly as I fought the urge to push her aside. Pushing old ladies wasn't going to earn me any brownie points with Tate, though. "What?"

She raised her chin. The old lady had balls. I'd give her that. She'd just watched me slaughter an entire unit of soldiers, and she still intended to confront me, and I knew full well what it was going to be about. She might be old but she wasn't stupid. She spoke with deliberate firmness. "Something went missing last night... from my bedroom while I was sleeping."

I felt Tate jolt at my side but I ignored it. "You should lock your door. You never know who might be sneaking around."

Her wrinkled lips formed themselves into a shape that was almost a smile. "I did. They made short work of the locks. They obviously knew what they were doing." Her gaze swept the street again, skirting over the dead bodies. "I guess I should be relieved that they only stole from me rather than murdering me in my bed."

"Probably."

She nodded, tension draining from my shoulders at the realization that we had an understanding of sorts. That meant I wasn't going to have to add her body and that of her grandson's as well to the growing pile. And more importantly I wasn't going to have to do it in front of Tate. It was a new experience to care what others thought, but I was beginning to get used to it being there, like a nagging headache that wouldn't quite go away.

Tate was understandably confused, his brow furrowed as he tried to make sense out of the conversation. "What did they steal?"

Talon's gaze slipped over to him. "Nothing important. Not to me, anyway. Seems like it was important to someone else though."

I cut in before Tate could ask any more questions. "Let's go."

"What about your bag?" Talon's brow was raised as she gestured at my empty back.

"I had to leave it. Roof jumping and backpacks don't mix."

"Psyche will get it."

I raised an eyebrow. I could understand her backing down from confrontation, but being prepared to help us further was another thing entirely. She seemed to follow my train of my thought, her gaze returning to the bodies. "You already paid me. These might not be the same bastards who killed my son, but I got to pretend they were, eight times over. That's payment enough."

At the mention of his name, Psyche had dragged himself away from a close inspection of one of the corpses, bounding over to us like an expectant puppy waiting to play fetch. Which I supposed in some strange way he was about to do. He bounced on his heels. "Where do I need to go?"

I relayed the name of the street, along with details of where I'd hidden the bag, and then told him where to meet us. I managed to resist the urge to tell him to stay out of sight. He might act like a kid but he wasn't one. He hadn't survived this long without knowing not to take stupid risks. And there I went giving a damn again. The old X wouldn't have given a flying fuck if Psyche was vaporized by the DTP, and I could tell myself all I wanted that it was about getting my possessions back, but that wouldn't make it true. Being with Tate was warping me in ways I'd never anticipated, and I wasn't sure whether that was a good thing or something completely disastrous given the situation we were in.

I quickened my pace to reach the end of the street, Tate directly behind me. The conversation with Talon might have only taken a couple of minutes, but that was two minutes longer than we should have hung around. I was dimly aware of Tate turning to say an awkward farewell to the old woman while attempting to keep pace with me. I left the niceties to him. I didn't do hellos, and I sure as fuck didn't do goodbyes, not even the new and improved X was going to go that far.

The end of the street was clear, allowing us to slip down a side street unnoticed—by soldiers anyway, the curtain-twitchers were back with a vengeance. I paused for a moment to listen, but the city was silent. Just as I thought that, there was the distinctive blue flash of laser fire, Tate jolting so violently that I had to grab onto him in order to steady him. I increased our pace to a jog.

"What if it was Psyche?" Tate's whisper was so quiet that I almost didn't catch it.

"Then I guess lighting fires without the lighter in that bag is going to be a problem, and we'll be down to sharing one flashlight and eating less."

"It—"

"Not now, Tate." His eyes flashed, a hint of the anger from earlier returning, but then he seemed to catch himself, nodding once before going silent. He could have a go at me for being an unfeeling bastard later. In fact, he could rail at me to his heart's content once we were out of this godforsaken city. Voices came from our right, and I pulled Tate back into a doorway, blocking him from view with my body. They were real voices though, not tinny ones synthesized through a mask. I peered out to see two men sauntering down the street as if they were completely unaware of what had been happening in Urstone for the past hour.

Tate's body heat bled into my back and he slipped a hand in mine as we waited for the two men to pass, their voices growing fainter as they continued their journey to wherever they were going. I let the moment linger for a few glorious extra seconds before reluctantly pulling my hand from his.

It took another five minutes to reach the place where we'd agreed to meet Psyche. Instead of being dead, the grinning idiot was already there, my backpack dangling casually from one finger. His grin grew wider as we approached. I snatched the backpack from him, Tate thanking him when I didn't bother.

Psyche crossed his arms over his chest. "So I guess this is goodbye, like for real this time. You two take care. You're going to be famous in this city for the way you…" I didn't stop to listen to the rest. The amount that Psyche talked, the DTP would probably have caught up with us before we'd heard it all.

21
X

Years of prowling around city streets and honing my senses to each and every noise meant I picked up on the fact that we were being followed straight away. I placed my finger over Tate's lips, waiting until he'd nodded to show he understood before removing it. He was still shaky, but since leaving the city over an hour ago some of the color had returned to his cheeks, enough that he no longer looked like a walking corpse ready to keel over at the slightest breeze.

We'd reached tree cover a few minutes ago, which was good on two counts. There was no option to bring a tank through, and there were enough dry leaves underfoot to alert us to anyone else's presence, which was the noise I was currently listening to despite the fact that both Tate and I were still. I held a single finger in the air to demonstrate to Tate that I could hear one person. Could Psyche have followed us? Given the amount of hero worship that had been written all over his face after witnessing me taking out the DTP soldiers, I wouldn't put it past him. Kid obviously had a dark side hidden beneath that puppy exterior. Well, if he had followed us, he was in for a shock.

With Tate's eyebrows raised in a question, I leaned forward, placing my lips right next to his ear so that my voice wouldn't carry. "I need you to carry on walking." I raised an arm to indicate the direction I wanted him to go in, hating the fact that for the second time in a day I was separating myself from him. If it was up to me, I'd glue him to my side forevermore. But it was necessary. "Keep walking. Make noise but not too much." I didn't want him doing an impression of a brontosaurus or it would be too obvious.

Tate didn't say anything but his eyes blazed blue murder at being used for bait twice in one day. I dropped a kiss on his lips and gave him a gentle push. The glare grew more pronounced for a few seconds before he turned and disappeared out of sight. I slid my bag off my back in slow degrees, lowering it silently to the ground before pressing my back against the tree, knives already in my hands. I regulated my breathing, muscles coiled and ready as I listened to the approaching footsteps.

They paused as if the person was listening for Tate's footsteps and couldn't hear them over the sound of his own. Then they started up again, growing ever closer. I closed my eyes and concentrated on gleaning as much information as I could. Heavy tread, which meant the person was on the larger side. Probably not Psyche then. He was tall but wiry. There was evidence of the person trying to tread more lightly, that telltale hesitation of them trying to pick the best place to step before each one. They just weren't having much success with it.

The footsteps came closer still, the person now only meters away. I didn't dare look out. It would have been helpful to know what I was dealing with, but it wasn't worth giving away the element of surprise. I gripped the handle of my knife, the familiar feeling of adrenaline and expectation building to a crescendo inside me. I'd have been lying if I said I hated it. Before Tate, it had been the only thing that made me feel alive. There was a hesitation to the person's gait now as if they'd sensed that something wasn't quite right. Perhaps they'd worked out that Tate's footsteps, though perfectly audible, had changed in some way. I would have been able to tell that two people had become one. But could they? Is that why they'd slowed? Were they trying to work out what had happened to the other person? Well, the answer to that was simple, right here waiting for you, you bastard, so step a little closer, why don't you?

I turned my head to the side, waiting, breathing with my mouth open so I didn't make a sound. And then there they were. I whirled around, aiming my blade for the place where their head was. Except they'd ducked so it met nothing but air. The answer to who they were was in the full military garb and familiar mask covering their face. Somehow despite me being on my guard, one of the remaining soldiers from Urstone had managed to tail us. It didn't quite add up. But then neither did the fact that I'd never seen one without a gun before. Was he unarmed? I discovered the answer to that the hard way as the six-inch blade he carried sank deep into my right shoulder. There was a moment of cold numbness before flames of heat engulfed it, exacerbated as he twisted the blade before removing it.

Cold, hot fury seeped through my entire being. I stabbed. I didn't get stabbed. It was the worst sort of insult to fall foul of my own weapon of choice. It could only have been worse if it had been my own blade used against me. His arm lifted with the intention of sinking the knife into another part of my body. I blocked it with the arm that didn't feel like it was bathed in fire, giving him a shove at the same time.

He stumbled backwards, and I didn't give him time to regain his balance, ignoring the pain and pressing forwards. I grabbed the back of his head, forcing it down at the same time as bringing my knee up. He wore too much armor for the move to be fully effective, but it caught him off-guard enough for me to keep driving him backwards. He fell to the floor and I was on him in a flash, straddling him. Despite the inferno in my shoulder I kept on him as he struggled, pressing him down into the leafy ground and using my body weight to keep him under control. Only once I'd worked the point of my blade between the edge of his armor and the mask to press against his throat did he go still, recognizing that movement would only hasten his death.

A crunching noise preceded Tate's arrival. His face was a picture of concern as he peered down at us. If I hadn't been so busy, I might have been annoyed at him for not keeping his distance. Either he'd decided from the commotion that I needed help, or he'd thought it was all in hand. The truth probably lay somewhere between the two. Tate's eyes grew wide. "What happened to his mask?"

I hadn't even noticed the crack down the front. "My knee."

He nodded. "I've always wondered what…"

Even though he didn't finish, I knew what he'd been about to say. If I was honest, it had crossed my mind too. The DTP prided themselves on being a faceless entity. No one knew who they were, where they came from, or anything about them beyond what they wanted you to know, which was basically nothing. The same questions were asked from all quarters. Were they young or old? Was it voluntary or forced? Were they taken? Or born into it? If anyone had ever discovered the answers, they hadn't lived long enough to share them, so it had remained a mystery.

Beneath my hands was the perfect opportunity to answer at least some of those questions. I kept the blade at the soldier's throat, trying to show no signs of discomfort as I grasped the bottom of the mask with my injured arm. I glanced at Tate to see if he really wanted me to do this, but his attention was focused on the soldier, his eyes wide with expectation.

I ripped the mask off in one fell swoop.

Tate came a step closer. "Fucking hell!"

I didn't have to ask what had caused his shock. It was obvious. Hatred burned in the gray eyes staring back at me, his mouth twisted into a sneer. But it wasn't that. It was the fact that the soldier couldn't have been a day over eighteen. Sweaty blond hair curled over his forehead and his face was red. I guessed the masks had to be a bastard to wear all day. God knows what had possessed him to follow us on his own. And he had to be alone because just as the commotion had drawn Tate back, had he had any nearby companions they would have been drawn to us too. Perhaps he'd been hoping for a huge slice of personal glory. Either that or he had a death wish. "Can you speak, baby soldier?"

"Fuck you!"

Nice. His mouth started to move in an obvious attempt to gather saliva which was presumably destined for my face. I'd already been spat at once this week, so I really wasn't up for another dose. I pressed the blade harder against his throat, blood starting to well up from the resultant wound. "I wouldn't."

"You're going to kill me anyway."

That was a valid point. I leaned closer. "Yes, but it can be fast. Or I can remove all your skin first. Find out what's underneath this baby-faced exterior."

His belligerence lessened slightly. While I wouldn't have said the look on his face was fear, it might have been described as caution. He might not care about dying, but nobody was up for dying in excruciating agony if it could be avoided. Not even me. I sat back and stared at him for a few seconds, considering what the unmasking had revealed. His age and proficiency in fighting definitely answered one question. There was no way he could have been that good from a short period of training, so either they were recruited as young children or they really were born into it. At the thought of them having little to no choice, a stab of something that I might have thought was empathy if I was capable of it lanced my chest. I shook him slightly, more droplets of blood welling up as my knife bit deeper into his flesh. "How long have you been a soldier?"

"Fuck you!"

Baby soldier was at least consistent. He wasn't going to answer any questions, which meant that questioning him was a waste of time.

"What are we going to do with him?" Tate scanned our surroundings. "We could tie him to a tree. Gag him so that he can't shout for help."

The soldier started laughing, his chest shaking beneath my knees. I pressed the blade even harder against his neck until the laugh turned into a strangled cough. He still managed to force words out through his compressed windpipe, and for a change they weren't the words, fuck you. "Yeah, why don't you tie me to a tree? I could have a nap while I'm waiting for them to find me." His glance in Tate's direction conveyed the words "fucking idiot!" loud and clear.

I ignored him, focusing my attention on Tate and speaking softly. "Why don't you go and wait over there?" It wasn't Tate's fault that idealism ran all the way through him. He'd never had to face the harsh reality of life before, never been forced into a kill or be killed situation. I'd thought that the past week might have awoken him to that fact, but I couldn't bring myself to mourn the innocence that still remained. It was one of the ingredients that made Tate who he was. The man I'd fallen in love with and devoted most of my adult life to. I neither wanted nor needed a clone of myself.

Tate stared at me, realization finally dawning, followed by multiple emotions that flickered across his face at rapid speed. He swallowed as his gaze darted back to the soldier. I shouldn't have removed the mask. It had answered questions, but it had also humanized him, made him all too real. Tate hadn't seemed to have a problem with the soldiers I'd killed back in Urstone, not when they were just faceless killers. The next words out of his mouth confirmed the accuracy of my theory. "He's just a kid."

"Tate?" I waited until he dragged his gaze back to mine before continuing. "He's not a kid. He's a trained killer. He wouldn't think twice about murdering either of us." The searing pain in my shoulder confirmed that. If I hadn't taken him down, that same blade would have gone into another part of my body without a second's thought. And then he would have left me for dead and gone after Tate—the DTP's trained attack dog ready to deliver a prize at his master's feet. Whoever the master was. The driving force behind the DTP was another unanswered question. I begged Tate with my eyes not to make a bigger thing out of this than it needed to be. If he asked me not to kill him, I'd have to go against him, and I didn't want to do that. A few short hours ago he'd claimed to love me. Would one simple action cause that so-called love to shrivel and die? Tate continued to stare at me, his expression one that clearly said how much he was struggling with what needed to be done. I tried once more, displaying a patience I would never have shown anyone else. "Don't look at his face. Look at his uniform. Remember who he is. What he is."

Tate did as I asked, his gaze slowly trailing down over every inch of the soldier apart from his face. I was glad he didn't look at his face. It meant he was blissfully unaware of the smirk on the soldier's face as he seemed to find the conversation about his impending death amusing.

Finally, after what seemed like an age, Tate gave a terse nod, walking a few meters away to stand with his back to us.

I let out a slow breath, relieved that there'd been no pleading or histrionics, just a calm acceptance. The man beneath me wasn't a stinking old man who lived in a bunker. He was a living, breathing threat, or at least he was for the next few seconds.

"Make it quick, please." Tate's words were barely audible, just a whisper carried on the wind.

I turned my attention back to the soldier. Where before his face had been red, now it was waxy and pale, belying the bravado he'd been exhibiting. Hatred still gleamed in his eyes, the will to survive strong. I removed the blade from his neck, turning his head to the side and plunging it straight into his ear. Death was almost instantaneous. He twitched. Once. Twice. And then he was still. I ran my hands over his body, searching for anything of interest, but bar the radio they all carried there was nothing.

A wave of dizziness hit me as I stood, reminding me of the wound I'd sustained. How much blood had I lost? I slid my hand beneath my jacket, the material of my T-shirt completely sodden. I guessed the answer was a lot. Darting a surreptitious glance in Tate's direction to check he still had his back to me, I managed to zip up my jacket to hide the worst of it, wiping the blood on my fingers onto the black trousers I wore. Tate didn't need to know about the injury. Not yet, anyway. There was still the driver of the tank not accounted for. And that was assuming it had only carried one person. The likelihood was that it had contained at least two.

"Is it done?" Tate still hadn't turned around as if he thought he might change his mind if he even so much as glanced at the soldier.

"Yeah, it's done." Relying heavily on my uninjured arm, I dragged the corpse into a bush so that it was at least partially obscured from view. It wouldn't fool anyone actively looking for it but at the very least it would buy us some time. A wave of weariness hit me, or maybe it was dizziness again. Buying time was all that we ever seemed to do. We were close, though. Only a few days away at most. I cleaned my blade on the grass before walking over to Tate, retrieving my bag on the way and ignoring the fact that as I heaved it onto my back the strap pressing on the wound was utter agony, like someone driving rusty nails into my flesh one after the other. I'd be okay. I had to be. Tate was relying on me. "Let's go."

22
TATE

Today had been the most difficult so far. It seemed like days since the events of this morning, rather than hours. Another day, another brush with death. If only I could actually be that flippant about it. There'd been a moment that morning when X had left me where making my legs move had seemed like the most difficult thing in the world. Even now, thinking back, I wasn't sure where I'd found the strength to follow X's instructions to the letter. But I had, stopping exactly where I'd been directed to, pausing for a moment to make sure the DTP had seen me before darting down a side street that took me out of sight, and more importantly out of the firing line. Arriving at the street we'd visited the day before, there'd been nothing to do but wait, my heart pounding so loudly in my ears that it was like being back under the waterfall. And all the time, there'd been a voice in my head screaming at me, demanding to know where X was, demanding to know why he wasn't there when he should have been.

Once the soldiers had appeared at the end of the street, I wouldn't have been capable of moving even if there'd been anywhere to go. X had wanted a dead end. He just hadn't shared the reason why or where he was going to be. Fear had stolen every one of my bodily functions away, and all I'd been able to think about was the fact that I was alone, my solid protector of the last week gone from my side when I needed him most. And for the second time I was on my knees, staring down the barrel of a gun and waiting for my life to end.

I'd been deadly serious when I'd told X that I'd prefer to be stabbed rather than vaporized. Nothing scared me more than the knowledge that with one flick of a finger I could cease to exist in less than a second. And then the scene in front of me had changed, soldiers falling to knives the same way they had back in the club when X had been a stranger. I knew what he was capable of now, but that didn't make it any less impressive. I dreaded to think just how much practice it had taken to hone his skills to that level of accuracy and precision. I should have gotten up, tried to hide somewhere and at least take myself out of the firing line. But I couldn't. Someone had replaced my once functioning limbs with a material that couldn't bear weight. By the time X had swooped down from the sky like some sort of avenging angel, there'd been a trail of corpses, X dispatching the last two with ease.

Things had blurred after that. I briefly remembered acting like an ungrateful wretch toward X, but I couldn't recall what I'd actually said. Whatever it was, X had brushed it off with his customary patience when it came to me. Talon had appeared out of nowhere, as had Psyche, some sort of conversation happening that hadn't made the slightest bit of sense—something about a break-in and then the dash out of the city. That would have been enough drama for one day, but oh no, being used as bait once in a day wasn't enough. I'd had to play the role for a second time, giving X the chance to lie in wait for whoever it was that had been following us, which had turned out to be yet another soldier, like they were coming out of the woodwork.

I'd regretted letting X remove the soldier's mask almost immediately. I'd expected a grizzled old man, not someone who looked like they'd barely started shaving. It made me wonder about the corpses we'd left back in Urstone. What if they were all kids? What if that was standard practice for DTP soldiers? Despite knowing that X was right, it had taken every ounce of willpower I possessed to walk away and let him do what he needed to do.

Deep down, I'd known that the soldier had to die, but that didn't make it any easier to be there, to be complicit in ending someone's life even if I wasn't the one wielding the blade. My whole body had been rigid as I'd stood and waited for something that would clue me in to the fact that the deed was done. I'd even had to blink back tears. I didn't even know what the tears were for, whether they were for the soldier or for myself. Was it guilt for not having tried harder to stop X? Or was it just the crushing realization that the DTP would forever be changed in my mind? They were human beings now rather than faceless monsters. People like X and me. They walked, talked, and probably shared jokes when they weren't following orders. If I could have rewound time and asked X not to remove the mask, I would have done so. Even after X had done it, I hadn't been able to look at the soldier's body. I didn't want to see that youthful face with all the life removed from it. That would have been the face that haunted my dreams. Therefore, I was a coward and I didn't look, letting X shoulder the burden.

We'd continued on our way as if nothing had happened, apart from X being even quieter than usual, his face pale and drawn. Did he think I was mad at him? That I resented him doing what I'd never have been capable of doing? I didn't know and I didn't ask, stewing in my own silence and wrestling with my own chaotic thoughts. When we'd stumbled on an abandoned cabin, I'd been grateful for the chance to stop for the night and try and gather myself, try and work out what was going on in my head. We were both tired, even X slowing considerably over the last couple of hours.

Of course, there was one glowing bit of euphoria from the

day hidden among the chaos: X had said he loved me. The words I wasn't sure he'd ever be able to say had actually spilled from his lips. I smiled as I recalled the moment, playing it over and over again in my mind. And I'd said it back. X's face had been a picture. It didn't take a genius to work out that he hadn't believed me. That was fine. I'd just need to repeat it again and again until the words finally sank into his skull. That could be my mission for the next couple of days, shower him with declarations of love and watch him grow more and more uncomfortable. Emotions were clearly something that X didn't have a lot of experience with. Well, tough. I was going to drown him in emotion until he either accepted it or stabbed me.

X had gotten a fire going but it was still in its infancy, barely casting enough light to see by. I switched my flashlight on, shining it around the one-room cabin until I located him. I'd expected to find him busy doing something, but he was leant against the wall, far too still. I'd put his earlier pallor down to our disagreement, maybe even a reluctance to kill someone so young. But pale didn't even begin to describe his current appearance. My heart began to pound as I kept the flashlight trained on him. His eyes were closed and he looked like death, his stance against the wall giving the idea that it was all that held him up. What was going on? Had I been so wrapped up in my own thoughts that I'd missed something crucial?

I made my way over to him, my heart beating so violently in my chest that my whole body trembled. He looked even worse close up, with dark shadows under his eyes and his brow beaded with sweat. His breathing was far more rapid than it should have been as well. Something definitely wasn't right. "X?"

His eyelashes flickered several times before he managed to lift his lids to reveal the familiar amber gaze. Only, where it was usually calm and steady, it was laced with pain. He attempted to smile, but it was labored, barely staying on his lips for a second.

"What's wrong?" I couldn't hide the note of panic in my voice.

X slowly lifted his arm, unfastening his jacket with a belabored movement that looked far from natural. Confusion knitted my brow as he pulled one edge of his jacket back to expose the opposite shoulder. I stared at it, trying to work out what I was seeing. The material from neck to waist was darker than it should have been, a long tear in the material where there hadn't been one that morning. I knew there hadn't been one because we'd donned the new clothes provided by Talon. The tear was large enough for me to be able to see the skin stained red beneath it.

"Fuck!" I laid trembling fingers on his chest, my fingers coming away red from the damp material. I couldn't make sense of it. How? When? Why hadn't he said anything? I'd put him being quiet down to him being… well, him being X, really? But I should have known there was something more. Only I'd been too busy wallowing in my own self-pity. Oh yeah, poor Tate had to let someone else kill a soldier while he looked away like a Victorian damsel in distress. Well, poor Tate needed to toughen the fuck up and be a bit less blind. I shook my head, struggling for words before finally managing to force a single one out. "When?"

X grimaced. "The soldier. I didn't even know they carried knives. They don't usually. He knew I was lying in wait… bastard."

I took a long, slow breath, trying to tamp down on the nausea threatening to bubble up. That had been hours ago. "Why didn't you say anything? We've walked for miles since then. I could have helped. I could have…" I sought around for something I could have done that might have been remotely useful. "… at least carried your damn bag." My fingers hovered over the wound without touching. "You must have been in so much pain. We should have stopped earlier. We should have…" I didn't even know what we should have done so I left the sentence unfinished, frustrated by my own uselessness.

X leaned his head back against the wall and closed his eyes again, cold panic starting to claw its way up my throat. How bad was he? How much blood had he lost? What if he died and I was left alone? It wasn't just a fear of being unable to survive, though. In a few short days he'd become a part of me, wrapping his way inexorably around my heart, my words of love completely truthful. I couldn't manage without him, practically or emotionally, and it wasn't the practicalities making me feel like I had an army of ants marching across my skin.

I took a deep, steadying breath, my eyes fixed on X's face. Was he breathing too fast, or was that my imagination? "Right!" The word sounded far too loud within the confines of the cabin. X's eyes drifted open again, the amber depths clouded with… what? Pain? Knowledge of the probable outcome? Something else? "You're a stupid bastard. Do you know that?"

This time he managed a smile, lifting his uninjured arm to brush gentle fingers across my cheekbone. "For what? Getting stabbed? Sorry. Wasn't intentional."

I grabbed hold of his wrist and used the grip to pull him away from the wall and over toward the fire which had finally decided to start burning with a little more gusto. The stupid idiot had spent the last thirty minutes sorting that out as well when he should have made me do it. I pushed X down into a seated position, staring at him for a moment as I geared myself up to sound like I knew what I was doing. "Okay. What do we need? Hot water. Some sort of fabric." The fabric was easy. I got a spare T-shirt out of my bag and set about tearing it into strips. Hot water was a bit more of a challenge. I had water and I had fire, but finding something clean to boil the water in was the problem. After virtually ripping a cupboard at the back of the cabin apart, I finally unearthed a pan. I said a silent thanks to whoever was in charge of leaving cookware in deserted cupboards. Hurrying back over to X, I filled it with bottled water, managing to find a way of balancing it precariously over the flames. "How much blood do you think you've lost?"

"A lot."

I didn't know what was more worrying, the fact that he wasn't even trying to downplay his injuries or the way he was slumped against the wall as if even sitting upright was too much effort. X must have been operating on the last reserves of his energy for hours to deteriorate so rapidly. What did I need to do next? I guessed that I needed to take a proper look and find out what I was actually dealing with. Not that I had any experience to compare it to. Nursing had never exactly loomed large in my life. It would have been nice to start with something minor like a small burn before moving on to knife wounds. But I was all X had, so I needed to learn fast.

Pulling him forward away from the wall, I leaned him against me while I carefully removed his jacket, tackling his good arm first before starting the much slower and more laborious job of managing to extricate it from his other arm without hurting him. Even with me being careful, he went rigid as I eased it over the injured shoulder and peeled it down his arm until he was free of it. There was no way I was going to be able to get his T-shirt off the same way though. It was tighter and would mean lifting his arm. "I need to use your knife." I didn't wait for permission, reaching down and easing it out of the sheathe it rested in. I held my breath as I sliced the fabric down the middle with the sharp blade, staying well away from his shoulder. "He just stabbed you once, right?"

"Yeah. *Just* the once."

"You know what I meant. I wanted to check there weren't any other wounds you were keeping secret."

"You're always mad at me."

It felt better when X was talking. "Not really. It's just a coping mechanism."

"I know. I don't mind."

I'd managed to separate the material into two halves. From

there it was much easier to remove it altogether in a similar way as I had the jacket, X's clammy skin pressed against me as I supported his weight again. I sucked in a breath at the sight that met me. The whole right-hand side of his chest was covered in blood, most of it dried, but some of it fresh, which meant the wound was still bleeding and would continue to bleed unless I did something to stop it. The positive was that it was his shoulder which meant we weren't dealing with any major organs. What would they do in a hospital? Stitch it, I guessed. But we weren't in a hospital. We were in a shitty cabin in the middle of nowhere with zero medical supplies.

I wanted to hit something and rail against the world for putting yet another obstacle in our way. I ran my fingers through my hair, the action not helping one little bit. This was hopeless. Except… I raised my head, the beginnings of a smile on my lips as I remembered the items I'd taken from Jim's bunker, thinking that they might be useful, with a heavy emphasis on the might. One of them had been needle and thread. At the time, I'd thought I might need to repair clothes, not skin. But it was the same concept, right? Picking up one of the strips of material, I folded it into a pad, ignoring X's hiss of pain as I pressed it to his shoulder. "Yes, I know it hurts. But the wound's still bleeding so we need to try and slow it down. Can you hold it in place?" X shifted position so that he could bring his opposite hand across his chest in order to do so. "Press hard."

"Fuck off."

I grinned at the insult, reassured by the fact that he still had some bite in him. "I'm just waiting for the water to heat up, and then I'll clean you up and we'll get you sorted." I was impressed by how confident I managed to sound when I was anything but.

While I waited, I couldn't stop myself from sliding my fingers across the space to interlock them with X's. He gave them a gentle squeeze, even though it must have hurt him to do so with that arm. "You know… when I commented on you not having any scars, I didn't expect you to go out and get one for me."

X made a sound reminiscent of a snort. "Still upset that I killed him?"

"No." I was surprised to realize it was the truth. "If I knew that he'd stabbed you, I probably would have done it myself." Amber eyes fastened on mine as if he was searching for the truth in my statement, prompting me to elaborate. "Honestly, I would have. It would have made me so angry. I am angry. Can we reanimate him so that I can kill him myself?"

"I'll save the next one for you."

"The next one that stabs you?"

"Not planning on anyone else doing it."

"Good." I reluctantly disentangled my fingers from X's as the water in the pan started to bubble. Luckily, it had a wooden handle so I could extract it from the fire without adding another injury to the list. Dipping a strip of fabric in the water, I began the task of cleaning him up, starting at his waist where the blood was dried into his skin. It was strangely satisfying to unearth clean, unblemished skin, the muscles rippling beneath my fingertips. I worked silently, only stopping now and again to swap the fabric for a new piece. X's eyes had closed again. "You're still with me, right?"

"Still with you."

"Talk to me."

"About what?"

"Anything you want."

"We nearly met once. Before, I mean."

My fingers stilled. "What? When?"

"Remember when you were mugged?"

Of course, I did. I remembered it in vivid technicolor, the man appearing out of nowhere to demand my money when I'd been on my way home from work. I'd frozen in complete fear, unsure whether I was supposed to give in to his demands, try to run, or some third option that my brain hadn't even been able to come up with. There was so little petty crime in Cofield with the sentence still being death that I'd never had any reason to plan for such an eventuality. And then a door had opened close by and the man had heard the noise and run away, disappearing as quickly as he'd appeared in the first place. "How close were you?"

"Close."

"Did you kill him?"

The silence and lack of a denial answered the question without X even having to speak. I wondered how many other people had met a premature end simply for wronging me in some way. That was two so far, my would-be-mugger and Niles. If I dug deeper would there be more people? Maybe the man who'd sworn at me once for getting in his way? And despite what X had said, I still wasn't completely convinced that Niles hadn't seen something in my eyes and misread it. That he hadn't been trying to provide something he sensed I craved. But I didn't want real violence. I never had. I just needed the threat of it, someone who would make me believe that he could always go further. Only X had been able to deliver that, which was what made him the perfect man for me.

First though, I needed to keep him alive long enough to convince him of that fact. I pulled his hand away to clean the skin directly around the wound. The trickle of blood had slowed but not stopped, which meant I was going to have to stitch it. I cleaned it as best I could, doing my best to ignore X's sharp intake of breath every time I caused him pain, telling myself it was necessary. Once it was clean, I could see the wound better, enough to tell that it was bigger than I'd initially thought, more of a ragged circle than an incision.

"He twisted it."

Yeah, that would explain it. "I'm going to have to stitch it."

"With what?"

"Ah!" I scooted over to my bag, locating the needle and thread I'd stashed there and pulling it out with a flourish. "Well, that would be courtesy of our friend, Jim. I may have helped myself to a few things from his collection of junk."

"And how many wounds have you stitched?"

"Oh, you know, loads. That's how I spent most of my evenings."

"Funny how I always missed that."

"Yeah, you should be more observant. Take your stalking a bit more seriously."

I threaded the needle I'd already sterilized with hands shaking so badly that it was quite a trial. I tried to tell myself that it was just like mending a hole in fabric. Only fabric couldn't move or scream, or beg me to stop. This was X though. He was stalwart to the extreme. I doubted he was capable of begging. I knelt in front of him. "This is going to hurt, but I need you to keep as still as you can. I'll try and do it as quickly as I can."

"Your hands are shaking."

Yeah, thanks for pointing that out, X. That really helps. "All the best doctors shake. It's how you know they care."

X looked less than convinced. "As I'm guessing there's no anesthetic, give me something to hold on to."

That was a good idea. One I should probably have thought of myself. I scanned the surrounding area for inspiration, my gaze falling on the knife I'd used to remove his T-shirt. I lifted the handle and pushed it into his hand. "Here. Hold this. You can think about how much you love it. Just don't stab me with it when I hurt you."

I was fully aware that the type of needle I had wasn't designed for skin, but it was all I had so it would have to do. The next ten minutes were intense as I blocked out every telltale wince and groan from X as I concentrated on what needed to be done. By the time I'd finished and the wound was closed, it was a toss-up who was sweating more, myself or X. I didn't think I could have felt more exhausted if I'd just run a marathon, but the main thing was that the stitches seemed to be holding. I'd quadrupled the cotton thread trying to get a strength comparative to suture thread. "Bet you didn't know I was such a good nurse?"

X let out a shaky breath. "Shame you don't carry any anesthetic around with you."

I wet the cloth again, wiping around the now closed wound to clean the last vestiges of dried blood away. "You can't have everything. Besides, I thought someone like you wouldn't want to bother with something as petty as anesthetic. It won't do your street cred any good if it gets around that you not only don't have impervious skin but you need pain relief."

X managed a wan smile, his eyes closing seconds later. I studied him. As well as the sweat beading his brow, he was still incredibly pale. I wasn't fooling myself that he was anywhere close to being out of the woods yet. There was still the small matter of blood loss, the water in the pan I'd used to sponge it away mocking me with its sheer redness. And then there was the likelihood of infection. There were a hundred things that still could go wrong. I needed to dress the wound and then… then what? I was flailing around in the dark. There was no pretending I wasn't, no matter how confident I made myself out to be. "X?"

He answered without opening his eyes. "Yeah?"

"How are you feeling?" It was a stupid question, but I asked it anyway.

"Like crap."

I'd hoped he might lie. "So, erm… blood loss. You got any idea how that's normally treated?"

There was a long pause as if X were searching for the information somewhere in the recesses of his mind. "Water. My fluids are low. My heart's beating too fast."

I couldn't help myself. "That's probably just because I'm close to you." X made a sound, half snort, half something else. "What else?"

"Food. Rest." His eyes opened to slits. "The last one isn't possible, but the others."

"Shhh…" I lay my finger over his lips. "We'll talk about that later. Just… don't… die. I need you. I can't find this supposed safe place without you, so you have to be alright so that I can be too." It sounded dreadfully selfish when I put it like that, but I knew that thinking about me would be a better incentive than trying to get X to think about himself.

X reached out and grabbed my hand, the expression on his face strangely intense. "Just head north. It's only two days from here according to the map. Take them, and my knives. Keep to the same pace that we've been traveling at. Make sure—"

I couldn't listen to any more. The picture X was painting was way too upsetting. Did he really think he might…? I tugged my hand from his. "Alright, Mr. Drama. Enough." I busied myself with grabbing a bottle of water, refusing to even look at him until I was back by his side. I removed the cap of the bottle before curling the fingers of his good hand around it. "Drink all of that."

"Tate?" There was an urgency to his tone.

I shook my head, shushing him for the second time. "Don't! I don't want to hear it. Just… concentrate on resting. Think about how you can avoid the pointy bit of the knife next time."

His stare was heavy, laden with things he obviously wanted to say, but I pretended not to notice, and he eventually gave up. I needed to believe that everything was going to be alright, or else the urge to just curl up and die would become too strong. "Right! Food next. With me in charge, you're going to have a real treat coming up." The brittleness in my forced cheery tone wouldn't have fooled anyone, including myself. But even so, I kept it up, prattling about nothing as I prepared a makeshift meal of pasta and sauce, throwing some canned vegetables in for good measure as if extra vitamins could magically cure a knife wound.

Maneuvering X away from the fire and into the sleeping bag took quite some effort. It was scary just how weak he was. I had no idea how he'd managed to keep going for as long as he had. It must have been nothing short of sheer bloody-minded determination. Once he was securely tucked in, I curled my body around his, wrapping my arm around his waist while being careful not to knock his shoulder. After we'd eaten, I'd dressed it as best as I could without access to bandages, a safety pin or any medical knowledge that wasn't gleaned from films.

I couldn't stop myself from overanalyzing every tiny thing that I could take as a positive. He'd remained conscious. He'd eaten all the food. The wound wasn't bleeding any more. But even as I did so, I couldn't quite silence the voice of dissent which reminded me about his irregular breathing, his pallor, and the muscle tremors he couldn't manage to hide. Never mind the fact that he could barely sit up without help. Tightening my arm around his waist, I buried my face in the short hair at the nape of his neck. "Tell me about this place we're going to."

X sounded sleepy but he still answered. "It's an underground city. Everything's below ground."

I trailed my fingers down his arm. "And why is it safe from the DTP? I don't understand."

"Years ago, they tried to stamp their presence on it but it's all twisting tunnels and narrow corridors. It didn't end well for them when they tried to regulate it. They were sitting ducks, so they withdrew and announced it as a lawless no-go zone. They've left it alone ever since."

"And what's it like down there?"

"I have no idea."

Of course he didn't. It wasn't like he'd been there. Everything he'd just told me was hearsay. "I guess we'll find out."

"Tate?"

"No." I knew what he was going to say, and I still wasn't having any of it. "*We* will find out. No arguing. Not tonight.

Go to sleep, X. You need it so that your body will heal."

I waited until I was sure he was asleep before reluctantly extricating myself from him. Tucking the sleeping bag more firmly around him, I took up a cross-legged sentry position next to him. There was no way I could try and sleep. What if he stopped breathing? What if I went to sleep only to wake up next to a corpse? Even knowing that there was very little I'd be able to do if his condition took a turn for the worse didn't change my mind. If it happened, I at least wanted to know about it, wanted to be there with him so he wasn't alone. Tears pricked at my eyes and I made an effort to pull myself together, to man up. He'd watched over me for years. I could manage it for one night without falling to pieces.

I sat like that for hours, just watching the rise and fall of his chest, every breath a victory in my mind. Sometimes I held his hand. Sometimes I checked the wound, making sure there was nothing seeping through the makeshift bandage. Throughout it all, he continued to sleep soundly. I told myself that that was good, that it meant he was sleeping deeply, ignoring the voice that reminded me how unusual that was for him. He was one of those people who usually stirred at the slightest noise, ready to fend off attackers.

By the time the first rays of light started to make themselves known through the grimy window of the cabin, my eyes were aching and hot from the effort of staying awake. Yet, I still didn't take my eyes off him.

23
X

Fingers squeezed mine as I struggled to fight my way through the quagmire holding me back from consciousness. I didn't know why it was so difficult, until I tried to shift position and a red-hot poker lanced my shoulder, bringing it all back to

me in a rush. The soldier sinking his blade into me, the struggle to keep going until we found shelter, the overwhelming exhaustion that had enveloped my body once we'd reached the cabin, meaning I couldn't keep it a secret from Tate any longer, and the fear on his face when he'd seen the wound.

But after the initial shock, I'd seen a different Tate, one determined to take charge despite being completely out of his depth. He'd produced needle and cotton from nowhere to stitch the wound as if he were a magician, and then he'd fed me and tucked me in as well.

I opened my eyes to find him watching me. I studied his face, noting the dark circles under his eyes and the fact that they were bloodshot. "Did you sleep at all?"

He hesitated as if considering a lie before shaking his head. "I wanted to keep an eye on you. How are you feeling?"

How was I feeling? Tate hadn't been the only one concerned that I might not make it through the night. I'd known myself that it was a distinct possibility. So—alive was the first thing that came to mind. My shoulder hurt like hell if I tried to move it, but apart from that, and apart from having little to no strength, I felt better. "I'm okay. We should…" I made an attempt to lever myself to a sitting position, a wave of dizziness forcing me back almost instantaneously.

Tate's look was full of disapproval as if I was a particularly ornery patient, his words clipped. "We're not going anywhere today. Maybe tomorrow. We'll see how you are then."

I didn't mince my words. "We can't stay here. We're too close to Urstone, too close to the corpse of the fucker who stabbed me as well. You should go!"

Tate stared at me incredulously for a few moments before breaking into loud laughter. "On my own! Right, like that's going to happen. Like I'm just going to walk out of here and leave you here with no one to look after you. No, that's not going to happen. *We're* staying." His chin lifted mutinously. "And that's final. You won't get me to change my mind either, so don't start with that head north crap again. We both know I'd manage to get lost. Besides, I don't even know how to recognize an underground city when it's *underground* and you presumably can't see it. We'll take our chances here until you're well enough to make the journey, whether that's tomorrow, the next day, or next week."

The light in his blue eyes dared me to argue with him. How had I gone from barely conversing with anyone to being told what to do? Love—that's how. Despite my protestations to the contrary, I'd always known it was a powerful force. It just wasn't one I'd ever expected to be reciprocated. But even if I hadn't quite been able to believe Tate's words the day before, all his actions had backed them up. He'd looked after me, even going so far as to keep an all-night vigil. And it wasn't just because he was too scared to go it alone. If that was the case, he'd be trying harder to get me up and moving, not insisting that we stay here as long as we needed to. I sank back onto the makeshift pillow. "Tomorrow. We leave tomorrow."

Tate's mouth firmed into a straight line. "We'll see." But then his eyes softened. "What do you need? You have me at your beck and call today."

"Breakfast."

He nodded.

"A kiss."

His lips curled into a smile which was the exact reaction I'd been aiming for. "Oh, you're that sort of patient, are you?" He wasted no time in leaning across to drop a lingering kiss on my lips. He didn't pull away, instead shifting slightly to brush another kiss across my cheek before doing the same to my forehead, the skin tingling wherever he touched.

His fingers rested on my neck, gently stroking the skin there. It was such a shame to ruin the moment. Lord knows that tender moments in my life had been pretty non-existent up to this point, but the pressure in my bladder was reaching a point that was impossible to ignore. "And something to piss in."

Tate snorted but shuffled backwards across the floor, returning with an empty plastic water bottle a few seconds later. "That's good, right? That you have to go… means your body is working as it should and that there's enough fluid in it." He stared intently at me, the look reminiscent of a proud father about to watch his infant son use the potty for the very first time. I paused with my hand midway to my crotch. "Are you just going to watch?"

Tate did a double-take, a rosy blush appearing on his cheeks as his lips twitched into a smile. "Sorry. I guess I got carried away with the whole nursing thing there. I'll get breakfast sorted. Although…" The smile was replaced by a distinctively seductive gleam to his eyes. "I'll be back to give you another bed bath later." His gaze dropped to below my waist. "We should probably do everything this time, though."

If I hadn't already known how shitty I felt, the fact that my dick didn't so much as twitch at the thought of Tate's hands all over me confirmed it. How much blood had I lost? How close had I come to deserting Tate when he needed me the most? In retrospect, keeping the stab wound a secret had been a terrible idea. If we hadn't stumbled across the cabin I probably would have blacked out in the middle of nowhere, saddling Tate with an impossible dilemma. I guess I'd learned an important lesson, that I wasn't invincible and that my blood ran just as freely as anyone else's did when I was on the opposite side of the blade. If the wound had been a little lower, it would have been lights out for me.

Relieving myself quickly, I fastened the lid on the bottle and put up with the pain in my shoulder required to place it out of arm's reach. Tate hummed to himself as he opened up two cans and dumped them into another saucepan he'd found. I wished I could share his optimism that staying put for the day wasn't one hell of a risk. If we were discovered… I struggled to try and remember how obtrusive the cabin had been, but by that time everything had been a blur, and the fight to just keep putting one foot in front of another instead of keeling over had taken all of my energy. I couldn't even remember collecting the wood for the fire, never mind lighting it. There'd been a gray area between arriving at the cabin and Tate finding me leaned against the wall. "We need more branches for the fire."

Tate nodded without turning. "I'll get some after we've had breakfast. It'll stay alight until then."

I nodded even though he couldn't see. "You need to sleep today."

He glanced back over his shoulder and gave me a saucy wink. "Yes, sir. Anything else, sir? Need your pillows fluffing, sir?"

I lifted my head from the T-shirt stuffed with rolled up clothing which constituted a pillow. "If I had a pillow, then yes, I probably would need that."

I was awake at dawn the following day, Tate still fast asleep beside me. Our location had remained secret with no one stumbling across it. Most of the DTP's intel seemed to be based around predicting where we would go next, which led me to assume that they knew we were heading to Maimos. I guessed it didn't exactly take a genius to work out that our aim would be to reach a place beyond their jurisdiction.

Given that they were unaware of my injury, they'd have calculated that we'd be long gone from this area, so staying put might even have even worked in our favor. Until we reached Maimos that was, and we found the units there waiting for us. They knew as well as I did that once we were underground, there was no getting to us. I hadn't shared the theory about them lying in wait with Tate. There was no point in worrying him until I needed to.

He'd managed to grab a couple of hours sleep in the afternoon while I'd kept watch. Although, what I would have done had the DTP walked in, with only one functional arm and an untested ability to stand, I had no idea. It was completely alien to feel like I couldn't defend myself. I didn't like it one little bit.

We'd spent the majority of the day talking, or should I say I'd listened while Tate had told me lots of things I'd already known about people whose deep, dark secrets I was already fully aware of. I hadn't given a fuck. Watching Tate be animated was a medicine all of its very own.

We'd taken a huge risk by not keeping watch during the night, but Tate couldn't spend two nights awake, and I wasn't stupid enough to think that my body didn't need the rest to recover. There hadn't been a workable solution, and both of us had known that.

Tate had taken to sleeping with his arms and legs wrapped around me, so it took a bit of work to untangle myself before I gingerly eased myself upright. So far so good. I couldn't say that my shoulder was fine, but at least it was more of a dull throb rather than the white-hot agony of the day before. Gritting my teeth, I managed to heave myself to a standing position, glad that Tate wasn't awake to witness how much effort it took.

I leaned against the wall, working through a wave of dizziness and nausea. After several deep breaths, it eased enough for me to convince myself that it was more a reaction to twenty-four hours of being horizontal than anything else. The weakness though, the way my limbs felt like jelly, that was all down to the blood loss. But I wasn't going to give in to it.

Tate stirred as I made my way over to the pile of clothing strewn around the cabin floor. "What are you doing?"

I reached down, tugging a T-shirt off the floor and managing to ease it over my sore shoulder, the slow, deliberate effort taking far longer than it should have. "Getting dressed."

"Why?"

"Because like I said yesterday, we're leaving today."

Tate went from drowsy to fully conscious in the blink of an eye, sitting bolt upright to stare at me aghast. "We can't. You need to rest. Regain your strength a bit more."

"I did rest. I am rested."

"You can barely move."

"I can walk." The statement was true. But how fast was another matter entirely.

"X." Tate was on his feet now and making his way toward me, my dick twitching at the sight of him in only his underwear. Yesterday, my libido had been dead and buried and the funeral had already taken place, so life being breathed back into my cock had to be a good sign. Tate halted in front of me, tipping his head back so he could look me in the eye. "What if you collapse and we're in the middle of nowhere? What if…" He gestured at my shoulder. "… the wound opens up and you start bleeding again? What if we run into the DTP? You're hardly in death-defying-leap-from-roofs-and-stab-them-all form."

"I'll be fine."

He arched his eyebrow, managing to drip condescension with just that one gesture. "Like you were fine when you didn't bother telling me you'd been stabbed in the first place, and you almost died." Tate's voice cracked on the last word, but he simply raised his chin higher as if he was refusing to register his own distress.

I played my ace card. "There's two options. Either you leave on your own today. Or we both do." I put just enough steel into my words to let him know I was serious. I didn't like having to do it, not to Tate, but it was necessary.

A variety of emotions flickered across Tate's face as he visibly struggled with the ultimatum. "You can't force me to leave."

"Watch me."

He held my gaze for a few moments before looking away. "I guess you're the one who knows what you're capable of."

"Exactly."

"We eat first. You can't be missing meals in your condition."

I nodded. I could give him that much. "You cook. I'll pack."

Despite Tate's acquiescence, I could feel his gaze on me as I moved gingerly around the cabin, collecting up items one-handed to shove in either Tate's bag or my own. Neat packing and organization wasn't a priority for people on the run who'd already stayed in one place for too long. Tate lasted about a minute before he broke the silence.

"Any fever?"

I answered without looking his way. "No."

"Sickness?"

I turned to face him. "There's no infection, if that's what you're getting at."

He spooned some beans angrily into a pan. "Yet!"

"Tate…" I walked over to him and squatted down beside him so that we were both on the same level. "I've noted all your objections about leaving, but there's too many reasons against staying, infection being one of them. If it does set in, its likely to be a couple of days from now. If we leave today, we can be safely underground before then. If we hang around, then there's a chance of my physical condition deteriorating."

He thought about my words for a moment before letting out a long drawn out sigh. "Will they have antibiotics at this place where we're going?"

I didn't have a fucking clue. I knew nothing about it besides it being a place out of the DTP's reach. God knows what stage of civilization they were at. But that paled into insignificance next to being alive. "Sure."

Tate went back to cooking breakfast, seemingly mollified.

We left an hour later, Tate still not convinced we were doing the right thing.

I pulled Tate behind the wall of the building, which looked like it had once been a palatial house before a bomb had reduced it to rubble many years back. The only reason I could tell was from the elaborate archway that still stood, the swirls and curls of the architecture looking incongruous next to the desolate terrain. It had taken us three days to get here. It should have been two, had the fast pace of earlier days been possible, but blood loss and weakness had gotten the better of me. I'd regained more movement in my shoulder, and there was still no sign of infection so all in all, things could have been worse.

Until now that was. My theory about the DTP lying in wait for us had just been proved to be true. It was easy to tell where the entrance to the underground city lay, signposted as it was by the swarms of DTP soldiers milling around it. From what I could see there were three units, the most we'd come across so far. Two of them had probably been stationed here ever since the first day we'd left Cofield just in case all else failed.

"It's not fair!" Tate had his eyes screwed tightly shut as if he could eradicate the image of the soldiers from his mind simply by not looking. "We've come all this way, gone through so fucking much, and they're right there, X. Fucking bastards! Do I really matter that much to them? Do you? I didn't even do anything. How is that fucking justice?" He opened his eyes again, pain reflected in the blue depths of his stare. "I can't stop thinking about how many other executions they carried out, that I *saw* carried out… how many of those people were innocent just like me?"

I could mollycoddle him, or I could give him the pure unadulterated truth. I went for the latter. "Probably more than you think. The system was never set up to provide justice. Not really. It's population control and a deterrent all rolled into one. It always has been for as long as I can remember. Sure, they might kill a few criminals while they're at it, but do you seriously think they can't frame whoever they want to?"

Tate exhaled slowly. "Fuck! I'm so naïve. I used to believe the crap they spouted. I used to think they made it a better world to live in. Yes, it was harsh, but…" He trailed off, shaking his head before releasing a humorless laugh. "I guess it took finding myself on the wrong side of it to recognize the truth. How stupid am I?"

It was a rhetorical question, so I didn't bother to answer. He'd had his eyes well and truly opened to the truth about the world we both lived in. He didn't need me hammering it in. "You're no different to most people."

"But not you."

I shrugged, regretting it when my shoulder gave the now familiar twinge. "I see more than most."

Tate gave a wry smile. "You certainly do. There's only one X, that's for sure." I was still trying to work out whether that was a compliment when he changed tack. "So, what do we do?" He was silent for a moment but then his eyes sparked with a sudden light, his voice rising in pitch. "We can go back to the cabin and shelter there. They can't stay here forever. We wait them out and then we come back once the coast is clear."

Even as I shook my head, I admired his ability to think that things could ever be that easy. "Think of all the units they have. All they need to do is keep swapping them out. We've become the splinter in their finger, the one they're determined to eradicate no matter how deep they have to dig. I've killed a number of their men." I thought back over the journey we'd endured. "So many I've lost count."

"Twelve." Tate delivered the number flatly. At least one of us had been counting. "Three in the club, eight in Urstone, and one in the forest."

I nodded, figuring that he was probably right. Not that I gave a fuck. I'd kill double that number if it bought us our freedom, or whatever amounted to freedom these days.

Tate rubbed at his eyes with the heel of his hand, lines of fatigue clearly discernible on his face. "So… if we can't go back to the cabin and we can't make ourselves invisible, what are we going to do?"

I didn't know. That was the fucking problem. One I'd been wrestling with ever since predicting this exact outcome days ago. "I'm thinking."

"I could be bait again. Lead them away to…" Tate's voice faltered as we both surveyed the surrounding area. We were hidden behind the only cover there was between ourselves and the soldiers. All that stood between us and them was one stubborn wall which had refused to fall when the bombs hit, and an archway determined to look as fancy as fuck for the whole of eternity, or until it eventually crumbled. The only reason we'd gotten this far without being seen was the blind spot it had provided during our approach.

"If anyone's going to be bait this time, it's me." The plan had merit. All I needed to do was draw enough of them away so that Tate could gain access to the underground city. Then they could do whatever they wanted to me—vaporize me, torture me, I didn't give a fuck as long as Tate was safe. I suspected that after murdering twelve of their comrades, torture would be high on their list.

Tate's hand shot out, grabbing hold of the lapel of my jacket and dragging me forwards until we were nose to nose. His voice was low with intent when he spoke. "If you even think about doing that, let me tell you what will happen. I'll just walk up to them and give myself up. There's not going to be any self-sacrificing bullshit going on. Let's get that clear. Either both of us are getting in that damn city, or neither of us are. Are we clear?" He gave me a little shake to punctuate his point, his expression fierce.

"Ow! Shoulder."

He scowled at me. "The same shoulder that you've spent days telling me is absolutely fine. The same shoulder that you wanted to carry your own bag on yesterday."

I had, but it hadn't done the slightest bit of good. Tate had been determined to treat me like an invalid, and at least it had given him something else to think about besides the DTP. Also, if I was a hundred percent truthful, it had been nice. I wasn't used to anyone showing concern for me so I'd let him, to an extent. "Relapse."

He gave me a gentle shove, his face clouding over seconds later as reality hit home. "Tell me you've got some other sort of plan besides sacrificing yourself, X?"

"Let me think."

Tate nodded and went quiet, chewing on his lip as if doing as I'd asked required great effort on his part. I closed my eyes and tried to picture the scenario. The only way to gain access to the city was to draw their attention elsewhere. Only that required not being there when they went to investigate, which could only be done using some sort of timed apparatus, which we didn't have. Except… "Turn around."

Tate raised an eyebrow but did as I asked, although as usual his tongue had a mind of its own. "If this is a farewell fuck then I'm not exactly averse, but I'm not sure this is the best place."

I untied the backpack he wore on his back, extracting what I needed before retying it and spinning Tate back to face me. His eyes widened as his gaze fell on what I held in my hand. Then his brow furrowed. "We sold those to Talon."

I held up two grenades and a small amount of plastic explosive. "I took some back. Her prices were extremely overinflated."

Tate's eyebrows almost met in the middle as he worked through the series of steps needed to bring him to the right conclusion. "So that's why you went out that night in Urstone? That's what she was referring to the next day when you were having your little coded conversation when I was too busy trying to get over almost being executed for the second time?"

I didn't respond, too busy running several different scenarios through and only voicing one aloud, despite Tate's obvious impatience, when I found one that could work. "I start a fire. Even if they do notice it, I doubt they're going to deem it important enough to investigate. The fire's going to spread though, to this." I held up the plastic explosive. "The fire will work as a primitive timer so that by the time it explodes, I'm already going to be back here. They're not going to be able to ignore an explosion. They'll have to send units."

"How many?"

Tate had asked the key question. My guess would be two, which would still leave one guarding the entrance with no rooftops to drop from, no way of gaining the element of surprise. I'd be facing eight armed men with a shoulder nowhere near its prime. But I didn't see any other option. "I don't know."

"If it's not enough, maybe then I might need to be bait?"

"Maybe. We're going to have to play it by ear."

Tate nodded, and it was all I could do to resist wiping away the deep furrows on his forehead. I reached into my pocket, closing my fingers around the piece of metal I'd been planning on returning to him for days. There just hadn't been quite the right moment. But given what we were facing, it could be now or never. I pulled it out, placing it in the center of my palm before holding it out to him.

He stared at if for a moment as if he wasn't sure what it was that he was looking at. Finally, he raised his gaze to mine. "Are you proposing?"

The question hit me like a tidal wave, my tongue suddenly unable to curl itself into any shape where it was capable of making words. It took several attempts before I could spit one word out. "No!" Was I? "It's your—"

Tate's face creased into an expression of extreme mirth. "Your face! I know what it is, you idiot. I guess you helped yourself to more than the explosives when you paid Talon a midnight visit, the poor woman. But"—he waggled his eyebrows— "you need to be careful offering rings to men. They could take it completely the wrong way, and the next thing you know you're married." He plucked the ring from my palm, slipping it into his pocket. "It's a yes by the way."

"What? I didn't…" I decided to concentrate on the part of the conversation that didn't make my head spin. "Talon didn't care, not once I'd paid her in DTP blood."

Tate's knowing smirk said he was well aware of what I was doing, but he didn't push it. "Well, some people are strange, and I have a feeling that Urstone had more than its fair share. So…" His expression turned serious. "I just want to check I've got this right. You're going to leave me here while you go and set up your little explosion, but you'll be back before it goes off."

"I should be."

Tate winced at my use of the word "should." "I could come with you?"

I shook my head. "No. There's less risk if you stay here as long as you keep out of sight. Just… wait."

He nodded but reached out to grab hold of my sleeve as I went to turn away. "X?"

"What?"

"Thank you... for the ring. I know that's the reason you broke into Talon's house, that the explosives were just a while you were there thing. And I appreciate it, really, I do. And..." A slow smile spread across his face. "I know you weren't proposing. I just... I guess I like to see you uncomfortable. I'm not expecting you to marry me, not ever, even if we're still together in twenty years' time."

Twenty years! Tate knew exactly how to steal my breath away. I'd lived most of my life barely planning twenty minutes into the future, and he glibly threw out twenty years as if it were nothing. I shut him up the best way I knew how, crowding him back against the wall and pressing my lips to his. The kiss was long and slow, Tate winding his arms around my neck to press our bodies closer together. We were both breathing hard by the time I finally pulled away, Tate's cheeks sporting a rosy blush that made me want to push him down on the ground and make up for the last few days, where the pain in my shoulder and Tate's concern about hurting me had meant that we'd done nothing but sleep. Stupid, really, when there was absolutely nothing wrong with my other arm. The lost hand jobs I could have given him were a damn shame.

I backed away, keeping my gaze on him for as long as I could until I was forced to turn around. The wooded area I needed was a good ten minutes away. As I jogged the distance, I ran the logistics through in my head. Ten minutes meant I needed to allow at least that much time for the fire to reach the explosive. The problem was that I was far from an expert on how fast fires spread. Knives had always been my thing, not pyromania.

Reaching my destination, I cleared a space and set the explosive, the fuse ready to catch once the fire had gotten close enough. Had I made the right decision to leave Tate where he was? At the time it had seemed the sensible thing to do. But what if they did a patrol while I was gone? What if they stumbled across him and I returned to find he wasn't there? I worked faster, all the what ifs causing my fingers to be slightly less steady than I needed them to be.

Working backwards from the C4, I set a trail of branches and leaves, ensuring it was wide enough that the fire wouldn't go out. When I ran out of loose branches, I hacked them from the trees above, the action vibrating through my injured shoulder and making my teeth clench.

Ten minutes.

The words kept going through my head, but they may as well have been words from another language because I couldn't get them to fit the concept I was trying to create. Tate probably thought I knew exactly how long the trail of branches needed to be. But then he was trusting in that way, too ready to have blind faith and see the good in everyone, and I wouldn't change that character trait for the world. After all, it had worked in my favor: he was certainly viewing me through rose-tinted glasses. *Twenty years!* They were just words though. It didn't mean he believed it.

I stood back to survey the snaking trail I'd made, scraping wayward leaves away with the side of my foot where it looked as if the fire might head in a direction other than where I wanted it to go. Short of chopping a tree down, I'd used up all the available materials so it would have to do. Crouching down, I extracted the lighter from my pocket and held it to a patch of dried leaves until I was satisfied that it had caught fully. There was nothing else I could do but hope that it went to plan and created as much of a disturbance as we needed. The rest was down to luck.

Walking backwards, I watched the progress of the flames as they started to lick at the logs, the logs catching fast. Faster than I would have liked. I turned and ran, the pace much faster than the one I'd used to get here. Pain didn't matter. It was secondary to getting back to Tate before the explosion happened. Ten minutes were reduced to seven, Tate exactly where I'd left him. He grinned at me as I came to a stop in front of him, his hand lifting to rest on my chest. "Hi. Missed you. Nothing happened by the way. Which I guess was good… but boring." He gestured over my shoulder. "I see you made smoke."

I turned, but barely had time to consider the fact that the smoke was darker and therefore more visible than I'd expected it to be before a loud *boom* rent the air, flames shooting up into the atmosphere. Instinctively, I grabbed for Tate, pulling him into my chest as I turned us both into the shelter of the wall, hoping it would hold as the ground seemed to shake. "Fucking hell!" Tate's words were mouthed against my neck. "That *must* have gotten their attention. I'm glad you didn't use that on Jim's bunker now."

Letting go of Tate, I flattened myself back against the wall to peer around it, adrenaline surging through my veins. Tate squeezed himself next to me, his body warm against mine. "What's happening?"

"They're moving."

"How many?"

"Two units."

"And the other unit?"

I took another peek. "Not going anywhere."

"So what do we do?"

"We wait." At the telltale rumble of a vehicle getting closer I pulled us both back into the shadows. Not a tank this time, but a truck, the soldiers' featureless faces searching the passing terrain from the cargo bed.

"What if they head this way?"

"They won't. They'll go straight to the site of the explosion. They'll assume that whatever is happening is happening there." Sure enough, the truck passed by without stopping, Tate's exhale seeming to echo loudly in the stillness. I wished I could share his relief but that had been the easy bit. The last unit were going to be the biggest obstacle to overcome. Especially seeing as we had a limited time to deal with them before the other units found nothing more than burning wood and returned. I thrust my hand into my pocket, running my fingertips over the bumpy metal of the two hand grenades I had left and wishing I'd reclaimed more from Talon. Two hand grenades and six throwing knives. There had to be a way.

24
TATE

It was always difficult to tell whether X's silences were a good thing or not. But I respected it, even as my chest thrummed with the need to ask him a million questions. He'd gotten us this far against the odds. There was no reason he couldn't overcome one last step. I had to believe in him, had to believe that his brilliant mind could make the impossible happen. We were so close that I could almost taste the underground city and the safety it would apparently bring.

"I'm going to surrender."

I blinked twice but before I could treat X's foolish notion with the scorn it deserved, he held a hand up to stall me. "Wait! Let me finish. I need a way of getting close to them. They're not going to kill me straight away. I've killed too many of them for them to be prepared to give me a quick and easy death."

Cold fear inched its way through my body. "You don't know that."

Amber eyes fastened on mine, a steely determination lurking in their depths. "I do. I know how they think. I saw the look in that soldier's eyes before I killed him. I'm not just a target to them, not anymore. I'm a symbol of their failure. They'll want to make a spectacle of me, parade me in front of the media and make the execution public to show that no one's beyond their reach." X's eyes brightened more with every word he uttered as if he was convincing himself rather than me. "And that's their weakness. If they had any sense, they'd kill me straight away. Instead they're going to let me get close to them." His lips curled up into a smile, and I suddenly found two hand grenades pressed into my palms. "And that's where you're going to come in, when all of their attention is focused on me. Common misdirection. How good are you at throwing?"

My mouth went dry at the implication behind the question, the hand grenades clutched in my palms feeling as if they weighed a ton. I stared at X, shaking my head back and forth in denial. His gaze never wavered from mine, and eventually a strange sense of calm pervaded my body. If X thought I could do this, then I could. I would. I had to. Because that little picture he'd conjured up of him being publicly executed for all the world to see wasn't going to happen. Not while I still had breath in my body. I took a slow inhale, letting it fill me with a clear sense of purpose. "What do I need to do?"

"Wait until they're in a group. Take out as many as you can. Four or five ideally. I should be able to take care of the rest."

My gaze automatically dropped to X's injured shoulder, but I didn't say anything. I could tell we were both thinking it though. This wasn't the same X that had taken out a whole unit the other day. It was an X operating at seventy-five percent, and that was probably being generous. I knew for a fact that he'd gone to great pains to hide a lot of his discomfort from me. There'd been several occasions where I'd been able to see it as clear as day in his face when he hadn't known I was watching him. X grasped hold of my hands and curled my fingers around the grenades. "You've got two chances. If the first one falls short or you overshoot, try again with the second."

"What if I hit you?"

X's lips quirked. "Then… I won't have to worry about being publicly executed, and I guess you're on your own getting inside."

I didn't appreciate the rare flash of humor, not about something as important as this. I'd never be able to live with myself if I was responsible for the death of the man I loved. Even the thought had me paralyzed with fear, the earlier calm deserting me. "I don't know if I can do this."

X pulled me against him, my body sagging against his, desperate to leach what comfort I could from the hard muscles. "It's the only plan I have."

The stark truth in the words had me pushing him away and standing straighter. I nodded, burying all the concern I had about whether we could pull this off. I pulled the ring out of my pocket, holding it out to him, his brow furrowing. "Give this to me later, once we're underground." I couldn't resist adding, "Down on one knee would work for me."

He shook his head but took it anyway, slipping it back into the pocket where it had presumably spent the last few days. "Are you ready?"

I lunged forward, stealing a kiss. Our lips barely brushed for a few seconds, but it was better than nothing. At least it was one last opportunity to breathe him in, to feel the heat of his skin against mine before he walked straight into the lion's den and I let him. I nodded, making the movement as definitive as I could. "Ready as I'll ever be."

X returned the nod before slipping out from the shelter of the wall. Blood pounded relentlessly in my head as he began to make his way across the empty space in that surefooted way of his that I'd gotten so used to seeing. The gap between ourselves and the soldiers couldn't have been any more than twenty-five meters. In terms of distance, it felt like none at all, whereas in time, it felt like forever.

At first it was almost comedic, X in plain sight walking toward them with his hands raised in the air, and not one of them looking the right way to notice him. And then all of a sudden, a gun swung his way, the rest quickly following suit.

The muscles in X's back went rigid as he continued to walk toward them. In that moment, I prayed like I'd never prayed before. If one of them pulled the trigger, then that would be it. Game over. No more X. Therefore, every second that there was no burst of blue light was a blessing.

How X could just keep going, I had no idea. I would have been a nervous wreck. I had been a nervous wreck whenever I'd faced them. I'd barely been able to breathe. There was no way I'd ever have been able to maintain the casual stride that X was, as if he had absolutely no cares in the world.

Apart from leveling their guns on him, the DTP hadn't moved. X's angle was such that he'd left a clear trajectory, a clear trajectory where I was supposed to be able to throw an explosive projectile despite having never done it before or had so much as a practice throw. In fact, I couldn't even remember the last time I'd thrown anything at a distance. He was putting an awful lot of trust in my physical abilities, ones that I'd never given him any evidence of possessing.

"Stop!"

The tinny voice rang out across the open space. X came to a sudden halt, his fingers locking behind his head to reinforce a casualness that I knew he was far from actually feeling. He shifted slightly so that rather than having his back to me, I could see him in profile. "I'm here to give myself up." Even his voice sounded steady and sure. If it was possible, I loved him even more in that moment.

The hand grenade dug into my palm as I did a quick inventory of the assembled soldiers. There was too much space between them; the largest group was two. That wasn't enough. There was no way that X would be able to take on the rest, especially not in his current weakened state. A wave of dizziness hit me, my heart racing so fast that I had to fight the urge to be sick.

One of the soldiers stepped forward, and I held my breath. "Do not lower your hands."

X shrugged, the muscles in his back bunching with the movement. "Wasn't planning on it."

I pressed myself back against the wall as the same soldier scanned the direction X had come from. "Where is your accomplice?"

"I dumped him back in Urstone. No idea where he is now. Probably dead. He wasn't exactly proficient in keeping himself alive."

"You expect us to believe that?"

X lifted his shoulders in another shrug.

Some of the soldiers shifted position, their guns never moving from X, as if they were expecting him to make a move at any minute. There still wasn't enough of them together. I needed a plan… and quick. Or even if they didn't kill X straightaway, which it seemed as if he'd been right about, there was only a certain amount of time before they bundled him into the one remaining vehicle and drove away. Maybe that had been X's plan all along. If the last unit left the area, it would leave me free and clear to enter the city. Had he pretended to abandon the self-sacrificing bullshit only to disguise it as something else? I wouldn't put it past him. Well, fuck that. He wasn't going to get to do that. I was going to throw the fucking grenades, and I was going to do a good job of it even if it killed me.

X tilted his head to one side. "Why don't you lose the mask? I know you're just men beneath it. I saw that when I killed the bastard who was stupid enough to go rogue and follow me in the woods. You found his body, right?" He paused for dramatic effect. "Are you barely out of nappies as well, or do you always send the babies to do the difficult jobs? Like sending a lamb to the slaughter, really. He had no chance."

Fuck! Why was he provoking them? What was that going to achieve?

Except just as I thought that, one of the soldiers who'd been separate from the rest at the back of the group moved closer as if he wanted to make sure that the crap coming out of X's mouth was actually what he'd thought it was. I had a group of three to aim for now, but it still wasn't enough.

To my surprise, the soldier X had been addressing lifted his arms to remove his mask. He couldn't have been any further from the soldier X had killed in the woods, grizzled features and gray hair placing him somewhere in his fifties. A vicious scar snaked its way down one side of his face, twisting his lips into even more of a sneer than it was already. "I'm a long time out of fucking nappies, you cocksucker, and I'm going to enjoy making you eat those words. If you were hoping for a quick death, then you're going to be disappointed. I'm going to take my time with you."

X inclined his head toward the rest of the group, his fingers still laced behind his head. "What about them? Surely, they get to have a go? One man's not really enough for me." X's lips curved into a cold smile. "I say *man*, what I really mean is cowards who hide behind a mask and a gun. Where do they breed you? I've always wondered. Are you like cockroaches? Yeah, that's it. That's a perfect description. You don't have a base. You have a hole that you all crawl out of to infest the earth. A bunch of fucking cockroaches who wrap themselves up in hard armor because they're too chickenshit to face people without it."

Grizzled soldier was almost shaking with rage, I could see it in the set of his jaw and the tension in his shoulders. If X's intention was to make him see red, he was succeeding with flying colors. Another soldier stepped forward. That made a group of four. Chances were that was as good as it was going to get. If I waited, there was just as much probability of one stepping away as there was of another joining them. And by that time, head soldier would have tired enough of X's insults to either forget his orders and gun him down anyway, or to dole out some sort of physical punishment just to shut him up.

I held the grenade tighter, taking a precious second to try

and calm myself, X's voice floating back to me from a time that seemed so long ago but was actually just over a week. *"Don't pull the pin out and if you do, don't hang onto it for longer than three seconds."*

I could do this. I had to do this. Worried that I'd succumb to a paralyzing bout of self-doubt if I waited any longer, I stepped out from behind the wall, my gaze fixed on the group of four soldiers. I pulled the pin, throwing my arm back and letting go. Watching the grenade arc through the air was the ultimate torture. I already knew it was going to fall short even before it landed, but I'd already prepared for that eventuality. It was like X had said I had two chances. The first grenade told me that I hadn't put enough force into it, that I needed to correct that, so even before the earth-shattering explosion that had all the soldiers turning toward it, I'd unleashed the second grenade. The throw was better than the first. But was it good enough? Had I thrown it too hard? Was it going to go sailing over their heads? The soldiers had scattered when the first explosion had gone off, but not quick enough, the second grenade dropping perfectly into their midst.

X had already used the distraction of the first explosion to release a flurry of throwing knives into those who weren't grouped together, one of them managing to stagger a few steps before falling to the ground. If they'd had any sense, they'd have stripped X of his weapons straightaway. But they'd been too arrogant, too sure that with eight guns trained on him, he had no chance. And that was their downfall.

Hopefully.

The sensible thing would have been to step back behind the shelter of the wall, to wait it out and see what the score was when the dust settled. But how was I supposed to do that when two soldiers, the grizzled one and one other, were approaching X from different angles. They were the only ones left standing. The rest might not be dead, but they were injured enough to look like they weren't going to be getting up any time soon—if ever.

Two on one, and X not in the best physical condition. My breath came in pants as X swung around, plunging one of the blades from his waist into the still masked soldier's neck. He dropped like a stone, but grizzled soldier was already on X, both of them tumbling to the ground, rolling over and over as they battled for supremacy. X was briefly on top but then the soldier, by means of a heavier body weight, managed to flip them. X had a knife between them but didn't seem to be able to make enough space to be able to use it.

I'd seen enough. Grabbing the backpack, I ran toward them. Grizzled soldier was obviously strong, his gloved hands digging into X's face as he went for his eyes, the gun forgotten next to him on the ground. Either he was still determined to injure without killing, or it was something more animalistic than that—a man reverting to base instincts, rage taking over from common sense. Whatever it was, it gave X a chance. But how long was he going to be able to hold out? The soldier was bigger than him, broader than him, heavier than him. X might be muscular, but he was still lean. And that was before you took into account his injured shoulder. If the soldier got wind of that, then he'd forget about the eyes and go for the shoulder—use it as X's Achilles heel.

I didn't know what I was going to do once I got there. All I knew was that I couldn't leave X on his own fighting for his life while I simply stood and watched. The smell of charred flesh clogged my throat as I got closer, the moans of soldiers still alive reaching my ears from behind their masks. I knew that later it would hit me that I'd done that, that I'd have to start keeping my own body count on top of X's, but right now I didn't have time for guilt when there were more important things to think about.

X was back on the bottom as I drew close, the soldier's fingers still not quite able to reach his eyes. He'd managed to hold him at bay so far, his fingers wrapped around the soldier's wrists. But he was tiring. I could see that from the strain on his face and the pronounced tremble of his muscles. The soldier could see it too, grim determination etched on his face as his fingers inched closer to their target.

I cast around for something to use, my gaze skirting over the death and devastation surrounding me before finally alighting on one of the throwing knives embedded in a soldier's neck. I didn't stop to think, dropping the backpack before running over and tugging it free. There was only one thing that mattered and that was freeing X. Knife in hand, I ran over to the struggling pair. I'd never stabbed anyone, had never even considered it before, but I didn't hesitate, didn't even stop to consider the best target. I grabbed the back of the grizzled soldier's head, yanking it back by the hair as I plunged the knife straight into his eye as deep as I could.

His body went still, and he let out a howl of either pain or surprise. I wasn't sure which and it didn't really matter. It had done what I'd set out to do, which was buy X enough time to extricate himself from the soldier's grip. With one sweep of his arm, he brought the knife up and slit his adversary's throat, blood arcing into the air to fall in ruby red drops on the ground, the life seeping from the soldier within seconds.

My legs gave way, and I sat in the dirt, the pounding of my heart so loud in my ears that for the first few seconds it was all I could hear. Saliva pooled in my mouth, and I fought the nausea, dimly aware of X's movement around the surrounding area as he checked for soldiers who were still breathing. If they were, it didn't last long, their moans gradually ceasing until it was so quiet you could have heard a pin drop. And then a firm hand hooked itself under my elbow, pulling me to my feet and tipping my chin back to meet X's stare.

He was bruised and had an abrasion on the right side of his face, but apart from that he looked okay. He lifted his arm, wiping the blood that smeared his face away with his sleeve as he turned to check that the returning units weren't already on top of us.

"So where do we go?"

X inclined his head behind me and I turned, noticing the hatch in the ground for the first time. Small, round and metal, it was easy enough to miss if you weren't looking for it. I didn't know what I'd expected—a sign proclaiming 'Welcome to Maimos' maybe. There'd been so many hatches throughout this journey, X's home, the sewers, Jim's bunker, that it seemed to be strange to be staring at one that was supposed to be our home. Forever.

I walked over to it on legs that were still the wrong side of shaky. "What do we do, knock?"

X did just that, lifting his foot to pound on the metal surface.

25
TATE

Nightmare scenarios of the city existing but being abandoned had begun to circulate in my brain by the time the hatch finally started to move. I steeled myself for whoever was about to appear. If they turned us away, we had nowhere to go. Back to the cabin, or back to one of the other less welcoming places we'd sheltered in over the past few days, I supposed. But how long would we survive there? We'd probably run out of food before we even got there.

The man who appeared looked to be in his early twenties, his keen brown eyes sweeping the still smoldering ground before settling on us. "We usually prefer people not to set off explosions above our heads."

"Are we welcome here or not?" X's voice was gravelly, his tone making it clear that he wasn't about to take any crap.

I inwardly winced. Shouldn't we be being as polite as possible? I waited for the man to tell us where to go and slam the hatch shut. Instead he grinned. "Well… despite the noise, and the damage to the ceiling you've caused in one tunnel, we quite like your gift. Price is usually only two dead DTP bastards for entry, so you've more than met the criteria. Come in."

He disappeared out of sight, and I found myself descending yet another ladder, X closing and locking the hatch behind me and bringing up the rear as was customary. This ladder was shorter, and within a minute I was standing in a dimly lit corridor, X arriving a moment later to stand next to me.

The man crossed his arms over his chest, regarding us silently for a moment before he spoke. "Name's Mac, by the way." He raised a finger to point to the sky, or at least where the sky would be if we were still able to see it. "I'm in charge of the gate and therefore new arrivals."

I couldn't hold back my questions any longer; they all came bubbling out of me all at once. "So you get new arrivals? It's not just us? How many? Is it often? Are we really welcome here? Just like that. How big is this place? How many people live here? Is it really true that the DTP have no access? How do you keep them out? If you're in charge of the gate, does that mean people have jobs? How does that work? Do people get to choose or are they assigned to them? I have pharmaceutical experience but not much else. I can't cook or anything."

Mac blinked twice before his gaze drifted across to X. "I like you. You don't talk much. Makes it peaceful."

I grimaced. "Sorry. I just… I'm Tate, by the way, and this is X. That should have been my starting point. I've got a lot of questions."

Mac nodded slowly. "And they'll all be answered in time. But first, I need your weapons. First rule of living here is no weapons allowed. I'm sure you understand, stops people from killing each other." He scratched his head and looked thoughtful. "Most of the time anyway."

X's shoulder turned to stone next to mine and I cast around for some sort of compromise which didn't involve him telling them where they could stick their underground city. There was no way X was going to be separated from his knives, particularly when his adrenaline was still running so high. It was like asking him to cut off his own arm. "Is there some sort of compromise?"

Mac's brow furrowed. "What d'ya mean?"

"I don't know." What did I mean? Inspiration struck. "Some sort of lockbox or something. So that we can keep them with us, but you know, we can't access them without the key. They've kept us alive. We're kind of attached to them." X stayed silent next to me. At least he wasn't arguing.

"Huh!" Mac tapped his finger on his lips. "Scarlett, we got anything like that? Big box that locks?"

A girl detached herself from the shadows. She didn't look any older than sixteen and I wondered if she'd been there all along. I guessed she must have been. She was scrawny and pale, her thin shoulders bare. Mousy brown hair tied back in a ponytail swung from side to side as she walked toward us. She seemed transfixed by X, her gaze never moving from him to me. He must have looked even more fearsome, smeared in blood as he was with a bruise slowly darkening on the side of his face. I'd gotten used to him. I never noticed anymore. He was just X to me now—an amazing and complex man that I couldn't get enough of.

Mac coughed. "Scarlett?"

She made a valiant attempt to look somewhere other than X, but it lasted no longer than a second. "What?"

"Go and look for a box that locks."

"Sure. I can do that."

She walked backwards for as long as she could manage it before turning and darting down the tunnel, an uneasy silence filling the space left behind by her departure. As usual, I felt the need to fill it. "Sorry to be awkward and you know, we're really grateful that you're going to let us stay here, but…" I ran out of words at that point, not even sure what I'd been going to say. Luckily, Scarlett arrived back at that moment clutching a large metal box. She held it out to Mac and then went back to staring at X. I was beginning to think that rather than finding him scary, she was weaving adolescent fantasies about climbing him like a tree. Well, the bitch could back off if that was the case.

Mac flipped the lid of the box back, held it out, and waited.

X didn't move. Mac tipped his head to one side and raised an eyebrow. X still didn't move. I turned to find X eyeing the box like it was a pit to hell. I decided that the only thing for it was to take my life in my hands as I began to slowly divest him of the two longer knives at his waist, doing my best to ignore the streaks of red that still marred them. X didn't look pleased by my actions but he didn't do anything to stop me. Placing them in the box, I went back for the throwing knives, extracting them from their various hiding places and depositing them in the box along with the larger blades.

Mac flipped the lid shut, turning the key in the lock and pocketing it before holding the box out. He didn't seem to know which of us he was supposed to offer it to. I wasn't sure myself. When X didn't make any move to grab it, I reached out, taking it off Mac and hugging it to my chest. "What happens now?"

He gave us a toothy grin. "Now, I give you a quick tour, emphasis on the quick, and then I show you to your living quarters. I'm assuming that you only need the one room?"

"One room." X's first words since his opening gambit aboveground were delivered in the same not exactly friendly tone. But then, he was probably still sore at the loss of his knives.

I nodded to confirm his words.

"Follow me." Mac turned his back on us and started off down the tunnel. I did, aware of the sixteen-year-old shadow at our back who seemed determined to go wherever X did. Regularly spaced lanterns were used to light the tunnels. Every now and again, one would flicker, casting an eerie glow and threatening to plunge us into darkness. Eventually, it would rally. Given that Mac never mentioned it, I assumed it was normal. I guessed I'd have to get used to things like that. The walls themselves were reinforced with wood and a dark material that looked like clay. I glanced up at the ceiling nervously, recalling Mac's words about the explosion damaging one tunnel, but they looked solid enough. The tunnel forked into two at the end, Mac leading us off to the right. He paused midway down it, his head cocking to the side as if he was listening. "You can go now, Scarlett. You're not needed anymore." The girl slunk back the way she'd come without a word, disappearing down the other fork of the tunnel. Mac rolled his eyes. "Sorry about that. She has many good qualities, but discretion and lack of curiosity aren't among them." He continued to lead us down a succession of winding corridors, most of them sloping slightly downwards to give the impression of heading deeper and deeper below the earth's surface.

I was beginning to think that the journey would never end when Mac finally stopped in front of a door. He opened it to reveal a man sitting at a desk, the sight strangely incongruous. After a brief explanation of it being some sort of reception area, Mac continued on. I had no idea what its purpose was, or why it had to be manned, but I guessed I couldn't expect to discover everything all at once and there didn't seem to be any point in asking when my initial round of frenzied questions had rendered nothing but silence.

After the reception room, there were more tunnels and then we stepped into a large room with actual people in it. I blinked in the brighter light, trying to take in as much as I could. It seemed to be some sort of dining room with long tables, some of them inhabited by a rag-tag bunch of people who shared no similarities in age, gender, or physical characteristics. A few glanced our way, X predictably getting the lion's share of their scrutiny. But most simply carried on with whatever it was that they were doing. I tuned back into what Mac was saying. "… where we eat. Meals are served three times a day at set times. If you're late, you miss out. It's as simple as that. Most people have already eaten and gone to their living quarters. Food is rationed, of course. What there is depends on what we can grow and what we can trade or scavenge."

That got my attention. "You grow food down here?"

Mac's answering frown said he thought it was a stupid question, but he humored it with a nod anyway. "Course we do. Or we'd starve. I forget sometimes that you surface dwellers don't know a thing about living underground. We've got animals as well, cows for milk, chickens for eggs, some pigs. To answer one of your earlier questions, that's one of the jobs available." His expression turned hopeful. "Either of you any good with animals?" His gaze skirted quickly over X as if the answer was obvious to focus on me. I shook my head, and he looked disappointed. "Oh well. There's plenty of time to sort out roles for you both. We normally give the newbies a week to get settled in and used to routines before we place you. Then it's like any other job, you know nine to five, break for lunch. Depending on the job, you might need to work some weekends, or it might be shift work. You can't just stop cooking or feeding the animals because it's the weekend. Rest of the time is your own to do with what you want."

"What is there to do?" My question came out harsher than I'd intended. I attempted to soften it with a smile.

A furrow appeared on Mac's brow. "Read. Sleep. Wank. Fuck, if you're lucky enough to have a partner." He shrugged as if there might be more on the list but he couldn't be bothered to think about it. "Oh!" His face lit up as if he'd suddenly recalled something obvious. "We have a poker night every Tuesday if that's your sort of thing."

As he hadn't phrased it as a question, I didn't bother to tell him that it wasn't. I'd played before, but I'd never been able to wrap my head around what beat what. Was it X's sort of thing? I glanced his way, but he was staring off into the distance as if he hadn't been paying attention to the conversation.

The tour lasted about another ten minutes, taking us through more tunnels and numerous rooms including the poorest excuse for a library I'd ever seen, some sort of common room which was apparently where the poker game took place, a large room where crops were grown using heat lamps, and other rooms which in all honesty started to blur into one.

Once the adrenaline had worn off from the confrontation with the DTP, even I hadn't been in the mood for polite chit chat. All I wanted was a shower, a private space to possibly fall apart, and X.

Instead, I kept forcing a smile and trying to say all the right words about sickly looking crops. At least, I'd gotten an answer to the question of how many people were down there: one hundred and fifty. I wondered how long it took until you were sick of seeing the same people day after day.

Mac took us down another tunnel, halting in front of the door. "This'll be your room. It's one of the smaller ones but it's got all the basics: bed, light, toilet." He scratched his head. "That's about it really. Lights go off at ten until six to conserve electricity. There's a shower but it's on a timer so it'll only run for ten minutes. Make sure you read the rulebook before lights out. It'll go through some of the nitty gritty stuff that I haven't had a chance to mention. There'll be a meeting scheduled for you in the next few days that you'll need to attend where we'll go through the rules and check that you understand everything. I'll come and get you for breakfast in case you can't find the dining room. I wouldn't want you to miss it." He paused, his face screwing up as he thought hard. "That's it, I think. Welcome to Maimos."

I nodded, adding a hasty "thanks" as he walked away, Mac raising his hand in acknowledgment. X pushed the door open, and we both entered the room. Mac hadn't been kidding when he'd described it as small. It was a square room, and I calculated that wall to wall would only take about six steps. Most of the space was taken up by a bed only slightly bigger than a single. The only other thing in it was three empty boxes which I assumed were what passed for storage. A door in the opposite wall led through to a tiny bathroom with a sink, shower and toilet all crammed together in a way that meant whichever of the three things you were trying to do, it was always going to be difficult.

There was no getting past what it reminded me of. I might have only seen them in films, but it screamed prison cell. I reminded myself that it didn't matter, that safety was the important thing, the means to breathe another day without being executed. Besides, we'd stayed in worse places throughout the last couple of weeks, but then we'd always known they were temporary. This was… a huge wave of emotion I couldn't even identify hit me.

Lowering the lockbox that contained X's knives, I turned blindly into X's arms, letting the mask I'd somehow maintained all through Mac's little tour slip. X pulled me closer, his arms enfolding me, one hand cupping the back of my head to hold it more firmly against his chest. I closed my eyes, but opened them again, shuddering, when all I could see was the blade I'd driven into the soldier's eye. I was no doubt going to relive it again and again in numerous nightmares.

X's lips brushed over my temple. "Thanks."

"For what?" My response was automatic. Of course I knew what he was thanking me for. But perhaps I needed to hear him say it, needed the acknowledgement that it had actually happened.

"For doing what needed to be done, even though it's not in your nature."

"Did it need to be done?"

"Yeah, it did. I was losing."

Was he? Or was he just saying that to make me feel better? We'd done it again, somehow wiped out another DTP unit. And this time I was going to claim the "we," not because I wanted acclaim but because I needed to take responsibility for the part I'd played, the blood that was now on my hands, both literally and figuratively. "I killed him."

"No, you maimed him. I killed him."

"I killed the others... with the grenade."

X dropped another gentle kiss on my temple. "You did what was necessary. If they'd left us alone, if they hadn't blocked our route, we wouldn't have been pushed to that point. You're a good person, Tate. You only did what I asked you to do, and I wouldn't have asked it of you if there'd been any other way."

I pulled away slightly, far enough to be able to see his face, X's expression earnest. I knew that what he said made sense but it was going to be a long time before I could look at it that pragmatically, if ever.

"They'd have killed me if you hadn't."

"I know." I forced a smile but couldn't hold on to it for more than a few seconds before it slipped away. "How's your shoulder?"

"It's fine." From the grimace when he tried to roll it back, it was a long way from fine, but we had time now for it to heal. I took a deep breath and did my best to shove the bloodshed from my head. X was right. It was either them or us, so with a choice like that, I'd vote for us surviving any time. "This room is..." *Is what?* I couldn't say it was a prison cell, but I needed to change the subject. "It'll be easy to clean."

X's only response was a grunt, his gaze fixed on something across the room. I followed it to the lockbox. Was he still sore about being separated from his beloved knives? "Don't tell me you're upset about that?"

"Why shouldn't I be?"

"Because..." I let my gaze drop slowly to his left boot. "You could have that box open in a second using the knife you still have, you know, the one I deliberately left there, not to mention the fact that you have lockpicks."

X held my gaze for a second before his lips slowly curved into a smile. "Possibly."

I reached up, laying my hand against his cheek and turning

his head to the side so I could examine the bruise on his cheek more closely, my fingers trailing over the smear of blood close by. Slipping his jacket off, I tugged his T-shirt over his head so that I could give his shoulder the same scrutiny. I probed the wound cautiously. "The stitches held. Tomorrow, we'll ask about a doctor and antibiotics."

"Tomorrow."

There was no mistaking the look in X's eyes, my cock reacting to it with equal enthusiasm. Only problem was we were both bloody and sweaty. "Shower." I fumbled with the fastening on his trousers, the rapidly growing bulge behind it making them all the more difficult to undo. I backed him toward the so-called bathroom.

X's gaze radiated heat as he obediently followed my directive. "You haven't touched me for days."

I divested him of his boots and trousers in record time. We'd both foregone underwear—there was only so many times you could wash and wear the same couple of pairs before you gave up. "I didn't want to hurt you." I started to rip my own clothes off, tossing them over my shoulder and not caring where they landed. "But given that you were fine to roll around with that soldier…" I tamped down on the immediate wave of guilt for referring to a dead man so flippantly. "… then I figure you can roll around with me instead." I shoved X into the shower before squeezing myself in with him, my erect cock finding a natural home next to his.

The controls for the shower were easy enough to work out, a trickle of lukewarm water greeting us moments later. And apparently, we only got that for ten minutes. We settled into a pattern of washing each other, fingers sometimes getting distracted when they delved into interesting places. I rose up on my toes, grinding my cock against X's abdominal muscles as his fingers slid between my ass cheeks and grazed my hole.

Despite all of my churning emotions, there was a lot to

celebrate: being safe, getting one over on the DTP, both of us being relatively unharmed. And right now, I couldn't think of a better way of doing it. I gave up on bathing, sliding my hands up the taut muscles of X's abdomen and over his pectorals, avoiding the wound on his shoulder until I could wind my arms around his neck.

X met me halfway, his lips parting beneath mine as we both opened up to taste. It was surprisingly gentle considering how aroused we both were. I didn't want kinky tonight though. I wanted straightforward and honest. No games. No roleplay. No props. Just both of us taking what we needed from the other.

When the water slowed to a stop, neither of us made any move to leave the shower, too lost in each other to care. Besides, we were making enough heat of our own. My hands worked independently of my brain, sliding over every inch of X's skin that I could reach with our mouths still fused together, from the curve of his biceps to the place where back met the first swell of ass. It was like discovering anew just how perfectly the man was put together.

X's hands weren't still either, stroking down my back to grasp my ass and prove it was the perfect fit for his hands. I squeezed myself even tighter against him, the slide of my cock against his skin making me feel like I could come just from that.

Forgoing his lips, I turned myself around in his arms, X's cock finding a natural home between my ass cheeks. I watched his fingers stroke over my chest while I ground myself back against him, goosebumps erupting wherever he touched. There was something almost poetic about his darker fingers against the pale skin of my torso as he traced my abdomen and my nipples, painting pictures from sensation. Only when he'd finished his exploration did he wrap me up tight in his arms so that there wasn't a whisper of space between our two bodies. It was like being one person. "X?"

He lowered his mouth to my neck, my head lolling to one

side to give him better access as he scraped his teeth over the skin before using his lips and tongue to soothe the same area. "Hmmm?"

I didn't even know what I wanted to say. There was no way of putting the mixture of emotions bubbling inside me into anything approaching words. It was relief. It was a release of tension. It was lust and love all rolled into one. I settled for the part that screamed louder than the rest. "I love you."

X's mouth stilled for a moment on my skin, before returning to the same teasing caress of teeth and tongue. I smiled, despite the fact he couldn't see it. "You already said it once, remember? I heard it. Loud and clear. I'll get you to say it again." He didn't offer a comment. I shuddered as he moved from my neck to my ear, his tongue exploring the sensitive skin within it. "Fuck! I didn't think my ear was an erogenous zone."

"Want me to stop?"

"No."

I felt his lips curve against my skin. Maybe now that we were safe, that we had a home of sorts, that's something I could have every day—X smiling just for me. I didn't give a damn if he scowled at everyone else. In fact, I'd positively encourage it. He was mine and mine alone. I was surprised by the hot burn of possessiveness that flooded my body. But then, it had been just the two of us for so long that it wasn't surprising that I didn't want the status quo to change. I'd probably stab anyone who tried to come between us.

Questing fingers drifted lower, dancing along my treasure trail as if it was some sort of mystical map before wrapping firmly around my cock. I gasped, arching my back in order to push my cock more firmly into X's grip. There was still enough water to ensure a slick slide as he stroked me from root to tip. I closed my eyes and laid my head back against his shoulder, giving myself up to pleasure as X continued with the perfect hand job.

"Moan for me."

That I could do. I had no idea how thick the walls were in this place, how easily noise could spread. But with X's hand driving me quickly toward orgasm, I didn't give a damn. Let them listen. It might give them a bigger thrill than poker night. X's mouth was back on my neck, his hips moving so that his cock rode the crease of my ass. I covered his hand with my own, whether to speed him up or slow him down though, I wasn't sure. Whichever it was, X took no notice, maintaining the same knee-buckling slide of callused palm over my sensitive glans.

My balls were tight, the orgasm starting to make itself known in the tingles radiating from my groin and trickling through my veins. If I wanted to stop him, I needed to do it soon. "I'm going to… come."

X's hand gripping harder and moving faster was all the answer I needed about what he wanted. Writhing against him, I hovered on the precipice for what felt like forever, my breathy gasps of pleasure filling the small room. And then there was no holding back the torrent of sensation any longer, X continuing to stroke my cock as my body shuddered through the orgasm. I went lax against him, only his arms holding me up. Squirming as he continued to stroke me, I finally had to push his hand away when my dick was too sensitive to take it. X didn't seem to mind, burying his face in the curve of my shoulder to drop gentle kisses on the bare skin.

For a minute we stayed like that, X eventually reaching over to the small sink to turn the tap on and rinse the cum off his hand. At least there was still water in the taps then. Whatever timer system they had rigged up for the showers didn't seem to extend to the rest of the plumbing.

X turned me in his arms, capturing my mouth for a long, slow kiss, the throbbing heat against my hip reminding me that there was still important business to attend to. "What do you want?" I whispered the question against his lips, unable to resist punctuating it with another kiss. "Do you want me to blow you, or do you want to fuck me?"

Hands slid to my ass to lift me. I quickly got his intention, obediently wrapping my legs around his waist and my arms around his neck, X carrying me as if I weighed nothing. Progress to the bed proved slow despite the short distance as we both took it in turns to initiate kiss after kiss. When we finally reached it, X lowered me gently onto the bare mattress. I watched him with hooded eyes as he left me for a moment to locate the lube that Psyche had sourced for us from the front pocket of one of the backpacks. And then he was back with me on the mattress, my thighs automatically parting as he crawled between them. "I'm guessing you're going for the fucking option then?"

"Is that okay?"

I nodded, unable to look away from the naked desire throwing his features into stark relief. I lifted my hand, tracing my fingers gently over his cheekbone before moving to his jaw. "More than okay. You can do anything you want to me."

A glint of amusement sparked in his gaze. "Anything?"

"Anything."

He lowered himself on top of me until his chest was flush with mine, my hips tipping up to bracket his body more comfortably. "Good thing I only want to do pleasurable things to you then, isn't it?"

"I'm fully on board with pleasurable things."

There was another hint of a smile as he coated his fingers in lube. I could barely breathe as he eased it between us, one slick finger wasting no time in locating my hole. He played around the rim for a few seconds, teasing and tormenting before it dipped inside. I watched his face, loving the look of intense concentration on it as he opened me up. To think that this was the man who'd been scared he couldn't be gentle. He was probably the most considerate lover I'd ever had. He was certainly the most versatile: rough when I needed it and equally soft when I didn't—like now. Yeah, it was official, we fit perfectly.

One finger quickly became two, my dick starting to plump

again as he teased my prostate. Soon fingers weren't enough, X continuing to torment me as I begged for more. Only then did he give me what I wanted, lubing himself up and replacing his fingers with his cock, my legs wrapping around his waist to pull him deeper. Even if I couldn't come again, I wanted everything he had to give me.

There was something freeing about not chasing my own orgasm. It meant I could concentrate on him, enjoying everything from the flex of his muscles as he held himself above me to the myriad emotions that crossed his face every time he withdrew, only to sink deeper into me. He was beautiful—every powerful inch of him, every muscle, every sinew, every little noise of pleasure he made. I could tell when he got close from the way his thrusts became much less controlled and his breathing more ragged. I tightened my ass around his cock, laughing at the expression akin to pain that briefly crossed his face. "You're going to kill me."

I laughed again, feeling like the most powerful man on earth. "But what a way to go."

His lips found mine, our kisses almost as frenzied as the movement of his hips. And then I was swallowing his moans and stroking his trembling limbs as his cock pulsed its release inside me. I held onto him, stroking gentle fingers across his skin as he continued to shudder before collapsing on top of me. I didn't mind his weight. In fact, I relished it.

Finally, X lifted himself up onto one elbow, searching amber eyes examining my face. "You didn't come."

I ran my thumb across his bottom lip. "I didn't come *again*. There's a huge difference. Doesn't mean I didn't enjoy it." I figuratively bit my tongue for a moment before letting the words spill free. If he was going to be with me, he needed to get used to my adoration because I'd never been great at holding back. "I watched you. You were beautiful. I've never done that before, just watched someone come. Besides, we've got the rest of our lives. It's too early to start a tally chart of our orgasms."

X rolled off me in one swift movement and onto his back, his gaze fixed on the ceiling, which was a muddy brown color and didn't deserve even an iota of the attention that X was giving it. Had he found what I'd said too creepy? But then, he was the man who'd stalked me for years. Something else then? Or was I just being

paranoid?

I scooted over and laid my head on his chest, feeling better when he rested his hand on top of my head and began to stroke my hair. One of us should probably get the sleeping bag, but not yet. It could wait a few more minutes.

As usual, I filled the silence. "So, what did you make of the tour? You didn't say much. I know it's quite cramped down here, and this room is… well, quite frankly the tiniest shithole I've ever seen, but I guess we'll get used to it. And we can ask Mac about the room. Maybe the newest arrivals get the shittiest one. He called it small so there must be bigger rooms. We might be able to get an upgrade once we've been here longer. People might leave or… I guess people must die sometimes."

X's fingers continued to stroke my hair, plucking at the strands before letting them slip through his fingers. It made me want to grow it, the thought of him grabbing onto it while fucking me bringing new life to my flagging dick. When he didn't offer anything to the conversation, I carried on. "Not sure about the job thing. I definitely don't fancy spending the day cleaning up animal shit so that's definitely out. God knows what you're going to do. I picture you doing that even less than me."

"You'll find something."

"Maybe they have a pharmacy of some sorts that I can get involved in. Drugs is about the only thing I know. Name a drug and I bet I could tell you the ingredients. I might miss a couple, but I know most of them. I could…" I stopped, X's comment finally sinking in and something tickling at my brain at his phrasing. "What do you mean *I'll* find something? Don't you mean we'll find something?" I tipped my head back so that I could see his face. "Or is this your way of telling me you're planning on being a kept man? I go off to work every day and you stay here polishing your knives, is that it?"

X didn't answer, and every second he stayed silent with his face a blank mask, was another second where panic got a firmer grip on me until my body felt like one vibrating nerve. "X, talk to me. You might pull this non-communication thing with everyone else, but please don't do it to me. Not now, after everything we've been through."

"I can't say what you want me to say."

"Which is?" But I already knew the answer deep down. I levered myself away from him to sit upright. I needed to think, and I couldn't do that when I was so close to him.

X shifted himself backwards until he was propped up against the wall. My mind raced as I stared at him, gathering every little bit of evidence together to ensure that I wasn't traveling down the completely wrong path with my assumptions. "You never had any intention of staying here, did you?"

He didn't need to say a word, the way he couldn't even look at me spoke volumes. A multitude of emotions all slammed into me at the same time. Panic at the thought of being left on my own, grief at the thought of losing what I might only have had for a while but was already so important to me. Hot on the heels of those emotions came the anger, burning fiery hot from my toes to my scalp. It made me want to throw something. It made me want to snatch up one of X's knives and use it on him for real this time. It was probably a good thing that they were locked away.

I scrambled off the bed, settling for putting some distance between us instead. Keeping my eyes focused on the floor, I pulled my trousers on with short, jerky movements.

"Tate?"

His voice was soft and pleading. I remembered when I'd first met him and I'd found his tone hard and lethal. It had been one of many things that had made me want to run from him. Only, he'd been the one thing standing between me and the DTP. It had been like being stuck between the proverbial rock and the hard place. How times had fucking changed. Well, he could take his soft use of my name, the way he could get me to do whatever he wanted with just the right inflection, and he could stick it up his ass. "Don't Tate me!" My voice vibrated with an anger that I couldn't disguise. "In fact, don't talk to me. Not now. Not ever." Even as I said it, I didn't mean it. Not really. But it seemed to do the trick, X falling silent.

I started to pace, words falling from my mouth almost automatically. They weren't even aimed at X. They were just my brain's way of trying to piece things together. "So that was the plan, was it? Rescue me, spend time with me, *fuck* me…" I risked a glance in his direction when I said the latter, but he was still staring sightlessly into space. For all I knew, he wasn't even listening, a fact which sparked another wave of anger. So, okay, maybe the words were aimed at him after all. "… make me fall in love with you… and then just dump me here and leave me."

The words were unfair, I knew that. Especially the part about him fucking me and making me fall in love with him. X had done everything in his power to stay away from me despite his feelings. I was the one who'd kissed him. I was the one who'd pushed and pushed when he'd said no. Only it was becoming more and more clear that there'd been an additional reason for his reticence, one I hadn't figured out. Until now.

Pacing was proving very unsatisfactory when there was so little space to do it in. I'd estimated six steps earlier, but it was actually only five. There was no place in the room that I could go that took me more than two meters away from X. The room was a fucking cupboard. Most of the places we'd stayed in on the way here, apart from the cave, had been bigger. Full of junk and dilapidated in some cases but definitely bigger. I swallowed as a startling truth slammed me between the shoulder blades. X would go crazy in here within a week. He was built for racing across rooftops like he had in Urstone, for skulking through streets, not for being penned up in a tiny underground room and forced to work a normal job.

Somewhere in my subconscious, I'd already known it deep down, had recognized the true reality of our future existence at some point during the tour and had been unable to see X in it. Neither had he, and that's why he'd paid so little attention. It would be like trying to cage a wild animal. He'd be miserable and eventually he'd snap, and God knows what he'd do then or how high the body count would be as a result.

Anger leached out of me to be replaced by resignation. X had saved my life and uprooted his whole existence in the process. He'd kept me safe and protected me, had faced down whole military units and taken a knife in the shoulder that had almost killed him. And on top of that, I expected him to stay with me just because I loved him. Who the hell did I think I was to be that selfish? He deserved better.

Stepping around the mattress, I placed myself firmly in his eyeline so that he couldn't avoid looking at me. His gaze slowly lifted to mine, the familiar amber eyes full of wariness. For a second, we just stared at each other. I swallowed, and then took a deep breath. "I didn't mean it when I told you not to talk to me. I get a little... wound up sometimes."

His lips twitched as if threatening a smile. "I've noticed."

"Where will you go?" It hurt to even ask the question, but I needed to know. When he didn't immediately answer, I was left having to guess. "Will you go back to Cofield? You can't, surely?"

X shook his head. "And spend all my days hiding from the DTP... it wouldn't work. I might be able to evade them for a few weeks, but they'd find me eventually."

I frowned. "So where? There's nowhere you can go where

they can't go… apart from here. You said so yourself. You said this was the only place I'd be safe. So it's the same for you. Unless…" Something whispered in my brain and I couldn't quite let go of it. I shook my head as if it might somehow manage to dislodge it and rid myself of the truth slowly sneaking into my consciousness, cold dread already starting to inch its way along my spine. X didn't flinch from the hard, penetrating gaze I threw his way. I studied him, hoping some other explanation would come to mind, that there was somewhere else I hadn't yet thought of, but there wasn't so I was forced to put it into words and give it life. "You're going to look for that place. The one beyond the desert that there's stories about."

X's slow nod set me off pacing again, the words tumbling out of my mouth more rapidly than my steps. "You don't even know if it's real. You said yourself that no one's ever come back from there, which I guess if it's real means that it's a wonderful place much nicer than here so why would anyone return. But if it's not real, you'll die in the desert, and no one will even know about it. You'll just be a pile of bones." I closed my eyes against the stab of pain that image evoked. "Is it really worth the risk? Might as well just open up a wardrobe and try and find Narnia."

X climbed off the bed and walked over to me without stopping to put on any clothes. "I have to try."

The four simple words reverberated around in my brain. I would have given anything in that moment to have somewhere to go, or at least a window to stare out of. But short of holing up in the bathroom, which wasn't really a bathroom, there was nowhere, so I simply turned away as tears threatened to make an appearance.

But X wasn't having it, pulling me back around to face him. I lay my palms against his chest, the firm heartbeat beneath it somehow reassuring. He sighed. "If I could stay, I would. You know that, right?" His thumb brushed my cheek, wiping away a tear that had managed to escape. He gestured around the room, pointing at the rulebook we hadn't even bothered to open yet and the lockbox containing his knives that someone else held the key to. "But this... this is not me. It'll never be me, no matter how hard I try, no matter how long I give it. But *you*. You can make it work. You can find yourself a job where you're happy"— his lips twisted— "something that doesn't involve pigs... and you'll find someone, maybe not straightaway, but eventually. Someone nice. Someone..."

I wrenched my head back, putting all the venom I could muster into my glare, the fingers on his chest curling involuntarily as the anger I'd felt previously came back with a vengeance. "Someone nice! Are you fucking serious? You know that's not what I want... what I need. I need someone like..." I cast about for a way of finishing the sentence, but there was only one thing that worked. "...you. I need you."

A strange sense of calm invaded my body once I'd said the words aloud because all of a sudden, I knew what I needed to do, and it was so fucking obvious that I had no idea why it had taken me so long to realize it. X couldn't stay; that wasn't up for debate. Therefore, there was only one possible solution. He wasn't going to like it though. Not one little bit. But then he didn't have to. It was my decision. "Okay... so we leave."

X jerked so violently that it was as if I'd slapped him. "No." He continued to shake his head as if the word itself wasn't sufficient.

I smiled, heady with the newfound prospects that my decision wrought. "I'm not asking you. I'm telling you. If you leave, I leave." I shook my head. "Wait... I didn't phrase that right. This is not an ultimatum. I know you have to leave, that you can't stay here. But when you do, I'm coming with you." I kept on talking when it looked like X might have been going to interrupt. "And if you've got any crazy ideas about sneaking out in the middle of the night and leaving me behind, then you should know that I'll come after you. I'll probably perish on my own in the desert because we both know that my best chance of survival is with you, but I'll do it anyway. I'll wander around and try and find you until I die of dehydration." X stared at me and I raised my eyebrows in a challenge. "So we'll leave, but not yet. We stay here for a week. We both need rest, and we need to make sure your shoulder is healed properly before we go anywhere."

"Tate!"

I ignored him, picking up the rulebook and laying back on the bed before opening it up and starting to read. I didn't look up even when I felt X's presence as he came to stand next to me. It didn't matter what he said. He could threaten, he could cajole, he could refuse to talk to me. My mind was made up. He didn't get to leave me here. Whatever fate awaited him out there, he was going to share—good or bad.

"I might die out there."

I did lift my head then, looking him straight in the eye as I shrugged. "Then we die together."

26
X

After three long days of doing everything I could, I had to concede that there was no talking Tate out of it. I recognized that steely look of determination in his eyes. I'd seen it many times throughout the years when I'd been watching him at a distance, and never once had he backed down when it was present. It was a trait that he'd inherited from his father. The same stubborn streak that had led his father to continue to help me when he should have walked away. I'd even bitten him once like the feral cat I was. He'd just smiled and said it was a good thing he was a doctor, calmly wrapping a makeshift bandage around the wound. Yeah, he and Tate were definitely similar, only Tate had that initial flare of anger to accompany it, presumably inherited from his mother's side of the family. But whatever I said, he wasn't shifting on his insistence that wherever I went, he'd go too.

Truth be told, I was conflicted. Could I have been more persuasive? Possibly. Was there a part of me that couldn't bear the thought of being separated from him? Most definitely. Tate seemed to think that leaving had always been the plan for me, but that wasn't true. I'd hoped I might be able to stay. After all, this was Tate—the man I'd loved since I was a teenager, and I was willing to do whatever it took to keep him safe. But it seemed that there were limits even for me. I'd leave the only home I'd ever known for him. I'd change my whole life. I'd kill an army of soldiers. But I couldn't live underground in cramped conditions, squeezed together with people I had no wish to see, never mind speak to. Not even for Tate.

I'd known that from the first moment I'd set foot in there, every additional room on the tour just adding another layer of certainty. I'd deserved Tate's anger, knowing that I should have raised the possibility from the start. But when exactly would have been a good time? By the time he'd stopped looking at me as if I were the devil incarnate, he'd already started to look at me as if he wanted a taste of the forbidden fruit. I might have tried to convince myself at the time that it was just wishful thinking on my part, but subsequent events showed that for the farce it was. And then there was the fact that I'd been more concerned with keeping us both alive than worrying about what might happen once I'd delivered Tate to a safe place. The future where I might have to make that decision had seemed like an abstract concept. No, things had unraveled the only way possible.

Life in the underground city had turned out to be the hell I'd expected it to be. It was always too hot, the proximity to the desert ensuring that even deep underground the temperature didn't alter that much, the ground holding enough heat for there not to be much of a dip during the night. Add to that the rationed water and it didn't smell too pretty most of the time either. If avoidance didn't mean starving to death, I would have been quite happy not to mix with the other people that lived there. But the communal meals meant there was no chance of that.

As for the people, they ranged from overly friendly to downright surly, and I wasn't sure which was worse. One man wore a permanent sneer whenever he looked my way—which was often, my hand automatically straying to the knives that weren't there, ready to surgically remove the expression from his face in the most painful way I knew. Luckily, Tate seemed to know when he needed to intervene, pulling me away at the point where I remembered that I didn't need a blade. I was perfectly capable of killing a man with my bare hands. It was just slower and not as fun.

Then there were all the damn rules. You could barely take a shit without asking for permission first. The list was never-fucking-ending. I hadn't read them; I'd rather have removed my own appendix without anesthetic. But Tate, like the good member of society he was, had, and had insisted on relaying them to me. Lights out at a certain time. Limited water. Set meal times. Books and games had to be signed out and back in again so that they didn't go missing. Alcohol was permitted but only on a Friday and only in limited amounts. No drugs allowed apart from weed, which incidentally Mac usually stank of, so it didn't take a genius to work out how that rule had managed to sneak in, given that Mac's father was the big cheese of the underground hellhole. No one was allowed in anyone else's room unless they'd signed a form to say they were courting—and the rulebook had actually used that word.

Tate had stopped me from scribbling it out and writing fucking instead, reminding me that we were supposed to be keeping our heads down until we left—a fact that we hadn't actually gotten around to telling them yet. The meeting that Mac had mentioned on our arrival was due to happen the next day. From what I'd gathered it was mainly an opportunity to discuss the fucking rules and to talk about what line of meaningless servitude you intended to devote the rest of your miserable life to.

That's where Tate was at the moment, informing Mac of our future plans in the hope that that would negate the need for the meeting. He'd decided that it was probably better that he went on his own, and I hadn't bothered to argue. But alone in the tiny cupboard of a room where we were supposed to spend the majority of our day, the walls were starting to close in.

Three fucking days, and I was already starting to go insane. I needed to get out of here; even walking into certain death had to be better than this. Tate had concocted a balm to soothe my jagged nerves with a ninety-five percent success rate. As it involved the two of us fucking like rabbits until I was too tired to be restless, I'd raised little objection.

Except Tate wasn't here now. He was making nice with Mac, which meant I needed an alternative distraction. Maybe I'd go and find my friend with the permanent sneer. I didn't need to touch him. I could just whisper a few choice words in his ear and let him know what I'd like to do to him given the opportunity. That would fill five minutes.

I was halfway to the open doorway when Tate appeared in it. He raised a finger in a way that I assumed was meant to be threatening but looked more like a child pretending they had a gun. "And where do you think you're going?"

"To find you."

The look in his eyes said that he didn't buy that even for a second, but he let it go. I walked over to the bed, lying down on it and lacing my fingers behind my head. Tate straddled me just as I'd hoped he would, his fingers absently tracing over the fabric on my chest as he looked thoughtful.

"Did you find him?"

Tate nodded but didn't seem too happy about it.

"And?"

His fingers stilled. "Well, I'll give you the abbreviated version of it. He thinks we're a pair of absolute fucking idiots, that we're chasing a dream and that we'll both die in the desert."

I tipped my head to one side, considering Mac's blunt prognosis for a few seconds. "He's probably right."

"Then he spoke to *Daddy*…" Tate's voice dripped with derision as he talked about the man that neither of us had actually met yet. "… and he wants us out sooner, in the next couple of days apparently. I have no idea why. I assume they're just miffed that we don't want to stay."

"Suits me."

Tate's mouth settled into a tight line. "We said a week."

"*You* said a week."

Tate sighed, his hands moving to the bottom of my T-shirt and tugging it up until he could pull it over my head, his gaze homing in on the wound on my shoulder. It was a hundred times better than when we'd first arrived, the movement much freer now that the swelling had gone down. Tate had managed to source antibiotics from somewhere on the second day, and I'd been dutifully taking them with only the minimum of complaints ever since. We'd left Tate's makeshift stitches in because it hadn't seemed worth replacing them when they were holding together just fine. Besides, I wanted the reminder that it was his handiwork that had saved my life.

I let him probe the wound, knowing that it made him feel better to see that if he pressed it, it no longer hurt me. Eventually, I grabbed his hand and tugged it away. "It's fine. No pain. No swelling. No infection." I ran my fingers up his chest, hooking my hand behind his neck to pull him closer so that we could share the same breath. "I didn't see you worrying about my shoulder last night when you asked me to fuck you standing up against the wall."

Tate's nostrils flared at the memory, his groin shifting over my stiffening cock as the reminder backfired on me. "I had more important things to think about."

I lifted my head to steal a kiss. Although technically there was no thievery required when Tate responded so sweetly. We kissed for the next few minutes until I remembered what we were supposed to be discussing. "So, we leave tomorrow."

Tate propped his elbows on my chest and stared at me, his blue eyes full of something I couldn't decipher. Finally, he nodded. "Tomorrow."

I held his gaze. "You can still change your mind. I'll understand if you want to stay." Something clenched in my chest as he considered it. I should want him to stay, but in the last few days, despite my protestations to the contrary, I'd gotten used to the idea of having him with me. We'd started this journey together and it seemed right—however it ended—to do that together as well.

Tate shook his head. "Not happening. Besides…"

He hesitated, some undefined emotion flickering across his face.

"Besides what?"

"I have a good feeling about it. It's going to be okay. The place we're heading to is real. I can feel it. After everything we've been through, there's no way it couldn't be. This is not the end of the line. I know it."

I stared up at him, bathing in the unrelenting optimism that shone from his eyes. I just wished I could share it.

Mac strolled back down the corridor. "Coast is clear. Course, we can only see so far away." He shrugged. "DTP filth could be lurking a mile away ready to leap on you at the first opportunity."

Tate rolled his eyes. "Yeah? Well, maybe we should have stayed for a whole week then. They might have got bored by then."

The comment seemed to roll off Mac like water off a duck's back. "Hey man, if it was up to me you could have, but Dad, he's old school and doesn't like what he sees as timewasters. He sees it as you throwing his hospitality back in his face."

I expected Tate to have some sort of witty retort, but he simply shook his head. Either he was more nervous than he was letting on, or he just couldn't be bothered. Instead, he held the lockbox that we'd brought with us from the tiny bedroom we'd been relieved to leave up in the air. Although, given the amount of sweaty bone-shakingly good sex it had seen, it would always hold some fond memories. I almost felt sorry for whoever got that room next. It couldn't have seen more action if we'd been on our honeymoon. I guess boredom and celebrating safety were a lethal combination. Either that or Tate was just so fucking hot that I couldn't resist him. The truth probably lay somewhere between the two. I'd never been driven by my cock before, sex more like scratching an itch. But Tate... well, I couldn't get enough of him. He only had to look at me a certain way and I'd be ripping his clothes off within seconds.

"Key." Tate's demand prompted a piercing whistle from Mac, the same girl as on the day of our arrival slipping from the shadows to run over and give it to him. He fitted it in the lock and then flipped the lid back. My lips curled in amusement as Tate lifted them out gently as if it was some sort of sacred ceremony. In a direct reversal of when he'd stripped them from me, he placed each knife back in its proper place before standing back to peruse me from head to toe, a huge grin appearing on his face. "Now you look like you again."

I had to admit that I felt complete for the first time in days, my fingers automatically curling around the hilt of the knife, the cool carbon fiber handle fitting as perfectly into my hand as it ever had. Tate's gaze followed the movement, his grin widening. "Aww, what a sweet reunion. Shall I give you a few minutes alone?"

I gave him the glare he expected but we both knew there was no real antagonism behind it. I was concerned by how chipper he was though, considering what we were about to face. Either he really was as optimistic about the outcome as he kept making out, or he was playing ostrich with its head in the sand. I moved closer to him, turning us slightly so that my back blocked us from Mac's view, my palm finding a natural resting place against Tate's cheek. "It's not too late to stay."

Tate lifted his hand to cover mine, the action completely at odds with the next words out of his mouth. "Fuck off." He raised an eyebrow. "Stop trying to keep your mythical utopia to yourself. I know your game. You want to get there and find some nubile twink to stalk, don't you? Probably some squeaky-clean eighteen-year-old who can't even grow facial hair yet. Well, tough…" He thumped my chest but was careful to hit an area nowhere near the healing wound on my shoulder. "…you only get to stalk me. For the rest of your life." His blue eyes held mine for a long moment as if he was daring me to argue.

"That wouldn't be a hardship." My voice was husky and filled with emotion, the audience of two, who were no doubt watching us with interest, the last thing on my mind.

Tate smiled. "Right answer." He inhaled slowly, the release of that same breath sounding loudly in the enclosed space. "So… let's do this."

I nodded, feeling like there was something else I should be able to say, some words of comfort I should be able to offer, but we were heading into the unknown. The only information I had about the desert or the place that supposedly lay beyond it was from hearsay, scraps of conversation picked up from one place or another. There were people who'd claimed to have gone there and returned, but their stories never held weight for long before they were revealed as bullshitters and con artists. Therefore, there was nothing I could say to Tate, no reassurance I could give him. There was only moving forward and hoping that I wasn't leading him to his death. Mine didn't matter, but his…

Mac coughed, pulling my attention back to him. "Sorry guys, but I've got stuff to do. The heat lamps for the tomatoes are acting up, and I have to go and check on them, and one of the goats has had diarrhea for the past few days. So…"

I moved over to the ladder, pausing when Scarlett appeared in front of me. She held out her hand, slowly unfurling her fingers until I could see something silver in the center of her palm. Her smile was shy. "It's a good luck charm. It'll keep you safe."

I highly doubted that but the gentle shove in my back from Tate told me that I should take it. I plucked it from her hand, holding it up to one of the lanterns so I could see it better, unable to hold back a snort of amusement when I saw what it was, the silver rat painstakingly crafted to show every feature.

"Look, Tate, it's a..."

He batted my hand away, the expression on his face as disgruntled as if the rat had been real. I slipped it into my pocket anyway. We needed every bit of luck we could get, even if a rat wasn't exactly the most traditional of good luck charms.

I placed my hand on the first rung of the ladder, Mac still talking. "... and you can come back, you know, if you get so far in the desert and realize it's just a sandy wasteland with nothing for fucking miles. Dad won't mind as long as you intend to stay. Unless someone arrives in the next couple of days, your room will still be empty. And if that happens, we'll find somewhere. You can always kip with the pigs."

Tate mumbled something in response, but it was too indistinct to catch when I was already making my way to the surface. Mac got smaller as I continued to climb. He'd need to hang around to fasten the hatch after we'd gone. Speaking of the hatch, it was easy to undo, but more difficult to open, bright sunlight blinding me when I finally managed to achieve enough leverage to throw it open.

I covered my eyes with my hand as I heaved myself out, pulling Tate out after me. Tate was struggling as much as I was with the bright light so at least a minute had gone by before he raised watery eyes to mine. "The bodies are gone."

They were. In fact, there was no evidence at all of what had happened five days ago apart from a scorch mark on the ground where the second grenade had gone off. I turned in a slow circle, scanning the vicinity until I was sure there was no sign of the DTP. Their absence wasn't a surprise. They would have assumed that we'd never come out again, that we were out of their reach for good. I swung around to where the horizon changed to one of never-ending sand. Squaring my shoulders, I set off in that direction.

It took us an hour just to reach the desert, the temperature seeming to rise a few degrees with every step we took. Tate had been quiet. Too quiet. I wondered if his unshakeable optimism was finally wavering. Whatever thoughts were going through his mind though, he kept them to himself. Yet, when we reached the border, he was the first to set off across the sand as if he needed to prove something to himself. Never having walked on sand before, I was more cautious. Doubt set in almost immediately as I discovered that it was harder going than I'd expected. That meant that we were covering less ground and drinking more water than I'd anticipated. We'd brought as much as they'd been prepared to give us and that we could carry. We weren't stupid; water was a priority. But I was already beginning to suspect that it would run out within a couple of days. Would that be long enough to get us where we needed to go?

"How do we even know we're heading in the right direction?"

I wiped sweat off my brow before it could sting my eyes as I turned in Tate's direction. He wasn't faring any better, his T-shirt soaked through and his hair hanging in sweaty clumps. A pang of something hit me. It took a moment to identify the emotion I wasn't used to feeling—guilt. I should have been doing this on my own while Tate stayed somewhere safe. There had to have been a better solution if only I'd been less selfish and tried harder. I could have gone back for him if I discovered the place was real, or at least have led him to believe that was an option. Only, now it was too late. There was only one direction and that was forward. "They all said north."

"Who said?"

I almost let out a laugh. Tate was finally asking the questions he should have asked earlier. Maybe then he'd have realized that my hunt for this place was based on smoke and mirrors. "Anyone who talked about it."

"Which was?"

Drunks. Druggies. Criminals. Conspiracy theory nuts. But I couldn't tell him that. Not unless I wanted Tate to lie down in the sand and give up there and then. "Anyone who talked about it."

"What's it called?"

"I don't know."

"What's it like?"

I had to concentrate on freeing myself from a particularly deep sand dune before I could answer that question, so by the time I did it came as quite the anticlimax to just repeat the same three words again.

Tate went quiet. I could almost hear his brain whirring as he picked through the information—or lack of it—I'd just given him. That was all I could give him because it was all I knew.

"It's real. I know it is."

I wasn't sure whether he was trying to convince me or himself.

27
TATE

I'd seen deserts in films so I thought I'd known what to expect. I'd known it would be hot. I'd known it would be desolate. But the reality was something else. It wasn't just hot, it was baking, the sun a blazing weapon relentless in its intention to bring me to my knees. I'd tried to shed my jacket, only for X to insist I kept it on or I'd burn. If history had taught me one thing it was that X was always right, so I'd left it on even though it felt like I was wearing a blanket. And as for desolate, I would have settled for that if it had been flat. But the sand dunes were like mini hills, each one taking an eon to climb and expending twice as much energy before the whole thing started again for the next one.

I paused to take a drink, my throat permanently feeling like I'd swallowed the sand, which wasn't beyond the realms of belief given how the slightest breeze caused it to whirl and eddy around us. I was constantly stuck in a place midway between the need to ration the water and to assuage my raging thirst, the latter never going away no matter how much I drank.

When I looked back now, there was nothing but sand. In fact, whichever direction I looked in, that was all I could see. It was no wonder that the DTP didn't venture into the desert. I was beginning to see why. Only a complete idiot would do that willingly. Yet here we were, heading north, on the say-so of men who X hadn't been willing to name. Did they even exist? Or was this some fantasy that he'd conjured up one night? I pushed that thought down. X wouldn't do that. It was just my exhausted brain starting to play tricks on me.

Darkness seemed to come quicker in the desert. When it did, we had to stop, the flashlights not providing enough light to prevent us from tumbling down a sand dune and possibly getting separated. The temperature dropped just as fast, and I went from being far too hot to freezing cold in a matter of minutes. During our journey to Maimos, we'd always been able to rely on a fire at night. But here in the middle of nowhere, there was nothing to burn, not unless we were going to start burning the few clothes we had. Therefore, the only option after eating cold tinned food from one of the cans we'd brought with us was to huddle together in the sleeping bag and try and sleep until morning came and it was back to being roasting hot.

Pressing my face against X's chest, I listened to the firm beat of his heart, hoping to take comfort from it. He seemed to be coping with the drop in temperature better than I was, his body not wracked by the same shivers that I found it so difficult to control. "I'm cold." It was stating the obvious, I knew it was. But even so, X wrapped his arms more tightly around me and I tried to get closer, despite the fact that we were already sandwiched together as tightly as possible. Everything ached as well, my legs, my arms, my back. I was one great big throbbing nerve—a cold one.

I'd hated the shitty room in Maimos, but right now I would have given anything to be back there. I'd even agree to look after the pigs. X lifted his hand to cup the back of my head, his fingers stroking through my hair. It helped some, the shivers starting to subside as his body heat gradually leached into mine. "Get some sleep, Tate. We'll have another long day ahead of us tomorrow."

"What if it's not north?"

The fact that X didn't answer my question spoke volumes.

I awoke with a smile on my face from the dream I'd been having. I couldn't remember the details, only that it had been full of fun and laughter. But then someone had lit a fire and I'd been too damn close to it. No matter where I'd tried to move to, I hadn't been able to escape its heat. Only of course it wasn't a fire, it had been the sun rising, back to torment us for another day.

Struggling to a seated position, I blinked myself awake as I searched for X. It didn't take long to locate him, his deft hands making short work of opening up another can of food which would serve as breakfast. He looked like shit, his face and hands red with sunburn and sand clinging to any exposed patch of skin. I lifted my hand to my face, wincing at how sore it was, the discovery making me realize that I probably looked just as bad as he did, if not worse.

X lifted his head and stared at me as if he'd only just registered that I was awake. I could either allow myself to wallow in a world of misery and pull us both down, or I could suck it up and continue to be optimistic even if it was false. I went for the latter, pasting a huge smile on my face. After all, it wasn't as if X hadn't been perfectly transparent that we could be walking to our deaths. He hadn't dragged me here under false pretenses—far from it. He'd tried to change my mind. I was here because I'd insisted on it, so it was nobody's fault except my own. "So…" I kept my tone as upbeat as possible. "What's the plan today? Bit of walking… bit of sunbathing… and then another night in Casa Del Sand?"

Amber eyes scoured my face as if he was searching for the real emotions hidden beneath the mask I wore. I refused to let him find them. I was going to be cheery even if it killed me. He gave in before I did, passing across the can he'd opened, along with a fork. "Yum… my favorite, cold beans." I ate a mouthful.

"Correction... warm beans, but not quite as warm as they'd be if you cooked them. They taste alright, though." Truth be told I would have eaten anything, even the dog food good old Jim had once jokingly wished on us.

X opened another can and began to eat. He was brooding, but then when wasn't he? X and brooding went together like strawberries and cream or bread and butter. I surveyed the surrounding area now that it was light, searching for anything of note. But as usual there was nothing. The view was completely identical no matter which direction I looked in. "I've decided something."

"What?"

"I hate sand."

At least that raised the ghost of a smile on X's lips. "I'm not a huge fan of it myself. It's a bitch to walk on."

I raised my half empty water bottle, trying to push down a pang of panic at the fact that we'd already consumed half our water supplies in one day. "I'll drink to that."

Even the most optimistic person could only hold out so long. My optimism lasted until the third day when, even after rationing it for the last twenty-four hours, we were on our last bottle of water, and there was still no sign of civilization. We had food, but without water and given how much we were sweating, it wouldn't do us any good once the water ran out. My lips were dry and cracked, my skin burnt wherever it wasn't covered, and the pounding in my head was now such a regular feature that I couldn't recall the last time it had been pain-free. In fact, I couldn't recall anything except this damn desert. Even the DTP seemed like a fanciful story I'd dreamt up to keep myself entertained. I'd probably have smiled at the sight of a tank had one appeared in front of me, glad that someone was going to put me out of my misery.

I stumbled, falling to my knees for at least the third time in the last hour. Or maybe it hadn't been an hour. I didn't know anymore. Time had long since lost all meaning. There was just day and night and the monotony of putting one foot in front of another. I'd taken to looking at my feet because it was a better alternative than looking up at the sun. I shook my head as a water bottle with precious little fluid left in it was shoved in front of me as I struggled to my feet. "Drink it, Tate."

I wanted to give some sort of witty retort, or at least form a spirited refusal but spirit took energy and I had precious little of it left. My brain felt like it had been dipped in treacle, so all I managed was to push his hand away and even that left me feeling breathless, like any action beyond walking was just too much. It took me three attempts to form my lips into the word "no."

"You're dehydrated."

I laughed, but it was a dry, hacking sound barely resembling one. "No shit, Sherlock." I started walking again, X following closely with the bottle still held out.

He shoved it forward again. "I want you to have it."

"And I want you to..." I didn't even know how I planned to finish that sentence... go to hell? Stop talking? Leave me alone? None of them were true so I settled for leaving it unfinished. I sighed. "We share it. You don't get to die first and leave me alone in this stinking shithole."

The emotions that flickered across X's face were like a slide show, encompassing everything from sorrow to guilt. "I'm sorry."

I lifted a hand which felt like it weighed a ton, finally managing to wag a finger at him. "Don't say you're sorry. Don't..." I shook my head. "Just keep walking. We must be close now. We'll be there before nightfall." I didn't believe a fucking word of it. Not anymore. The desert was endless. Beyond the desert there was just more desert—a never-ending world of sand. Nature's fuck you for not doing more about global warming. There was nothing on the other side of it. No city. No people. For all I knew, we'd been walking around in circles for days. X assured me that we hadn't, that he'd been using the sun to navigate, but in my beaten down state I'd come to believe that the sun was our enemy. It was out to get us so of course it would lie. Deep down, I knew my thoughts weren't rational. I just didn't know how to correct them, or if there was even any point correcting them.

All I knew was that we were going to walk until we collapsed, and then we'd both die. The end. But I'd been deadly serious when I'd told X that he didn't get to die first. I couldn't bear to see that; my heart would break. It was breaking already just from witnessing his physical deterioration. He'd already come close to death after the knife wound so I recognized the signs no matter how much he tried to hide them. The sunburn might hide the pallor, but it didn't disguise the unfocused gaze, or the way his usual gait that I'd admired so many times had slowed to a shuffle. We were both going downhill rapidly, which begged the question why we were bothering to ration the water when we were dead men walking.

I snatched the bottle from his hand, gulping half of it down in greedy mouthfuls. It wasn't enough—nowhere near, but at least I could stop thinking about it once it was gone. I shoved the bottle back at him. "Drink the rest."

X's gaze held mine, but for once he did as he was told, his eyes never once leaving mine like it was some strange sort of ceremony. Maybe it was. It was likely the last water either of us would ever drink. I took the bottle out of his hand and tossed it over my head without bothering to see where it landed, and then I started walking again.

I had no idea how many more hours passed before it was nightfall, only that it seemed like forever and when we were able to stop, we both fell down, rather than the organized bedding down of previous nights. We didn't eat. Everything we had was too salty anyway and would just make us more dehydrated, if that was even possible. X pulled the sleeping bag over the top of us and we slept, or lost consciousness, one of the two. At least I wasn't aware enough to be cold.

It was the sun that woke me. It was always the sun. I spent a moment staring up at it, imagining for a moment that I had the power to make it disappear and conjure up rain. Rain would save us, but there was barely a cloud in the sky. Besides, it would only be a short-term fix, and then we'd be back to wandering aimlessly. It was probably better to get it over with rather than to suffer false hope.

My head hurt even more and even the slightest of movements seemed to take forever to carry out given the disconnect between my brain and my body. Therefore, it took several minutes and just as many attempts before I managed to struggle up to one elbow to check on X.

His eyes were closed, but I could tell somehow that he wasn't asleep. His breathing was far too rapid, his heart struggling to keep pumping oxygen around his body when it didn't have enough fluids to do it efficiently. I knew exactly how it felt because my body was doing the same.

I attempted to speak but nothing came out, my lips moving but my mouth struggling with producing sound when my throat felt like a dried-out husk. I swallowed, an action that used to be so simple but was now incredibly painful. Finally, I managed to croak out his name. "X?"

There was movement beneath his eyelids for several seconds before he finally opened his eyes. It was worth his effort when I could finally meet his gaze. He didn't speak, just stared at me. I managed to force more words from my lips. "We can't walk anymore."

There was the tiniest inclination of his head in an acknowledgement that I assumed passed for a nod. Whatever it was, it was enough. I let my head drop onto his chest, the rapid hammering of his heart even more apparent when my ear was pressed up against it. I didn't know whether it was a relief or a disappointment that he hadn't tried to argue. Maybe I'd secretly wanted him to drag me to my feet and demand that we couldn't give up. He'd always been the strong one though, so if X was done then I didn't need to feel guilty about it. I could just accept my fate and enjoy the moments I had left—moments with X. Besides, I was so damn tired, ready to just close my eyes, go to sleep, and never wake up.

"I'm sorry." The words were whispered against my hair.

"You've got nothing to be sorry about."

"I..." There was a long hesitation, as if X were choosing his words carefully. "I've killed you."

"You saved me." I tried to move my neck into a position where I could see his face, but I'd expended all the energy I could for at least the next few minutes. "If it hadn't been for you, I'd have been dead long ago—vaporized on a nightclub floor for something I didn't do, would never do." I managed something approaching a laugh. It still amused me that I, Tate Gillespie, a goody-goody from the day I'd been born, had been accused of industrial espionage. I wouldn't have known where to start. I guess that was what had made me the perfect fall guy. Malcolm must have thought all his prayers had been answered when I blundered into his late-night machinations. "And then I would have been dead another several times over between Cofield and here." I managed to make my arm move, steering it across X's chest inch by slow inch and feeling blindly until I located his hand. Our fingers slid together, his closing around mine. "You saved me." I hoped that by saying it again he might believe it. "You showed me possibilities I'd never have known. I wouldn't change it for the world. Not even now. Not even if our last moments are right here, right now."

X's fingers squeezed tighter. "I should have made you stay in Maimos."

"You couldn't have. I meant every word I said about sneaking out. I would have done it, would have come after you. There was no changing my mind so you're not to blame."

"I could have stayed."

I smiled against his chest. "No, you couldn't. You were already planning one guy's demise. He wouldn't have survived the week, and then they would have thrown you out anyway. Rule number five hundred and six, no violence of any kind."

"I don't know what you mean."

He was so full of shit. It was almost endearing. "So the guy with the beard didn't bother you?"

"He kept sneering at me."

"He had something wrong with his mouth. It was twisted. He looked at everyone the same way."

"Maybe."

I took a deep breath, my lungs feeling as if someone had filled them with the sand that we were surrounded by. "Anyway, let's not spend the time we have left talking about some random guy."

X's other hand landed heavily on the back of my head, his fingers stroking through my hair. "What do you want to talk about?"

The caresses felt nice. What more could I want but to hold the hand of the man I loved and feel his touch before going to sleep forever? "Us."

He went still, the muscles under my chest taking on their usual rigidity whenever I brought emotions in play, but it didn't last long, X seeming to realize that holding back was pointless when there wasn't a future to save it for. It was now or never. "I think I loved you from the very first time I saw you."

"Tell me about it, please." I closed my eyes, wanting to concentrate solely on the words. Yes, it was needy, but I figured I was owed it. It wasn't like I could return the favor. I'd known X for a couple of weeks, but he'd known me—sort of—for years.

"You were on your own, just walking down the street. You looked annoyed about something, but I have no idea what…"

I tried to remember a time when something might have pissed me off when I was twelve, but of course it could have been any number of things. Twelve-year-olds weren't exactly known for their sunny disposition. I'd been as moody as any other soon-to-be-teenager and given that it had to have been soon after my father's death I'd had more excuse than most.

"Yeah, I sound irresistible."

"I don't know. There was just something about you."

I smiled. I could hardly dispute X feeling some sort of chemistry given how quickly we'd gravitated together years later. Granted, due to X's stubborn determination to remain in the shadows, it had taken a life-changing event to trigger our meeting "I wish we'd known each other sooner." There was an unmistakable note of longing in my voice.

"It wouldn't have worked. You wouldn't have looked at me twice."

I thought about it—not for the first time. "I think... I would have been scared of you at first because you're, well... you, but then, I'd like to think that I'd have seen that we were perfect for each other, because we are, X. You're the yin to my yang. You're the..." I couldn't think of anything else with my brain having been replaced by cotton wool. "I love you."

I painstakingly levered myself back up, slow movement by slow movement, the whole process taking even longer than it had the first time, my head spinning so much that it felt like I was going to pass out. It would be worth it though when I finally got to do what I was aiming for.

"Tate?" He accompanied the question with a squeeze of my hand, our fingers still entwined.

"Shhh." I was finally face to face with him again, pressing my dry lips over his in what would be our last kiss. We made it count, our lips pressed together for as long as we could manage until I had to pull back for oxygen that was already in short supply.

X's lips attempted to curl into a smile. Although, I could tell it was painful for him. "I love you too."

I slid back down his chest, resuming my earlier position with a smile on my face. "One day you'll say that when we're not about to die." Except that he wouldn't, would he? But I could pretend. My eyelids were too heavy now to keep open, so I let them drift closed. "Going to tell… your knives… that you… love them too?" My voice sounded slurred, each word more difficult than the last to get out.

X's chest moved as if he was attempting to laugh but no sound came out. "Love you… more than them."

"Can I have… that… in writing."

"Don't have… a pen."

I think I dozed for a while then. At least it seemed that time had passed, the blazing heat of the sun seeming to come from a slightly different position. "X?" My voice was barely a whisper. I squeezed his fingers and said it again, managing to add a bit more volume. His chest still rose and fell so I knew he was still breathing, but there was no response. I hoped for his sake that he'd just go to sleep and not wake up again, and that it would be the same for me. I let myself slip back into a dreamworld, my last conscious thought the old quote that it was better to have loved and lost than never to have loved at all.

28
TATE

Something wasn't right. I felt cool. In fact, I was bordering on being too cold. Yet, something told me that it wasn't dark. It was like the laboratories at work where they used to keep the air-con on all day long. Was that where I was? Had it all been some strange sort of dream where I'd never been accused of a crime I didn't commit and sentenced to death. No journey. No sewers. No DTP. No desert. No... X.

I sat bolt upright and opened my eyes. I wasn't in a laboratory but beyond that I couldn't make any sense out of where I was. I concentrated on gleaning as much information as I could from my surroundings, hoping it would all start to fit together in a way that solved the puzzle. I was on a bed, the mattress soft beneath me and the sheets a pristine white that I hadn't seen since leaving Cofield. It was a double bed, but the opposite side of it was empty. The room I was in was large, the walls painted a soft yellow and the furniture far more opulent than any I'd ever seen before, most looking like it had been carved from wood by hand. Not the cheap stuff either but the expensive type that I couldn't even remember the name of.

The room was empty apart from me, air con just as I'd suspected blowing cold drafts of air from vents above my head. On the far side of the room, there was a window, the curtains just a shade darker than the walls.

Once I'd done an inventory of the room, I started on myself. My hands were bandaged, which was another thing that didn't make sense. I hadn't hurt my hands, so why would they be bandaged? I lifted a tentative hand to my face, but through the thick fabric of the bandages I couldn't feel a thing. I was naked apart from a dark pair of boxer briefs which weren't my own, which meant that someone had undressed me and put them on me. But who? Why? Where were they?

There was a slight throb in my temple, like the last vestiges of a headache disappearing. But apart from that, I felt fine. Confused, but fine. The last thing I remembered was the desert and the knowledge that I was about to die. But I wasn't dead. At least I didn't think I was. Not unless heaven was a hell of a lot different than I'd always imagined it to be.

I swung my feet over the edge of the bed to find soft carpet. Wherever I was, there was no expense spared on the décor. Maybe it was heaven. I certainly couldn't think of anywhere that looked like this room did. Or maybe it wasn't heaven and I was still in the desert, having some sort of lucid dream. It seemed like a strange thing to conjure up though: a room I'd never seen before with no people in it. And if it was a dream, why could I feel things? I shouldn't be cold. I shouldn't be able to feel the plush carpet between my toes, and my head shouldn't ache. Eyeing the window on the other side of the room, I contemplated my chances of being able to make it over that far. What would I see if I looked out of it? A scenic view? A dark void? A brick wall? Nothing would have surprised me at the moment. Well, there was only one way to find out.

I'd barely started to shift my weight onto my feet when the door flew open. I froze, staring in disbelief at the pretty woman who stood in the doorway. She was blonde, her hair long but tied back in a ponytail. Her flowery dress and the apron she wore over the top of it made her look like the pictures of the 1950's housewives I'd seen in history books.

She seemed just as surprised to see me as I was to see her. Her lips formed a silent "o" before she seemed to catch herself and it transformed into a huge smile. "You're awake! We thought you'd be out for at least another day."

Despite her apparent friendliness, I couldn't help but scramble backwards on the bed in an effort to put some distance between us. "Am I dead?"

The smile trembled on her lips before changing to a frown. She stepped closer, the door closing behind her. Placing her hands on her hips, she stared at me for a minute before letting out a loud tut. "Now, why would you go and say a thing like that?"

Blood roared in my ears and all I wanted was for everything to go away. The room. The woman. The goddamn cold draft. Everything. It was all too much. "Am I?"

"Of course not."

I swallowed with difficulty. My throat felt dry, but it seemed like more of a memory of my time in the desert than anything else. "So where am I?"

She nodded, understanding dawning on her face. "I'm so stupid. Of course you're confused. Why wouldn't you be? What's the last thing you can remember?"

I forced myself to breathe more evenly. At least that was a question I could answer. "The desert. We'd been walking for days, trying to find a place beyond the desert that probably doesn't even exist." *If I wasn't dead, then where was X?* "We ran out of water, and we couldn't go any farther and it was so hot. I went to sleep." That was all I could say.

She nodded. "Well, you found us. Indirectly at least. I guess you could say, we found you really. You weren't that far out though. You'd nearly gotten here."

"You found us in the desert?" *Us! Where's X? Why haven't you mentioned him?*

She smiled again. "We did. And in the nick of time. We

weren't sure for a while that you'd make it. You were extremely dehydrated, and you were unconscious." She inclined her head towards my bandaged hands. "And extremely burnt everywhere that wasn't covered. We had to bandage them because even unconscious, you kept scratching." She lay a hand against her chest, which made her look even more like she should have been in a black and white film. "Forgive me, I haven't even told you my name. It's Clara."

She raised an eyebrow and waited. Eventually, it dawned on me that she was expecting me to return the favor and tell her my name. "Tate." *Ask me what my companion's name is.* But she didn't, hurrying over to the window instead to pull the curtains wider so that more light flooded into the room. Something she'd said suddenly occurred to me. "So this place… this is where we were looking for? It's the place we were trying to get to?"

She turned back around with a nod. "Yes, this is Kalboa."

I sagged back against the pillows, a tumult of emotions swirling through my body. X had been right all along. It was real. We hadn't been chasing an invisible dream after all; we'd just seriously underestimated how far it was and how difficult it would be to get there. "How did you find *us*?" I kept stressing the us, hoping it would spur her into mentioning X. The longer she spent avoiding the subject, the more a heavy sensation settled in the pit of my stomach. There was only one reason I could think of that would cause her not to mention him. Had I survived, and he'd died? Tears pricked my eyes at the thought. X was stronger than me, but he'd still been recovering from the knife wound, so…

Oblivious to my inner turmoil, Clara continued with the answer to my question.

"We do patrols sometimes. We've had people arrive from there before…" She said there like it was a dirty word. "…not many though. We find more, that… well, don't make it than people who do. At least then we can give them a proper burial.

That's why we started the patrols in the first place. Normally, we're still too late. The desert is such a harsh environment." She didn't need to tell me that. I'd had a fight with it and lost. "But sometimes..." She gave me a beaming smile. "... we're lucky and we find people like you."

"How many days has it been since you found me?" Even I was switching from us to me now.

"Two days."

I lowered my foot to the floor gingerly. Two days. That wasn't that long. There was absolutely no reason why my limbs shouldn't work properly after only two days. And if Clara wasn't going to tell me anything, then I'd just have to search for the answers myself. She was too busy chattering to notice as I eased myself to standing. "I think you'll like it here. It's very different from the world you're used to so it may take a period of adjustment, but once you do get used to it, most people seem to prefer it." She gave a musical laugh. "Although... it's not like anyone's going to head back across the desert, so I guess there's a little bit of bias there."

Tuning her out, I took careful steps across to the door that Clara had come in through, feeling stronger with every step I took. The door creaked slightly as I pulled it open and she whirled around with a confused look on her face. "Where are you going?"

I didn't stop to offer her a response, taking off down the long corridor that lay beyond the door. There were a multitude of doors, and I flung open every one that I passed that wasn't locked. Empty room. On to the next door. Another empty room which was some sort of makeshift gym by the looks of it. Next room. Two men spun around at my entrance, their expressions somewhere midway between confusion and surprise. As neither of them were X, I ignored them and continued my search. It dawned on me that it would have been far easier just to ask, but whether it was because I'd only just regained consciousness, or because I couldn't bear to put the question into words, I didn't know. Besides, I'd started now. I may as well continue.

"Tate?" That was Clara, who'd been trailing in my wake the whole time. "If you tell me what you're looking for, I might be able to help?"

Next came a storage room with things piled up to the ceiling in boxes. The room made me think of Talon. No gold cupids in sight though. Clara was getting closer to me, her pretty face full of bemusement. What did she think I was looking for? She must know, surely? I flung open another door and froze for a few seconds in the doorway staring at the bed. Or more specifically the dark hair on the pillow. And then I was rushing toward him. Not even the proverbial wild horses could have held me back.

He was still. Too still. But the main thing was that he was alive, a flutter of warmth in my chest expanding to a full-blown inferno within seconds. There was a chair next to the bed, so I sat in it, grabbing X's hand and pulling it into my lap. It was bandaged just as mine was so I had no chance of any skin to skin contact, but it was still better than nothing.

Clara appeared next to me. "Oh! I should have realized, sorry. He hasn't woken up yet."

Emotion choked my throat for a few seconds. "I thought he was dead, and you just weren't telling me."

"Oh God, no! I just… I guess I was only thinking about one thing at a time, and I wasn't sure what the relationship was between the two of you."

I dashed away the tears of relief which had insisted on spilling down my cheeks. "He's my boyfriend." I laughed at my own statement, the words sounding way too simple to sum up our relationship, and it also struck me as absurd that we'd never even had that conversation. Uttered words of mutual love, yes, but discussed the fact that we were in a relationship, no. I lifted his hand and kissed it, the fabric bandage rough against my lips.

In the background, I was dimly aware of Clara reassuring

the two men who must have followed me that everything was fine before shooing them away.

Everything *was* fine now that I'd found X. I stroked my fingers across his forehead, the skin still red. But then I guessed it would take longer than a couple of days for the burns to heal. "Wake up, X." As he wasn't *Sleeping Beauty*, and I wasn't a visiting prince, the words had zero effect.

I cast my eyes around the room, searching for something in particular. When my scrutiny came up empty, I turned to Clara, who still looked a little dazed. "Where are his knives? He'll want them close when he wakes up."

To give her her due, she barely blinked at the somewhat strange request. I had a feeling that I'd end up liking her eventually, strange fifties fashion sense and all. "I'll see that they're brought here. You should go back to bed. You need to rest and get your strength back."

I shook my head. "No, I'm staying here. I want to be the first thing he sees when he wakes up."

She stared at me for a minute but seemed to work out from my set expression that it was pointless arguing with me. Finally, she nodded. "Okay. I'll have some food sent here for you. You're probably hungry?"

I hadn't even considered it, but after a brief moment of self-evaluation I had to concede I was. Starving, in fact.

"Maybe clothes as well?"

I blushed. In all the rush to find X, I'd completely forgotten that my only covering was borrowed underwear. As to who I'd borrowed them from, that was still up for debate. It was probably one of those questions that it was better not to know the answer to. Along with who'd stripped me out of my clothes and put me in them. "Please... and the knives."

Clara bustled out of the room, leaving me alone with X. Shuffling the chair even closer to the bed, I enfolded his hand in both of mine. "Hey, gorgeous. Just us again. Just the way we like it, right? You and me against the world. Well, mainly you, but I can pass you weapons or something. Or offer my body as a reward for a job well done."

If I'd hoped that my voice might cause him to suddenly re-enter the world of the living, I was in for a huge disappointment when X didn't even stir. What was it Clara had said? They'd been surprised that I'd regained consciousness so quickly. Therefore, I didn't need to be unduly concerned about the fact that X was still out for the count. Not yet, anyway. "I can wait for you. I've waited twenty-six years. I can wait a couple of days longer."

The next forty-eight hours passed in somewhat of a blur. I resisted all attempts to make me return to my own room, no matter who made them. Clara had tried, and at one point she'd appeared with a gray-haired man in tow who'd tried as well. He'd told me his name, but either I hadn't listened well enough to take it in, in the first place, or I couldn't remember it. It was probably rude, but I couldn't concentrate on anything else, not while X still lay in the bed, breathing but unconscious. Clara had kept her word to retrieve the knives, watching me curiously as I'd counted them to make sure that none were missing before arranging them carefully on top of an elaborately carved chest of drawers close to the bed.

At some point, clothes had been given to me—not my own, but then my own hadn't really been mine either. They'd been Talon's and someone else's before that. The clothes were a little big, but they did their intended job of giving me something to sit around in apart from underwear. At night, I squeezed myself into the bed with X, retreating back to the chair in the light of day.

It took until the third day before he woke up, dark eyelashes fluttering against his cheek for a few seconds before I was rewarded with the beautiful amber gaze I'd been longing for. I squeezed his hand, unable to keep the smile off my face. "Hey! About time you woke up, sleepyhead."

X's gaze flitted around the room before finally settling on me. His lips moved soundlessly as if he was testing out their ability to form words before he finally spoke. Even so, his voice was thin and raspy. "Am I dead?"

My smile grew wider. "That's exactly what I thought when I woke up, which may I add was two whole days before you. Ever since then I've been sitting here waiting for you, lazy bones."

X lifted his free hand, the one that I wasn't holding captive between mine and stared at the bandages wrapped tightly around his hand. "I look like a fucking mummy."

A bark of laughter escaped from my throat. "I better tell you what happened because, trust me, if I leave it to Clara, you'll be going crazy waiting for her to get to the point."

"Who the fuck is Clara? Where the fuck am I?"

He was starting to sound better already. "They found us in the desert. Brought us back here. This is the place we were looking for. It's called Kalboa. We found it, X. Or..." I grimaced. "... they found us before we died if you want to really split hairs. However, it happened, we're here."

X stared at me as if he was struggling to process the information. "What's it like?"

I shook my head. "I have absolutely no idea. I've been waiting for you to wake up so that we can find out together. The people I've met so far have seemed nice though. Oh, and..."

I let go of his hand and ran across to the chest of drawers, snatching up one of the longer blades and waving it in the air. "Look, who's here to see you." I picked the other one up. "Betsy and Barbara."

X blinked before lifting his hand and curling his fingers into a come-hither motion. "If they had names, which they haven't, I certainly wouldn't call them Betsy and fucking Barbara." I passed them over to him, his fingers immediately fastening around the handles. Although the sight of X clutching the knives whilst in bed was slightly incongruous, it was strangely right at the same time.

I took my place in the chair again, fighting the urge to drape myself across him to check that he wasn't just some sort of delightful hallucination. He turned his head on the pillow to face me and for a moment we just stared at each other. When he dropped the knife and lifted his hand, I leaned forward and met him halfway, his fingers curling around my cheek. "I thought…"

I didn't let him finish. "Yeah, me too. But we've got a second chance. And whatever this place is like, we can find a way to make it work. I'm sure of it." I gestured over to the window at the light streaming in. "Look, we're not underground. That's a great start."

I'd ventured over to the window on a couple of occasions when restlessness had gotten the better of me, but the scenery hadn't really provided much information about what lay beyond the house we were in. And if I was being completely honest, the sight of the desert in the distance had made me sick to my stomach. It would be a long time before I could think about those days in the desert with anything close to dispassion. There were some moments though that I'd hold onto, like the naked honesty of the conversation that I'd thought would be our last. That's assuming it hadn't been a hallucination, my dying brain conjuring up what it needed to hear during a time of great stress.

X's gaze homed in on the furrowing of my brow, his thumb sweeping across my cheekbone. "I love you, Tate."

I could have sworn that my heart swelled to ten times its size until my chest could barely contain it. I turned my head to the side, far enough to enable me to kiss his bandaged palm, even though I knew he wouldn't be able to feel it. "Is there some sort of danger I don't know about? A snake under the bed, maybe? Ninjas about to burst through the window?"

He raised a questioning eyebrow and I grinned at him. "You've only ever told me that before when there's a high possibility of us both dying."

X's gaze didn't waver from mine. "And you told me that one day I would say it when we're not about to die…" My breath caught in my throat. It hadn't been a hallucination then. "… so here I am, proving you right. I'll say it every day if you want." He sagged back against the pillows as if the words had left him completely spent. Either that or the fact that he'd gone without food for even longer than I had before regaining consciousness, had finally caught up with him.

I smiled at him. "No, you won't. But that's okay. I'll know it's true anyway. I don't need to hear it all the time. Just every now and again."

Clara had been right when she'd said there'd need to be a period of adjustment. Kalboa was worlds apart from what we were used to. Everywhere we looked we were surrounded by a freedom and equality we weren't used to seeing. Yes, the people had jobs. But they didn't seem to dominate their lives to the extent that they had in Cofield. And people were happy. Even in Cofield, which had been a positive fairy tale in comparison to the slums—and in retrospect most of the other places we'd passed through during our journey—there'd been a permanent air of dread with people on edge, living in fear of the DTP brandishing their heavy-handed justice.

X had been up and about within a day, and we'd been left to explore on our own. No tour. No rule book to scrutinize that we'd be tested on at a later date. Just "Have a look around and come and speak to us if you have any questions." The "us" in question was Montague, the gray-haired man I'd virtually ignored, and his younger brother, Melvin. Melvin was married to Clara, and together with his brother they headed the council who ran the city.

There was no getting away from the heat in the city. But that was to be expected given its proximity to the desert. And from what we'd seen so far, that was its only downside. The buildings were nicer than Cofield, all glass and polished metal. It wasn't hard to see that it was a city untouched by war. There were things there that I'd seen in old films but had never expected to see in real life, such as the large as life police station that X and I had stood and stared at for quite some time with uniformed policemen and women going about their daily business.

There were shops and businesses and parks where children could play. Basically, anything you could think of was tucked away in Kalboa somewhere. You just had to know where to look.

As for living arrangements, we'd been allocated a house in the northern part of the city. I'd laughed for ages the first time I'd seen it, unable to stop myself from comparing it to the tiny room in Maimos where I'd nearly ended up living out my days. The house was huge in comparison. It seemed crazy to have all that space just for the two of us, but I wasn't about to look a gift horse in the mouth. There were even two bedrooms, not that X had any chance of sleeping in a separate room if I had anything to do with it.

There was a question mark in the air over whether the house was permanent or not. During the meeting we were about to attend with the two brothers, it was one of the many questions I intended to ask. I was hoping to see Clara as well. I'd never really gotten a chance to thank her for playing nursemaid to the both of us. I'd been so wrapped up in X that all I'd really given her was a great deal of grief.

X lounged back against the wall and I couldn't help but stare, my gaze roving greedily over every inch of his body. The hot weather definitely had its perks, one of them being X's muscular arms being permanently bare. He still wore black, people looking at him as if he was mad. Although, that might have had more to do with the twin knives he still wore. No one had tried to take them off him. Not yet, anyway. So… he'd carried on. I guessed that would also be addressed during this meeting. It wasn't like I'd seen anyone else wandering around Kalboa armed to the back teeth.

"Tate, don't look at me like that."

I hid my smirk, projecting as much wide-eyed innocence as I could muster. "Like what?"

"Like you want to strip off all my clothes and find out what's underneath."

I let my smile free, lowering my voice to a seductive purr. "I already know what's underneath. I've explored it many times with my hands… with my fingers and with my… tongue. Refresher courses are always welcome though, so feel free to lose the clothes. I certainly won't complain."

X's chin tipped up in a clear challenge. "Why don't you try to take them off me if you want it so much. Let's see how far you get?"

It was probably a good thing that the door opened at that point to reveal Montague standing in the doorway. Five more minutes and I wasn't sure either X or myself would have remembered where we were. His gaze moved between us as if he'd picked up on some of the tension and was trying to work out where it had come from. Luckily, his eyes never dropped below waist height, or he'd have been treated to a free demonstration of my burgeoning arousal at the thought of a naked X.

He waved us into the office where Melvin was already seated. Although, it wasn't like any office I'd ever seen before. There was no desk or computer, only opulent furniture, including the most decorative three-piece sofa I'd ever seen.

It was to this that Montague gestured us over, indicating that we should take a seat. I shouldn't have been surprised at the décor really. It was after all the same house that X and I had awoken in. I lowered myself gingerly, resisting the sofa's attempt to swallow me whole, and not even bothering to try and hide my amusement at the sight of X perched on a pale pastel cushion. Yeah, this was definitely a whole new world.

Melvin waved a hand at a nearby table that contained a teapot and dainty little cups. It had Clara written all over it. "Tea?" I shook my head, X doing the same. Shame! I would have given everything I owned—which granted wasn't much—to watch him sip tea from delicate bone china.

Crossing his leg over his knee with his hands resting loosely in his lap, Montague's gaze swept over us both. "So, you've had a chance to look around. What do you think?"

"It's nice."

I nearly choked on my tongue as the words came out of X's mouth. I wondered if the brothers realized that X saying something was nice was akin to someone else saying spectacular. Any minute now a pig would fly into the room and the moon would turn blue. At my silence, Montague's gaze swung my way. I quickly nodded. "Yeah, it's different. But different in a good way."

He smiled. "Good." He reached across to pour steaming liquid from the teapot into a cup. "You've probably got lots of questions?"

I struggled my way out of the plush cushions to sit farther forward. "A few."

"Well…" Montague smiled, but it was notably cautious. "…I thought I might start with a quick history lesson and then tell you where I see you fitting into our little civilization."

"Okay." I threw a quick glance at X, wondering if he was getting the same vibes as I was. As usual though, his expression was inscrutable so I couldn't tell whether he too thought that Montague was picking his words carefully, almost as if he thought we might not like what he had to say. Was our new life about to come crashing down already?

Montague cleared his throat. "We know quite a lot about the world you come from and how things are done there. You will probably have seen already that we do things very differently here. We arrest, rather than execute, and we have a rigorous court system to ensure a fair hearing. However..." His gaze fastened on X. "... like any civilization that has its limitations. There are certain regrettable situations that sometimes call for, let's say more immediate action, either as a deterrent, or as a..." He grimaced as he struggled to try and find the right words. "... I suppose you would say a cure. Occasionally situations arise that threaten the safety of thousands of our citizens. Situations where all other solutions have been looked into and found not to be viable. They are few, but they do crop up."

A gleam appeared in X's eyes as he tipped his chin up. "You need an assassin?"

Color crept into Montague's cheeks as his gaze dropped to linger on one of X's knives. "Basically, yes."

"And you think I might have the necessary skills you need?"

Montague looked sheepish, but in the end, it was Melvin who answered, the first words out of his mouth since we'd entered the room. "We've talked about it, and we suspect that, yes, you could be the person we've been searching for, for years. But..." He held up a hand. "If you said yes, it would be council-approved targets only. You're not entitled to take the law into your own hands and go around killing people willy-nilly. And if you do agree to take on this role, we can discuss payment, which will of course be suitably generous for such a... challenging position. The house where you've been staying will also be part of the package."

I couldn't help but voice the question on my lips. "What if he says no?" It was a stupid question really. One of my biggest fears had been how X was going to manage to keep that part of himself in check. Yet here he was being offered a golden opportunity to harness it, rather than bury it altogether.

Montague tipped his head to one side as he considered the question. "Then we'll have to discuss other possibilities. We would probably need to find a viable alternative for the overt knife carrying, something a little more socially acceptable."

X interjected. "I'll do it."

Melvin's eyebrows shot up. "You probably want to consider it for a bit longer." He waved a hand in my direction. "Talk it over between yourselves, make a collective decision. There's no rush."

I smiled. "He doesn't need to think about it for longer or discuss it with me. He knows that whatever he wants to do, I'll support him. If X is happy, then I'm happy too." I didn't care if I sounded like some sort of sappy housewife when it was true. I added a shrug. "So…"

Montague sat back on the couch looking like the cat that had gotten the cream, or I guess the council member that had gotten the assassin. He'd probably never dreamed that one would fall right into his lap. After a few seconds of looking pleased with himself, he turned his attention to me. "And don't worry, we haven't forgotten about you. There's plenty of possibilities that we can discuss."

I nodded. "As long as it doesn't involve pigs." The two men looked understandably perplexed, comprehension gradually dawning as I launched into a brief explanation.

X
Epilogue

Walking down the busy street, I smiled to myself as someone automatically crossed over to the opposite side to avoid me. A month after arriving, I still couldn't get used to how different things were here in comparison to where I used to live. Back in the slums, I'd spent most of my time in the shadows aiming not to be seen. But here, I was a figurehead. They wanted me to be seen—and feared. And that was a role I was never going to struggle with. My 'job' so far had mostly consisted of appearing in the places they wanted me to be—a silent threat on the edge of society, a reminder to the people who were lucky enough to live in Kalboa that their justice system was fair and that other places weren't so just. Nine times out of ten it worked with whatever situation had arisen, de-escalating to the point where the police could deal with it through the usual channels.

I'd be lying if I said there wasn't a slight itch under my skin, a desire for someone to go rogue so that I would be asked to deal with it using more persuasive devices. It would happen. There was no doubt in my mind. They hadn't gone to all the trouble of hiring me just to have me standing around looking scary. That itch, that need to free myself from the restraints of polite civilization, would die down, though, as soon as I was around Tate.

Tate. Even thinking about him brought a smile to my face. He'd changed me in ways I couldn't even begin to quantify. He'd always been my world. But there was a big difference between sharing it with him and lurking on the outskirts looking in. He was everything that I'd never known I needed. Kind. Funny. Patient until he wasn't, which never ceased to be entertaining. And, of course, so damn sexy that it only took one look from him to bring me to heel. If the X I'd been before was feral, well, then Tate had tamed me without even having to try. He would no doubt argue that point. But then Tate liked to argue as much as he liked to breathe. Mostly to provoke, to push me into that headspace where I'd treat him the way he yearned to be treated, the two of us coming together like the purest of chemical reactions.

One month living with him had been worth more than my entire life up to that point, and I knew that I'd never grow tired of him. I'd never had any desire to grow old and gray before. But now I did. I wanted to see what Tate would look like a few decades down the line. And that was a revelation, something worth every moment of pain and suffering we'd endured to get to this point.

Tate had settled into working three days a week. He didn't need to work full-time, given my more than generous salary. It was his choice. It wasn't as if I had any desire to keep him at home like a good little housewife, and I'd never have dared use that term to him even in jest. It wasn't worth the risk of waking in the middle of the night to find him contemplating chopping my balls off.

In the end, he hadn't wanted to go back into the pharmaceutical trade, saying that it reminded him too much of things he'd rather forget. Instead, he'd taken a position at the local town hall dealing with daily inquiries that would have made me want to hang myself within the first five minutes. But Tate seemed to like it, especially the social aspects of the role. I didn't want, or need, to talk to anyone—except him. But he wasn't me, he needed to discuss the weather. Although, that was a damn short conversation in a place where it was roasting hot ninety-eight percent of the time. The other two percent consisted of the torrential rain we'd wished for in the desert and never gotten.

Unlocking the door of our house, I pushed it open, my mind flicking back as it so often did to the days when part of that routine would involve disarming a shotgun. It was nice to have evenings which didn't consist of getting rid of corpses. I slipped my hand into my pocket, pulling the silver rat charm free that I always carried around. I smiled as I left it in full view on a table where Tate would find it later and freak out. As traditions went, it was a strange one, but one I intended to keep up. Besides, we'd survived the desert, so who was to say that it didn't bring good luck. Tilting my head to the side, I tried to get a sense of whether Tate was there. He hadn't been working today, but that didn't necessarily mean anything. Faint noises from the kitchen told me that he was most likely in there. I headed that way, pausing in the doorway to admire him for a moment while he had his back to me. In this climate, his hair was lighter and his skin much more tanned. The most important thing was that he looked happy and relaxed.

Sensing my stare, he spun around, his eyes narrowing when he saw me standing there. "Oh my God! I've got a stalker."

"Not just any stalker."

Predictably, the pseudo annoyance that he'd managed to muster lasted no more than a few seconds before his face creased into a grin. "*The* stalker."

"And don't you forget it."

He winked. "I've got a surprise for you."

I crossed my arms over my chest. "Is it in your trousers?"

He snorted, his eyes dancing with merriment. "Not this time. It's in the living room… sort of."

When he didn't elaborate, I headed in that direction to find the table that we hardly ever used set up as if we were having a dinner party. Covered dishes lined the center of the table. "What's this?"

Tate waved a hand at an empty chair as he eased himself into the one opposite. "I made a promise once that I'd take you out on a date. Only…" He rested his chin on his hands, waiting until I'd sat down before continuing. "… I decided that I didn't want to take you out. I prefer having you all to myself."

My gaze slid to an empty chair positioned at right angles to mine. "Who's the empty chair for—your girlfriend?" I was referring to Clara, the two of them having become as thick as thieves over the last few weeks. I suspected that was where the food we were about to eat had come from. Tate was many things, but a good cook wasn't one of them.

Tate rolled his eyes. "No, it's not for *my* girlfriend. It's for *your* girlfriends."

I shook my head, understanding only dawning when Tate reached across the table to divest me of my knives before laying them gently on the empty chair. "There you go, Betsy and Barbara. Once upon a time, I promised a very grumpy man just because he was so damn sexy that I'd include you in the date. So… you just sit there and be quiet."

I bit my lip to keep myself from laughing. Yeah, X laughing. Fancy that. Tate really had changed me in mysterious ways. "I asked you not to call them that. They don't have names."

Tate's gaze stayed fixed on the knives. "Don't listen to the nasty man. He'll stroke you and caress you and make you feel special, but he won't give you names."

"Are we still talking about the knives?"

He ignored me. "And how are you two doing anyway, now that you're not getting anywhere near as much action? I bet you're finding it hard?"

I stiffened. There'd been an unspoken mutual agreement between us not to discuss it, which I'd been only too happy to go along with. Only, it seemed we were going to talk about it, just not directly. "They're... finding that they have different priorities. That this world is very different to the one they're used to. But they're adjusting, and they're..." I hesitated, rolling the word I wanted to say around on my tongue first and checking if it fit, especially when I couldn't remember ever having used it before. Not to describe myself at least. I went ahead and said it anyway, dropping any pretense that we were talking about the knives. "I'm happy."

Tate's head whipped up, his gaze meeting mine with a dazzling smile on his lips. "Good. I'm happy too." He waved a hand at the dishes in the middle of the table. "Now eat before it gets cold. I want to remember my first date with my gorgeous boyfriend."

Dinner hadn't been dinner, not really. Sure, we'd eaten. But it had been more about foreplay, Tate doing everything he could to flirt and tease, using the food as a weapon in his ongoing mission to drive me crazy, with his tongue making an appearance far more than it needed to. Well, it was about time he paid for that. I placed the dirty plates down on the kitchen counter before calling back to the room where we'd eaten. "Tate, come here?"

There was a long pause before the answer floated down the hallway. "Make me."

Oh, it was like that, was it? A few strides had me back in the living room. In one quick motion, I'd snatched up one of the knives from the chair and had the point pressed under Tate's chin. His reaction was instantaneous: his cheeks flooding with color, and his breathing turning decidedly ragged. I took a slow step backwards, giving him no option but to follow. We continued in that slightly awkward fashion until we'd reached the kitchen. There was no particular reason to be in the kitchen, apart from that being the room where I'd originally made the request that Tate had decided to refuse.

Despite his obvious arousal, I watched him closely. I'd learned his tells for when he wanted it rough and for when he needed something more measured, something softer. I was equally happy to provide either. Whatever Tate wanted, he got. I altered the position of my wrist slightly to force the knife blade higher so that Tate not only had to tip his head back but also had to stand on tiptoes. He didn't hesitate, the gleam in his eyes telling me that he definitely was in the mood for something a bit kinkier. Good. Because so was I.

I backed him over to the far side of the kitchen where the window was. Gathering both of his wrists with my free hand, I pinned them to the wall above his head, the point of my knife still pressing into the soft skin of his neck. I might draw blood, but it would be nothing more than a pinprick. Tate swallowed as I aligned my body with his, the movement of his throat teasing the blade. Any doubt that there could be any real fear there was assuaged as he shifted his hips to better bracket mine, the heat of our erections burning just as hot for both of us.

He held my gaze as he moved his wrists within my grasp to test how firmly I held them. As the answer was pretty damn firm, he didn't get far. His gaze skittered toward the window, his breath catching. "Anyone can see us."

I gyrated my hips against his, letting him feel the length of the cock desperate to be inside him. "So let them see."

Tate exhaled slowly. "But what if they make a complaint?"

I trailed the point of the knife over his Adam's apple. "Then I'll shut them up so that they're not capable of making another one." They were just words. I had no intention of silencing our neighbors. Given their advanced age, they were more likely to have a heart attack if one of them happened to pass by and glance through the window. The idea of them mustering enough courage to come round and complain was quite frankly ludicrous. "Clothes off."

Tate's tongue darted out to moisten his lips. "Here?"

"Here."

"You'll need to move your knife then."

"I could cut them off." Tate's breathing accelerated that little bit more and I filed it away as something to revisit in the future when he hadn't gone to the effort of dressing up. I smiled, letting the blade drift away from his neck, only to turn my wrist and lay the flat part of the blade against his lips. "Kiss it goodbye."

"Perverted fucker."

"Takes one to know one."

He pursed his lips to deliver an overexaggerated and noisy kiss to the cold metal. But Tate being Tate, he couldn't leave it at that. "Bye, Betsy. See you later."

Letting the knife clatter to the floor, I silenced him with my lips, my kiss hard and dominant, forcing his mouth open whether he wanted it or not. Except he did. Of course he did. He gave back everything I dished out with interest, his captured wrists straining as he writhed against me.

When I finally pulled back, I gave myself a few precious moments to admire him, taking in his moist and reddened lips, his flushed cheeks, and his dilated pupils. This was a Tate I would never tire of seeing as long as I lived. Especially knowing that all that pent-up passion was for me and me alone.

His lips curled into a provocative smile, one that promised I'd get everything I was currently fantasizing about and more. "I thought you wanted me to take my clothes off?" His eyes flicked upwards, a reminder that I still held his wrists, which made my directive impossible to follow. I stole one more bruising kiss just to let him know I was in charge before letting go of his wrists. Then I stepped back and watched, reveling in every inch of bare skin that was revealed as Tate stripped until he was naked, his beautiful cock curving against his abdomen.

I wanted to drop to my knees and worship his cock, to let the contractions of my throat slowly tease an orgasm out of him until I could taste his cum. But that wasn't the game we were playing today so it would have to wait. Later, I could take him to bed, and we could do gentle and slow. But that wasn't what Tate needed right now. Wrapping my fingers around the back of his neck, I directed him over to the window, pushing him up against it so that his fingers splayed against the glass. "Not here, X."

I lowered my lips to his ear. "Yes, here."

"Shit!" Despite his epithet, he made no attempt to move away from the window.

I backed off a couple of steps. "Don't move." Keeping my eyes on his tight ass, I wasted no time in extracting the lube from the kitchen drawer, long since having learned that it was better to keep some in every room for just such an eventuality. Halfway back across the kitchen, I slowed to a stop, letting the seconds tick away as Tate pressed himself more firmly against the cold glass, his thighs parting in an unmistakable invitation. He was different with me than with anyone he'd ever had sex with before. And lord knows, I should know, having watched him so often. The knowledge was heady—a precious gift that no one could ever take away from me.

"X." He elongated my name, dragging it out in an impassioned plea for attention.

Unzipping my fly to release my cock, I lubed myself up before I got back to him. I wrapped my arms around him, letting him feel that I was still dressed, the material of my trousers rasping over his bare skin. His head lolled back against my shoulder as my hands explored his body without once touching his cock where he wanted them the most. Even when he tried to shift himself so that I had no choice, I managed to evade his manipulation. Pushing him harder against the glass to keep him immobile, I slid my cock between his ass cheeks to tease his hole.

Tate let out a little moan. "Aren't you going to take your clothes off?"

I nipped at his neck. "And display myself at the window

where anyone could see? Not fucking likely."

I swallowed the protest that I knew was coming from his lips with my own, easing myself inside him at the same time so that I could taste the moans and whimpers that came from his lips as his body adjusted to the cock pushing into him.

He still had plenty to say when I eventually released his lips though, even with the slow rhythm that I'd started up, his ass feeling just as perfect wrapped around my cock as it always did. "Fucking bastard! It's alright for me to display myself like a cheap whore though, isn't it? It's alright for everyone to see me. What if Clara comes round?"

I hid a smile against his nape, my hips moving more urgently. "Then I guess she'll get to find out what your cock looks like."

"She—"

Whatever he'd been going to say was lost as I sped up, concentrating on giving Tate what he needed, my grip punishing enough to give him that slight edge of pain that he needed today. Every grunt he gave, every pant, every breathy exhalation was music to my ears. Our hips moved in unison as we found the perfect rhythm that would push us both over the edge.

"X! Hurry up. Someone's coming."

I was close anyway, biting down on his shoulder hard enough to leave teeth marks, I thrust twice more before spilling myself into him. Taking only a couple of seconds to recover from my orgasm, I pulled him away from the window, the smear on the glass revealing that I wasn't the only one who'd come. I might have told him that I didn't care who saw him, but at the end of the day only one person got to see him naked and that was me.

Hauling him over my shoulder, I carried him up the stairs and into the bedroom, dropping him onto the bed before joining him. "Was there really someone coming?"

Tate threw his head back and laughed. "No. I just wanted us to finish before someone did."

I propped myself up on one elbow, exploring all the places

on Tate's body where I'd left marks. They'd fade quickly, but while they were there, I had every intention of enjoying them. When I finally made my way back up to his face, it was to find a faraway look on it. "What are you thinking about?"

He turned his head to face me. "I was thinking about how one lost wallet changed my life beyond any recognition. How if I hadn't have gone back for it none of this would ever have happened. That we wouldn't be here now."

I contemplated his words before phrasing my question carefully, my heart beating rapidly. "And if you had the choice, if you could go back and remember your wallet that night, would you?"

To be fair, he gave the question its due. I could almost see him replaying everything we'd gone through which had brought us to this point: all the times we'd hid, all the times we'd run, all the times I'd had to kill and the time that he'd had to as well. Finally, after what seemed like an age, he shook his head. "That's a really stupid question, X. If I hadn't left my wallet, I would never have met you." He threaded his fingers with mine, lifting our hands so that he could view them both together. "No, I wouldn't change a thing. We have more freedom here than we could ever have had back there. We have each other. We have love. We have everything we could ever want. Whatever pain we suffered was worth it in the end."

I couldn't have agreed more as I bent over to kiss him softly. I might have started in the shadows, but with Tate I was more in the light than I could ever have hoped for. There would be no separating the two of us.

Not for anything.

He was mine and I was his.

Till death do us part.

About the Author

H.L Day juggles teaching and writing. As an avid reader, she decided to give writing a go one day and the rest is history. Her superpower is most definitely procrastination. Every now and again, she musters enough self-discipline to actually get some words onto paper—sometimes they even make sense and are in the right order. She enjoys writing far too many different subgenres to stick to one thing so writes everything from rom-coms to post-apocalyptic sci-fi. She also has a dark pen name (H.L Night).